THE EAGLE & THE LYNX

Destined – Book Three

Michele James

2

PRAISE FOR THE DESTINED SERIES

The Lion & The Swan

"What an amazing book! Well developed characters, complex and entertaining plot, beautifully described details and settings. Very difficult to put down. It cries for a sequel! Book two, hurry! ~ conniecutie

"The purity of love between Assad and Oona is undeniable and beautiful. I adore Oona's strength and dedication to her sister. Assad was the perfect alpha, sensitive, strong, and passionate. Great, and moving tale." ~ Andrea

"Full of romance and adventure, The Lion & The Swan *is a story of forbidden love between a prince and the exotic Northern slave he vows to help escape from his cruel father, the king."* ~ MCB

"Great love story! Well developed with strong female characters. Thoroughly enjoyed the surprise HEA!" ~ jwrvt

The Stallion & The Tigress

"Love these books! Fun, witty, sensual and adventurous!!! Should be made into movies!!" ~Laura L. Sockey

"The strong woman (and the way her chief rival woos her) is wonderful. Especially because the leading lady is every bit as strong as her suitors! She chooses! I love the horses and the races and the way historical places and people are shown. This book stands alone, but it's also so cool that when you read Book 1 The Lion and the Swan, you get some of the backstory of this romance. Can't wait for Book 3 in this Destined Series. ~Kathleen Canney Lopez

"In this myth, the heroine, as her nickname suggests, is as powerful if not more so than any man. The men melt at the sight of her, but only one man will do, no matter the obstacles and there are many. The races by themselves are beautifully rendered. Kudos to the author for this romantic masterpiece. The book although number 2 of 3 is complete and stands alone." ~Plume Sobriquet

"I really liked this book, it drew me in and I read it in a few days. Well developed characters. I'm looking forward to the third book.." ~JK Surfs

4

www.BOROUGHSPUBLISHINGGROUP.com

THE EAGLE & THE LYNX
Copyright © 2021 Michele James

ISBN: 978-1-953810-31-1

For Jim. My man.

ACKNOWLEDGMENTS

Thank you to Elizabeth Archer and Michelle for the honest reads and critiques. And to KCL for all the tech help.

THE EAGLE & THE LYNX

8

CHAPTER 1

Promises Made

"I, Bard, King of Sea Ridge, name Jerrik, son of Anders, king upon my death." Bard's rheumy gaze fixed on Jerrik's. "Do you accept, brother?" he wheezed. "Will you take the throne and save my sons and Tryggr's from our family curse?"

Jerrik glanced at the faces of those gathered in his brother's sick room. At Dagny, Bard's soon-to-be widow, her eyes red and swollen from crying. At Tryggr, Jerrik and Bard's younger brother, who had pleaded with Jerrik to accept his rightful place as Bard's successor before they entered the sick room. At Trine, Tryggr's wife and mother to his young son, whose eyes were wide with the same fear that Tryggr had spoken to Jerrik of. If Jerrik didn't accept, the cursed throne would go to either Tryggr or to Bard's eldest son, who was only ten years of age.

Jerrik looked to his uncle, Fenrir, his father's younger brother, who had been King's Counsel to his father and both brothers, and who stood watching Jerrik with his counselor's mask of neutral study firmly in place.

Born the third son of King Anders, Jerrik had never expected or wanted the throne. He had reveled in a freedom his two older brothers, the heir and the spare, had never known. He'd chosen to sail on the *Sea Eagle*, his uncle Knut's trading ship, the summer he turned ten and two. A choice he'd never regretted. For the past ten and four years, he'd sailed the world's waterways trading for goods, and adding coin to his uncle's and his own coffers while learning the ways and tongues of lands known and unknown.

Knut, also third son to a king who had chosen the life of a trading sailor at the same age as Jerrik, had passed three years ago, making Jerrik skeppare of the *Sea Eagle*, and a wealthy trader in his own right.

He loved his ship, his crew, life on the open seas and moving rivers. He had no need to become king, no desire to be stuck on a throne in a palace ruling over thousands. If he denied his brothers' requests that he take the throne, he was certain that Fenrir would continue to counsel the new king, whoever it turned out to be. It was only by a happenstance of fate that Jerrik was even here now, for the *Sea Eagle* was seldom in its home port, and then never for more than a moon's time. What would his brothers have done had he not been here?

"Jerrik?" Bard gasped for what little air he could suck down his diseased lungs.

"It should be someone who is married, someone who has sons," Ermelinde, Fenrir's wife, said. "Jerrik has neither. Not unless they are hidden away in some foreign land."

"None that I am aware of," Jerrik said.

Fenrir almost smiled. "A wife is easily enough found for a king," he said. "Jerrik is a strong, virile man capable of siring many sons."

Jerrik walked over and pushed open the shutters to the window. He gazed out across the gray sky filled with storm clouds scudding from west to east and breathed in the fresh, brisk breeze of early spring. He looked down at the *Sea Eagle* anchored in the bay, bobbing and beckoning him to sail away, free of politics and entanglements like marriage and children, beholden only to his ship, his crew, the tides, and the winds.

Still, he was a king's son. Raised to always consider his familial duty. There was fear, true fear, in Tryggr's eyes. Fear if he became king, he would leave his wife widowed and his young children orphaned, or worse, next in line for a cursed throne. Perhaps the fates had landed Jerrik here for a reason.

His father, King Anders, had ruled the kingdom of Sea Ridge for over twenty years before dying in his sleep, an early and unexpected death for a hale and hearty man of forty and two years of age. In the four years since his death, his oldest son, Alviss, had ruled for only three years before falling off a cliff in a hunting accident, with no sons to succeed him. Bard, their father's second son, had sat on the throne for only one year before becoming afflicted with the moon's-long wasting sickness that was mere days from taking his life. Then there was their mother's death by her own hand when Jerrik was six years old. He still had nightmares about finding her, her bed linens red with her life's blood, her blue eyes that had smiled so brightly at him dulled and fixed.

He rolled his shoulders and rubbed the bristles of his short beard. If he truly hated being king, he could always abdicate the throne to Fenrir, who claimed to have no qualms about a curse, and who had two healthy sons, both of whom were already married and with young sons of their own to continue the royal line. Fenrir, who had comforted Jerrik after his mother's death, when his father was wrapped in a shroud of grief.

He nodded to Tryggr, who let his breath out in a great rush, and took Bard's clammy, limp hand in his. "I accept," Jerrik said.

"Will you marry me, Jerrik?"

He gazed down into sea-green eyes fringed with thick, sooty lashes, eyes of uncommon beauty and clarity, a woman's eyes in a pretty young girl's face.

"I tell you what, little lynx," he said, "I will consider your proposal, and let you know in ten years' time."

"I dreamt of your sister last night," Jerrik told Aaron as they rode along the crest of the craggy ridge that sat high above the palace and the city below, overlooking the sea's port. "Of the feast on Winter's Eve in your father's palace the night I first met you and your family."

Sailing for southern climes as winter approached, the *Sea Eagle* had dropped anchor in a port on the shore of the Mother River, the city where King Aleksandr and Queen Sahar, Aaron's parents, ruled. The king had invited Knut and the entire crew to the feast in the palace that night, where Aaron had approached Jerrik and asked him endless questions about life on a trading ship. Named after his seafaring great-grandfather, Aaron had inherited more than his name and his fair-haired northern looks; he had the sailor's wanderlust. His parent's fifth son, Aaron had been given the gift of choosing his life's course, and that night he'd decided he was going to sail with the *Sea Eagle* when it left port.

After the last of the feast had been cleared and the warmed, spiced wine brought out, as thanks for the king's and queen's hospitality, Knut had asked Jerrik to sing to the gathering. Having grown up singing for his family, and then the ship's crew, and being drunk enough to douse any nerves, Jerrik had sung "The Sailor's Tale," accompanied by an eight-year-old Alyssa on the harp. The youngest child and only daughter of Aleksandr and Sahar, the precocious imp had played the harp as if born to it, plucking each note as pure and true as her sweet, lilting voice that had melded with Jerrik's lower bass like rippling water over stone.

When the song was sung and the applause died down, she had turned to Jerrik in front of a hundred pair of watching eyes and listening ears and asked him to marry her.

"The night she proposed to you?" Aaron asked.

"The same."

"Have you dreamt of that night before?"

"No." Though he had dreamt of Alyssa many times since he'd last seen her four years ago, a girl on the verge of womanhood at ten and six, and the decidedly unchaste kiss they'd shared. Those dreams, he would not tell her brother about.

"Why do you think you dreamt of that night now, so many years later?" Aaron asked.

Jerrik laughed, short and harsh. "Because Uncle Fenrir and Aunt Ermelinde have mentioned my need to marry and produce sons daily since I became king two moons ago."

"Do they have a bride in mind?"

"The widow Marianne."

Aaron frowned. He and Jerrik had been fast friends since the day Aaron had joined the crew of the *Sea Eagle*, when they were both young, eager boys of ten and four, and that hadn't changed in the ten and two years since.

They'd watched each other's backs and saved each other's skins too many times to count through the years. When Jerrik had become skeppare of the *Sea Eagle*, he'd named Aaron his second in command, and now that Jerrik was king, Aaron was his special counsel, along with Fenrir. There was no one in this world Jerrik trusted more, no one who would tell him the truth as they saw it like Aaron would.

"Out with it," Jerrik said.

Aaron eyed Jerrik evenly. "Your uncle says you must marry and produce sons, so why has he selected the widow Marianne, who is childless after five years of marriage to a man who had children with his previous wife?"

"Marianne told me it's because she had no desire to conceive her husband's children. That he was a dried-up old worm whom she'd had to drink herself blind with beer to sleep with."

"Do you believe her?"

Jerrik shrugged. Marianne was a beautiful woman of twenty and five years, with white-blonde hair and eyes the blue of cornflowers. She was a passionate woman too, a generous lover well versed in how to please a man. They had taken precautions to keep her from becoming pregnant with his child, so it was likely she'd told him the truth.

"Do you want to marry her?" Aaron pressed.

"I may as well marry her as anybody. Her father is a landed jarl."

Aaron nodded, his lips pressed tight and his jaw clenched.

"You don't approve," Jerrik said, more statement than question.

"It's a good match, politically," Aaron admitted as they rounded a blind, narrow curve that led up to the top of the ridge, Jerrik's favorite vantage point for overlooking his kingdom and the wide-open sea beyond. "Do you love her? Can you trust her?"

Jerrik had learned at a tender age that love was a rare and precious commodity in a royal marriage, and trust even more so. His father had loved and trusted his mother, and she had sworn she loved him, right up until she had been unfaithful to her marriage vows. Untrustworthy to the end, she had taken her own life, leaving her sons motherless, and their father a changed man.

Three years later, he'd married a widow with two young daughters. A woman who had not borne Anders any children, and to whom he'd never shown any of the trust or tenderness he'd bestowed upon his first wife, at least as far as Jerrik had ever witnessed. Between his father's marriages as examples and the freedom his life as a sailor had given him, Jerrik had never seriously considered marriage before, despite his promise to Alyssa when he was still a lad and she a young girl. As king, it was a decision he was bombarded with daily.

"The question for me," he told Aaron, "would be can I love her, and do I trust her?"

Aaron raised his brows, waiting for Jerrik to answer his own question, when a great rumbling filled the air.

"Rock slide," Aaron yelled as a great cloud of dust and rocks and boulders came tumbling down. He shoved his mount into Jerrik's, pressing them both against the wall. There was nowhere for them to go, nothing they could do but hug the wall as debris rained down all around them. As the flood of rocks and logs and dirt finally began to ebb, a huge boulder knocked Aaron from his horse, pinning the poor beast under it.

"Aaron," Jerrik shouted over the horse's screams. "Aaarron!"

He jumped off his mount and knelt by Aaron's side. Coughing and choking on the settling dust, he lifted Aaron's head onto his lap and listened to the horrible sucking sounds as his best friend in the world tried to draw air into his crushed chest.

"Aaron?"

His friend's brown eyes focused on his, grimacing with the pain and effort it took to breathe. "Remem…member," he gasped, "how Alyssa cried so, wh…when I told her, I, I was, sailing, wi..with you?"

"You were always her favorite," Jerrik said.

Aaron closed his eyes. "We bo…both were," he sighed, and his sigh turned into a wet rumble. He opened his eyes, and they wandered before finding Jerrik again. "Re…remember how, she…she snuck on…onto the *Sea Eagle*?" he gurgled. "How…how she hid, and al… almost sailed away with us?"

Jerrik nodded, his tears falling freely and unashamedly onto Aaron's ashen cheek, mixing with the dirt and the bloody spittle bubbling out of Aaron's graying lips.

"I remember," Jerrik said. "She would've done it too, had your mother not found her missing and sent your father after the *Sea Eagle*." He tried to smile through his tears. "Your father was so angry he wouldn't even let us lower the rope ladder. He made her jump off the side of the ship into the freezing river and swim to his boat."

Aaron coughed up more blood than spittle and grabbed a handful of Jerrik's tunic. "A-lyssa," he whispered. "You can trust Alyssa."

His hand dropped and he was gone.

CHAPTER 2

Promises Kept

Alyssa sat at the open window of her bedchamber, staring out into the blue sky of Summer's Eve day without really seeing, plucking a tune on her harp without really hearing, yet feeling each melancholy note from her fingertips to her soul.

"'The Boat Man,'" her mother said, as maidservants bustled about the bedchamber, preparing her bathing tub and scented oils. "That's a rather sad song to be playing on your wedding day."

"It was one of Great-Auntie Lyrra's favorites," Alyssa told her, as if that explained why she was playing such a sad song on what was supposed to be one of the happiest days of her life. "You always said I was her spitting image in looks as well as temperament."

"Yes, well, somehow I don't think she was playing that song on her wedding day."

"That's because she loved Great-Uncle Nasim from the first moment she saw him," Alyssa said. "As Great-Grandmother Oona loved Great-Grandfather Asad, and you loved Father."

"I hated your father on first sight."

"That isn't how he tells it."

Her mother laughed. "That's because he was, is, and always will be an arrogant ass." Her green eyes sparked, as they always did when she and her husband were sparring over some inconsequential thing. "But he is my arrogant ass."

"And you are his tigress."

"Just don't call her Kitten," her father's deep, teasing voice said as he entered Alyssa's sitting chamber, giving his wife's backside a playful swat as she was laying Alyssa's wedding gown of jade green worm weave on the sofa.

He sat down on the chair opposite Alyssa and stared hard into her eyes, the only physical attribute she shared with her mother and her grandmother. Where they were both tall for women, with strong, angular features, Alyssa, though not short, was smaller and more delicately built, and her face was heart-shaped. Her grandmother's hair, grown as white as snow with age, had been what her grandfather called moonbeam yellow in her youth.

Alyssa's mother, Queen Sahar, was as renowned for her mane of black and auburn curls as her grandfather, King Asad, once called the Black Mane, had been for his. Alyssa's hair, an unruly mass on the best of days, was more like her father's, a mix of golds and browns, depending on how much time they spent under the sun's rays. But her eyes, they were all her mother's. Catlike in shape and green in color. As with her mother's eyes, all her father had to do was look in them and know what she was feeling.

"What's the matter, little lynx?" he asked, using the endearment he had given her when she was a toddler. The name only he, her mother, Aaron, and Jerrik had ever called her.

At the thought of her brother and Jerrik, neither of whom she'd seen in over four years, her eyes welled with tears.

"Out," her father shouted, and the maidservants stopped what they were doing. "Out, I said." He pointed for emphasis, and they all scurried out the door.

Only her mother remained. She pulled a stool over and sat beside her husband, exchanging a quick, worried glance with him.

"Tell me, my princess," her father said.

Alyssa loved and admired her mother. She was the strongest, most passionate woman Alyssa had ever met, and the queen was a good mother. Fiercely protective of all her children. As the youngest of seven and the only daughter, Alyssa was her father's "little princess," and had been from the day she was born, which her entire family, and especially her mother, teased him about.

When her father and mother first met, he was a king's bastard who had declared his disdain for all the soft, proud, spoilt rotten princesses of the world, not realizing that she was the Princess Sahar. She, of course, had shown him the fault of assuming all princesses were the same.

Now he sat across from Alyssa, his own little princess, who he doted on and had definitely spoiled. Alyssa had never wanted for anything, especially her father's love and protection. Both had shielded her for her entire life. Until now. They couldn't shield her from her current dilemma.

"I miss Aaron," she said. "And Jerrik."

Her parents shared a long, lingering look between them.

"As do we," her father sympathized. "We haven't seen or heard a word from them in over four years. None of us know why."

Alyssa knew. It was the kiss. The last day of their last visit here, the autumn Alyssa had turned ten and six. She had thrown herself at Jerrik and kissed him with every fiber of her being, holding back nothing of what she had felt and dreamed since she was eight years of age.

He'd kissed her back, one strong arm pressing her close to his lean, sea-hardened body, his other big, calloused hand twining through her hair and holding her head while his mouth plundered hers, soft and demanding, hungry and giving.

A strange heat had stirred in her belly and risen to her breasts and then escaped from her lips in a throaty mewling. Jerrik had stopped kissing her and stepped back, his sharp, angular features drawn tight. He'd run both hands back through his sun-bleached hair and then he'd turned away without a word and returned to the *Sea Eagle*. Though ship and crew had always dropped anchor in their city's port every two years for the previous eight, and had stayed a fortnight at least, she'd not seen Jerrik or Aaron again.

She'd heard rumors that the *Sea Eagle* had sailed to the far east three years ago. It was now two years past the ten that Jerrik had promised Alyssa he'd answer her marriage proposal, which they'd teased each other about over the years.

Until she had kissed him.

"We only hope and pray," her mother said with a catch in her throat, "that they are still away exploring some far-off part of the world and not…"

Dead.

None of them would say it out loud. Only the twins, Vladimir and Viggo, who were three years older than Alyssa, and best friends with Kostya, her husband-to-be, had ever voiced it, telling her she was being foolish, keeping Kostya at bay while she waited for a ghost.

"Do you love him, Alyssa?" her father asked.

"Jerrik?"

Her father shook his head. "Kostya. The man you are about to marry."

It wasn't the first time her parents had asked her that, and always before she'd answered them with a quick "of course."

She'd agreed to marry him, and it wasn't like she had to. She had family and wealth and rank of her own.

No one in her family had pressured her to marry other than Kostya and the twins. Still, she was twenty years old, well past the age of consent, and she had always wanted to marry and have children, but she always wanted it with Jerrik, who was either dead or steadfastly avoiding her.

Kostya, a younger son of Pyotr, her father's stable master, and Ursula, head cook of the palace, had grown up alongside the twins, becoming such fast friends that the entire household, from chambermaid to king, called him the third twin.

Alyssa had never known life without him, and it had been Kostya who had scolded the twins, stopping them from teasing her when she was still in side braids. Kostya who had talked the twins into letting her tag along on their adventures after Aaron had left. Kostya who'd saved her from being savaged by a drunkard who had come upon her alone in the woods when she was ten and three, killing the man who held a blade to Alyssa's throat, blowing his foul breath into her ear as he told her all the horrible things he would do to her.

She had fallen asleep under the summer sun along the lakeshore and had woken to the suffocating weight of a man whose horrid stench of sweat and stale spirits could still make her retch, pinning her under him. The man had been three times her size, and flail and scratch and bite as she had, it had made little difference as he tore at her clothes, ripping her tunic down the front, exposing her breasts to his scratching beard and grabbing hands.

Unable to hold her thrashing body still long enough to untie his breeches and free the disgusting proof of his intent, he held his blade to her throat and Alyssa had gone still and numb, closing her eyes and her mind against her attacker.

One moment the sound of his heavy breathing was all she heard, and then a loud crack, and the man had rolled off her and lay dead and unseeing, the side of his head caved in by a rock in Kostya's hand.

He'd saved her and promised to always protect her and never leave her.

It was also Kostya whose kiss left her…well, left her. She felt little more than a strange curiosity when he kissed her, like she was observing the kiss rather than participating in it. Once his kisses were over, she hardly ever thought of them again.

Unlike Jerrik's kiss. One long, searing, single kiss that she could still feel in her marrow four years later.

But Jerrik wasn't here wanting to marry her. Kostya was. Kostya, who was familiar and constant and dependable, all the things that Jerrik was not. Kostya swore he loved her enough for the both of them, and had proposed marriage for twelve moons straight until three moons ago, when he'd found her weeping angry tears over Jerrik's and Aaron's long absence. She'd agreed to marry him in a moment of weakness, and couldn't break her word.

Kostya, who had never directly asked her if she loved him, because somewhere deep down inside, he had to know.

"Alyssa?" her mother urged.

"Kostya has been a true friend to me my whole life," she said. "He's promised to always protect me and never hurt me. I trust that love will grow between us."

Her father shifted uneasily on his chair and looked to her mother, who, as a young woman Alyssa's age, had foresworn marriage altogether, until she met her father.

Her mother held Alyssa's gaze with kindness and understanding. "It's your decision, my darling daughter. Your father and I will stand by you no matter what you choose."

The sun was setting on Summer's Eve as Alyssa walked along the path to the courtyard where her wedding would soon be taking place, her mind on a Winter's Eve night ten and two years ago, the night she had first seen Jerrik, a tall, broad-shouldered Northman with hair the color of winter wheat and eyes as blue as a summer sky. He had sung "The Sailor's Tale" in his deep, resonant timbre, and Alyssa had joined him, playing her harp and singing along in her child's voice.

The last, long, lingering note of the song hadn't yet ended when she'd turned to Jerrik and asked him to marry her. To this day she couldn't have said why. Perhaps it was as Aaron claimed. He'd often teased her about her catlike tendency to change moods or directions with no more warning than the quick twitch of her tail, which would always make her turn around and look for a tail somehow magically attached to her backside, leaving Aaron laughing.

Yet no matter how impulsive her marriage proposal had been, she'd never regretted it.

The only thing she regretted was that she wasn't walking toward Jerrik, that it would not be him reciting vows before the priest with her.

But the ten years he had promised to consider her proposal had come and gone without an answer. At one point, right before their one and only kiss, she'd thought that his answer would be yes when the time came. That was four years ago. All she had of him now were the trinkets he'd gifted her with from his travels, and her memories of his visits, which had consisted of four fortnights over eight years.

She had known him, spoken with him, reveled in his company for a total of two moons' time. Kostya, she had known her entire life. Kostya was her friend. He swore he loved her. Loved her enough that it didn't matter that she didn't love him in the same way.

Kostya stood before the priest now, watching her entrance into the torchlit courtyard, the smile on his face growing as she approached him until it almost split his broad face in two as she took her place beside him and let him take her hands in his.

"You are so beautiful, Aly," he said, using his pet name for her. "I'm so happy."

Alyssa gave him a shaky smile, truly wishing she felt the same.

Kostya was a good man. A handsome man. Though not tall, he was strongly built and sturdy, made to last, as he often said, with light brown hair and warm brown eyes that were quick to laugh. Like his father, he too had a way with horses, and had earned his position as the royal stable's breeder and trainer. As a dowry gift, her parents had presented him with enough land and coin to build his own stables, along with three broodmares of his choice and access to any stallions in the royal stables for stud.

Alyssa's smile faltered as she wondered, not for the first time, if Kostya wasn't more enamored of her pedigree than of her.

She shook it off and blew out her breath. He was her friend, first and foremost, and people always said that when the passion in a marriage dwindled, friendship remained. Their marriage would simply start where most marriages, good, solid, committed marriages, ended up.

She glanced over at her parents, whose marriage of thirty-plus years was still as passionate as newlyweds, and she thought of her mother's parents, King Asad and Queen Oona, whose love and marriage were legendary.

A love Alyssa had witnessed and aspired to. With Jerrik.

Her grandmother, Queen Oona, had understood. When Alyssa was a girl of ten and two, she'd been visiting her grandparents with her mother. She'd confided in her grandmother about Jerrik, and after hearing her granddaughter's tale, Oona had kissed her cheek and hugged her close.

"I am sorry it happened to you so young, Lyly," she'd said, calling Alyssa by the endearment she shared with her Great-Aunt Lyrra. "It seems to be the fate of our line, falling in love at first sight with our men." She'd smiled, not as queen, but woman to woman, and had whispered in Alyssa's ear, "Our men fall in love with us at first sight as well. Being so young, you may have to wait a little longer for yours to realize this."

It'd been the last time she had seen her grandmother and grandfather. They had passed away the next winter, the Swan following her beloved Black Mane only three days after he died peacefully in his sleep, his devoted wife of fifty years by his side.

Brought back to the present by Kostya squeezing her hands, Alyssa focused on his steady gaze as the priest began his recitation, of which she heard perhaps one out of ten words, until he spoke the vows.

"Do you, Kostya, son of Pyotr and Ursula, swear before these witnesses and the gods, to strive to keep your marriage vows to Alyssa, daughter of Aleksandr and Sahar?"

Kostya smiled and squeezed Alyssa's hands tighter. "I do."

The priest turned to Alyssa. "Do you, Alyssa, daughter of Aleksandr and Sahar, swear before these witnesses and the gods, to strive to keep your marriage vows to Kostya, son of Pyotr and Ursula?"

A cold, creeping dread spread through Alyssa at the priest's words. Once she spoke her vows, she would be bound to Kostya for life. She would be wife to a husband she didn't love. Not as a wife should love a husband. Not as she wanted to love hers.

The smile plastered on her face cracked, as did her heart for what she was about to do to Kostya. "I…cannot."

"What?" Kostya snapped, his hands squeezing the blood from Alyssa's.

"I can't marry you, Kostya," Alyssa said, her own voice strangely calm and steady.

"Why not?" he erupted, his face turning a mottled red.

"Because," a man's voice boomed from the back of the courtyard. "She foreswore herself to me ten and two years ago."

Jerrik stood in the middle of the pathway Alyssa had walked up a few moments ago, moments that Jerrik had spent cursing himself for being two years too late and boring holes into Kostya's head with his heated glare. He'd recognized the man as soon as he saw him, for the boy Kostya had been inseparable from Alyssa's younger set of twin brothers, and followed Alyssa around like a sick puppy whenever Jerrik and Aaron had visited.

Standing still and silent as Kostya pledged his troth to Alyssa, Jerrik had decided to turn around and sail right back to Sea Ridge before anyone recognized him. Then Alyssa told Kostya she couldn't marry him, and Jerrik's chest swelled with renewed determination.

The fates and Aaron had sent Jerrik here not a moment too soon.

Alyssa turned toward him as the shocked gasps and whispers of the gathering swept across the courtyard like wildfire, her eyes big and round, her heart-shaped face breaking into a smile as bright and mesmerizing as sunlight on water.

He'd missed that smile, how it brightened her beautiful face and made him feel as strong and powerful as the gods of the sky and the sea combined. He had missed her.

"Alyssa." His voice lowered at the sight of her.

"Jerrik." Her voice was as sweet and melodic as he remembered it.

She shook her hands free of Kostya's grip and took a step toward Jerrik before Kostya grabbed her by the upper arm and held her there.

Jerrik's feathers ruffled as he shouldered his pack and strode forward, his jaw clamped and his hands fisted, ready to tear Kostya limb from limb.

Jerrik had never been a possessive man, especially over women. He'd sailed the world's waterways and lain with women in every port, from ale houses to palaces, without caring in the least what man came before him or after, as long as they weren't married. That was a line he wouldn't cross. A pain he'd never cause another man. He'd seen what it had done to his father. But Alyssa was his, by her own words and kiss, and Jerrik wasn't going to stand by and let anybody manhandle her.

Red-faced and chest out, still holding Alyssa by the arm, Kostya stood waiting as Jerrik approached. The twins, Viggo and Vlad, stood to Kostya's side glaring at Jerrik, their stances stiff and erect, their jaws set, their alliance clear.

Jerrik glared right back at them, and was no more than three strides from them when King Aleksandr stepped in front of him, stopping him in his tracks. Still a large, well-muscled man who had always treated Jerrik kindly, the king was not a man Jerrik wanted to challenge.

"King Aleksandr." Jerrik dipped his head. He glanced at Alyssa, whose wide eyes never left him, and dipped his head to her as well. "I've come to ask for your daughter's hand in marriage," he said, his chest swelling at her instant, open smile. He looked back to the king, hating what he had to do. "I bring grievous news of your son."

Queen Sahar stepped up and stood beside her husband. "What of Aaron?"

Jerrik cleared his throat and met the queen's knowing, pleading eyes. "Is there someplace more private we can speak?"

King Aleksandr nodded and took his queen by one hand and Alyssa by the other, eyeing Kostya until he let go of her.

"Friends, family, honored guests," King Aleksandr addressed the whispering, watching gathering. "While there will be no wedding ceremony this Summer's Eve, the feast will commence shortly. Please, enjoy our hospitality."

The whispering grew to a loud buzzing as the king indicated that Jerrik and Kostya should follow him. The king and queen walked abreast of Alyssa, with Kostya and the twins right on their heels, making sure that Jerrik walked behind them.

Jerrik was followed by Alyssa's three other brothers and their wives, and an older couple he presumed were Kostya's parents given their looks and manner.

They walked past the rooms that Jerrik knew were the king's council chambers and along the hallway that led to the family quarters, where King Aleksandr ushered them into the family's common room, a room Jerrik had spent time in with the royal family on his visits with Aaron.

A room that brought back happy memories of songs sung, conversations had, and games played. Of a big, boisterous family that had welcomed him and made him feel a part of them, something that Jerrik hadn't felt since that horrible day his mother had passed, other than with the crew of his ship.

Alyssa's sunny smile, melodic harp, and lilting laughter were a large part of those memories. As were their long walks and deepening talks, along with the lingering looks and undeniable connection that had grown between them through the years. A connection that Jerrik had never been able to explain, even to himself, and that he had severed four years ago out of sheer panic.

Their gazes met and she gave him a tremulous smile as he took a stool situated at an angle to the long sofa that she sat on between her mother and father. The queen gave the servants directions to bring food and drink.

Kostya's parents sat down on another sofa next to them as Kostya, his meaty hands clenching and unclenching, paced back and forth behind them.

The brothers and their wives pulled sofas and stools up to complete the half circle, and Jerrik took the lull between waiting for the servants to bring the refreshments and the start of the conversation to observe the people in the room.

Kostya wanted to kill him, that much was obvious. The twins, Viggo and Vlad, remained loyal to their friend.

The older twins, Asad and Asim, were on high alert, watching everything and everyone closely, while Maksimillian, the oldest son and heir to Aleksandr's throne, sat prepared to judge.

Kostya's parents glared angrily at Jerrik one moment and then with sadness at Alyssa the next. Alyssa's parents, the king and queen, kept their thoughts and emotions close, though their hands were clasped tightly with Alyssa's in her lap.

And Alyssa, sweet Alyssa, who wore her heart on her sleeve, sat staring at him with wide eyes welling with tears, waiting to hear how the older brother she adored had died.

Jerrik adjusted the pack at his feet and sat with his spine erect and his shoulders back. As hard as the news of Aaron's passing would be for his family, at least his had been an honorable death. The last of the servants set down trays of fruit and cheese and shut the door behind them.

Everyone in the room leaned forward in their seats. Jerrik took a drink of wine to ease the words from his throat, and met the queen's mournful gaze. "Aaron died saving me," he told her, for there was no way to soften this blow. He looked to the king. "One moon ago, in my home port of Sea Ridge, he pushed me aside and took the full weight of a boulder that crashed down the mountainside." Jerrik's voice caught, despite the wine. "He gave his life to save mine."

Jerrik looked to Alyssa. "He is buried high atop the ridge, as is your custom, overlooking the bay and the open sea."

The king nodded, his jaw clamped tight as his wife's tears fell silently.

Between them, Alyssa cried softly, burying her face into her father's shoulder. Aaron's older brothers looked from their parents and sister to each other, holding their weeping wives close. Vladimir and Viggo cursed Jerrik and his heathen gods. Kostya's parents looked upon the king and queen with sympathy, while Kostya continued to pace, his face growing redder and more mottled by the lap.

Jerrik picked his pack up and opened it, reaching in and pulling out a small package. He leaned forward on his stool and handed it to the queen. "A lock of Aaron's hair," he said, as she unwrapped the braid of light brown hair. "And a brooch he bought you on our last voyage to the far east."

She held the braid to her nose, closing her eyes and breathing in the scent of her dead son before laying it back on the linen square and lifting the brooch of seeded pearl and silver with a sad smile. "It's beautiful," she said. "Thank you, Jerrik, for bringing these last gifts from my son." She smiled through her tears. "I am glad that Aaron, so like his grandfather and namesake, was able to live the life he wanted with a good and true friend by his side."

Jerrik bowed his head to the queen. "It was my honor to be his friend and share in his journey," he said, his voice breaking.

Clearing his throat of the knot threatening to strangle him, he pulled another package from his sack and handed it to the king. It was a bridle of fine goat leather embedded with stones of amber, onyx, rubies, and emeralds. The reins were woven of the same leather with beaded tassels at the ends. "Aaron traded for this in the western lands of Ebros, a land of fine craftsmen, whose horsemen, Aaron proudly told them, only dreamt of comparing to you and his grandfather, King Asad."

King Aleksandr nodded, coughed, and rubbed his nose. "Thank you, Jerrik."

"I am truly sorry that I, and not Aaron, am the person presenting you with these."

The king nodded once and said nothing further.

Jerrik pulled out a small packet and handed it to Alyssa, whose bottom lip trembled as she took it from him and unwrapped the bone carving of a wild cat, its eyes wide and ears and tail erect. "Aaron bought this in the land of the pharaohs. He said it reminded him of you."

"Thank you," she sniffed. "I shall treasure it always."

Jerrik dipped his head and handed Alyssa another packet. "This is from me. It too is from the land of the pharaohs."

She smiled shyly as she unwrapped the packet. "Oh, Jerrik," she gasped as she lifted the comb of ivory and mother-of-pearl to the light. "It's beautiful."

"It will look even more beautiful in your mane of burnt honey, little lynx."

The apples of her cheeks blushed a most becoming rosy pink. "Thank you, Jerrik."

"It's only the first of many bridal gifts I intend to give you, Alyssa," he told her, smiling as her cheeks turned even rosier.

"What if she doesn't wish to marry you?" Kostya huffed, causing a roomful of heads to turn his way. "What if she does not wish to sit at home waiting for you years on end until you return from yet another sea voyage? To be the wife of a common sailor who brings home with him who knows what disease contracted from some foreign whore? Where will you live? What hut in what faraway port will be your home?"

"Valid questions all," Jerrik said with a calmness he didn't feel. "To be asked and answered by Alyssa, her family, and myself. While I have sympathy for your circumstances, whatever happens between Alyssa and me from this point forward has nothing to do with you. Do not presume to interfere again."

Kostya puffed out his considerable chest, stepped around the sofa, and up to Jerrik, who rose from his stool so that they stood eye to chin. Not a favorable position for Kostya, which he must have realized as he stepped away from Jerrik to face Alyssa and her parents.

"Is this what you want, Aly?" Kostya said, tossing his head toward Jerrik. "A man who sails in and out of your life? A man you barely know?"

"I do know him, Kostya," she answered soberly. She looked to Jerrik and spoke in his Northern tongue. "I know him in all the ways that matter."

"As I do you," Jerrik said in kind, dipping his head to her.

"Then take the little cheat," Kostya erupted. "Marry your ice princess. Make her your fishmonger, and may your marriage bed be as cold as your bride."

The room went dead silent, and Alyssa's cheeks went beet red.

Jerrik cocked his head, glancing between Alyssa and Kostya. Why the man would call Alyssa cold and icy was beyond Jerrik's ken. She was as warm and openhearted a woman as Jerrik had ever known. All a person had to do was look at her to know what she was feeling. And what she felt, she felt deeply.

He could still taste the heat and passion of their one and only kiss. The desire it had stirred in him had scared him into staying away from her, away from the temptation of her for the past four years.

Not only had she been his best friend's sister, but she was the kind of girl you married, not one you dallied with for a night or two. A princess. He hadn't been ready to marry her, or any woman, back then. Now, he needed to marry.

Aaron had been right. If Jerrik was to marry, he would marry Alyssa. If she agreed to marry him, it wouldn't be under false pretenses. "Alyssa would be no common sailor's wife," he said. "She would be my queen."

"Queen," Kostya snorted, as King Aleksandr and Queen Sahar looked from Jerrik to each other, and Alyssa's big, round eyes widened. "What would she be queen of?" Kostya's laugh was crude and guttural. "Some shanty town built on a crumbling bridge over a swampy marsh?"

"I became king of Sea Ridge three moons ago," Jerrik told King Aleksandr. He looked to Alyssa, who sat in stunned stillness. "I sit on the throne of Sea Ridge, and would have you, Alyssa, daughter of King Aleksandr and Queen Sahar, rule beside me." He took a knee before her. "Will you marry me, Alyssa?"

CHAPTER 3

Vows Given

Alyssa sat at her open window gazing out into the clear morning sky. The same sky she'd stared into yesterday, feeling as dull and heavy then as she felt sharp and light today despite sleeping little and fitfully. Her flitting dreams were filled with Jerrik's sky-blue eyes smiling over his sharply angled cheekbones and his deep, resonant voice calling her little lynx and asking her to marry him.

She'd said yes, of course. She'd accepted Jerrik's marriage proposal without thought or hesitation. It was what she'd been waiting for. *He* was what she'd waited ten and two years for. Though her joy at his proposal was tempered with her sorrow at losing Aaron, she couldn't help smiling through her tears each time it came to her anew.

She was going to be Jerrik's wife at last. She was going to be Jerrik's queen.

Through all the years of waiting, her dreams had always been of sailing off with Jerrik and Aaron on the *Sea Eagle*. Of traveling to far-off, exotic lands and exploring the world their tales had teased her with a taste of. That was where her dreams had ended.

As she grew older, she realized that once babies started coming, she wouldn't be able to sail. She also knew there were ways to prevent pregnancies, and had dreamed of enjoying a few years of adventures together before experiencing motherhood.

She'd loved growing up in a large family, and she enjoyed her brothers' children, but like her brother, Aaron, and his namesake, she'd always had wanderlust.

Her happiest memories, other than of Jerrik's and Aaron's visits, were of traveling with her family to visit her grandparents in their city on the southern shore of the Great Inland Sea, and of the hunting trips they took a different season each year, camping in varying climes for a fortnight at a time.

Alyssa knew her stars as well as any sailor, and could track, trap, shoot, skin, salt, and cook anything from squirrel to elk as well as any huntsman. Skills her parents had taught all their children, as well as how to fight with knives, swords, and sticks.

Skills that had saved her parents' lives once, and that would've served Alyssa well on her adventures with Jerrik and Aaron.

Not so much with Jerrik the king, stuck in his palace, which he was expected to fill with children as soon as possible. Heirs to a cursed throne.

Alyssa picked up Meadowlark and plucked the harp's strings, filling the air with a contemplative tune. After Kostya and his parents had left last night, Alyssa and her family were alone with Jerrik. He'd told them the details of Aaron's death, as well as Alvis's and Bard's. They heard about Bard's and Tryggr's pleas for Jerrik to take the cursed throne and save their sons. Jerrik had shared all this because he wanted Alyssa and her family to know what she was agreeing to. Alyssa had said yes, again. All she cared about was that Jerrik had come for her. Jerrik wanted to marry her. The rest of it could be dealt with as long as they were together.

From the time she was a little girl to now, she'd heard the tales of her parents' and grandparents' love stories, of the trials and tribulations they went through to be together, to marry and to rule their kingdoms and raise their families. She'd learned from them that a great love could conquer anything as long as the lovers kept faith with each other.

Alyssa had put her faith in Jerrik years ago, and then she'd doubted it. Doubted him and doubted herself. She'd relied on the advice of others, when she'd known her heart and mind and ignored what they told her. Her parents, her brothers, and Kostya had been watching over her and protecting her for her entire life. Her whole coddled life, she'd done what everyone wanted her to do and thought she was being dutiful. It had almost caused her to make the biggest mistake of her life.

She wouldn't do that again.

A knock on her door announced her maidservant's entrance. "Come, Princess," Olga said, "time to get dressed."

Time to discuss the terms of her marriage.

Alyssa sat beside her parents on the sofa in the family's common room while Jerrik sat on the sofa opposite them waiting for her father to speak. Jerrik looked more at ease than he had last night when he'd been confronted by her brothers, Kostya, and his parents. They all did.

"You will marry here before you sail to your home at Sea Ridge," her father said.

Jerrik nodded his assent. "Of course, King Aleksandr." He turned to Alyssa. "Our wedding here can be as large or small as you wish, Alyssa, but it must take place soon. We need to sail within a fortnight in order to reach Sea Ridge and plan our wedding there, which traditionally takes place mid-autumn, and, necessarily, will be large."

"Small and soon here will be fine," Alyssa said. She smiled at Jerrik. *The sooner the better.*

He smiled back, holding her gaze with those piercing sky-blue eyes.

"Jerrik?"

"Huh?"

The king chuckled as Jerrik and Alyssa turned their attention to her father. "Will seven nights from tonight do for the wedding ceremony?"

"Yes, of course, King Aleksandr."

"Please, call me Aleksi," her father said. "We are both kings, and are soon to be father and son."

"Thank you, Aleksi," Jerrik said with a strange hitch to his voice.

"Good. Now that's settled, let us get to the business of my daughter's dowry."

Last night, her mother and father had generously offered to let Kostya keep the horses and the land they had promised as Alyssa's dowry, and Kostya had ungratefully accepted. Alyssa sat with a cold pit in her belly and waited to hear Jerrik's demands, to find out what he wanted to marry her.

"Have you any requests or requirements?" her father asked.

Jerrik glanced at Alyssa and shook his head. "I request nothing more than a few bolts of worm weave to make summer gowns worthy of your daughter to wear and make the women of my land green with envy. Perhaps some furs for winter as befit a queen."

Her father nodded his approval, and a lock of hair fell down onto his forehead. Her mother reached up and pushed the lock back with a tenderness that brought a smile to her husband's face as he took her hand in his and kissed her open palm.

Alyssa noticed Jerrik watching her parents as her father kept hold of her mother's hand and held it tucked in his, an occurrence so commonplace between them that the rest of the family barely took notice.

"My daughter and I will choose ten bolts of worm weave," her mother said, "with enough left over to make the women of your family gowns as well. I do not think it wise to make the women my daughter will be living amongst too jealous right off."

"Thank you, Queen Sahar," Jerrik said, "for the offer and the advice. I still have much to learn of politics and palace life, having lived among sailors for so many years."

"You're most welcome. Please, from this day forward, I am Sahar or Mother to you."

"Thank you, Sahar," Jerrik said with another strange hitch in his voice.

Alyssa knew from Aaron and the few times that Jerrik had spoken of his family that he considered the crew of the *Sea Eagle* more his family than his blood relatives. He'd always envied Alyssa's family's closeness. A closeness that she hoped to emulate with her own. With him.

"Is there anything you wish to bring with you to your new home?" Jerrik asked.

Reeling her thoughts back in, she considered his question then said, "My mare, River. Will she be able to travel on the *Sea Eagle*?"

"I'll have the crew build her a pen on the deck."

Alyssa smiled. She had claimed the foal the night she was born six summers ago, and had saddle-broken the mare herself. Since then, she'd ridden her every day for the past five years. Next to her family, she would have missed River the most.

"How much more difficult would it be to sail with two horses than one?" her father asked.

Jerrik shook his head. "Not much."

"Then my wife and I would like to give you a saddle-broken, two-year-old stallion we call Seryy, the Gray. Together with River, they will bring a fine bloodline to your royal stables."

"Thank you, Father." Alyssa knew the honor her father had paid them. Seryy was a direct descendant of Zolotoy's and Lasair's bloodline, her parents' stallion and mare that had created their royal stables. A bloodline that Kostya had been drooling over. She looked to Jerrik, who likely wasn't aware of his stallion's pedigree, though he did seem aware of her pleasure at the gift.

"Thank you again, Aleksi, Sahar," he said with a respectful dip of his blond head. "I'm honored."

Her father patted his wife's hand. "Is there anything else you request as a dowry?"

Jerrik met Alyssa's gaze. "You will gift me with the most valuable treasure of all," he said, "when you give me your daughter's hand in marriage seven days hence." Alyssa blushed and Jerrik's gaze sharpened. "If I may be so bold," he dipped his head to her father before his gaze retuned to Alyssa, "to ask my betrothed to walk with me along her favorite wooded path alone?"

Alyssa didn't wait for her father to answer. "I would welcome a walk," she said, standing, and forcing herself to keep from leaping across the space between her and Jerrik and grabbing his hand and running from the salon out to the palace grounds and into the seclusion of the woods beyond. "Alone, with my betrothed," she added in his Northern tongue.

Jerrik stood and held his hand out to Alyssa, then looked to her parents, who nodded their assent with knowing smiles. As with all things concerning Jerrik, Alyssa set her hand in his without hesitation, thrilling at the feel of his large, calloused fingers closing around hers, closing the chasm of four years apart between them.

"You speak the Northern tongue well," he said in that same tongue as they headed for the door. "Better than I remember."

"A traveling tutor has been giving me lessons whenever he is in port for the past three years," Alyssa answered.

Her father's low chuckle followed them out the door, and then there was nothing except the sound of their footfall in the hallway and the rhythmic thumping of her heart in her ears.

At last. At last. At last.

With the unerring memory and direction of a sailor, Jerrik led them out of the palace and into the courtyard, neither of them speaking a word until they were outside the palace grounds and well into the wooded path that led to the lake.

"I'm glad you came for me," Alyssa said, the quick squeeze of his hand giving her courage. "I feared my kissing you the last time we were together caused you to stay away."

"It did," he stated matter-of-factly, and Alyssa stopped still as her heart dropped to her feet. Jerrik gently chucked her chin, closing her gaping mouth. "That kiss scared me to my marrow."

Alyssa shook her head, wondering what she'd done to frighten him. She thought the kiss was wonderful. Extraordinary. Life-changing. It seemed she was horribly wrong. "I don't understand."

"I was afraid of the passion your kiss stirred in me. Passion I didn't wish to feel for any woman, and especially not for my best friend's sister."

"I still don't—"

"I wasn't ready to feel that way about anybody."

Oh. Well, in that case… "And now?" He'd already asked her to marry him, yet she was nervous about his answer.

"Now I'm king and it is my duty to wed and raise a family. Aaron was right. If I'm to take a bride, it should be you."

"Aaron?"

Jerrik nodded and held her gaze, his own dead serious. "His last words to me were, 'Alyssa, you can trust Alyssa.'"

Alyssa's heart dropped. Trust. She wasn't the exchequer. She was his future wife. "What about love?" she stuttered.

Jerrik cocked his head and held Alyssa's waiting gaze. "I've always liked you, little lynx." He grinned. "You know that."

Alyssa nodded as her throat constricted. *Like.* Not love. Like. Friendly. Compatible. A sensible emotion that didn't drive him wild, make his blood boil, or force him to go to extremes for her. The person he was supposed to *love.*

"I knew I could trust you, even without Aaron telling me. I knew, and know, you have no motives for marrying me other than marrying me, Jerrik. The man." He smiled and reached out and pushed an errant lock of her hair behind her ear. "Don't ever doubt that I desire you," he said, his voice deep and low. "I have since our kiss four years ago." He ran his hand through her hair. "You've grown into a beautiful woman. I would be proud to have you as my wife. Friendship, trust, desire… A marriage can be built on such a foundation."

How perfectly reasonable. She wanted to scream and pound her fists on his chest. Instead, being the well-brought-up princess she was, Alyssa swallowed past the lump in her throat. She found herself in the horrible position Kostya had been in: loving and adoring a betrothed who did not love her back. Now knowing how Kostya felt, she couldn't blame him for his bad behavior. Actually, she envied him the freedom to express it. She, on the other hand, had to process what she was hearing while keeping a neutral expression on her face when she wanted to knock Jerrik on his arse and give him a good thrashing.

Impassive because she had to be, she kept her gaze on Jerrik as she decided her fate. Much as Kostya had, she had to decide: should she marry Jerrik and hope her love for him would be enough, or walk away? Could she marry a man she had loved since she was eight years old knowing he didn't love her?

True, he'd admitted to trusting her, to desiring her. To having been shaken to his marrow by her kiss. Could love grow from that trust and desire? If it didn't, she'd live her life in a marriage where she was the only one in love until that love turned to resentment, and inevitably disgust and hate.

This was NOT the way this was supposed to be, and she really, truly, absolutely did not want to walk away from Jerrik.

What had her grandmother said? *Sometimes it takes our men a little longer to realize their love.*

Alyssa had put her faith in what her brothers, whom she loved with her whole heart, told her was her best option, and almost made the mistake of marrying Kostya.

Now, and by the heavens she hoped she was making the right decision, Alyssa would put her faith in her own judgment.

"Kiss me," she ordered.

"What?"

"Kiss me."

Jerrik knew Alyssa'd had a young girl's crush on him since she was a mere child. She'd never tried to hide it. In truth, he wasn't sure she was capable of hiding her feelings about anyone or anything. All a person had to do was look in her eyes to see her true feelings, even when she was trying to hide them, as she was now. Jerrik had hurt her when he spoke of marrying her for duty's sake. He knew this as surely as he knew his response to her request to kiss her would determine whether they had a future together.

Tall even for a Northman, Jerrik stood head and shoulders over her, and something about her slim, delicate features and big, expressive eyes made him feel a tenderness for her that he'd never felt for a woman before. He was in uncharted waters, and although he looked forward to exploring her depths once they were married, until then he was determined to wade slowly and carefully while navigating her shallows.

Cupping her chin, he tilted up her head and lowered his own. "It'll be my pleasure to kiss you, my little lynx," he breathed against her lips.

She smelled of the first lilies of winter and soft summer rain. Her minty sweet breath caught and then let out in a sigh as he brushed his lips along hers, tender and featherlight. Her felt her lush lips rise in a smile, and he smiled too, and took her head in his hands.

Weaving his fingers through her tawny mane, he slanted his lips along hers, tenderness giving way to the desire coursing through him.

Running a hand down her back and pressing her slim, taut body close to his, he breached her lips with his tongue, groaning with pleasure as she opened to him. He probed the warm, wet contours of her mouth, tasting the salty sweetness of her, and when the tip of her tongue touched his, the rope of his tightly wound self-control unraveled.

He plundered her mouth, and she gave herself to him, hiding nothing, holding nothing back, the treasure of her passion his for the taking.

Already hard with desire, Jerrik claimed her with one last, long, lusty kiss, and then pulled his mouth from hers, though he still held her close. By the gods, he had never been driven to such need by only one kiss. Two, if he counted their kiss four years ago, and he did.

He'd worried that his memory of that first kiss had left him with unrealistic expectations. A needless worry as it turned out. He gazed down through a haze of pulsing, wanting need into the swirling, mossy green of Alyssa's heavy-lidded eyes, and at her slick, swollen lips. He smiled.

She'd grown from a skinny waif of a girl with eyes too big for her rose petal face into a beautiful sylph of a woman with eyes as deep and wide and unfathomable as the sea. The fates had offered him a wife he desired, and as Aaron had said, a wife Jerrik could trust.

He held his hand out to her. "Shall we continue our journey?"

She smiled as bright and warm as sunlight on water and put her hand in his. "Yes," she said. "We shall."

"Where would you like to go first?"

Alyssa laughed lightly. "You know, you're the only male in my life other than my father who ever asks me what I want to do?" She smiled sadly. "Even Aaron never asked, though he did let me tag along whenever I wanted."

"Aaron adored you," Jerrik told her. "There are royal courts all over this world who have been entertained by his stories about his little sister, his little lynx."

"Truly?"

Jerrik cupped her quivering chin and placed a tender kiss on her lips. Lips he suddenly couldn't get enough of. "Truly."

"Thank you for that," she said, her voice and expression wistful.

"So," he said, swinging her hand in his. "Where to?"

Her eyes lit up. "Would you like to meet my mare and your new stallion?"

"I would," he said. "After we see the horses, we can go to the *Sea Eagle* and plan how and where we'll build their pens."

And their life together.

They walked hand in hand into the palace yard, greeted by many openly curious stares and congratulations as they passed through the grounds to the stables. They approached the one-story building of stone and wood that was almost as large as the palace, and Alyssa led Jerrik to a sleek, leggy mare so black she almost shone blue in the sunlight.

"I don't claim to know much about horses," he said as Alyssa rubbed the mare's velvety muzzle, "but I know beauty when I see it, and she is beautiful."

"Aye," Alyssa said, "that she is. There is more to her than her looks. She runs as swift and untiring as a mountain river after a spring rain."

"Hence her name?"

Alyssa nodded as a gray tabby ran up, chirping and mewing and rubbing up against her legs. "Good day, Queenie." She picked up the cat and touched noses with her. "How are your babies today, mama?"

She put the cat down and signaled for Jerrik to follow as she pushed open a door to a tack room. The creak set off a chorus of furious mewling from a nest of straw in the corner. The cat trotted over and lay down in the middle of her litter, who crawled on unsteady legs to nestle up against her, rooting for milk.

"Are they not precious?" Alyssa said. She pulled a piece of dried meat from her skirt pocket and gave it to the proud, purring Queenie. "They started walking a few days ago. Soon enough they'll be running and jumping all over the place."

Jerrik bent down and rubbed a finger up and down one of the kittens' furry backs. "I'd forgotten your family's affinity for cats," he chuckled. "Though I shouldn't have." He gave Alyssa a sad smile. "Aaron was always the one to take in a stray and turn it into a ship's cat."

He swallowed a stinging lump and held his arms open to a teary-eyed Alyssa, who stepped into his hold and buried her face into his chest. "I miss him," she sniffed.

"So do I." He laid his chin on top of her head, content to hold her in his embrace, breathing in the scent of winter lilies and spring water.

"Do you have a ship's cat now?" she asked, leaning back and looking up with watery eyes.

"No." He shook his head. "We were in Sea Ridge for so long that the last cat jumped ship and never came back." He eyed Alyssa. "Why?"

"There is a young male tabby hanging about where Seryy is stabled. Unfortunately, another big male has been ruling over the same territory for a while now, so poor Bones is having a hard time of it."

"Bones?"

"That's what I call him because he was nothing but skin over bones when he first showed up."

"Well then." He placed a smacking kiss on the top of Alyssa's head. "Let us go meet my new horse and the ship's new cat."

Jerrik stood back from the stall's gate, admiring the big gray who was contentedly munching the carrot that Alyssa had given him.

"He looks as strong and sleek as a warship," Jerrik said. "Even the proud arch of his neck looks like a ship's prow."

"He too is as fast and strong as he looks," Alyssa told him. "He and River will bring good blood to your...our line of horses."

"I may have to start learning about breeding and bloodlines," Jerrik said with a grin that grew wider as Alyssa's cheeks flushed a rosy pink.

"What will you name him?" she asked, swiping at her pink cheeks.

Jerrik eyed the slate gray stallion for a long moment. "Storm," he said, and the stallion nickered and bobbed his head and shook his mane of an even darker gray. Jerrik chuckled. "I think he likes it."

"It fits him," Alyssa said, "and his bloodline. Storm Chaser was the name of his great-grandsire, the sire of his dam, Lasair. He was the stallion my mother's father, King Asad, started his stables with."

"Storm it is then." Jerrik offered the stallion another carrot and ran a hand along the arch of his neck. "I hope you take to traveling on a ship, young man."

A raspy meowing grew louder and more insistent as a bow-legged orange tabby came running up to Alyssa, who scooped up the cat and nuzzled his neck. The cat, who Jerrik assumed was the aforementioned Bones, rubbed his head against Alyssa's cheek, purring loudly and patting her arm with his paw, his claws sheathed.

"Bones," Alyssa said, holding the cat to face Jerrik, "meet Jerrik, skeppare of the *Sea Eagle*, soon to be your new home."

Jerrik eyed the skinny cat askance. "He's terribly scrawny," he pointed out.

Alyssa tucked the cat into her chest. "I think he was a runt who had to fight for his mother's hind teat and every scrap of food he has gotten since," she defended Bones. "Which proves his tenacity and will to live." She kissed the cat on the top of his head, and he chirped in response. "He promises to be the best ratter the *Sea Eagle* has ever had," she said, her big sea-green eyes pleading the scrapper's case. "All he asks for is a clean bed of straw, a fresh bowl of water each day, and a fish head now and then to supplement his diet of vermin."

Jerrik held his fingertip out to the cat, who sniffed it and licked it with his raspy tongue. "I'll hold up my end of the bargain if he holds his," Jerrik said, and was rewarded with Alyssa's bright smile. He chuckled and fixed a purposely chary eye on her. "Are there any more animals sailing with us that I should be making plans for?"

Alyssa stood on her tiptoes and gave Jerrik a kiss on the cheek. "I'll be sure to let you know when there is," she told him saucily. She tucked Bones under her arm. "For now, I'll go gather Bones' things to set him up in his new home while you and Storm get to know each other."

Jerrik touched his cheek where Alyssa had kissed him, admiring the twitch of her skirts as she disappeared into another part of the stables. He rubbed his cheek and grinned at Storm. "The cat has things?" he asked, incredulous that a barn animal had anything needing retrieving. He reached down into the bucket and offered the horse another carrot. "I suppose you have things as well." Rolling his shoulders back and shaking his head, he leaned closer to the munching stallion. "It seems we have both found our mates, my new friend."

"At least your stallion's mate has never been mounted by another," a man's snide voice said.

Jerrik turned to face Kostya, who stood no more than ten paces from him and whose sneer was as full of insinuation as his words had been. "Say again?"

"You may take Alyssa as your wife and make her your queen, King Jerrik, but I made her my bride when I took her maidenhead, or rather, when she gave it to me, willingly if not warmly."

"You lie."

"Do I?"

It was obvious that Kostya was telling Jerrik this hoping it would keep him from marrying Alyssa. Though Jerrik had presumed Alyssa was still a maid, the possibility that she wasn't wouldn't change his mind. She'd belonged to Jerrik since she was a child. Belatedly, he knew it was his fault she'd turned to another man. He should have come back sooner to claim what was his. The fact of the matter was, he was here now. He'd proposed and she'd accepted and he wasn't going to dishonor her, her family, or Aaron's memory by backing out.

It pricked his male pride to think she may have lain with another man, but his pride would survive it. At least that's what he told himself. What really concerned him was Kostya's description of how she had relinquished her maidenhead, *willingly if not warmly*.

"You called Alyssa an ice princess," Jerrik said. "Explain." The kisses Jerrik had shared with her were the opposite of cold. Then again, she'd been his from the first kiss.

"You do know about the drunkard attacking her the summer she was ten and three?"

Jerrik nodded. King Aleksandr had told Aaron, who'd told Jerrik all he knew of the attack, including how Kostya had killed the man and saved Alyssa from almost certain rape.

"Well, the memory of it has left her indifferent to intimacy with men," Kostya said. "She will do her wifely duty, but she will not enjoy it." He eyed Jerrik, who stood silent, and then added, "This I know from experience." Jerrik stopped himself from grabbing Kostya by the neck of his tunic as the bastard turned and walked away.

As satisfying as it would feel to beat Kostya to a bloody pulp, it would serve no purpose other than to anger Kostya's and Alyssa's families.

All Jerrik had to do was ask her if what Kostya said was true. But what if she lied, as he expected most women would. The lie would be worse than the truth. With his dying breath, Aaron had told him he could trust Alyssa, yet Jerrik had trusted his mother, as had his father, and she had lied to them, and then taken her own life because of her shame.

Did it really matter if Alyssa was a virgin? In his land, a woman wasn't required or even expected to still be a maid on her wedding night, as long as she wasn't breeding with another man's child. Which would be simple enough to discover if Jerrik waited to consummate their marriage until after she'd bled. If her belly grew with Kostya's babe, Jerrik could always divorce her and ship her back to her family and Kostya's waiting arms.

Fucking Kostya.

CHAPTER 4

Vows Taken

"Do you, Jerrik, son of King Anders and Queen Alina, swear before the gods and these witnesses to strive to keep your marriage vows to Alyssa, daughter of King Aleksandr and Queen Sahar?"

Jerrik's gaze held Alyssa's, sober and serious, the lights of the torches in the courtyard reflected in their blue depths. "I do."

Alyssa let her breath out, breath she had been holding for days. Jerrik had changed. She could pinpoint the moment to when she'd returned to Storm's stall with Bones, his food dish wrapped up in the holey old blanket he slept on. She had no idea what had caused the change, and it gnawed at her.

Like, not love. Desire was evident, but lust was a far cry from love. Alyssa had lived her whole life with parents and grandparents who adored each other to distraction. She didn't get that from Jerrik, and she didn't know if she ever would.

When she'd left to retrieve the cat's meager belongings, Jerrik's eyes had been dancing with delight, as clear and blue as a summer day, but when she'd returned, his smile had disappeared and his gaze was clouded over. Since that day, though his smile had returned and the clouds cleared on occasion, he hadn't kissed her once.

"Do you, Alyssa, daughter of King Aleksandr and Queen Sahar, swear before the gods and these witnesses to strive to keep your marriage vows to Jerrik, son of King Anders and Queen Alina?"

Alyssa smiled into Jerrik's serious gaze, letting all that she felt for him shine through. "I do."

Jerrik took both of Alyssa's hands in his. He rubbed his calloused thumbs over the backs of her fingers and gave her a soft smile that brought a lump to her throat and tears to her eyes.

"Then by your vows before the gods and these witnesses here," the priest intoned, "you are husband and wife."

Jerrik stood silent and stunned, and then seemed to recollect himself. He reached into the pocket of his indigo blue tunic that highlighted his sky-blue eyes and held up a necklace of warm copper filigree with a single teardrop pearl swirling with iridescent sea green at its center. "Rings are being made at the smithy in Sea Ridge for our ceremony there," he told Alyssa, clasping the necklace around her neck. "I wanted to give you this tonight, as a token of our union," he spoke softly, so that only she could hear him, his stormy gaze fixed on hers. "Green pearls are prized because they're so rare," he said. "They symbolize purity and integrity, loyalty and trustworthiness."

Alyssa clasped the cool, smooth jewel in her hand. "All worthy attributes, especially in a marriage," she spoke so that only he could hear her, and she smiled at him, only him, and the warmth of her feelings looked to burn the clouds from Jerrik's eyes as he leaned forward and kissed her, sweet and tender and lingering, their first kiss as husband and wife.

He started to pull away, and Alyssa threw her arms around his neck and deepened the kiss, her breath a throaty sigh as Jerrik's hands roamed up and down her arms and around her waist, his strong arms holding her close as his mouth took hers, seeking, demanding, claiming.

Alyssa surrendered to his kiss, to him.

"Keep kissing like that," one of her brothers called out, "and our mother and father will be grandparents again in nine moons' time."

Jerrik broke from the kiss abruptly and eyed a blushing Alyssa, the clouds skittering across his gaze once again.

"Jerrik?" she said softly, calling him back from wherever he'd gone.

He shook his head and glanced around at his crew, at her family and friends heading for the tables set up in the courtyard for the wedding feast. "This all happened so fast."

"Fast?" Alyssa said, taken aback. "You call ten and two years fast?"

Jerrik laughed, short and quick, and not unkindly. "Not us," he said. He waved his arm around. "This. I have gone from sailor to king to husband to prospective father." He shook his head. "This is not where I saw myself four moons ago."

Alyssa understood what he was saying, yet it still made her heart bang against her ribs and her throat to constrict. She gazed down at her feet and smoothed her gown of amethyst worm weave, newly made for what should have been the happiest day of her life. "I know you wouldn't have married me if you were still skeppare of your own ship and life."

"That's not what I meant, Alyssa. I chose you of my own free will."

"Aye, once you were made king and forced to marry." He opened his mouth to object, and Alyssa held up her hand. "I'm glad you chose me, even if it was at Aaron's urging. I'm sure there were many maids in your homeland who would've been happy to marry you." He clamped his mouth shut, and Alyssa gave him a rueful grin, sure she had the right of it. "Still, you chose me, and I you, and I swear to you here and now, I will hold to our vows and be a loving and faithful wife to you and give you as many children as the gods bless us with."

"And Kostya?" he asked, giving her the full slant of his piercing blue eyes. He'd shaved for the ceremony, and she could see a muscle twitching along the side of his jaw. "Would you have gladly given him children?"

Alyssa held his gaze for a long moment. Was Jerrik jealous of Kostya? "If I had gone through with the marriage, yes, of course," she said. "But I didn't, because I never felt for Kostya what I feel for you."

"What do you feel for me, wife?"

Alyssa smiled and placed her open palm over Jerrik's heart. "Kiss me, husband, and you will know. You will always know."

Alyssa entered the bridal chamber—her bedchamber adorned with summer blooms of lilies, jasmine, and roses—dressed in a night shift of sheer worm weave the color of moonlight, her hair down, her heart beating triple time as Jerrik stopped his pacing to stand and stare at her, his mouth slightly open. She touched the green pearl dangling between her breasts, her nipples hard and sensitive from the male approval in his smile, and the fact that he was dressed only in his tunic and a breechcloth, his tanned, muscular legs bare.

He held his hand out to her. "Come to me, my little lynx," he said, "my bride, my queen."

Alyssa placed her hand in his and stepped into his arms, burrowing her nose through the gap in his night tunic and nuzzling the light furring of his chest, breathing in the scent of sun-dried linen, open seas, and musky male. The scent that was his and only his. He was hers. Her husband. Soon to be her lover. Only hers.

He tipped her chin up so her gaze met his and pressed a tender kiss to her forehead, and then he stepped back and took her by the hand and led her to the bed, sitting down and patting the space beside him. Alyssa sat down next to him, her arm pressed against the brawny length of his, loath to leave any space between them. In truth, she couldn't get close enough in her eagerness to join their bodies together and become man and wife in deed as well as word.

Jerrik took both her hands in his and held them in his lap, rubbing the backs of her fingers with his thumbs. "I'm glad we married, Alyssa," he said.

"I'm glad too."

He smiled, as unsure as Alyssa had ever seen him. "I want to make you my wife in all ways."

Alyssa shifted toward him and tilted her head.

"However," he said, "I will not breach your maidenhead until we have reached Sea Ridge."

Alyssa's heart fell with her voice. "I…don't understand."

"I want you, Alyssa," he said, squeezing her hands. "I desire you, as a man desires a woman, a husband a wife, but I don't want to plant a babe in you until we're safe and sound in Sea Ridge. It would be neither wise nor safe for you to sail pregnant, and I won't chance losing you, a babe, or both on the voyage." He raised her hands and kissed the backs of each in turn. "We've waited ten and two years," he told her, "we can wait another two moons to consummate our marriage."

Tears welled in Alyssa's eyes. She didn't know what to say, but she knew how she felt. Liked. Not loved. She'd been dreaming of her wedding night with Jerrik since she was eight years old, and though the dreams had changed through the years from innocently vague to intimately detailed, none of them had prepared her for this rejection.

"It will happen, my treasure," he said, pulling her onto his lap and nuzzling the nape of her neck, sending shivers down her spine. "I promise." He nipped her throat above her collarbone. "There are still many pleasures we can give each other," he whispered, his voice low and raspy. "All of which I plan to teach you, one," he nipped her collarbone, "by one," he nipped her shoulder, "by one."

"Well," Alyssa sighed, her disappointment tempered with each delicious, tender nip, "if you promise."

"I do," he vowed, kissing and nipping his way up her throat. "I promise."

"What will tonight's lesson be?" she asked while she could still think, for with each nip and kiss, she was losing her ability to hold on to anything past the feel of his lips on her skin.

"Kissing," he murmured low as his lips met hers, moving over them, nipping, tasting, the tip of his tongue trailing wet heat across them. He shifted her on his lap so that she was facing him, straddling him on bent knees, her thin gown tucked up under her. "Just kissing."

He deepened his kisses, his mouth covering hers, his tongue searching, seeking hers, exploring, plundering, stealing her breath and her soul. Thoughtless, boneless, nothing except warm, salty lips and raw nerves, Alyssa fell back, panting, gasping for air, for sanity. Heat from Jerrik's lap, along with something long, thick, and hard, barely contained by his breechcloth, singed her. Dazed, she gazed into eyes as blue as the sky and as deep as the sea, eyes that watched hers, searched hers.

"Alyssa?" Jerrik's voice was low and rough and resonated from her ears to her core.

She smiled, slow and sure. There was no *just* to kissing Jerrik. There never had been, and there never would be. She swayed a little and ran her hands up his arms to his shoulders, licking her lips. "Hmmm?" she hummed.

"Kiss me now, Lyssa," he rumbled. "Kiss your husband, my beautiful bride."

She leaned into him, her breasts pressed up against his chest before her lips met his, nipping and licking and suckling his until he clasped her to him with a groan. He kissed her then, hard and slaking, and it was Alyssa who moaned.

He nibbled kisses down her throat, stopping and playing where the pearl hung above the swell of her breasts, and then he ran a thumb over the peak of her nipple, and Alyssa gasped and went still. So did Jerrik. Then he lay back on the bed, taking Alyssa with him and rolling them onto their sides facing each other and holding her at arm's length.

"We should stop, Lyssa," he rasped, "before we go any further."

"Nnnooo." She gave Jerrik her best pout and he gave a quick, hoarse laugh.

"A man can only take so much temptation from such a woman before he gives in," he said, his voice low.

Alyssa went still for several breaths. "I tempt you?"

"Me and every other male from the age of eight to eighty who looks upon your beautiful face and delicious body."

She giggled at the put-upon expression on his handsome face. "I will try not to tempt you too much, my husband," she said. "At least not until we reach your…our home."

He took her hand in his and kissed it. "You don't know how much I wish it could be otherwise, Lyssa. It will be as soon as we're off the *Sea Eagle* and in our royal chambers at Sea Ridge."

She smiled and tucked their hands to her chest. "You call me Lyssa," she said with a sigh. "Only you. I like it." She snuggled in close enough to tuck her head under his chin and burrow her nose into his chest.

"Lyssa," Jerrik's low voice roused her as she was drifting off.

She lifted her head and focused on him. "Hmmm?"

He sat up and swung his legs over the bed and walked over to the chest that held his belongings, opened it and pulled out his waist blade. Alyssa's eyes opened wide as he held the blade to the tip of his little finger. "Do you want me to leave some blood on the bed linens?"

She sat up, her eyes widening as she understood what he was asking her. She bit her lower lip and nodded. "It would save us both from having to answer certain questions in the morning," she said.

"Sooo?" a bevy of women cooed as Alyssa entered the family's private dining salon late the next morning.

She blushed, remembering the night that had passed, her wedding night, and how the maidservants had nodded with approval at the bloodstains on the bed linens and her night shift when they had come into the chambers, waiting until after Jerrik had left to see to his ship. Which meant her entire family and all the palace servants already knew about it as well.

She smiled, remembering how she had woken, her backside tucked into Jerrik, his arm holding her tight, his hand resting on her breast, how he had kissed her before leaving their bed this morning, and then her smile turned inward as she remembered their kisses last night. Kisses that still made her flush.

"That good, eh?" Evgenia, Asad's wife, said with a knowing grin as she filled her bowl with juicy melon, and the salon filled with the knowing laughter of married women.

Alyssa's cheeks flamed, and the women's laughter grew, though not unkindly.

"Come, daughter." Her mother offered her a seat on the sofa beside her, her eyes smiling with understanding and affection. She tucked Alyssa into her shoulder and planted a tender kiss on her forehead. "I'm glad your wedding night makes you smile," she said. "I never expected otherwise, not between you and Jerrik." She leaned in and whispered into Alyssa's ear. "After all, you are my daughter." She chuckled as Alyssa flushed even hotter.

Her wedding night had pleased her a great deal, even though it hadn't been consummated; still, she felt guilty letting her mother believe the telltale lie of Jerrik's blood on their marriage linens.

The uneasy look on Jerrik's face when she'd agreed to it had left her worried too. Still, she'd agreed to the subterfuge, they both had, and she wouldn't go back on her word. She understood his manhood would've been questioned as much as her lack of virginity had they not bloodied the linens.

As disappointed as she was about Jerrik's determination not to consummate the marriage until they made Sea Ridge, she understood his reasoning for not wanting her to be sailing pregnant, which could indeed prove uncomfortable or worse. She'd heard of women bleeding out after a difficult miscarriage, and there would be no midwife on the ship.

"I know you idolize Jerrik," her mother said, jolting Alyssa back to their conversation, "and that you'd do most anything for him, but remember he is only a man—"

"A big, strong, handsome, virile man," Evgenia said, wagging her eyebrows for emphasis. If Alyssa and all the other women there hadn't known how much Evgenia loved Asad, Alyssa would have gladly clawed out her big doe eyes.

"A man nonetheless," her mother continued, nonplussed by her daughter-in-law's comment. "Not a mind reader." She looked at her three daughters-in-law, all of whom were nodding in agreement. "What I am trying to say is, don't be afraid or ashamed to ask for what you want and what you need as a woman, a wife, a mother, and a queen. Don't lose yourself."

Alyssa's mother was a tigress who fought as fiercely for what she believed as for those she loved. She not only believed that women were men's equals, but she had spent her life proving it, leading and teaching her children and her kingdom by example. Her wisdom was deep and hard earned, her lessons not lost on her only daughter. Surprised to see tears welling in her mother's determined eyes, Alyssa squeezed her mother's hand and said, "I promise."

"Asad loves it when I tell him what I want in bed," Evgenia offered, unasked. "Especially when I want to be on top."

Her sisters-in-law burst out laughing and her mother-in-law rolled her eyes. Alyssa flushed from head to toe, remembering how much she had liked straddling Jerrik last night, which did not go unnoticed by the incorrigible Evgenia.

"Look at our little sister's face," she said, pointing at Alyssa. "Apparently her husband likes to be ridden as well."

"Look lively, men," Sven, Jerrik's second-in-command on the *Sea Eagle,* called out. "Skeppare's aboard."

Along with Alyssa's entire extended family and a few close friends, Jerrik's crew had been at the wedding and the feast last night, and though he and Alyssa had left as soon as the food had been cleared, his crew stayed until the last of the wine and beer had been drunk.

He waved off the men as they staggered to line up, groaning and grimacing, their eyes squinting against the late morning sun.

"Take the day to recover," he told them, receiving muted, mumbled thanks as they stumbled back to whatever dark, shady corner they could find. He'd come to the ship to escape the curious stares and confining walls of the palace, to breathe fresh air and be only Jerrik for a while, not king or husband. "The crew seems to have enjoyed my wedding feast," he said to Sven.

"And you, lad," Sven asked. "How did you enjoy your wedding night with the lovely Alyssa?"

A big, burly Northman from the eastern wetlands who had sailed under Jerrik's uncle Knut for at least ten and five years before Jerrik had become skeppare, and who had taught Jerrik and Aaron as much about how to handle themselves in strange ports as he had about sailing, Sven was the only man besides Knut who had ever called Jerrik "lad." As thickly muscled as an ox, but much quicker thinking and moving, he'd saved their skins more than once through the years. Aside from his Uncle Knut and Aaron, both of whom were dead now, Jerrik trusted Sven more than anyone.

"As well as could be expected," Jerrik told him.

"Aye, well, virgin brides can be tricky, so I've been told," Sven said. "You must treat them kindly and with patience." He eyed Jerrik. "You did treat her kindly and with patience, did you not, lad?"

"Of course I did."

"Because that sweet girl worships the ground you walk on, lad. You are her true north."

"I know." He did. "I would never hurt her." Not on purpose.

He was fairly certain he'd hurt her last night. Deeply. Though Alyssa had seemed to accept and understand his excuses for not consummating their marriage until they reached Sea Ridge, she hadn't been able to hide her dismay. Which added to Jerrik's confusion, for if she truly were indifferent to intimacy with a man, why had she looked dejected instead of pleased? Why had Kostya called her cold in bed?

Alyssa and Jerrik had only kissed, yet her kisses were more passionate than most women's lovemaking.

Fucking Kostya. If it hadn't been for his claim that he'd taken, no, that Alyssa had given him her maidenhead, Jerrik would have been stones deep into his bride last night. It occurred to him for about the thousandth time that Kostya had lied, but Jerrik couldn't take that chance.

Thanks to Kostya, the only way that Jerrik could make sure that Alyssa wasn't pregnant with the bastard's child was to not consummate the marriage until after she had bled. Which was why he'd come up with the excuse of not wanting her to sail pregnant.

It wasn't that Jerrik couldn't wait until then. He'd been with Marianne fairly regularly right up until the night before he'd left Sea Ridge, when he'd retired to his chambers only to find her waiting in his bed, knowing full well he was sailing for Alyssa to bring her back as his bride. He hadn't missed Marianne since the day he'd left. She was an experienced lover who knew how to please a man, yet Jerrik found himself craving Alyssa's innocent, passionate kisses over Marianne's skilled performances. If Alyssa's kisses were, indeed, innocent.

Ask her, Jerrik told himself for about the hundredth time since Kostya had claimed she'd given her maidenhead. *Ask her if she's slept with Kostya.* Jerrik would know if she told him the truth.

But what if the truth was that she had lain with Kostya, and she truly disliked being intimate with a man? Or worse, if Kostya had lied about Alyssa being cold in bed to keep Jerrik from marrying her, and she had enjoyed sex with Kostya.

Jerrik rubbed his jaw and told himself it didn't matter. He'd had sex with hundreds of women, sex that had meant nothing more than the physical pleasure of the moment. What did it matter if she'd had sex with Kostya, good or bad?

She had sworn to be a loyal and faithful wife to Jerrik, and that was all that mattered from now forward. He'd been telling himself this daily since that day in the stables. Problem was, he didn't believe a word of it.

The thought of Alyssa touching or being touched by Kostya or any other man except Jerrik was like a festering sore, one he knew he should leave alone but couldn't help but pick at, making it even more angry and purulent. The thought of her lying to him, as his mother had to his father, was even worse. Which was why he hadn't asked her flat out.

"Take a look at the horse pen," Sven said, pulling Jerrik from his unhappy muddle. "The men finished it yesterday as a wedding present."

Jerrik took in the sturdy fencing and the clean straw spread on the deck, the old sail stretched like a tarp over a corner for shade, the water buckets in the pen and the bales of hay and buckets of oats stacked out of a horse's reach. He looked around the rest of the deck, which was cleaner than the floors of most inns, at the tight coils of ropes, neatly stacked buckets, and tied-down sails, and he knew that if he went below deck, he would find the hold laden with a supply of food and trade goods, the crew's personal belongings in their chests and the oars gleaming with beeswax. His uncle had taught Jerrik to keep a tight ship, always at the ready.

"We'll load Alyssa's belongings tomorrow," he said. "Start getting the horses used to walking up and down the gang plank and spending some time in their pen, let them get the feel of a ship before we set sail." This had been Alyssa's idea. He liked how she thought of their comfort and welfare, as she had in setting up Bones in the hold of his new little kingdom that was the *Sea Eagle*. "Remind me to thank the men for finishing the pen when they're up to hearing it."

"Will do, Skeppare."

"Everything still on schedule?"

"Aye, Skeppare."

Jerrik nodded. They'd be setting sail in three days, heading north and then west up the Mother River, which would take twice as long as the twenty days it took them to sail downriver because they would have to tack from shore to shore as well as put the oars to use. It was still quicker than sailing south on the river and then west through the Great Inland Sea and across the Mid-Earth Sea. They wouldn't need to store fresh water until they made the Northern Straits. Once in the Straits, they'd sail west for another seven days before landing in their home port of Sea Ridge, where he and Alyssa would start their new lives together as king and queen.

Until then, he was looking forward to one last journey aboard the *Sea Eagle*.

One last time to be nothing more than skeppare.

His first time as a husband.

CHAPTER 5

The Journey Begins

Alyssa stood on the stern of the *Sea Eagle*, tears flowing down her cheeks as she waved good-bye to her family standing on the dock, their familiar, loving faces growing smaller and smaller as the ship tacked upriver. Jerrik tucked her into his shoulder and pressed his lips to the crown of her head.

"I've never seen a man, especially a king, cry so openly and without shame before," he said, "yet still maintain his dignity."

Alyssa smiled through her tears. "My father loves his children," she sniffed. "More than anything in this world except my mother."

"Did he cry when your brothers married?"

Alyssa shook her head. "I'm the first to leave him. My brothers all brought their wives into the family fold, and my father simply built a new wing onto the palace for each new couple and whatever children they might have."

"I was only six when my mother died," Jerrik told her. "I remember her. Her voice when she sang, her smile, her soft cheek pressed against mine, but I don't remember the feel of a family. Not since she left us. The closest thing to family I've had for many years now has been this ship and crew."

Alyssa turned away from the distant dock, from her home, and into Jerrik's embrace. She knew a little about his mother from Aaron, that she had taken her own life, and that Jerrik had felt her absence keenly ever since. She met his gaze and held it. "We will make a new family, you and I."

Jerrik nodded and tucked her closer into him. "We better," he said. "My family are counting on it, and I promised your mother that

I would send my fastest warship for her two moons before you're due with our firstborn."

Alyssa's cheeks flushed hot and Jerrik grinned.

"And," he said. "I promised your father that we would come back to celebrate his sixtieth birthday, and that we would stay a full moon."

Alyssa took a deep breath in and blew it out, turning her face to the north and east, to her new life. "It's strange," she mused aloud. "It's the women in my family who leave their homes to start new lives with their husbands in distant lands, my mother with my father, my grandmother and great-aunt with their husbands."

"I met them, you know," Jerrik said.

"Who?"

"Your grandfather and grandmother, King Asad and Queen Oona, and your great-uncle and auntie, Nasim and Lyrra. We sailed into their cities' ports twice after Aaron joined the crew, and stayed as guests in their palace." He smiled down at Alyssa. "You take after your Great-Aunt Lyrra."

"So I've been told."

"Did you not know her?"

"I only met her once, and my grandmother twice." Alyssa smiled, remembering her conversation with her grandmother about Jerrik, and how the women in their family fell in love at first sight. How, like her Aunt Lyrra, people who didn't know them well assumed that Alyssa was more delicate, physically and emotionally, than she actually was. "Even so, the three of us understood one another."

"You sing and play the harp as well as your aunt did, which will come in handy on this voyage. The crew are heartily sick of my singing and Han's flute."

Alyssa doubted that. Jerrik had a wonderful voice, low and deep, rich in timbre with an edge of roughness that resonated from her ears to her bones, whether he was singing a ballad or whispering sweet endearments in her ear. She watched the crew performing their duties with the ease of a well-practiced dance. The crew she would be living in close quarters amongst for the next moon and a half, and whom she had come to know fairly well over the past ten days.

There was Sven, Jerrik's second-in-command, a big, burly, gray-bearded Northman from the eastern isles who demanded no more from the rest of the crew than he was willing to put forth, which was his all. Yet despite his gruffness, he put Alyssa in mind of a mother hen watching over her unruly chicks, chicks that knew better than to ruffle his feathers too much.

After Sven, Jerrik looked to Bors, another big Northman, bigger than Sven, and a good ten years younger, whose eyes were the color and mettle of well-honed blades and who wore his dark blond hair and beard cropped close, which was how he kept his words, tight and close. A scar ran down the left side of his face from below his eye to his chin, a warning, Jerrik said, to any man foolish enough to challenge him in a fight.

Lev, who hailed from the northwestern shores of the Mother River, was the head carpenter. It was he who had overseen building the horse pen, and who was in charge of fixing and maintaining the ship's structure, all while cursing in the most colorful of Alyssa's mother tongue. He was also the ship's surgeon.

The most mysterious to Alyssa was Han. He had joined the crew on the *Sea Eagle*'s last voyage to the far east, and was the only member who hadn't sailed under Knut, Jerrik's uncle. He'd come to Jerrik's defense after a pearl trader accused Jerrik of cheating him, standing back to back with Jerrik and fending off a crowd of drunken sailors looking for a fight.

Slim and agile as a cat, with sooty black hair that fell to his waist when it wasn't pinned up in a topknot, Han was up in the sails and rigging almost more than he was down on the deck, and according to Jerrik, Han was as deadly throwing his assortment of blades as he was fighting with them.

The fifth member of the crew was Zoltan, the main cook as well as sail and net mender, who came from the Hellenes Isles and was as proud of his flowing black curls as he was of his tight seams and fish soup. He was also an incorrigible flirt. A harmless one, but entertaining nonetheless.

In truth, other than among the men of her own family, Alyssa had never felt so safe and protected as she did among Jerrik's crew. It was obvious that they respected him as skeppare and king, and showed her that same respect as his wife and queen.

Respect she meant to earn on her own merit during the voyage.

"Let's hope I have my grandmother Oona's sea legs," she told Jerrik, "and not my auntie Lyrra's. She got horribly seasick."

Alyssa splashed water in Jerrik's face, laughing as he dove underwater and grabbed her ankle, which she jerked from his loose hold with a playful yelp and then backed up a safe distance from the bubbles giving his location away.

Over the last fortnight of sailing and rowing upriver, they'd learned many things about each other and themselves, among them how ticklish Alyssa was. All Jerrik had to do was reach for her ankle and she would giggle and squirm, which he seemed to thoroughly enjoy causing. He pushed up and squirted a mouthful of water at her, and she rewarded him with another splash in his face.

"Come here, my beautiful bride," he said, pulling her close as she swam into his arms, their legs moving in unison beneath them. He kissed her and ran his hands up and down the goosebumps on her arms. "Time to get out of the water."

"No," Alyssa protested. "Not yet." She wrapped her legs around his waist and teased him with a smile.

"Your lips are turning blue, my little otter," he said, "and so are my bollocks."

Alyssa had heard her brothers talking about "blue bollocks" quite a few times through the years and knew the term could refer to either a man's testicles freezing, as was likely the case with Jerrik now, or to a lack of sexual release, which could also be the case. They'd kissed and petted each other plenty over the past fortnight, yet had gone no farther, and while Alyssa thoroughly enjoyed both, she was eager to do more.

She knew by Jerrik's pained grimaces and bulging breechcloth during their love play that he was as frustrated as she was, if not more so. She tightened her legs around his waist and bumped her pelvis against his. "We can do something about those blue bollocks of yours," she said with her newly practiced come-hither smile.

"Yes, we can," he said, setting his jaw and unwrapping her legs from his waist. "We can swim to shore and dry off."

Alyssa followed Jerrik as he swam for the shore, unsure of what she'd done to displease him. One moment he had been his playful, teasing self, and the next he'd turned staid and dour.

This wasn't the first time his moods had changed in an instant. His temper was like the sky, clear and warm and calm one moment and storm-tossed and cold the next. Yet another thing she'd learned about her husband over the past fortnight. Still, his smiles and laughter were worth putting up with his frowns and silences, and she figured she'd navigate how to deal with both as they continued to learn about each other.

Once on the shore, he shook himself off and then picked up the large linen drying cloth and wrapped Alyssa up in it as soon as she walked out of the water. She had cut the hem of one of her night shifts up to her thighs to swim and bathe in, and though his crew had shown her nothing but respect, he was careful of her modesty.

They walked into their tent, a comfort that Jerrik told her he'd never bothered with before in good weather, where Alyssa stripped out of her wet shift and he picked up another towel and began to rub her goose-pimpled skin dry, starting at her nose and cheeks and working his way across her shoulders and up and down her arms as she shifted from foot to foot, her teeth chattering.

He started to rub slow circles around her breasts, and she stilled as his thumbs gently rubbed even smaller circles over her pebbled nipples. Her chattering soughed into a sigh and Jerrik swallowed her breath with a kiss as he rubbed the towel down her back and over her backside, grinning into their kiss as her sigh turned into a soft moan.

Trailing kisses that left her panting down her neck, between her breasts and across her belly, he rubbed the towel down the backs of her legs and nuzzled the curls between her legs. He flicked the tip of his tongue through her curls, touching her flesh, and Alyssa went rigid, every sensation in her body pooling where his tongue had touched her. Pulling back, he finished drying the fronts of her legs and the tops of her feet and then he stood and wrapped the towel around her sopping wet hair.

He leaned in and placed an almost chaste kiss on her lips. "Did my touch please you?"

Alyssa nodded and licked her lower lip. It was the first time he had gone that far with their sex play. The first time he had touched her there. "Yes," she whispered.

He kissed her again, suckling her lower lip. "I'm glad," he whispered huskily. "Would you like to continue this later tonight?"

"Oh yes."

Alyssa stumbled out of the tent in her long tunic, her skin warm everywhere Jerrik had touched and kissed, her flesh aching where he had nuzzled and licked.

She walked in a daze over to the horses and triple checked the rope line even though she and Jerrik had double checked it after their afternoon ride. It had become their custom after coming ashore for the night to take the horses for a quick run while the rest of the crew set up camp. After stretching the horses' legs and staking them out, Jerrik and Alyssa would swim in the river while Lev prepared their supper.

She smiled, thinking of how Jerrik would always cover her with a drying linen as they walked from the river to their tent, shielding her half-naked and completely soaked body from his men. Not that any of them would dare to stare or gawk; they had too much respect for Jerrik, and treated her like a little sister, which was something Alyssa was used to.

What she wasn't used to was the raw hunger in Jerrik's eyes when she stood before him naked and shivering, more from the heat in his gaze than from the cold water. A heat that she knew was mirrored in her own eyes when he stood before her in almost all his naked splendor. He had yet to remove his breechcloth in front of her.

Alyssa had grown up amongst big, strong, handsome men, as known for their looks as for their brains and their brawn, yet not one of them compared to Jerrik.

He was all sharp-honed planes and angles, with muscles sculpted by the hard, physical life of a sailor and crowned with hair the pale yellow of the sun with a smile as bright and blazing, and eyes as blue and clear as the sky. Those eyes had watched and smiled into hers while promising her more of the blinding flash of pleasure his tongue had given her in their tent only moments ago.

"Are you ready for lesson?"

Alyssa whirled around to stare blankly at Han, her cheeks flaming as she tried to pull her thoughts from Jerrik's tongue to what Han was saying. "Lesson?"

Han flipped the waist blade he held in his hand a full circle, catching it by the hilt. "You ask me teach you throw knife."

"Knives," Alyssa said, gathering her wits. Her parents had taught her how to fight with blades from knives to swords, and she had grown up sparring with her brothers and had impressed the *Sea Eagle*'s crew by sparring with Jerrik and Han. But she had never learned to throw knives, and had asked Han to teach her. She pulled her skirt up through her legs and tucked the hem into her waist belt, freeing her legs for better movement. "I'm ready."

"We go there." Han pointed to a stack of logs washed up by the tides a hundred feet upriver. "So you not stab men instead of target."

Once Jerrik got his randy cock under control, he changed into a dry, clean tunic, and trousers, and made his way over to where Sven sat on a log by the fire where two rabbits roasted on a spit, chewing on his beard while carving on the piece of driftwood he'd been working into the shape of a mermaid for the past three nights.

"Smells good," Jerrik said.

"Aye. Bors claimed he was tired of fish stew and snared these hares whilst you and the missus were splashing around."

Jerrik eyed Sven. He'd known the big Northman most of his life. In truth, Sven had helped raise Jerrik along with his Uncle Knut. He knew Sven better than he ever knew his own father or his brothers.

"Out with it," Jerrik said.

"Out with what?"

"Whatever it is you're chewing on besides your beard."

Sven set his carving aside and glanced over to where Alyssa was watching Han flipping knives, nodding her head at what Han was telling her. "The men and me," Sven said. "We've been noticing how we drop anchor earlier an' earlier each evening and pull anchor later an' later each morning." He eyed Jerrik. "An' since we're losing time tacking upriver, we were wondering if there's a reason we're wasting daylight."

Jerrik watched the *Sea Eagle* gently sway and bob against her anchor line in the river, and then he looked to where Alyssa was mimicking Han's motions of aiming and throwing with the natural grace the women of her family were renowned for.

While Jerrik hadn't done it consciously, Sven and the men were right, he had been ordering the *Sea Eagle* to shore early and setting sail late for the simple reason he'd been enjoying this time with his new bride.

He liked being Jerrik, newly besotted husband and skeppare, and not king. He'd missed sailing the rushing rivers and open seas, the expansive sky and strange lands, the wind in his face and the stars to guide him.

More, he looked forward to his nights with Alyssa, especially when it was their turn to stay onboard ship overnight, only the two of them, away from the prying eyes and ears of the crew. He liked learning about his wife away from the crowds and politics of a palace. He liked how she took to the sailing and the camping, how she was teaching him to ride and he was teaching her the pleasures of sex.

He liked courting Alyssa, even though she was already his wife, something he had never done with other women. He liked getting to know her. He liked her.

He wasn't ready to share her with the rest of the world yet.

He chuckled as Alyssa let out a whoop of victory after sticking a blade into a log. "Truth is," he told Sven, knowing his words would make it back to the rest of the crew, "I'm enjoying my freedom and my bride. I'm in no hurry to return to the shackles of life in a palace."

"The roast rabbit and greens were delicious," Alyssa told Zoltan and Bors as she licked her fingers. Fingers Jerrik was eager to feel running over his skin later. "Thank you."

"You are most welcome, mistress."

Alyssa eyed Zoltan with raised brows.

"Alyssa," he corrected.

"Bones will be most appreciative when I take him a piece of rabbit tonight," she said.

Zoltan laughed. "With the weight that cat is putting on, you will need to rename him soon."

Jerrik nodded. With the steady diet of rats and mice he caught on the ship, and the choice bits of fish and meat the crew fed him, Bones was filling up and out and growing into a handsome tom.

"What is the male version of Bertruda?" Zoltan asked.

"Hey." Bors punched Zoltan in the arm. "At least I know my mother's name," he told Zoltan, "and who my father was."

The men all burst out laughing and Alyssa looked to Jerrik.

"Bertruda is the name of Bors' mother," he explained to her, holding out his arms and puffing out his cheeks.

"Ah." She laughed as the crew shoved, pushed, and taunted each other.

She was the first woman to ever sail on the *Sea Eagle*, and Jerrik was glad to see the crew had taken to her so well and so quickly. They'd even started telling her tales of Aaron around the campfire at night, and tonight Jerrik noticed a marked difference, a lightness to his crew, since Sven had related his and Jerrik's conversation to them before they'd gathered for supper tonight.

"Music?" Alyssa said, and the men stopped jostling each other.

Bors helped Zoltan wash the pots in the river while Alyssa took her harp from the tent. When she returned to the fire, Han had his flute out and Lev his sticks for drumming on the logs.

"'The Wedding Song'?" Alyssa said, taking a seat beside Jerrik.

Jerrik dipped his head to her. "Ladies first."

She strummed "Meadow Lark" as Lev began to tap the logs, warming up their wrists and fingers, for the way this group sang "The Wedding Song" could take half a night.

She'd told them all the tale of the Lion and the Swan, the story of her grandfather and grandmother, King Asad and Queen Oona, and of how Oona, a slave, had sung the song to Asad, the Prince Black Mane, the first night they met. How Oona had sung the song in the desert words the first verse, the traditional verse, and then how she'd sung the song in her High Land tongue the second verse, changing the words and calling him her prince, her darling, and how she would change the words each time she sang it to him after, sending him secret messages of love.

Since then, Jerrik and the others had taken to changing the words of each verse, trying to outdo each other with whatever theme the song took for the night.

Alyssa sang:

"Welcome, gentlemen,
Welcome, and here's a health to you,
Tonight, there will be a wedding,
Tonight, she will be a bride,
The Skeppare is my darling."
She nodded to Jerrik, who sang:
"Welcome, gentlemen,
Welcome, and here's a foretelling to you,
Tonight, there will be a taming,
Tonight, she will purr,
The Lynx is my darling."

Jerrik wagged his eyebrows at Alyssa, whose cheeks flushed a becoming pink, and the men hooted and whistled until Zoltan, always the showman, jumped up and danced a jig while he sang.

"Welcome, ladies,
Welcome, and here's a man for you,
Tonight, there will be dancing,
Tonight,"
he tossed back his long curls,
"you will swoon,
over me, my darlings."
Lev drummed a loud ba-da-bum on the log and the crew groaned to a man.

Zoltan gave over the stage of trampled grass with a flourish to Lev, and so it went, each verse getting bawdier and bawdier with each singing, until Alyssa missed plucking half the notes for wiping the tears of laughter from her eyes. After the third round of bawdy verses, Jerrik stood and offered Alyssa his hand.

"Gentlemen," he said, clearing his voice. "As it is our turn to guard the ship tonight, we will be retiring now."

"Spoilsport," Lev called out good naturedly as they headed for their tent to gather what they needed for the night.

"Braggart," Zoltan added with rather less good humor.

"Let's go below deck for a while," Jerrik suggested, though they usually stayed deck side on their overnights aboard the *Sea Eagle*.

"Is there something in particular you want to check on?" Alyssa asked.

"There is," he told her. "Something quite particular in fact."

What he didn't tell her was that the something was a particular part of her body. A part he had skimmed with his tongue earlier in their tent, and that he was eager to check thoroughly tonight. He didn't want the sounds he hoped to elicit from her carrying to the men on shore.

As king and skeppare, he could have easily commandeered the privacy of the ship all night, every night, yet as much as enjoyed their nights aboard ship, he was practical enough to know that keeping their nights aboard to every third night helped keep him from pushing his self-made boundaries with Alyssa.

Tonight though, if she let him, he would be pushing himself and her to the edge of those boundaries.

He followed her down the ladder and struck the flint to light a few candles while she petted Bones and fed him bits of rabbit. He chuckled as the cat's loud purring rumbled through the hold.

"That cat eats better than some people," he said.

"That's because he's such a good ratter, are you not, my handsome Bones?" Alyssa cooed to the cat, who was now licking his paws and rubbing them over his jowls.

"Butterball is more like it," he pretended to grouse.

"Don't listen to him." Alyssa scratched the cat's chin. "He's jealous."

"Aye," he said, striding over and scooping Alyssa into his arms. "I am." He dropped his giggling bride onto a soft pile of furs and lowered himself over her. "I am jealous of each and every pet and caress and cooing and tender tidbit you give that mangy cat."

"He's not mangy." Alyssa pouted prettily.

Anything else she tried to say Jerrik's lips stopped. He kissed her long and hard, intent on wiping any thought of anything except each other from both of their minds. He kissed her until she was purring deep in her throat and then he pulled back and his cock jumped at her little mewl of protest. "Lift your arms, Lyssa."

She smiled at her favorite pet name and languidly lifted her arms, sighing as he pulled her tunic up and over her head and tossed it to the floor, quickly followed by his own. She reached up and placed both palms on his chest above his erect nipples, and then slowly ran her palms over his shoulders and down his arms. "Kiss me again, husband," she soughed.

"As you command, wife."

He kissed her mouth, softly at first, then harder, more intent, his tongue tangling with hers until she was gripping his arms. He kissed his way down her throat to first one nipple and then the other, nipping and suckling as she arched her back to give him even more.

Jerrik trailed his hands down her sides, his thumbs pushing the waist of her skirt down below her hips, his mouth following, and he heard her soft, low moan as he ran his hands up the insides of her thighs, stopping as his thumbs touched her curls. This was as far as he'd ever gone with Alyssa, until tonight. He sat back on his knees and waited as her glazed eyes focused on his.

"I want to do something we haven't done before," he said. "I want to pleasure you with my hands and my mouth."

Alyssa licked her lips and nodded.

"Trust me," Jerrik told her as began to pull her skirt down the sleekly muscled length of her legs. "I think you'll like this."

He hoped. So far Kostya had been wrong about her fear of intimacy. Jerrik would find out if his run of good luck was about to end.

He started slowly, running his fingers from her ankles to her knees and then following with his mouth, kissing and nipping the tender skin up the insides of her thighs. Her belly twitched and her breath caught as his mouth met his hands at the top of her thighs, and then he parted her curls with his thumbs, brushing the pads over the sensitive flesh that his tongue had flicked over earlier. Alyssa released her breath with a sigh.

"Open yourself to me, my beauty," he rasped, his hands gently pushing Alyssa's legs wide. "Ahh." He blew his breath over her exposed flesh. "There's my pearl." He licked her, slowly, deliberately, and Alyssa gasped and tensed, and then he licked her again, and Alyssa melted and moaned. "There's my treasure."

His cheeks rose against her thighs in a slow smile and he lightly rubbed the soft bristles of his beard against her skin. He ran his tongue in delicious, deliberate circles around her flesh, closing the circles in on the little nubbin of flesh that he knew was the center of all sensation.

Sounds came out of Alyssa that Jerrik had never heard her make before, from soft, high-pitched mewling to low, guttural groans, primal, earthy sounds that urged him on.

He took her sensitive nubbin in his mouth and suckled and she fisted her hands in the furs and opened her legs even wider, opening her body, herself to him, whose pleasure it was to take her to the edge of her known world and beyond.

She wove her fingers through his hair and held on as he drove her through wave upon wave of pleasure until she peaked and crashed and lay spent and breathless on their newly discovered shore.

As she came back to herself with each slowing breath, Jerrik kissed his way up her belly to her mouth, sharing the taste of her on his lips and her scent on his beard. She lifted her pelvis, meeting the hard length of his erection still contained by his breechcloth and began to move her hips against it.

"Alyssa." Jerrik gave her a warning growl.

"You pleasured me," she said, her voice low and sultry. "How can I pleasure you?"

Jerrik lifted himself up onto his elbows and met her earnest gaze. "You want to pleasure me?"

"I do. I grew up with six older brothers, three of whom are married now. I've heard bits and pieces of their talk about the pain and danger of blue bollocks. I don't want to make you suffer such a malady." She smiled, her expression a sensuous mix of shyness and sexuality. "Surely, you need your release."

Jerrik groaned. "Keep talking like that and I will have it sooner rather than later."

"How do you mean?"

Jerrik sat back on his knees and Alyssa eyed his about-to-burst-at-the-seams breechcloth. He fixed his gaze on Alyssa's. "Do you really want to know?"

"I do."

He gave a short, quick snort of laughter. "Normally," he said, "after our sex play, I wait until you fall asleep and then I take matters into my own hand."

Alyssa tilted her head and then her eyes grew wide. "Oh," she said, blushing furiously. She bit her lower lip. "Can I watch?"

CHAPTER 6

Lessons Learned

"Can I watch?"

Jerrik stood at the helm of the *Sea Eagle* as they tacked upriver, half-hard simply thinking about Alyssa and their sex play last night. Thinking of how she had sat up on her knees, knees that had been around his shoulders as he brought her to climax with his mouth, of how she had watched intently as he freed his straining cock from the confines of his breechcloth.

How her big, beautiful eyes had grown even bigger and wider at the sight of him fully aroused. How she'd bit her lower lip when he smeared the milky drop of his arousal from his tip to his root, and then licked her lips as he started to slowly run his hand up and down his throbbing cock. He'd watched her watching him, never taking his eyes from her as he'd stroked faster and harder, imagining her wet, swollen lips wrapped around him, pulling on him, sucking him. Only then had he closed his eyes, his release pulsing into the cup of his other hand.

Before he could wipe his handful onto a rag, she had lifted from her knees and bent over his hand and dipped a finger into his spent seed and licked the drop from her fingertip as dainty as a cat tasting a bowl of fresh cream.

"Hmm," she'd said, her purr still vibrating through his cock. "Tastes like…beer."

Desire shuddered through him, and he shook himself from his reverie before he embarrassed himself in front of his crew.

He looked up into the rigging where Alyssa was helping Han tie off one of the lines, her hair braided into a thick rope that shone like burnt honey in the sun's light, her feet bare, and her skirt pulled up between her legs and tucked into her waist belt, creating a sort of pantaloons that enabled her to scamper around the riggings with her movement unimpeded. She saw him watching her and smiled down at him, as warm and bright as the summer's light reflecting off the water.

Fucking Kostya.

Jerrik didn't know if Kostya had lied about Alyssa being afraid of intimacy and cold in bed, hoping that Jerrik would decide not to marry her, or if she had truly been cold and unresponsive with Kostya. Which would've been the best answer to that riddle.

With Jerrik she'd shown no fear of intimacy.

In truth, she was the most naturally responsive woman he'd ever been with. Oh, he'd been with women who were better schooled, and better actresses, but never with one who was as sensitive to his touch, or whose touch he felt so fervently.

Whether the bastard had lied about taking Alyssa's maidenhead, he'd succeeded in planting the seed of a doubt in Jerrik's surprisingly jealous mind, causing him to set a course of denial for himself and Alyssa until they reached Sea Ridge.

A course he regretted more each day, yet one that he would keep to. As much as he wished he were still simply skeppare, he had agreed to become king, and a king's son and heir must be from his own loins and blood, leaving him honor bound not to spill his seed into Alyssa until she had bled. It was either that or admit to Alyssa that he had lied about why he wouldn't consummate their marriage before they reached his home.

Fucking Kostya.

Alyssa hugged River's sides tight as they raced Jerrik and Storm across the open meadow and felt a little thrill where her seat rubbed against the mare's back, a newly sensitive part of her body that had been dormant until last night that was now fully awake and aware.

The thundering of hooves approaching told Alyssa that Storm and Jerrik were gaining on her and River while she'd been daydreaming about her nights with her husband.

In bed, he was her dream man. Everything she wanted him to be: generous, adventurous, gentle, and not…but in the best way.

Yet, every now and again, she caught him staring at the water wearing a frown, or scowling at her, his expression fixed in a mask of consternation. When he realized she'd caught him, he fixed a smile on his face that didn't reach his eyes. Because of those times she wondered what churned in his gut, and if he was only playing the part of the happy newlywed. He seemed pleased enough with her, but she knew a man didn't have to love a woman to enjoy her in bed. Sometimes she worried their marriage was nothing but him fulfilling his duty to his family or keeping his word to Aaron.

Times like now, when they were lighthearted and happy, she felt foolish for allowing dark thoughts to trouble her, but she'd be a fool not to worry about what was troubling her husband.

Alyssa glanced over and grinned at him. He'd taken to riding as well and quickly as she had taken to sailing. He was accomplished at many things, but today she could focus on nothing but what they'd done last night.

She thought of his proud cock and ached to straddle it and ride him until they both fell tumbling down the cliff he had taken her soaring over last night. That particular dream would have to wait to be fulfilled. Disappointed as she was by his decision to wait until they got to Sea Ridge, she understood it. Still, she was learning there were many pleasures to be had without consummation, and had become an avid student.

Her mind on tonight's promised lesson, she came back to the here and now as Jerrik and Storm went racing by. Jerrik reined Storm into a loping loop and brought the stallion alongside Alyssa and River as they slowed to a cooling walk back toward the river.

"I'm sorry to be so blunt and indelicate," he said, "but when do you expect your moon flow?"

Surprised, but not offended, amused even that his mind seemed to have been on the same thing, Alyssa counted backwards. Her last flow had finished three days before her non-wedding to Kostya, which would have been twenty and eight days ago. "Any day now," she said, catching the quick uptick of Jerrik's brows. "Reconsidering your vow not to consummate our marriage before we reach your home?" she teased.

"Every waking moment of every day and night since."

Alyssa laughed, inordinately pleased by his confession. "I'm no sheltered innocent," she told him, testing his resolve. "I know there are ways to avoid pregnancy."

"How?"

Alyssa shook her head. Surely a man as worldly as he would know. "You're asking me how a woman avoids getting pregnant?"

"No," he said, all humor gone from his voice. "How do you know?"

"I have six, no, five older brothers," she corrected herself and caught his flinch. "Three sisters-in-law, numerous aunts, uncles, and cousins. I grew up in a palace full of servants. I would have to be deaf, dumb, and blind not to have learned of such things." She eyed his serious face and gave him a teasing smile. "I'm willing to chance it if you are."

"I'm not."

Alyssa sat back at the finality of his response, and tried to make light of the cold shiver that ran down her spine. "It's just as well, I suppose," she said. "My mother and grandmother both have spoken of how their moon flows were often set off course by long journeys."

His hooded eyes fastened and held onto hers. "As you say, it's just as well."

He said nothing more, and here was one of those times Alyssa sensed he was angry at her, though she wasn't certain about what or why. She was about to ask him when he pulled Storm to a halt and cocked his head first one way and then the other.

"Do you hear that?" he said.

Alyssa stopped River and listened.

"There," he said, jutting his chin toward a thicket of flowering brambles on the edge of the meadow.

Alyssa finally heard it, a soft, high-pitched whining. She jumped off River and started to follow the sound of an animal in distress.

"Alyssa, wait," Jerrik called after her, but she was already at the thicket's edge, bending down on her knees and offering the back of her hand to a quivering bundle of white and tan fur with liquid brown eyes huddled in a shallow hole freshly dug under the brush.

"Are you lost, little one?" she cooed.

She looked up and around the open meadow she and Jerrik had been exercising the horses in, knowing there were no farmhouses or fishing huts there, but somehow hoping to see signs of the pup's owner or mother or other litter mates. She saw nothing.

"Did some horrible, heartless person leave you here all alone?" The pup gave Alyssa's hand a sniff and a tentative lick, and she gently stroked the frightened creature's nose and forehead, working her way to its ears and the back of its neck. Jerrik squatted beside her and offered his finger for a sniff and a lick as well. "Are you injured, little one?" Alyssa said, her voice purposely high and soft. "Will you let me see?"

Slowly, carefully, she worked her hands over the pup's back and down his sides, applying gentle pressure along its spine and ribs, nodding with relief as the pup neither clenched nor cried out.

Scooping her hands under its belly, she lifted the pup, who was no bigger than a rabbit, up and out from under the bush and tucked it into her chest, whispering soothing endearments and continuing to stroke the frightened animal's head and neck.

"See if it can stand," he said.

Setting it on the ground, Alyssa let go of her hold and sat back as the pup stood on all fours and wagged its stubby tail.

"It doesn't look to be hurt," he said, eyeing the pup's protruding ribs and sunken belly. "Half- starved maybe."

"It's a boy," Alyssa said, cupping the dog's muzzle as it sniffed her hand. She lifted the pup's upper lips and checked its teeth. "Four to five moons old. See there," she showed him, "his adult incisors are in, but not his canines yet." She let go of the pup's lips, and they stuck to his gums, which were pale and tacky. "He needs water and food," she said as she picked up the pup and cradled him to her.

"We can feed him and shelter him until we reach the next port, which is only a day or two's sailing from here," he said.

"We can't keep him?"

"A ship is no place for a dog, Alyssa, especially once we reach the Northern Straits."

"But—"

"Where will he relieve himself? What if he falls off?"

"He can learn to relieve himself in his own box of dirt, as Bones does," she said. "I can make a harness and keep him tied up whenever he is on deck."

He eyed her and the pup.

"Please." Alyssa hugged the pup tighter and gazed up at her husband with wide, pleading eyes, something that almost always worked with her father and brothers.

He laughed, quick and short, and shook his head at her. "What are you going to name him, since Bones is already taken?"

Alyssa smiled and stood on her toes to kiss her husband's bearded cheek. "Digger," she said. She kissed the pup on top of his head and handed him over to Jerrik and untied her head scarf. "Those blackberries are ripe for the picking. I'm sure the crew will like fresh berries with their supper."

"Aye, they'll make a good bribe for taking in this flea-bitten mongrel," he said with a wry grin, scratching the pup's chin as he said it.

Alyssa fed Digger some dried meat and hard cheese while Zoltan gutted the fish for their evening stew, setting aside the entrails for Bones. Lev had pulled some pieces of lumber from his cache and was measuring and cutting for the pup's dirt box, while Han worked on fashioning a harness and leash from some old rope. Suddenly, the pup stood at full alert and let out a series of high-pitched woofs, and they all turned to see Sven and Bors returning from their afternoon hunt empty-handed.

"What a good little guard dog you are, Digger," Alyssa praised the pup, who then ran and hid behind her skirt as the two big Northmen walked up.

"What," Sven glared down at the pup, "is that?"

"It's a puppy Jerrik and I found," Alyssa told him as Sven turned a chary eye to Jerrik. "His name is Digger."

She coaxed the pup out from under her skirt and held him up to Bors, who cradled the pup to his chest, grinning like a lad who had been given his first sweet cake.

"I had a little ratter dog looked a lot like him when I was a boy," he said, laughing as the pup licked the stubble on his chin.

To a man, Jerrik and the crew watched gape-jawed as Bors planted kisses on the pup's nose before setting him down and playing tug with his leather archery glove. Alyssa grinned. The stoic, dour Bors was a softy.

"A cat, a dog, two horses," Sven hmphed. "What's next, a one-winged gull?"

"Why?" Alyssa asked the blustering Northman with a smile. "Have you seen one in need of aid?"

Sven hmphed louder, and Alyssa's smile grew wider. "You would help me take it in if you did, Sven," she teased. "You know you would."

"Aye, Mistress of Strays," Sven grudgingly admitted. "I likely would."

Laughing, Alyssa stood on her toes and planted a kiss on Sven's cheek. He harumphed again and Alyssa turned to Jerrik, a happy smile on her face. Jerrik was glowering.

"The pup stays," he announced abruptly, and then scowled at Alyssa. "But I'm not sleeping with the flea-bitten mongrel."

Alyssa snatched the pup up and clutched it to her chest. "I was going to bathe him tomorrow morning before we set sail, so that he'd have the heat of day to warm him while he dries," she told Jerrik, completely at a loss to explain his change in attitude toward the pup. "I'll bathe him now instead."

Lev stood and glowered at Jerrik. "I'll gather more wood for the fire," he said. "So it'll burn longer and hotter."

"I'll warm a little fish broth while you bathe the pup," Zoltan added. "He'll need it to help warm him from the inside."

"I have an old woolen vest he can sleep on," Bors offered.

"Thank you," Alyssa told the men before she carried the pup into the tent. When she came out with a tub of soap and a drying linen in one hand and Digger in the other, Han stood and escorted her to the river's edge, where he held the drying linen while she dunked and lathered the whining pup, her attention split between the wriggling pup and her husband, who still stood at the campfire, glaring at them.

Alyssa put the vest that Bors had volunteered at the foot of her bedroll and laid Digger on it, rubbing his belly, full of food for the first time in who knew how long. Then she kissed his nose. "This is your bed now, Digger," she told him. "You must stay and sleep on it, and if you need to relieve yourself in the night, give me a little whine and I'll take you out."

The pup wagged his stubby tail, licked Alyssa's nose, and settled into the soft wool with a contented sigh, letting out little puppy snores before Alyssa had doffed her tunic and skirt and folded them to use as a pillow. Jerrik, already down to his breechcloth and lying on top of his bedroll, watched her as she lay down on hers.

He'd been keeping an eye on her all night as they ate their supper and she and the others fed Digger pieces of stew and flatbread. After supper, when she sat away from him and close to the camp's fire, cradling Digger and listening to Han play a beautiful, haunting song of his homeland on his flute, Jerrik had watched and listened, but he hadn't said a word to her, other than "You're welcome," after she'd thanked him for deciding to hunt for fresh meat on the morrow rather than sail.

The crew had watched them the entire time, rolling their eyes and shaking their heads at each other.

Alyssa knew that Jerrik was angry with her. One moment he'd been his usual self, more amused than upset about the pup, and the next he'd been snapping at her. The only thing that had happened in between was that she'd kissed Sven on the cheek, and while she supposed it might've caused Jerrik to be jealous, she didn't understand why. It was a sisterly kiss on the cheek, or in Sven's case, more like a niece kissing an uncle. Surely, she'd never given Jerrik cause to be jealous of any of his crew, or man for that matter, not even Kostya, whom she'd told Jerrik she'd never felt any passion for.

She knew how quickly his moods could shift and change, and his sudden change tonight put Alyssa in mind of all the times in between when he acted as he had that day at the stables when she had left a happy, smiling Jerrik to gather Bones' things, and came back to a sullen, closed-mouthed stranger. Though *her* Jerrik eventually came back, she never knew why he'd left or where he'd gone.

One of the many pieces of marital advice that her mother had given her was that a husband and wife must always communicate, otherwise small misunderstandings became large hurts, which could grow into poisonous grudges, and that the small hurts of an argument healed, while poison festered and killed.

She rolled onto her side and met Jerrik's gaze. "I'm sorry I kissed Sven on the cheek," she said. "I didn't realize it would upset you. I won't do it again if you don't wish me to."

Jerrik opened his mouth to say something, closed it, and said nothing for what felt like an eternity. At last, he reached over and pushed a lock of Alyssa's hair behind her ear. "Thank you," he said, moving his hand to Alyssa's shoulder. He cocked his head and gave her a rueful grin. "You aren't one of those women who hold back their favors when their man has been an ass, are you?"

Alyssa shrugged her shoulder. "I don't know."

"You, ah, never got angry enough at Kostya to refuse him?"

"Kostya?" Alyssa had never refused Kostya's kisses, yet she'd never craved them the way she craved Jerrik's. She shook her head. "Kostya never gave me reason to be that angry. He always let me have my way."

"I see." He dropped his hand from Alyssa's shoulder. "I cannot promise the same, little lynx, though you seem to have my crew at your beck and call."

Alyssa laughed, which seemed to surprise him. "Truthfully," she admitted. "Kostya's always giving way without a fight was one of the things that drove me mad about him."

His grin was pure male, and Alyssa felt it all the way to her core. "So, you like a challenge, do you?"

Alyssa grinned right back at him. "Apparently," she said, "I'm more like my mother than I knew."

Jerrik sat on a log checking his arrows and arranging them in his quiver while Bors honed his spear's point and Zoltan packed them dried meat and flatbread as the sun rose over the eastern horizon. Sven, still groggy with sleep, ambled over and stood close to the morning fire, rubbing his hands briskly, though it was a warm summer dawning. Snagging a piece of flatbread for himself, he plopped down next to Jerrik.

"I've never known you to be jealous before," Sven said without preamble.

"I've never had a wife before." The more you cared about a woman, the more she could hurt you. A lesson he'd learned at a tender age and that he'd lived happily by, making sure he never got too close to any woman, until he'd become king and taken Alyssa as his wife.

"Do you want to talk about it?" Sven didn't say what the "it" was. He didn't have to.

"No."

He and Alyssa had talked it out last night, more or less. She'd thought him jealous of her kissing Sven on the cheek, and he was, a little. More than he liked to admit. He'd also been angry at her for the way that his men had rushed to defend her against him. It'd brought to mind her brother, Aaron, who adored his younger sister, telling Jerrik how adept she was at wrapping her father and brothers around her little finger with her big eyes and pretty smiles. Which was exactly what she'd done last night with his crew regarding Digger while making Jerrik out to be the bad guy.

Yet what was really bothering him, and had been since that day in the stables, was that he suspected her of having lain with Kostya and that she could be carrying the man's bastard. A suspicion her ingenuous answers to his questions yesterday about her moon flow, and then about Kostya as they lay in their tent last night had done little to allay.

He rubbed his bearded jaw, which was sore from being clamped tight as a vise most of the night. After their conversation, Alyssa had snuggled up to him and laid her hand over his heart and her head on his shoulder and had promptly fallen asleep, leaving Jerrik awake and wondering for the thousandth time since Kostya's boast if his new bride was as artless as he'd always thought her, or a clever liar.

"I was married once," Sven said, causing Jerrik, Bors, and Zoltan to stop what they were doing and stare gape-jawed at the gray-bearded Northman. "To a beautiful woman, as strong minded as she was strong limbed." He smiled to himself, sad and bittersweet. "We had a few rows in our short time together, usually because I was being stubborn about one thing or another, not a one of them that mattered in the end."

"I didn't know." Jerrik glanced at Bors and Zoltan, who were both shaking their heads no. "Ten and four years we've sailed together," he said to Sven, "and this is the first time I've heard this."

"Knut knew," Sven told him. "It was after she died in childbirth, her and our son, that I joined his crew."

Jerrik said nothing, yet he understood. Some wounds, some losses, ran so deep that a man dared not reopen them less he bled out.

"My point is," Sven said to Jerrik, "that girl you married thinks that the sun and moon rise and set by you, lad. Love her, enjoy any and all the time you have with her. Don't waste any of it being jealous over a puppy or a kiss on the cheek."

Jerrik nodded and clapped Sven on the shoulder. "You made your point, old man."

"Good," Sven said roughly. "Good."

Jerrik walked over to the bushes to relieve his bladder, wishing he could relieve his conscience of the nagging guilt he felt letting Alyssa, and apparently his men, think that he suffered from simple jealousy.

There was nothing simple about what he felt. He'd told himself over and over it didn't matter if Alyssa had lain with Kostya, what mattered was if she was pregnant with his bastard. Yet even as he told himself this, the thought of her letting Kostya kiss her, touch her, taste her, made Jerrik almost as angry as the thought that she was lying to him about it. Although, to be fair, she'd never denied it, because he'd never directly asked her. The last woman he'd asked directly about her faithfulness had lied to him and then killed herself.

Jerrik spat on the ground. By all the gods, he hated lies. He hated that he was lying to Alyssa about why they hadn't consummated their marriage yet. If he weren't a king, it wouldn't matter if she bore another man's child. He rolled his head and shoulders. If he were not king, he wouldn't be married to the lovely sylph of a woman who drove him mad for want of her.

He started back toward the camp, and Alyssa came out of their tent fully dressed, her loose hair hanging down to her waist, her cheeks still pink with sleep, the pup squirming in her arms as she carried him away from the tent to relieve himself. Jerrik altered his course and walked over to Alyssa and the pup, who was wagging his tail and running around sniffing clumps of grass.

"Good morning, wife," he said, pulling her into his arms and kissing her soundly.

"Good morning, husband," she said, smiling sleepily and kissing him in return. "I'm sorry I fell asleep last night before we—"

"You were tired," he said, tucking her under his shoulder. "We both were."

Digger ran over and jumped up and down, pawing at her skirts.

"Are you telling me you're hungry?" Alyssa asked as she picked up the pup. "This morning will have to be leftover stew, but tonight," she smiled into Jerrik's eyes, "tonight we'll all feast on fresh meat."

Jerrik's chest swelled at how she assumed his hunt would be successful, and he tucked her closer and kissed the top of her head, laughing as Digger shot his tongue out and licked Jerrik's chin.

"Oh," she said as they reached the others at the fire, which now included Lev and Han. "If you find any wild garlic, can you bring back a bulb or two?"

"Garlic?"

"It will help Digger get rid of any internal worms."

"Sure," Jerrik said, wiping his chin with his sleeve as Bors, who'd been letting the pup kiss him on the mouth last night, picked up a wineskin, took a big swig, swished and gargled and then spit it out onto the ground.

Jerrik and Bors shot a young buck and dug up five garlic bulbs at a lake a league from the river camp. They returned early enough for the buck to be dressed and a full haunch roasted before nightfall. After feasting on the venison roasted with garlic and mushrooms, bitter greens and sweet berries that Alyssa had collected, with Digger happily gnawing away on one of the buck's legs, Alyssa brought out her harp, and Han his flute.

"Are there words to the tune you played last night?" she asked Han.

"*Shi*," Han said. "Ancient, old love song. I know words."

"If you teach me the tune, I'll play while you sing."

He played the first refrain slowly, giving Alyssa time to find the notes on her harp, and then the next two in the same fashion until they were satisfied she knew the tune. As Alyssa played, Han sang the song of Niu Lang and Zhi Nu, the cowherd and the cloud weaver. He sang of how they were once stars in the night sky, and so much in love, though their love was forbidden by the Mother Queen of the Heavens. When the Queen found out, she separated the lovers, exiling Niu Lang from the heavens to be a lonely cowherd on earth. And though she spared Zhi Nu, her seventh granddaughter, from exile, she turned her into a cloud weaver, destined to create beautiful clouds in the sky.

One day, after years of unrelenting heartbreak, the Queen allowed Zhi Nu to go down to earth and bathe in the lotus gardens with the Queen's other granddaughters, where Niu Lang came upon her. Recognizing each other after all their grief-filled, lonely years apart, they ran away and got married. They lived happily in their little house with their two children, Zhi Nu weaving cotton and Niu Lang plowing the fields with his faithful cow, until one day a strong wind was sent down by the Queen Mother, who had discovered them, sweeping Zhi Nu and the children up into the heavens.

Niu Lang went after them, and almost caught them, but the Queen removed her golden hair pin and with a single stroke, rent the heavens, creating a river that would separate the lovers forever.

At that moment, the lovers cried out their undying love for each other, and the Queen took pity on them, allowing Niu Lang to remain in the heavens, only not with his wife and children.

Han pointed up at the River of the Heavens shining white as milk across the night sky and sang of how once a year, on the seventh day of the seventh month, Niu Lang is reunited with his wife and children when a flock of magpies create a bridge between the stars that allow him to cross over to be with his loved ones.

Alyssa, tears welling in her eyes, plucked the last, bittersweet note. "That was beautiful," she said. She turned to Jerrik. "Have you heard this love song before?"

He shook his head. He glanced at the sad-faced men sitting around the fire and then back at Alyssa. "None of us have. It seems you, my green-eyed enchantress, have bewitched my men into telling all their secrets."

Alyssa laughed lightly. "Not all of them, surely."

Jerrik raised his brows and said nothing. Besides hearing Han sing a haunting love song from his homeland, Sven had shared he'd been married once, and Bors had shown a soft spot for puppies, and all because of her. All she had to do was smile prettily at them and they were clay in her fingers.

Bors stood and yawned. "I'm off to bed on the ship," he said. "Traipsing around on land for half a day has worn me out."

Jerrik stood too, reaching down for Alyssa's hand and pulling her up onto her feet. "We're for bed as well," he said. "Another day and a half of sailing and we should reach the Rus port, which will put us halfway to the coast."

"Are we stopping there?" Alyssa asked.

"We are. Long enough to trade for a few supplies."

"Oh good," she said with a happy smile. "I've never traveled this far north and west before. It will be interesting to see the marketplace and meet some of the people." She squeezed Jerrik's hand and slipped her fingers from his. "I need to take Digger for his walk," she told him. "I'll be to bed shortly."

CHAPTER 7

The Rus Port

Jerrik woke with the graying dawn, fully clothed and lying on top of his bedroll. Alyssa, clad in her thin nightshift, was sleeping with her head on his shoulder and her arm across his chest, the rest of her tucked beneath her bedroll's linens. Slowly, so as not to wake her, he moved her arm and slipped his out from beneath her head, unable to resist nuzzling her unbound mane and inhaling the fresh, clean scent of summer rain and winter lilies.

Digger stirred as Jerrik stood and Alyssa burrowed her nose into his bedroll with a soft sigh.

"Come with me, you flea-bitten mongrel," he told the pup as he opened the tent flap. "Let your mistress sleep."

The pup trotted out and followed him to the brush, where they both relieved themselves. Then Digger sat and looked up as if to say, "What next?"

"Now we break our fasts, break camp, and hoist our sail," he told Digger as the pup cocked his head and ears. "Come on, we have a full day of sailing ahead of us and a crew still sleeping off their feast."

"Sven." Jerrik toed the Northman in his side as he snored away on his bedroll by the glowing embers of the campfire. "Sven, wake up."

Sven sat up with a yawn and a joint-popping stretch. He glanced around the camp, where only he and Jerrik were up and awake. "Skeppare?"

"After I retired to my tent last night, how long before Alyssa joined me?"

Sven scratched his beard and yawned wider. "Long enough to take the pup for a quick piss," he said. "Why""

Jerrik must have fallen asleep almost as soon as he'd lain down. Alyssa hadn't awakened him for their nightly sport.

"No matter," he said with a shrug. "I was only curious." Curious if she'd dallied with any of his crew around the fire.

Grumbling into his beard about jealous fools, Sven stood and eyed Jerrik. "If we make good time today," Sven said, wisely changing the subject, "we can make the Rus port by tomorrow noon, maybe even this evening if this wind holds up."

The wind not only held up, it blew north and west with such force that the *Sea Eagle* dropped anchor in the Rus port as the sun was setting in a brilliant red-orange sky.

Lev and Zoltan drew the short straws, so they stayed aboard the ship as the rest of them took the small boat to shore and headed for The Rus, an ale house that served food and whose owner, Tusya, always knew the latest news and gossip.

They claimed a table as far from the serving bar and as close to the door as possible, Jerrik glaring at the men they passed as they stared gape-jawed at Alyssa like she was a fresh, cool drink of pure spring water after three moons of nothing except stale, piss-warm ale.

Not that he blamed them; even dressed as she was in her workday tunic and skirt, with her hair braided and her face tanned by the sun, her natural beauty was obvious. Still, that didn't mean he liked them salivating over her.

He scooted her stool closer to his and laid a possessive arm around her shoulders as Sven, Han, and Bors stared down any man foolish enough to still be ogling her.

"King Jerrik," Tusya said jovially as he approached the table. He shook a finger at him and tsked. "You not mention little fact of becoming king when you come through here last, sailing south as if hounds of underworld after you." His quick eyes settled on Alyssa. "Who is lovely lady?"

"My wife. Queen Alyssa. Daughter of King Aleksandr and Queen Sahar."

Tusya let out a low whistle of approval. "No wonder you were in such hurry," he said. "She was to marry another, yes?"

Alyssa's jaw dropped. "How did he know that?"

"Tusya hears all the news and gossip," Jerrik told her. "It's that plain, unprepossessing face of his that makes people underestimate him."

"And my strong beer that loosen their tongues," Tusya said, laughing. Then he grew serious. "I am sorry for you, for loss of your brother Aaron." He doffed his cap to Alyssa. "He was good man."

"Thank you," Alyssa said, her eyes instantly welling. "He was. The best of men."

Tusya sniffed, and nodded, and plastered a big smile across his broad face. "Tonight, we must celebrate king and queen." He turned and spied a serving maid. "Natalia. Bring beer for my guests, King Jerrik and Queen Alyssa." To Jerrik he added, "I will tell cook only the best eel pie and fresh baked bread for you."

Alyssa watched as the brown-haired, sharp-nosed serving maid called Natalia sashayed her way over to their table and inserted herself between Jerrik and Bors. Cocking her hip into Jerrik's shoulder, she leaned over, exposing the ample flesh of her bosom as she smiled down at him with a knowing slant to her dark eyes.

"Anything else ye'd like asides the pie an' bread, skeppare?" she asked, licking her rouged lips suggestively.

Jerrik looked to Alyssa, who was doing her best to ignore the brazen hussy, though she was pretty sure she had teeth marks in her lower lip from biting it. "Do you wish for anything more?" he asked.

"Wine, please, if they have it."

"Such fine taste an' fancy manners you have, lady," Natalia said with an exaggerated dip of her head. "But then I 'spose that's what you need to catch yerself a king. 'Course, I knew Jerrik here afore he was king." She smiled at him with such coarse familiarity that Alyssa sucked in her breath. "When he was jes' a randy sailor lad."

Alyssa let out her breath with a slow, treacly smile and narrowed eyes. "My husband," she said, "has never been *just* anything."

Natalia shrugged, unaffected by the ice in Alyssa's manner, or her glare as the wench's tunic slipped down over a shoulder, exposing even more flesh. "King, peasant, skeppare, sailor," Natalia scoffed. "They all be naught but men." She smiled suggestively at Bors. "Now, few men's as big as Bors here."

"I wouldn't know," Alyssa said stiffly. "I don't have your wide range of experience."

Sven coughed and sputtered, Bors actually blushed, and Han let out a low whistle as Natalia's lips thinned and she turned on her heels and trounced away.

Jerrik's amused laugh stopped mid-chuckle at Alyssa's raised brows. "I was ten and three years of age," he said with a shrug. "Newly broken free of palace life and on my first journey as a sailor. I would've had sex with a squid if it was willing."

He looked to his crew, who all smiled sheepishly and nodded in agreement and understanding. Alyssa understood as well. She hadn't grown up with six older brothers without learning a few salient bits about the male species. She wasn't going to harangue or fault Jerrik for having had sex with who knew how many women before marrying her, nor was she going to pretend that she was indifferent to it.

"Apparently," she said, eyeing the purposeful sway of Natalia's backside, "it was more than willing."

They ate their meal as close to silent as any they had eaten together since Alyssa had set sail with them, with Sven and Han and Bors watching her and Jerrik like children whose parents had quarreled in front of them. She supposed in a way they were the crew's parents, much as they would be, as king and queen, to the people of Sea Ridge.

She was no longer simply Alyssa, or even a princess; she was a queen. Who had been raised by a queen. Using what she had learned from her mother, she made an effort to put the crew's worries at ease, laying her hand on Jerrik's forearm and asking him about the country they would be sailing through next and purposely ignoring Natalia's swishing skirts and sullen glares as she cleared their trenchers and refilled their cups.

After another round of beer, they returned to their more usual amiable conversation. Jerrik stood and offered his arm to Alyssa. "My wife and I will take the small boat back to the ship and relieve

Lev and Zoltan for the night," he told the crew. "I don't expect any of you back until the morn."

As soon as Jerrik pushed the small boat away from the dock and started rowing toward the *Sea Eagle* with smooth, powerful strokes, Alyssa spoke up. She wanted to say what she had to say before they made the ship and she lost her nerve.

"I'm not angry," she said. "I realize that the promise between us was more my youthful wish than your solid oath, and that you lived your life free of any such vows or constraints. We both did."

Jerrik kept rowing and said nothing.

"I am, I admit, jealous," she continued. "Jealous of Natalia and any other woman you have ever so much as touched or even looked twice at; however, that's my problem." She smiled and shrugged at the sideways cock of his head and bit her lower lip as she leaned forward toward him. "What I'm trying to say is, it doesn't matter who or how many women you have lain with before me, as long as from this moment forward, I am the only one."

Jerrik cocked his head the other way, giving her the full slant of his piercing eyes. "As I expect to be for you as well."

She sat back at the vehemence of his words. "As you are, husband, and always will be."

Jerrik said nothing as he continued to row toward the *Sea Eagle*, his strokes sure and steady, his expression unfathomable. Still, Alyssa was glad she had said what she did. She'd meant every word of it. She intended to keep to her word and not hold Jerrik's past dalliances against him. Not that it would be easy. The serving maid, Natalia, had brought out what Jerrik called the "bloodthirsty little lynx" in her, and while Natalia had been the first woman from Jerrik's past to confront her, Alyssa assumed she wouldn't be the last.

With one last deep pull of the oars, the small boat knocked up against the *Sea Eagle*, and Alyssa stood and started up the ladder Lev threw down, a happy warmth spreading from where Jerrik placed his hands on her hips to help steady her and easing the tightness in her chest.

He gave Lev and Zoltan the same orders to stay ashore until morning that he'd given the others while Alyssa checked on the horses and Digger, and then she met Jerrik in the middle of the deck.

He hooked a finger under her chin and drew her to him. "Kiss me," he ordered.

Alyssa lifted up onto her toes and wrapped her hands around his neck, pulling his head down until his lips met hers. She leaned into him with a sigh, and Jerrik splayed his big, strong hands across her back and pressed her even closer, rumbling with pleasure as he rubbed his growing cock against her belly, groaning as she rubbed her pelvis against him in response, their lips moving against each other's in the same tantalizing rhythm.

She ran her hands across his broad shoulders and down his hard chest and trailed kisses down the corded column of his throat. Jerrik stepped back long enough to shuck his tunic, and Alyssa sank to her knees and untied the stays to his trousers, which he quickly kicked aside.

He sucked his breath in as Alyssa untied his breechcloth, and let it out in a slow hiss as she freed his cock to stand at the ready in the cool night air. She ran her fingers from root to tip, tempering his rod to hardened steel until the first milky drop formed at the tip, which she licked with one quick flick of her tongue.

Jerrik went rigid, and then his hands were in her hair as she kissed and suckled his soft head, and he groaned. His hands stilled as she took him inside her mouth, wrapped her hand around the base of his cock and began to move, rocking back and forth on her knees, her mouth sliding, caressing, and sucking, as her hand kneaded and squeezed until Jerrik erupted with a shudder, and then another as Alyssa swallowed his hot seed.

"God's blood, Lyssa," he rasped, hooking his hands under her arms and pulling her up to him. "Where did you learn to do that?"

Alyssa smiled, happy to have pleased him and amazed at how arousing it had been to pleasure him. "I listened to the married women talk. Did I do it right?"

"Oh, you did it right," Jerrik half laughed, half groaned.

He kissed her, long and hard, and then he turned her and placed her hands flat on the mast before he lifted her skirts from behind, his low male growl reverberating from her ears to her core as she bent forward and thrust her shapely buttocks into his half-hard cock, still slick from her mouth. He ran his hands up and down the backs of her thighs, kissing and nipping the nape of her neck until she was squirming against him, and then he propped one hand against the mast and moved the other around her belly and down until he found her sex with his strong, talented fingers.

"Now it's my turn to do right by you."

Alyssa restrained herself from swinging the hand Jerrik held and skipping beside him like an eight-year-old girl in side braids as they strolled from the baker's stalls, her belly rumbling at the delicious aroma of fresh baked bread, to the farmer's stalls full of vine-ripened fruit and summer vegetables. Digger, sensing her excitement, jumped and tugged at the end of his leash, his nose and ears twitching at all the scents and sights.

They drew stares everywhere they went, male and female, young and old, everybody in the marketplace stopped to watch the progress of Jerrik, Alyssa, and Digger, accompanied by Han and Bors, Lev and Zoltan. Alyssa, dressed in one of her summer gowns of butter yellow worm weave, her hair pinned up with the beautiful mother-of-pearl comb Jerrik had given her and the sea-green pearl dangling above the cleft of her breasts, garnered the most attention, as Jerrik must have anticipated.

He'd asked her to dress as fine as the queen she now was for their day at the marketplace, claiming that the word would have already spread through the town of who and what they were, and that when, not if, word of them spread farther, he wanted it to be known how beautiful his queen was.

She did as he requested, and couldn't help but notice that if any man was bold enough to gawk too brazenly, they were quickly stared down by Jerrik or one of his crew. So as not to inflame the situation, she made sure not to smile too broadly or brightly at any man other than her husband.

She had pleasured him well last night, and he, her, and she wanted to keep him happy with her. One of the many things she was learning about Jerrik was that he had a jealous streak and did not completely trust her when it came to other men, which made no sense, considering he'd likely lain with hundreds of women, and she had only ever kissed one man other than her father and brothers, and a man more a brother to her than a lover at that.

That was all to be in the past after last night.

She smiled dreamily as she remembered their sex play on the open deck of the ship, of the cool breeze on her naked skin as Jerrik's strong fingers and hot mouth teased her into a heated frenzy until she had convulsed and melted into a boneless puddle of sated passion.

Still smiling, she wandered away from the stall where Jerrik and Lev had stopped to look at some woodworking tools toward a stall with a table laden with trinkets made of beads and shells, and where faceted crystals hung from a pole, catching the sun and reflecting all the colors of a rainbow.

"Pretty, ain't they?" the tinker, a middle-aged, portly man missing his two eyeteeth, said.

"Yes," Alyssa agreed. "They are."

"Not as pretty as you."

Alyssa nodded her thanks for the compliment as the tinker reached up and twirled one of the crystals. Gazing up at the spinning prism of colors, she felt a shadow move behind her. Digger growled and lunged at almost the same moment Alyssa's hair fell loose and a high-pitched yelp rang out.

She whirled around to find a stick-thin boy dressed in rags hopping around on one leg, rubbing at the calf of his other with a dirty hand, his other fisted tightly.

"Your dog bit me," he squawked at Alyssa, his voice starting low and breaking high, his blue-gray eyes, already too big for his spotty face, growing even larger as Jerrik, Bors, and Han surrounded him.

"I'm sorry," she said to the lad, reaching her hand up to where her comb should've been.

"Don't be," Jerrik told her. He motioned toward the boy's fisted hand. "Care to show me what you have there, boy?"

"N-nothing."

"Hand it over." Jerrik rapped the boy's white knuckles with the blade of his waist knife as a crowd grew around them.

The boy's hand shook as he slowly unfurled his fist to reveal Alyssa's comb in his grimy palm.

"Want me to cut off his thieving hand?" Bors asked with a quick wink at Alyssa as he pulled one of his short blades from the cross scabbard at his back.

The poor boy shook so violently that he dropped the comb onto the dirt. "P-please, ma'am, sir…" The boy looked from Bors to Alyssa to Jerrik to the tinker, who clamped his lips tight and gave a quick shake of his head.

Alyssa glanced around at the crowd of people watching and whispering among themselves. Some, she saw, feared for the boy, while others jostled for a better view of the potential hand severing.

She bent down and picked up her comb with one hand and Digger with the other. She looked to Jerrik, whom, though he could be a hard man when necessary, she had never known to be a cruel man, silently pleading mercy for the boy.

Jerrik cocked his head for a moment, and then turned the full slant of his hard gaze on the tinker. "Perhaps we should take the tinker's hand here instead," he said to Bors.

"What?" the tinker exclaimed. "Why?"

"Because 'e's yor son, ye thieven scoundrel," a man's voice yelled from the mob.

"Is this true?" Jerrik asked the tinker.

"What if it is?" The tinker, who still stood behind the table, spat onto the ground and shrugged. "Don't mean I put him up to it. Take his thieven hand—"

"Papa," the boy cried out.

"I got four more brats to feed," the tinker said. "I can't be worrying over this one 'ere turning to thieven. Take his hand, he deserves it."

Jerrik stiffened and Alyssa saw the muscle tic along the side of his jaw.

"What's your name, boy?" Jerrik asked the trembling youth.

"P-Pavel, sir."

"How old are you?"

"Ten and five last winter."

Jerrik's keen gaze took in the scrawny boy, who Alyssa would have guessed to be no more than ten and two. She glared at the tinker, who looked to be as well fed as the boy was not, and whose clothes, while not exactly clean, were at least well fit and mended, unlike Pavel's stained, overlarge tunic and tattered breeches, which only came to below his knobby knees. His sandals were a size too small and tied to his dirt-crusted feet by odd strips of leather bound around the thin soles.

"If I were to let you work off your thievery as a deck hand aboard my ship," Jerrik asked the boy, "do you promise never to steal again?"

The relief on the boy's face was palpable, as was the release of the crowd's collectively held breath. "Yes sir, skeppare."

"I will expect hard, honest work out of you, Pavel. In return you will be clothed and well fed, and learn a useful," Jerrik glared at the tinker, "trade."

"Yes, skeppare," Pavel said. "Thank you, skeppare."

"You have today to say your farewells," Jerrik told him. "Be on the dock before the sun sets. And Pavel."

"Yes, skeppare?"

Jerrik opened his purse and tossed a silver coin to the quick-handed boy. "Buy yourself a decent pair of sandals and a tub of soap and wash yourself and any clothes you bring with you before setting foot on my ship."

CHAPTER 8

The Bleeding

"Keep this up," Sven told Jerrik as they stood on the deck, watching Han and Lev teach Pavel how to tie off sail lines as they tacked upriver, "and you'll have to rename the *Sea Eagle* the *Ship of Strays*."

"I couldn't leave the lad to his father," Jerrik said. He met Sven's gaze head on. They'd both watched the half-starved boy eat three thick slices of bread and two full bowls of venison stew last night. "Neither would you have. Besides, with Han and Bors agreeing to become kapteins of my personal guard, and you my counselor, the *Sea Eagle* is going to need new crew members."

"Lev's agreed to keep the boy on then?"

They both watched as Pavel finished tying off the sail line by himself. A beaming smile split the boy's face in two as Lev slapped him on the back with a hearty, "Well done, lad."

"The fates led us to him for a reason," Jerrik said. If he hadn't asked Alyssa to dress the part of his queen, she wouldn't have worn her hair comb, and Pavel wouldn't have been ordered to steal it by his father and been caught by Jerrik and his men, who, rather than cut off the boy's hand, as many others would have done, were able to offer him a way out of a life that would lead to nowhere but ruin. "He was meant to become part of this crew."

"I suppose it had nothing to do with your bleeding-heart wife begging you to take in another stray?"

Jerrik liked to think he would've done the same for the boy even if Alyssa hadn't been silently begging him after Bors had offered to cut off the boy's hand, which he'd only said and Jerrik had only pretended to consider to scare the boy.

"Taking Pavel in is advantageous to both the *Sea Eagle* and the lad," Jerrik told Sven. "If my father taught me anything about being king, it was to weigh all options before making a decision, and to never act in haste." As far as Jerrik knew, the one time his father had ignored his own advice had resulted in his mother taking her own life. "A lesson I've taken to heart and try to live by."

Sven, who had known Jerrik since he was ten and two and had pulled him out of more than one sticky situation through the years, quirked his bushy brows.

"Sometimes more effectively than others," Jerrik admitted. He looked around for his wife, who wasn't on the deck with the horses, or up in the rigging, her favorite places to be. Digger, her constant shadow, was nowhere to be seen either. "Have you seen Alyssa?"

"Not since before we set sail. She weren't looking too good then," Sven said. "A little green around the gills, she was."

Jerrik headed below deck, worried about his wife. Alyssa had never shown any signs of seasickness before. He hoped it was nothing more than her having eaten something at the market yesterday that hadn't settled well in her belly.

He found her curled up on the pile of pelts with Digger tucked into her legs and Bones at her back, the three of them sound asleep. He touched the backs of his fingers to her forehead, which was warm but not hot to the touch, and then his fingertips to her throat, where he felt her pulse beating strong and steady.

He pushed a stray lock of honey gold hair back from her face, letting his thumb caress the soft rise of her cheek, and smiled as she sighed and burrowed her nose deeper into the pelts. Bones opened one green eye and stared at him for a moment before yawning and curling tighter into Alyssa's back, while Digger snored softly.

He smiled down at his sleeping beauty, who was likely exhausted from the events of the past moon. He knew his head was still spinning when he thought of all that had passed, and all that was still to come. In truth, he would've liked nothing better than to curl up and around Alyssa and sleep the day and night away.

But he was skeppare of the *Sea Eagle* and duty called.

Alyssa woke to the rolling motion of the ship and a throbbing head and cramping belly. She sat up on her makeshift bed of pelts and ran her hand down Bone's arched neck and back while trying to get her bearings. The last thing she remembered was coming down into the hold for something, though she couldn't recall what, right after the *Sea Eagle* set sail.

Digger, who must have been sleeping with her, jumped off the pelts and stood at the foot of the ladder leading up to the deck, whining.

"Do you need to relieve yourself?" Alyssa asked.

She stood to go to the pup and doubled over as her belly gripped and a wet warmth gushed between her legs. She pulled her skirt up and saw blood trickling down the insides of her legs. Her belly gripped again, even harder this time, and she watched, dry mouthed and heart pounding in her ears, as dark, wine-red clots of blood plopped down to the floor between her feet. Then the drumming in her ears turned to a loud buzzing and the world went black.

"Will someone shut that dog up." As soon as Jerrik said it, he knew that something was wrong. The pup had been sleeping with Alyssa down in the hold, and now he was barking up a storm, and Alyssa wasn't shushing him. "Sven," he yelled, running for the hold. "Lev, with me."

What he found there stopped his heart cold. Alyssa, crumpled on the floor, skirts up around her knees, her legs covered in blood, Digger whining frantically.

"Help me get her up on the pelts," he told Sven, as he lifted her from the shoulders. "Carefully, man, carefully," he barked, though he knew full well that Sven was being as gentle as possible as he lifted her limp legs. "Get clean towels," he yelled over his shoulder to Lev. "Have someone bring a bucket of water. Quickly, man. Quickly."

He felt her throat for a pulse for the second time that day, and though he found it, it was much fainter and weaker than before, and her skin was cool and clammy to the touch.

"Alyssa." Jerrik pushed the damp hair back from her face. "Alyssa, open your eyes. Open your eyes for me, Lyssa." He leaned in and whispered a desperate plea into her ear. "It's me, Lyssa, your husband, Jerrik. Come back to me, Lyssa. Please, please, come back to me, my little lynx." He felt her eyelids flutter against his cheek, and he sat back, clutching her hands in his. He couldn't lose her. Not like this. Not like his mother, in a bed soaked in her own blood. "Stay with me, Lyssa." Slowly, as with great effort, she turned her head toward the sound of his voice. "Stay with me." He lowered his lips to hers, and his breath was a prayer. "Stay."

Her lips warmed beneath his, and her eyes fluttered open. "I'm here, Jerrik," she whispered hoarsely. "I'm with you."

He buried his face in the crook of her neck, stifling a sob that threatened to unman him. He felt Alyssa's fingers in his hair, and he lifted his head and stared into eyes that reflected all the colors of the sea. "I thought I lost you," he said, his voice cracking almost as badly as his heart had at first sight of her lying in a pool of blood.

Alyssa smiled. The same pure, sweet, adoring smile she'd given him as an eight-year-old girl. "It will take more than a heavy moon flow to make me leave you, Jerrik."

She tried to sit up on her elbows, and Jerrik gently pressed her back down into the pelts. "You should lie still for a while. You've lost a lot of blood."

She felt the towel packed up against her with her hand and glanced down at the clots of blood on the floor where she had fallen.

"Digger alerted us with his barking," Jerrik told her. The pup, hearing his name, started pawing at Jerrik's legs. He picked him up and sat him on his lap. "That's the second time in two days you've come to your mistress's aid," he said, ruffling the pup's ears. "What a good guard dog you are, Digger."

"Of course he is." Alyssa held a hand out to the pup and smiled as he licked her fingers, then her smile turned to a grimace and she rolled onto her side and curled up tight.

"What is it?" Jerrik asked, his heart in his throat.

"A little after cramping," she said. "I'll be fine."

He might have believed her if she hadn't grabbed onto his forearm and grit her jaw as her body gripped. "Has this ever happened to you before?" he asked when the spasm passed.

"To me?" she asked as Jerrik wiped beads of sweat from her nose and cheeks. "No. But I've seen it happen to other women. They were fine after."

"Pardon me for being so blunt and personal," Sven, lurking over Jerrik's shoulders, said. "Could you have been with child? I've heard of it happening so, a woman losing a babe early on."

Alyssa shook her head. "No, I …" She met and held Jerrik's gaze for a moment. "I don't think so," she said. "Though I cannot be certain, either way."

Jerrik turned his head, unable to look her in the eyes.

"It happened to me mam," Pavel, who was setting a bucket of water down by a pile of clean towels, said. "Me mam lost two babes early on between me younger brothers." He met Jerrik's stricken gaze. "She went on to have three more babes after," he said encouragingly. "All of 'em born fit and fine."

"Pavel," Alyssa said, her voice thin and reedy. "Will you take Digger up to use his dirt box?"

"Aye, mistress."

"Sven," she said, "will you leave Jerrik and me alone for a bit, please?"

"Of course, lass," Sven said, his voice rough. He clasped Jerrik's shoulder and gave it a squeeze before he followed Pavel and Digger up the ladder to the deck.

Alyssa ran her hand up and down Jerrik's forearm. "I feel badly, letting them think…" She took a deep breath in and blew it out with a shaky laugh. "My moon flow was late in coming and extra heavy, Jerrik, nothing more." She smiled and squeezed his hand. "I'll be fine, I swear it." She lifted a hand to his cheek. "When the time comes, I will bear your children and raise them with all the love I can spare their father."

Jerrik lay in the trees' shade beside a slumbering Alyssa as Digger, true to his name and nature, dug holes in the loose soil of the creek's bank. River and Storm grazed on the late summer grass that grew thinner and browner the farther north and west they sailed. It'd been ten days since he'd found Alyssa passed out in a pool of her own blood, ten days since he'd done little more than kiss her, much to her growing discontent.

She'd kept to the ship's hold for the first two days and nights, sleeping or playing sad, melancholy tunes on her harp, subsisting on little more than a few bowls of broth and short visits by Jerrik and the rest of the crew, all of whom moped around with worried frowns and short tempers, taking their fears out on each other, which was easier than admitting them out loud. They could have lost her, they could lose her still, and they all knew it.

The third day, she'd asked Jerrik to help her climb the ladder up onto the ship's deck, where she'd sat on a bed of pelts tucked into the ship's prow so that she could feel the sun on her face and still be protected from the winds, which had held strong and steady enough that the *Sea Eagle* was now several days ahead in her journey home.

By the fifth day, Alyssa was moving about the ship on her own by day, and sleeping ashore with Jerrik in their tent each night. By the seventh night, she was getting angry with him for refusing to resume their sex play, insisting it would do nothing to cause her harm. Though Jerrik knew she was right, that as long as they continued to avoid consummating their marriage, nothing they did should cause her further injury, his nightmares were warning him not to tempt the fates.

He'd woken up every night for the past ten nights in a blind sweat after dreaming of Alyssa lying beside his mother in the queen's bed, both of them white-faced and blue-lipped, their eyes dulled and unseeing, their night shifts soaked in each other's blood. It was the same dream each night, a dream he couldn't fully shake even in the light of day. A dream he couldn't tell Alyssa or anyone else about, lest speaking it brought it to horrible fruition.

His crew thought he was grieving his and Alyssa's unborn child, and he let them. It was easier for everyone that way. At least, that was what he told himself. To Alyssa, he said nothing more about it, nor did she speak of pregnancy to him again.

Since they'd made such good time over the past fortnight, and all of them were strung taut as sails in a storm, Jerrik had declared today a day of rest and relaxation, and had been rewarded with Alyssa's happy smile when he saddled Storm and River for a morning ride. He hadn't missed her quick intake of breath when she'd swung her leg over River's back, or the way she'd shifted around until finding a comfortable seat.

After ten days of not being ridden, the horses were anxious to run, fighting their tight reins at first and eventually settling into the sedate walk Jerrik demanded, with Digger running between and around their legs and making Alyssa laugh. A sound Jerrik hadn't realized he'd missed until he heard it again.

They'd ridden a league or so up into the river valley before Alyssa had reluctantly admitted to needing a rest, and had stretched out under the trees and promptly fallen asleep with her head resting on Jerrik's shoulder.

Jerrik hadn't slept; he'd lain there with her tucked into him, enjoying a sense of peace and contentment he hadn't felt since finding Alyssa bleeding and deathly pale in the ship's hold.

Propping himself up on one arm, he watched her sleep, her brow smooth and unworried, her cheeks round and pink, her full, lush lips rosy and ripe for kissing. He leaned over her, bracing himself with his hands on either side of her and started to lower his mouth to hers when her eyes flew open, wide, wild, and frightened. She thrust her hands against his chest and shoved him away from her with surprising strength as she thrashed beneath him, her breath escaping in frantic gasps.

"Alyssa." He kept his voice low and calming. "It's me. Jerrik." He put all his weight on his knees so that she could scramble out from under him. "Look at me, Lyssa," he said, his voice gentle but insistent. "It's me. Jerrik."

She went still and her eyes focused on his and lost some of their wildness. "Jerrik." His name came out in a rush of breath, and then she sucked in another deep breath and blew it out, and another. She licked her lips and shook her head. "I dreamt... I thought..."

"That I was the man who attacked you by the lake when you were ten and three?"

Her entire body shuddered and she nodded. "Aye."

Jerrik sat back on his heels as Alyssa gathered her knees to her chest and laid her chin on them, her breathing finally slowing and her gaze fixed on his, her eyes still wide with lingering fear.

"You know I would never hurt you that way, Lyssa."

"I do."

Jerrik swallowed his own fear, the fear that had been eating at his insides since his conversation with Kostya, and plunged ahead. "Kostya told me the attack had left you afraid of intimacy with a man."

"Kostya?" She lifted her chin from her knees. "When did he tell you that?"

"That day in the stables when you introduced me to Storm. You'd taken Bones to gather his belongings when Kostya showed up and told me this."

Alyssa sat back. "That's why you changed toward me so suddenly that day," she said with wonder. "Why you've been so solicitous of me since. Is that why you won't consummate our marriage?"

"Yes," he admitted, "partly. But mostly because it would be dangerous for you to sail pregnant, the events of the past fortnight have proved me right about that." He didn't add that he still halfway believed that she'd miscarried Kostya's babe.

She smiled. "You are a considerate and honorable man, husband, thinking of my feelings and safety as you have."

"Yes, well," Jerrik hedged, "I hoped it wasn't true."

"About the attack leaving me fearful of intimacy with a man?"

Jerrik nodded. "It isn't, is it?"

Alyssa tilted her head, and then began to shake it, a slow smile spreading across her face. "Not with you," she said. "I've never been afraid with you. Perhaps a little nervous and shy at first." She shifted onto her hands and knees and crawled over to him. "Then eager and often frustrated." They were both braced on their knees, thighs to thighs, pelvis to pelvis, chest to chest.

"And now?" Jerrik rumbled.

"Now that I know why you've been so hesitant," she said, snaking her hands around Jerrik's neck. "I'm determined to show you how unafraid I am with you." She pulled his mouth to hers. "Kiss me, husband," she breathed into his opening lips.

She sighed as their kiss deepened and he moved his hands down her back, cupping her backside and pressing her closer, his eager cock growing against her belly. She leaned her head back, exposing her throat to him as he kissed and nipped his way down to her collarbone, arching her back as Jerrik continued south where he suckled first one pebbled nipple and then the other through the thin linen of her tunic.

She rubbed her pelvis against his erection, and Jerrik moaned. She let out a little mewl of protest when his mouth left her breasts, and then purred as he lifted her tunic over her head, and then doffed his own. She ran her hands across his chest and down his belly to the waist of his trousers. Licking her lips, she untied his stays, touching her peaked nipples to his and rubbing them in teasing circles that had Jerrik clutching her hips.

Freeing his straining cock from his breechcloth, she lightly raked her fingernails up and down the hard length of him. Jerrik groaned.

She stopped and smiled seductively. "Do you still think I'm afraid of this?" she purred, wrapping her hand around his fully erect cock and gently squeezing.

"I think," he growled, "I'm a damn fool masochist for swearing off consummating our marriage until we reach Sea Ridge."

"I wouldn't think less of you for breaking your oath," Alyssa said, her sultry gaze begging him to do exactly that.

He closed his eyes and gritted his jaw as Alyssa firmed her hold on his cock and began to move her hand up and down. "I would," he rasped as he pushed his cock back and forth in time with her hand.

He cupped her sex, and Alyssa gasped and began to move slowly, the two of them lost to everything but the play of their fingers.

Jerrik woke to Digger's sharp yipping, cursing himself for falling asleep as he saw three riders skirting the tree line along the far side of the open field.

"Alyssa," he said sharply, rousing her from sleep. "Riders approach." She sat up and followed his gaze to where the riders, realizing they'd been seen, were now coming straight at them. "Quick," he said as they both stood and he tied the stays of his trousers. "Take the horses and ride like the wind for the ship."

She scooped up Digger and ran for River, swinging her leg up and over the mare's back in one fluid motion, and then she reached over and grabbed Storm's reins. "Come on," she said, holding the reins out to Jerrik, who was right behind her. "No horse can outrun River or Storm."

Jerrik shook his head. Things could happen. Horses could stumble and fall. The brigands could have bows and arrows. He untied the horn from his saddle and pulled his long sword from its sheath. "I'll stay and make sure they don't follow you," he said. "Or at the least, slow them down, give you time to get away. Go," he yelled, slapping River on the rump and making the mare jump forward, "and don't look back. Blow the horn as you ride."

The crew might not even hear it, but it was a Northman's horn, known far and wide as a harbinger of battle and death, as was the long sword Jerrik swung in a circle, loosening up his arm and wrist. It'd been a few years since he'd engaged in any serious sword fighting, but he'd been trained by royal sword masters until he was ten and two, and made sure he and his crew kept their fighting skills honed with regular practice.

He glanced over his shoulder, smiling grimly as Alyssa and the horses disappeared into the wooded border of the field. She was safe. That was what mattered.

The approaching thunder of hooves turned his attention back to the three riders, and he strolled out into the field to meet them as the first blast of the horn sounded.

Strategically, he would have preferred to keep his back up against the trees, but he wanted to make sure none of the riders peeled off to go after Alyssa, and figured a bold approach to keep their attention was the best way to do that.

It worked. The three riders pulled their mounts up ten paces from him as the horn blasted again. The riders were as lean and rough as their horses, brigands who had no doubt meant to steal the horses and Alyssa, to use and abuse and sell them when they were done with them. Jerrik grinned as hard and deadly as the blade he rested on his shoulder. The brigands only had short blades, no swords or lances or bows and arrows.

"So sorry to deny you the woman and the horses," he said, speaking in the local Rus tongue. "Ride off the same way you came in, now, or I will also deny you the use of your limbs or your life."

"Or maybe we relieve you of yer clothes and weapons," the man in the middle said. He looked to be the oldest and the best fed, which wasn't saying much, and was obviously the leader of the raggedy pack.

Jerrik glanced at his tunic and boots lying in a pile on the blanket and back to the leader. "I give you my clothes and sword and you let me walk away," he said, knowing full well they would do no such thing, no matter what they told him. They would kill him as soon as he turned his naked ass on them. The talk was buying him time to size them up, and Alyssa to get farther away. "Is that what you're offering?"

"Sure, sure," the leader said. "You lay down that sword of yers and strip down and hand over those fine clothes and boots and we'll let ye go, won't we, boys?"

"Oh, fer sure we will," the scrawniest of the three snickered.

Jerrik rubbed his jaw, pretending to consider the deal. He thought about agreeing and stripping to buy even more time for Alyssa. It wouldn't be the first time he'd fought naked. But he had no doubt that this pack of curs would attack him while he was undressing and at his most vulnerable.

He had a good reason now not to fight naked and chance losing or injuring one particular body part. In truth, if he was meant to die today, the only regret he had was that he hadn't consummated his marriage to Alyssa.

Alyssa rode as if the baying hounds of the underworld were after her, Digger tucked safely into the special saddlebag Lev had made for him. She held River's and Storm's reins in one hand and blew the horn a third time, doing exactly as Jerrik had told her, riding away to save her own life while he sacrificed his to save hers.

It was what she'd always done, what her brothers and Kostya, and even her father had taught her to do, to let them fight her battles. She blew on the horn a fourth time, though she knew that even if the crew heard it and answered the call, they would be too late to save Jerrik if those men chose to fight him.

Why wouldn't they? They were three men on horseback against one man on foot. Granted, the one man stood head and shoulders above them and outweighed each of them by three stone at least, and he had a long sword while they looked to possess nothing more than short blades. Still, Alyssa would wager her soul on the brigands betting their numbers a good enough advantage.

It was Jerrik's soul she wouldn't chance.

She pulled the horses up and swung their heads around, keeping to the wood's edge and circling back to the field, where she could see Jerrik standing off against the three riders.

Her mother had faced her fear of water to save her father from a rushing, flood-swollen river once. Alyssa would be damned if she was going to let her fear of rape stop her from saving Jerrik.

She was more afraid of losing him. She led the horses deeper into the tree line, where they wouldn't be seen or hopefully heard, and when they were only a few hundred paces away, she dismounted and tied the horses off, leaving Digger in his saddlebag with a piece of dried meat to keep him busy.

Slowly, carefully, watching where she placed her booted feet, she crept through the trees, praying to her gods and Jerrik's that she wasn't too late, her throwing blade in her hand and at the ready. She stopped the moment one of the thieves' horses cocked its ears and head in her direction, waiting with her heart in her throat to see if any of the riders had noticed. If they had, they ignored it as the horse shook its head out and lowered it to the tasty grass at its hooves.

She let her breath out slow and quiet and steady as she bent low and crept closer, stopping and hiding at the tree line no more than ten paces from Jerrik's back and another ten from the riders. Whatever conversation they'd been having, they were silent now, glancing among themselves and shifting in their saddles.

Jerrik stood in the open in front of them, his stance careless and nonchalant to the casual observer. Alyssa felt a feral grin spread over her face.

She'd watched, studied, and learned her husband's mannerisms and moves since the day they'd set sail, and she knew how sure-footed he was on a rolling ship's deck, how quickly he could change his balance and direction. She'd watched him spar with Bors often, the two big Northmen handling their broad-bladed long swords in impressive displays of strength, agility, and cunning.

He lowered the tip of his long sword, which had been lying across his shoulder, to the ground, letting the cold steel of the blade catch the sun. Alyssa pulled her waist blade, holding it in one hand and her throwing blade in the other. These thieves would need more than numbers today.

"I'll give you one more chance to turn around and ride away alive and in one piece," Jerrik said in his booming skeppare's voice. He waited as they all three snickered and pulled their short blades. Jerrik shrugged his shoulders and swung his sword in a wide, singing arc. "Know this," he said, aiming the swords point at each man in turn. "Even if you do manage to kill me in the end, you will bleed, all three of you, and my men will track you down and kill you like the scavenging dogs you are."

Their snickers turned to wild whoops as two of the men swung their mounts around to circle Jerrik. If they'd expected him to stand and wait for them, they were gravely mistaken.

He charged straight for the rider still sitting his horse in front of him, and Alyssa stepped out from behind the tree. Never taking her eyes off the man circling around Jerrik's left side, she braced herself, hauled her right arm back, and slung the throwing blade with all her might, her grin growing even more bloodthirsty as it sunk into the thief's unprotected chest with a satisfying thunk. The thief grabbed at the hilt with a startled yelp, pulled the blade from his chest with an agonizing scream and then slumped forward in his saddle, a red stain spreading over his tunic as he slid off his mount onto the ground.

The rider Jerrik was charging kicked his horse forward, his short sword raised high. Jerrik waited until the horse was no more than a few feet from him, and then he shifted to one side, and then jumped to the other, placing himself on the opposite side of the thief's sword hand.

He let out a war cry that made the man's horse shy away from him, and as the rider fought to stay astride his frightened mount, Jerrik leapt straight for him and came down with a swinging arc of his broadsword and landed firmly on both feet, his blade dripping blood as the thief screamed, his arm dangling at an unnatural angle from his shoulder, which was split open from neck to chest. He slumped forward on his horse and fell to the ground with a deadened thump as his horse spooked and ran off.

The third thief whirled his horse around and kicked the poor beast into a headlong gallop back in the direction from where they'd come, running away from the carnage.

Alyssa stepped out from the tree line as Jerrik wiped his bloody blade on the dead thief's tunic. He stood and turned and watched her approach, wiping the sweat from his brow.

"I thought I told you to ride away and not look back." He sounded angry, but he was grinning and shaking his head.

"After all those years of waiting, I finally got you back," Alyssa told him. "I wasn't about to lose you again, not to the likes of them. Besides," she shrugged, "I didn't want Han to think his blade throwing lessons a waste of time."

CHAPTER 9

Sea Ridge

Alyssa stood on the prow of the *Sea Eagle* tucked into Jerrik's shoulder as the ship sailed through the deep, widemouthed inlet leading into the port of Sea Ridge. Unlike her homeland, where rolling hills grew into round-topped mountains, the mountains here jutted up into the sky, their jagged fingers reaching for the heavens, their faces stone gray except for the few hardy trees clinging to their steep sides at the highest points. Forests of spruce, fir, and pine starting to turn their early autumn reds and golds grew across the midline of the range, and below them were the thicker woods of oak, ash, and maple.

She breathed in the invigorating mix of salt-tinged sea and brisk mountain breeze, and gazed up into the cloudless blue sky. The weather and the winds had obliged them their entire journey, except for a late summer storm that had sent the *Sea Eagle* pitching across the brackish Eastern Sea. While not her favorite part of the journey, Alyssa hadn't suffered any ill effects from it, but poor Pavel had a rough time of it, his belly finally settling along with the sea when they made the smoother sailing of the Straits.

From the Straits they'd sailed into the North Sea, where pods of creatures that Alyssa had never seen before, called dolphins and whales, had swum and played alongside the ship. At night, she and Jerrik and the crew would sit in the ship's hold and listen to the whales sing their haunting songs, songs that Alyssa would imitate on her harp and Han his flute, and that the whales would answer, a thing that Jerrik and his crew all swore they'd never witnessed before, and earned Alyssa the new endearment of Sea Siren.

As they sailed farther up the inlet, they counted three trading ships at anchor in the bay and six warships at the docks. The port's town, nestled in the crook of the inlet, came into view, the buildings of wood and thatch laid out along the harbor's shoreline, where wagons, carts, and people could be seen moving about the day's business.

Jerrik pointed out the road leading from the town up to the base of the mountain, where the palace, which was actually a compound of longhouses, sat above the town. "There's our home," he told Alyssa.

Nodding, she nestled closer into his side.

"Are you nervous?" he asked, tucking her in tighter.

"A little," she admitted. She took a deep breath in and blew it out. "I am a princess born and raised. I grew up in a royal household. I know how the politics of palace life can be."

Jerrik chuckled. "I've no doubt you'll face my family as fiercely and fearlessly as you did the brigands in the field," he said. "Though hopefully there will be no need for knife throwing." He kissed the top of her head. "No matter what," he told her, "I'm glad it's you who'll be by my side, my bloodthirsty little lynx."

The grip that Alyssa had on Jerrik's arm as they entered the great hall, accompanied by Sven, Bors, and Han, belied the mask of calm she had plastered on her face. Despite her earlier assurances, she was far beyond a little nervous. She was teeth-chattering, knee-shaking terrified.

Three lines of people stood waiting for them in front of the high tables, arranged, as Jerrik had explained to her, by the ranks of jarls, karls, and thralls.

They stopped in front of a tall, slim woman with straight brown hair and the saddest brown eyes that Alyssa had ever seen, flanked on one side by a brown-haired boy with sky-blue eyes, and a younger, curly-haired blond boy with the same blue eyes on her other.

"Dagny, this is my wife, Alyssa," Jerrik said to the woman. "Alyssa, this is Dagny, my brother Bard's widow, and their sons, Anders and Davin."

"It is my pleasure and honor," Alyssa told the woman whose sad eyes were on the verge of tears. She stepped in closer and said softly, "I am so sorry for your loss, sister."

"Thank you, my queen."

Alyssa smiled and laid a gentle hand on Dagny's shoulder. "Please, call me Alyssa."

Jerrik gave his sister-in-law a quick hug and whispered something in her ear that brought a tremble of a smile to her drawn face, and then he took Alyssa by the arm and they stepped over to stand in front of a younger, stockier version of himself with darker blond hair and gray eyes. "This is my brother Tryggr, and his wife, Trine, and their children, Reidar and Elin."

Alyssa held out her hand. "I am so glad to meet you, brother."

"It is truly a pleasure, my queen and sister," Tryggr said, his grip as warm and steady as his smile.

Alyssa turned to his wife, who politely dipped a knee and her head.

"Thank you for coming, my queen and sister," she said, straightening and gathering her young son and toddler daughter to her skirts. "Truly, thank you."

Alyssa gave the young mother a heartfelt hug. "You are most welcome, Trine." She smiled down at her new niece and nephew. Elin hugged her mother's legs, while Reidar grinned right back at Alyssa, who knelt down and held her hand out to the boy. "Hello," she said. "I'm your Auntie Alyssa."

The lad took her hand and shook it as hard as he could three times. "I'm Reidar," he told her. "I'm four."

"Yes, I know." Alyssa made a show of checking her hand and arm for any damage, earning an ear-splitting grin from the boy. "Your Uncle Jerrik has told me how big and strong a lad you are."

"I am," he said, flexing his four-year-old muscles.

Nodding her head in admiration, Alyssa laughed lightly as she stood and met Jerrik's approving gaze.

"I think you've won yourself a new champion," he said, taking her by the elbow and guiding her to a tall, thin man with a stiff, unbending stance, shrewd gray eyes, and a long beard and hair the bright yellow of yarrow. "Alyssa, this is my uncle and counsel to the king, Fenrir. Fenrir, this is Alyssa."

Eager to make a good first impression on the patriarch of Jerrik's family, the man who Jerrik told her had taken him under his wing after his mother's death and had helped him navigate his new role as king, Alyssa smiled and held her hand out to him. "It is a pleasure to meet you, Fenrir," she said. "Jerrik speaks highly of you."

Fenrir took her hand in his and lifted it. "My queen," he said, his voice as smooth as his smile. He pressed his lips to the backs of her fingers. "My nephew has spoken highly of you as well." He let go of her hand and dipped his head to her. "It is a pleasure and an honor to finally welcome you to Sea Ridge."

"Thank you," she told him, breathing a sigh of relief. He was the one man above all others here whom she wanted to impress. "I'm glad to finally be here."

She turned to a handsome woman of late-middle years with a head full of thick brown hair shot through with gray who was almost as tall and thin as Fenrir, whom she stood beside. Though it was late summer and the hall warm, she wore an ermine fur slung over her shoulders, clasped with a stunning brooch of gold inlaid with a ruby the size of a dove's egg on one hem, and a silver brooch in the shape of a warship with an eagle head prow on the other and held together by a chain of multicolored beads.

"This is Ermelinde. Fenrir's wife," Jerrik introduced her. "Aunt Ermelinde, this is my wife, Alyssa."

If Fenrir's slow, purposeful movements and unblinking eyes put Alyssa in mind of a stork, then his wife, Ermelinde, put her in mind of a weasel. She had small, sharp, darting brown eyes, and her smile was a flash of clenched teeth. She dipped neither her head or knee to Alyssa, but eyed her openly, her gaze taking in Alyssa's raiment, from her soft leather boots to her butter yellow gown of worm weave to the pearl at her throat and the comb in her hair.

"Welcome, child," she said. "Welcome to our, your, new home."

"Thank you, Ermelinde," Alyssa said with a slight dip of her head. The woman was the matriarch of the royal family as it stood now, and had been acting as queen for the last few moons. Still,

Alyssa was no child; she was queen now, and while she had no desire to antagonize the older woman, especially on their first meeting, neither would she stand to be treated as anything less. Thankfully, her mother had taught Alyssa the nuances of queenly discourse, and when and how to use it. "Thank you for such a kind welcome."

Behind her, where she knew Sven and Bors and Han stood guard, Alyssa heard the unmistakable clearing of male throats, and beside her, Jerrik chuckled under his breath as he tucked her hand into the crook of his arm and led her away from his tight-jawed aunt.

The next group consisted of Fenrir's and Ermelinde's two adult sons, both of whom were different size and age versions of their father, and who, like their father, wore their long beards and hair dyed the same yarrow yellow, which Jerrik had explained was actually accomplished by dying their hair with lye.

As Alyssa greeted each of them, and their wives and children in turn, she noticed several more men with the same yellow hair and beards who were wearing lacquered vests and blade-heavy waist belts, standing behind Fenrir and his son's families, their hard gazes fixed on Sven and Han and Bors, who, Alyssa knew without looking, were staring right back at them.

So, not all one big, happy family.

She sighed and placed her hand on Jerrik's forearm, the heat and strength of him fortifying her as they stepped up to two women, both of them almost as tall as Jerrik, one of whom she recognized from the tales he'd told her as they lay nestled in each other's arms at night.

"This is my stepsister, Magna," he told Alyssa, introducing a woman with flaming red hair attempting to escape the many braids that started at the crown of her head and hung down below her shoulders. Hazel eyes smiled down at Alyssa from a round face sprinkled with freckles, and she wore an intricately etched leather vest over a linen tunic of woad blue and leather breeches rather than a skirt. "Magna, this is Alyssa."

"I've been looking forward to meeting you since your brother Aaron first told me about you," Magna said, her voice deep for a woman. She held her hand out to Alyssa, who took it and shook it.

"And I you," Alyssa said. "Jerrik's told me many tales of your childhood adventures together." Mostly of how they had bonded, each of them the same age when her mother and his father had married and both of them missing their deceased parents. How for the three years they'd lived as brother and sister, they'd roamed the countryside and plagued their more civilized siblings daily, and of how she had argued her way into being able to take sword fighting lessons along with Ander's sons, and was the best fighter among them, with the exception of Jerrik, of course.

Magna laughed, low and throaty. "Don't believe half of them," she said, wagging her finger at Jerrik.

"The other half she will deny with her last breath," Jerrik said, laughing and giving her a hearty hug and a smacking kiss on her cheek.

"Leave off, you big oaf." Magna pushed him away from her while grinning from ear to ear.

A tall, beautiful blonde who had been standing back from them stepped up to introduce herself to Alyssa. "I am Marianne," she said, her voice as cool and distant as her smile. "A close and intimate friend," she slid a sly, sideways glance at Jerrik, "of the family."

"Well then," Alyssa said with a smile that honey could have dripped from as she reclaimed Jerrik's arm. "I'm sure we too shall become fast friends."

Jerrik clamped down on the grin that threatened to split his face as Marianne's registered her surprise and displeasure at Alyssa's response. He met Marianne's cold glare and shrugged his shoulders. She'd asked for it, and his little lynx had given it to her.

"I fear the day has caught up with me, husband," Alyssa said, her storm-tossed, sea green eyes letting him know that it was about to catch up with him as well. "Will you show me to our quarters now, so I may rest up before the night's festivities?"

"Of course, wife," he said, tucking her hand tighter into the crook of his arm and addressing the assemblage. "My queen and I wish to thank you all for the warm homecoming," he told them. "We look forward to the feast tonight. For now, we are in need of a hot bath and a soft bed."

Alyssa's grip on his arm didn't loosen until the door to the hall shut behind them, and then she shoved his arm away and strode not in the direction of the royal longhouse, which he had proudly pointed out to her when they first arrived, but in the exact opposite direction across the grounds.

The longhouse that was to be his and Alyssa's residence was newly built according to the plans and instructions Jerrik had given before sailing to collect his bride.

He'd spent two moons living in the old royal longhouse, sleeping in the king's chamber where his father and brother had died, next to the queen's chamber where his mother had taken her own life, and he was damned if he was going to live there in that cursed house with Alyssa.

The old king's house sat nearest to the great hall and still housed his brother Tryggr and his family and servants. The new king's longhouse sat at the outermost southwestern edge of the grounds with windows that allowed a cross breeze and gave an unfettered view of the bay and the inlet leading out to the sea.

Unlike the other longhouses, their new one was built with an upper level of separate bedchambers for their personal guard along the wall facing the mountain, and an open hall along the other with windows of a size to draw smoke from the hearth fires and shoot arrows out of if necessary.

The base of the longhouse was built of hewn stone, which Jerrik knew from his travels would make the building stronger and keep it cooler in the summer and warmer in the winter.

His and Alyssa's chambers took up the entire southern end of the second level, with a private stairway leading down to the bathing chamber below their room so they wouldn't have to use the tubs in the common bathing house.

Jerrik had been looking forward to soaking in the big, new wooden tub all day. A tub large enough for him and his bride to bathe and play in together.

A bride who was striding away from him, skirts twitching and arms swinging.

"Alyssa," Jerrik called out as he picked up his pace to follow her. "Where are you going?"

"To check on River and Storm," she said loudly, and then muttered something under her breath.

"What?"

"I said, to check on River and Storm," she shot back over her shoulder. "To make sure they, at least, are welcome in their new home."

Jerrik stopped in his tracks. She was angry at him about Marianne.

A perverse grin spread across his face as he resumed following her at a brisk pace. It wouldn't do for the king to be seen chasing after the queen, not in public. He caught up to her in the stables, where she was being greeted by a strapping young man who looked closer to Alyssa's age than Jerrik's, with brown eyes, braided, curly brown hair, and a short-cropped beard who was introducing himself as Hamar Halvdanson, the stablemaster.

"You are Halvdan's son?" Jerrik asked as he stepped up beside his wife.

"Yes, King Jerrik," the karl said. "My father passed only one moon ago. Your uncle made me stablemaster, a position I shall strive to serve as well as my father did. If it pleases you, of course."

Jerrik nodded and clasped the man's forearm. "I remember your father, Hamar Halvdanson," he said. "He was a good man and stablemaster. I'm sure you will be too."

"Thank you, my king," Hamar said as they released each other's arms. He glanced at Alyssa, and Jerrik caught the gleam of male admiration in his brown eyes. At least the man had the decency to drop his gaze when he saw Jerrik scowling at him. To Alyssa he dipped his head and said, "My queen, I will take you to your horses now. You will, of course, let me know if they need anything that I have not been made aware of."

"Oh, she'll let you know," Jerrik said, earning an icy glare from Alyssa.

Satisfied that River and Storm were in good hands with Hamar, Alyssa refused the offer of Jerrik's arm as they walked past the horse and livestock kraals and around the kitchen gardens, which were situated in the middle of the compound's grounds to make the most use of the sun's light.

Though it was only early September, with the high mountain peaks to the east and the west, sunrise would be coming late and sunset early to Sea Ridge. Alyssa rubbed her hands up and down her bare arms as she walked quickly to the longhouse that was to be her and Jerrik's personal, if not private, residence.

"Alyssa, will you slow down?"

"Why?" she said, stopping abruptly and causing Jerrik to do the same. "Because people will see?"

"Yes." He glanced over at the feasting hall, from where he was certain people were watching them. "It is unseemly for the king and queen to be seen arguing. Especially on our first day here, our first day in our new home."

He reached for her hand, and she shrugged it off. "I don't care if people see us argue," she said. "My mother and father argue all the time in front of everybody and anybody. It does not mean—"

"Not my mother and father," Jerrik said.

"What?"

"I only saw my mother and father argue once. My mother died later that same day."

"Oh."

Jerrik stuffed his hands in his pockets and rolled his shoulders, embarrassed to have said what he did about his parents. It wasn't something he normally talked about to anybody.

Alyssa stepped up to him and laid her open palm on his chest. "We are married, and this is only the first of many arguments we will have, the gods willing, over many years together. It doesn't lessen what I feel for you. In truth, if I felt less, I wouldn't be so angry."

"About Marianne?"

Alyssa nodded. "You were lovers?"

"Yes."

"Did you love her?"

"No."

She sucked a deep breath in and let it out in a rush. "Did she love you?"

He shook his head. "Not really. I think she loved the idea of me being king and of her being queen more than anything."

"As did your aunt and uncle," Alyssa said. "She was their choice, I take it?"

He covered her hand on his chest with both of his. "She was more my aunt's choice," he said. "My uncle actually defended my choice, which was you, Alyssa." He pressed her palm closer, so that she could feel the beating of his heart. "I never sought

to marry before I became king," he admitted. "I thought it would bring me nothing but trouble and misery. But once it became clear I should marry, I chose you, my little lynx. I choose you."

Alyssa brought their hands to her lips and kissed the backs of his fingers. "I love you, Jerrik," she said, speaking the words to him for the first time. Words he'd known deep in his heart to be true, and that he'd been waiting to hear without realizing it. "I always have and I always will. No petty argument between us will ever change that." She smiled at him like she had the first night they'd met, making him feel like the gods of the sky and sea combined. "Now kiss me, husband," she said. "Kiss me so that all may see and know I am yours and you are mine."

More than happy to oblige, Jerrik gathered Alyssa in his arms and kissed her long and hard, letting his body tell her what he couldn't put into words. Not yet, but making certain the world that was their kingdom would see their marriage was more than a marriage of convenience. They had passion, a connection between them that Alyssa called love, and that was still new and unnerving and exciting, like sailing uncharted waters in a foreign land. A feeling Jerrik had come to crave through the years, as he had come to crave the woman in his arms. The sweet, willing, sensuous woman who was kissing him as intensely as he was kissing her, her body warm and pliant beneath his roving hands.

She moaned and pressed her pelvis against the growing heat of his cock, and Jerrik scooped her up and strode for their longhouse and the big, soft bed that would be ready for them in their private bedchambers with a blushing, giggling Alyssa in his arms.

He pushed the unbolted door to the longhouse open with his booted foot and located the stairs leading up to their personal chambers, aware that several servants stood at the ready by the main hearth in the middle of the house.

The kingly thing to do would be to set Alyssa down and make introductions, but there would be time enough for that later. Right now, his only duty was to make Alyssa his wife in all ways. They had waited long enough.

"The queen and I do not wish to be disturbed," he announced as he stopped at the bottom of the stairs, counted the number of steps to the top, and shifted Alyssa in his arms, slinging her belly down over his shoulder and holding on to her legs as she giggled and squirmed. He gave her lovely backside a playful pat and then mounted the stairs.

Behind him he heard Sven's chuckle. "Newlyweds."

Jerrik toed the door to their personal chambers open and chuckled himself as Alyssa, still hanging over his shoulder, slid the bolt shut behind them. He carried her through the sitting room, taking in the tapestries on the walls and the luxurious woven rug on the floor he'd bought in the trading market of the Great Southern Desert, along with two sofas from the far east covered in blue and green linen, and a small oaken table with two chairs carved by a local tradesman.

The furnishings had cost him a goodly amount of coin, and were well worth the price, for he planned to be spending a lot of time in these chambers with Alyssa.

He carried her through the door to the bedchambers and plopped her down on the bed, which had been built three times the size of a normal bed, according to his specifications, and was covered with the finest bed linens and a quilt that mirrored the blues and greens of the sitting room rug.

Alyssa spread her arms and legs out and purred. "Oh Jerrik, this bed is delicious."

"Always thinking with your stomach," he teased. For such a sylph of a woman, she had an almost ravenous appetite, and had on occasion out-eaten more than a few of the *Sea Eagle*'s crew.

She sat up and kicked off her boots and then unclasped the shoulder strap to her gown and let it fall to her lap. "Not always," she said with a sensuous smile as she shimmied the gown down over her hips and legs and tossed it to the floor alongside her boots. "Not now."

She lay back on the bed with nothing but her pearl necklace on, and Jerrik quickly doffed his clothes, his gaze admiring the lovely sight of his wife's lithe body bathed in the late afternoon light.

"By the gods, Lyssa," he said almost reverently. "You are beyond beautiful."

Alyssa smiled, slow and sensuous, as her gaze took him in from head to toe and then settled on his growing cock. She held her arms out to him. "Come, my husband," she said, her voice low and raspy. "Come make me your wife."

He climbed up onto the bed, his knees between hers, and placed his hands to the sides of her shoulders. Settling the sensitive head of his erection up against the crux of her heat, he kept his weight on his elbows as he began to kiss her mouth, her neck, and her breasts, slowly, purposely, nuzzling and licking and suckling each pebbled nipple until she was moaning and writhing beneath him.

He took himself in hand and rubbed the tip of his cock in tortuous circles against her eager flesh, pushing in a little deeper each time, until his probing head was nestled inside her. He stopped and gazed into her eyes, heavy-lidded and unfocused with the same desire coursing through him.

"Alyssa," he whispered hoarsely, the niggling worry that Kostya had planted in his ear not quite assuaged. He wanted her. He wanted her badly. But he didn't want to force himself on her. "If you want me to stop, now is the time to say so."

In answer, she lifted her pelvis and took more of him inside her. "I want you," she half gasped, half moaned. "I want all of you, now."

"As you command, wife." He took her mouth with his, swallowing her little yelp as he buried himself in her with one deep thrust. He held himself still, panting with the effort as he felt Alyssa's intimate muscles began to relax and fit around him. "Are you all right?" he asked, his voice thick with desire.

"I am more than all right," she said, her voice echoing his. "You fill a need I only felt the lack of before."

"Ahh, my Lyssa. I'm going to fill your need until we are both satisfied to bursting."

"And then, my love?"

"I am going to do it again and again, for the rest of our lives."

Jerrik woke with Alyssa nestled against him, her legs tucked up under his knees, one arm slung over his chest and her head cradled on his shoulder, her mane of tawny gold spread out like a veil over her shoulder and breasts. By the gods, he loved waking up with her naked in his arms, almost as much as he loved getting her naked and into bed.

He lay dozing and basking in the memory of their lovemaking, sweet and tender, and carnal and passionate. He was content, possibly for the first time since he'd agreed to become king. With Alyssa by his side as his queen, he found he didn't dread the daily grind of palace life quite so much. He chuckled, thinking of her run-in with Ermelinde and Marianne. If nothing else, life with his little lynx would never be boring.

"Jerrik?"

"Did I wake you, my sleeping beauty?"

"No." She snuggled in closer, burrowing her nose into his neck and nipping at his skin. "Do we have time for…?"

Jerrik ran his fingers through her hair. "Unfortunately, we only have time for that or a bath. While I would prefer making love to my wife, I fear the rest of our company would prefer we bathe before supping."

She nipped his neck and then kissed it. "A hot bath would feel wonderful," she said. She pushed herself up on one elbow and gave Jerrik a smile of pure sensuous promise. "After we sup, we'll have all night to ourselves."

Untangling their legs, Jerrik sat up and gave her a lusty kiss. "I like the way you think, wife." He stood and went to the door and unbolted it and opened it enough to poke his head out and see the household servants about their business. "Somebody prepare us a bath, please," he called out, and saw several heads nod. "Knock on our door when it's ready."

"Bring bandages enough for a cut hand," Alyssa added from the bedchamber.

"Bring bandages, enough for a cut hand," he repeated before shutting the door and hurrying back to find Alyssa, naked, on her knees in the middle of the bed, rubbing her hand on the linens. "What happened?"

Alyssa held both her hands up, one with a bloody cut along its palm, and the other holding her waist blade.

"Since we bloodied the linens on our wedding night to make my family think we had consummated our marriage," she said, "I thought I should be able to show a good reason for there being blood on our bed linens here today."

Jerrik stood over the bed and gazed down at the bloodied linens, unable to tell any difference in the small stains.

"I didn't think you'd want anyone knowing we hadn't already consummated our marriage," she explained.

"No." Jerrik shook his head. Her explanation was perfectly reasonable.

He'd felt her little yelp when he'd first thrust into her. Of course, women had been known to fake such things. "That was smart thinking."

Maybe too smart.

Bathed and dressed for their first supper in their new home as king and queen, Jerrik escorted Alyssa into the dining hall, where all conversation stopped as a hundred pair of eyes feasted on Alyssa in her shawl and gown of jade green worm weave. The gown she was supposed to marry Kostya in. The man who may have taken her maidenhead.

Jerrik had told himself over and over again since staring down at Alyssa's blood on the bed linens that it didn't matter if some of it had been her virgin's blood or not. It didn't matter if he was her first or not. What mattered was that she wasn't pregnant with Kostya's child.

Jerrik would be her last and only lover from the day they'd married. When he handed her to the seat at his left at the high table and she smiled up at him, he even believed it. He took his seat at the center of the table and took her bandaged hand in his and kissed her wrist, breathing in the scent of winter lilies and summer rain.

"What happened to your hand, Queen Alyssa?" Fenrir asked, always observant and seated at Jerrik's right.

"Oh." Alyssa flicked her bandaged hand this way and that before tucking it into her lap. "I cut myself practicing flips with my waist blade." She smiled and shrugged. "I can be quite clumsy at times."

At the low table to their left, Sven coughed loudly, Bors chuckled into his horn of beer, and Han's horn stopped and hung midair. They'd all watched her scamper about the *Sea Eagle* from hold to top sail with the ease and agility of a cat the entire journey, and had a healthy respect for her ability to wield and throw a blade. Her killing the brigand was one of their new favorite tales. They looked from Alyssa to Jerrik one by one, and Jerrik simply shrugged his shoulders and took a hearty drink of his beer.

"You should be more careful now that you are queen," Fenrir gently admonished. "You might have injured more than your hand."

"True." Alyssa nodded gravely. "Especially since the king and I were naked in bed at the time." Jerrik choked and sputtered on his beer, and Alyssa gave him a wicked grin as she handed him her linen napkin. "Luckily," she added, "the king escaped injury to any vital parts."

CHAPTER 10

Warrior Women

"Thank you, Borgny," Alyssa said to the head cook, a plump, pleasant woman of late middle years with streaks of gray showing beneath her cap, after being given a tour of the kitchens. Along with one main roasting pit in the center of the feasting hall and another outside in the courtyard, the kitchens were made up of two smaller buildings attached to the hall and each other by covered passageways. One building, with indoor and outdoor ovens, was for baking, and the other, located the farthest from the hall and closest to a separate cold cellar, was for preparing the greens and roots, and fruits and meats. "I can see that you and your staff keep a well-run kitchen."

"Thank you, my queen," Borgny said with a broad smile, a quick dip of her head, and an even quicker glance at Ermelinde. "We do our best."

"You'll need little to no input from me on the day-to-day workings, I'm sure."

One of the many things that Alyssa had learned from her mother about being queen was that it was best to choose good people and then let them do their jobs without too much interference. A practice she intended to follow.

Borgny nodded to Alyssa in acknowledgment. "I appreciate you saying it, Queen Alyssa. I'm sure we'd all be happy to learn recipes of your homeland."

"Unfortunately, unless it is wild game that I caught, skinned, and cooked over a campfire, I fear I have little experience preparing meals," Alyssa demurred. "Though I do enjoy eating a good meal."

She rubbed her full belly. "If this morning's breakfast and last night's supper are any indication, I'll be enjoying them daily here."

Borgny's round cheeks flushed with the compliment. "I will make certain you do, my queen."

In their private chambers after supper last night, Alyssa had asked Jerrik what he knew of the household staff, and he'd told her, between bouts of laughter each time he glanced at her bandaged hand and waist blade, that his stepmother, Edda, had made Borgny head cook over ten years ago. Which meant, Alyssa hoped, that the cook's loyalty would lie with whoever was queen of Sea Ridge, and not Ermelinde, who'd been acting as queen.

She'd chided Alyssa privately this morning about her "improper" behavior at supper last night, seeming to take Alyssa's flushed cheeks as an admission of guilt, rather than her body's warm memory of how Jerrik had asked her to wear her waist belt and blade to bed last night, and only her waist belt and blade. An assumption Alyssa had done nothing to correct, willing to let the older woman enjoy her sense of superiority, for now.

"Shall we see to the others?" Ermelinde neither gave Alyssa her proper address of "my lady" or "queen," or waited for her to answer. She simply turned her back on Alyssa and blew through the door to the hall as stiff as a sail in gale-force winds.

The lady was intimidating, Alyssa would give her that, but Alyssa came from a long line of strong, intimidating women. Women who had fought and won bigger battles than this.

Her grandmother, Oona, had survived being made a slave and became a queen. A beloved queen who had built a thriving city alongside her husband. Alyssa's mother had been the first woman ever to enter the Great Races, and had won the first and placed in the second before being kidnapped in the third, and escaped from her captors.

She'd killed a man in the fight to rescue her mare and had survived another fortnight in the mountain wilds. Alyssa had left her home and traveled to a faraway land to be with the man she loved, as had her grandmother and mother, and Great-Auntie Lyrra.

Alyssa lengthened her spine and squared her shoulders as she followed Ermelinde through the doors. She was a woman full grown, not a little girl, a queen born of queens. If Ermelinde thought Alyssa was going to roll over belly up whenever the older woman expressed her displeasure, she had another thought coming. Even if the woman did make Alyssa want to stick her tongue out at her like a petulant child in side braids.

Out in the dining hall, Ermelinde introduced the women gathered there, recommending two women whom she thought Alyssa should choose to be her housekeeper and maidservant, assuming that she, Ermelinde, would be the queen's counsel, as she had been apparently for the past four queens, all the way back to Jerrik's mother.

Alyssa listened intently and took in the two women whom Ermelinde recommended, both of whom had been standing with the group of yellow beards at her first introduction to the household yesterday afternoon.

With a regal nod of her head learned from her mother, Alyssa turned from the group of women and walked over to where Magna, Dagny, and Trine stood. With Tryggr still alive and two young children to raise, Trine had her own household to run, but as a widow with two sons in need of a father figure and no house to call her own, Dagny could surely benefit from becoming part of the king's household. Besides, she had been queen for a year, a well-liked queen from what Alyssa had learned in the short time she'd been here. She could help Alyssa as much as Alyssa could help her.

"Dagny, would you consider taking the position of housekeeper for the king's household, along with queen's counselor?"

Her widowed sister-in-law stood speechless for a moment, and then her brown eyes filled with the tears that had threatened yesterday and her lips trembled as she bent her knee to Alyssa. "I have no need to consider, my queen. It will be my honor and my pleasure to serve you and the king's household."

"Good," Alyssa said, clasping both of Dagny's hands as she straightened. "You and your sons can move into the king's house tomorrow." She let go of Dagny's hands and held her gaze. "As counselor, who would you recommend I choose for my maidservant?"

Dagny thought for a moment, and then inclined her head toward a pretty, round-faced blonde woman standing with the line of servants behind the royals. "Hulda is the younger sister of Helga, my maidservant," she said. "I'm certain she will serve you as well as Helga has served me."

"Thank you, Dagny." Alyssa stepped over to Hulda, whose brown eyes dropped to her feet as Alyssa stood before her. Of about twenty and five years, she was neither tall nor short, neither thick nor thin, and her clothes, while not fine, were clean and well cared for. "Would you like the position of queen's maidservant, Hulda?"

"I am a thrall, my queen," she answered with a quick glance up before dropping her gaze again. "I will do as you wish."

Jerrik had explained how the people here were either jarls, the landed freeborn, or karls, freeborn tradesmen, or thralls, slaves born or made, much as it was in most of the world, though not the one Alyssa had grown up in.

Her parents had abolished slavery in their kingdom, following in her grandparents' footsteps, who had founded their city on the belief that a person's worth should be the result of their labors, not their birth.

A city that thousands of people had immigrated to for the chance to prove their worth, and that had thrived and grown into one of the known world's richest trading ports. A belief that Alyssa agreed with, and planned to introduce to her new household and kingdom.

Jerrik, having traveled the world enough to see many different lands and cultures and to appreciate the differences, had agreed with Alyssa, even as he warned her to engage in her campaign step by slow, careful step. These Northlanders, he'd warned her, were slow to trust outlanders, and like any other people of any other land, would fight against their traditions being changed.

"I wish for you to choose freely, Hulda, without fear of either my displeasure or punishment."

Beside her, Ermelinde sucked her breath in through her teeth, and then let it out in a disapproving hiss. Before her, Hulda lifted her gaze and met Alyssa's, her brown eyes studying Alyssa as intently as Alyssa studied her.

"Then yes, my queen, I choose to be your maidservant."

"Good." Alyssa gave her a quick smile. "You may start your duties tomorrow." She started to step away and then stopped. "Do you have a husband or children, Hulda?"

"No, my queen."

Alyssa nodded. She wouldn't want to separate a family, even for the privilege of serving a queen. She moved to stand before Magna, impressed anew at the strength and fire that emanated from Jerrik's stepsister. "I would ask you, Magna, to be my counselor along with Dagny."

"I accept, my queen."

"And to be my personal guard."

Magna rose to her full height and breadth, a big grin splitting her freckled face in two.

"It would be my honor, my queen."

"I would have a word, nephew."

Jerrik stopped in the middle of the courtyard and waited for Fenrir to catch up to him. He'd been on his way to the stables to saddle Storm and ride down to the docks where he would oversee the unloading of the *Sea Eagle*'s hold. He smiled with satisfaction at the thought of the trade goods he'd be bringing back up to the palace, and was looking forward to helping Lev, as the new skeppare, take inventory of what supplies the ship would need to stock up on for the next voyage. His smile flattened at his uncle's stern visage.

"Your wife," Fenrir said without preamble, "chose to ignore the women whom your aunt, who has been acting queen, recommended for her new household."

"I'm sure she took Ermelinde's recommendations into consideration," Jerrik said. In his years of travel and trade, he'd learned to smooth many a ruler's ruffled feathers, as well as when to hold fast and when to give sway. "However," he told Fenrir, "Alyssa is queen now and knows her own mind."

"Yes, she certainly seems to," his uncle said with a chuckle. Then his expression turned serious. "But do you?"

"Do I what?"

"Know your own mind."

"What do you mean by that?"

"You are enthralled by her," Fenrir said. He smiled and splayed his hands. "It is to be expected, newly married to such a beautiful young woman."

Jerrik grinned. "I suppose it is."

"I'm glad," Fenrir said, "for the both of you. Passion in a marriage is a good thing, as long as you do not let her lead you by your passions, as your mother did your father."

Jerrik snapped his head back as if his uncle had slapped him back in time, back to his father's rage over his mother's infidelity. "What exactly are you saying?"

"I am saying that she is a pretty young thing, a princess, used to having her way and enjoying the fawning attention of many men, and that you are your father's son, with a jealous streak that you must learn to control."

Jerrik opened his mouth to say that he was nothing like his father, but as much as he hated to acknowledge it, he was. His mother knew it and used to tease him and his father about it. Fenrir, who had helped raise Jerrik after his mother's death, knew this about him. As did Sven, who had chided Jerrik for acting the jealous fool several times already. "I never was before Alyssa," he admitted.

"Yes, well, certain women can bring it out in a man."

Jerrik nodded. Alyssa certainly brought it out in him.

"I didn't intend to upset you or to bring back certain unpleasant memories," Fenrir said. "My only purpose was to provide counsel, as I have faithfully done for your father and brothers, and to break this curse with which our family has been burdened."

"As it is mine," Jerrik said, shaking off those memories as much as he was able. "Now, if we're finished here, I'm off to the docks. Is there anything you wish me to get for you there?"

Fenrir shook his head. "My only wish is for your happiness, and a long, prosperous reign, my nephew and king."

Alyssa was in the stables, braiding purple flowers into River's black mane, when Jerrik walked in, the mare's coat as sleek and shiny as pitch from the thorough brushing her mistress, dressed in her linen work tunic and skirt and covered in fine black horse hairs, had no doubt given her.

"We have stable hands for that, you know," Jerrik said, half teasing. He grinned, thinking of Fenrir's or Ermelinde's reactions if either of them had found their queen covered in horsehair and straw chaff.

"I know," Alyssa said, tying off a deep purple flower in River's mane and stepping back to stand by Jerrik and admire her handiwork. "It calms me, being with them."

Jerrik tucked Alyssa into his shoulder and kissed the top of her head. "I know it does," he said. "I have no issue with you tending them. Nor am I foolish enough to try to dissuade you from tending any other poor, dumb creature you take under your wing, including myself." He thought of her hands on him, of how her touch could either calm him or stir him. "In truth," he whispered huskily into her hair, "I give thanks to the gods daily that you are mine and I am yours. But..." He hated even mentioning it, yet it wouldn't be fair of him not to. Not to her, not to his aunt and uncle. "Fenrir told me you ignored Ermelinde's recommendations in choosing your household this morning."

Alyssa stepped out of Jerrik's embrace and lifted her chin to meet his gaze. "I didn't ignore her choices for me. I chose differently for myself."

"Which was basically what I told Fenrir."

"Dagny agreed to be keeper of our house," she told him, "and one of my counselors."

"Good." Jerrik had always liked his brother's wife. She had a calm steadiness about her and had been considered a good and fair queen for the little time she'd held the position. This new post would keep her and Bard's sons in good standing.

"Magna agreed to be my second counselor and personal guard."

Jerrik raised his brows. "Your personal guard? A woman?"

"You told me that she was as strong as a man and better with a sword than most, and as brave and honorable as any."

"I did."

"As a woman, she can go places with me that a man could not."

"True."

"So." Alyssa arched her brows. "You approve of my choices?"

"If I did not?"

"Then we would discuss it further," she said with a pretty pout that had no doubt swayed men her whole life, "until you did."

"You think you could persuade me so easily?"

"Perhaps," she said with a teasing smile. "Perhaps not." She stepped closer and slid her hands up his tunic's front and around his neck. "Either way," she said, lifting onto her toes and brushing his lips with hers, "I would enjoy trying."

You are enthralled by her. Do not let her lead you by your passions, as your mother did your father.

The little lynx can turn a man's head with nothing more than a pout and a smile.

Fenrir's and Aaron's words echoed in Jerrik's head, and he removed Alyssa's hands from his nape and stepped back from her, ignoring the confusion in her eyes. "Hamar," he called out, spooking Alyssa and River both. "Saddle Storm for me."

Two wagons pulled by a team of oxen each rumbled to a stop in the courtyard. Jerrik was driving one wagon with Storm tied off the back, and Pavel, holding Digger, sitting beside him. Lev drove the other wagon with Bors sitting beside him and Han sitting atop the pile of trade goods from the *Sea Eagle*'s hold. Alyssa watched from the paddock where she'd been exercising River with a training lead and trying to figure out the cause of Jerrik's latest quicksilver mood change. She untied River's lead and latched the gate as Digger, yipping with excitement, came running. Scooping up the wiggling pup and giving in to his wet kisses, Alyssa hugged Digger close as she approached the wagons.

"The tapestries and the rugs go to the storage room in my longhouse," Jerrik told the men unloading the wagons, "and the furs and cloths as well. The trunks of salt and spices go to the kitchens."

He met Alyssa's gaze for a brief moment, and then continued to direct what went where without outwardly acknowledging her presence. Not wishing to cause a scene by arguing with her husband in public for the second time in as many days, she strolled over to the wagon laden with bolts of worm weave and piles of furs and was soon joined by the other women of the palace, who had come out to admire the exotic cloths and thick, rich furs.

"This will bring good coin to the king's coffer," Ermelinde said as she ran her fingers down a bolt of midnight blue worm weave. "I can only imagine what it cost Jerrik."

"It cost him nothing," Alyssa told her, setting Digger down to run around. "It was a wedding gift from my parents."

"Well then," Ermelinde said, glancing down her nose at the pup. "Jerrik will be able to make a pretty profit from your dowry."

"My parents gifted the cloth to me, not Jerrik." Alyssa met and held the older woman's pinched gaze, and tried not to gloat. "Jerrik didn't ask for any dowry."

Ermelinde tsked. "Much like his father before him."

"How so?" Alyssa asked.

Ermelinde drew herself up to her full, haughty height. "He took only his own selfish wishes into consideration when choosing a bride, rather than the good of the kingdom."

Only a lifetime of royal training kept Alyssa from either slapping Ermelinde into the next fortnight or clawing the bolt of blue worm weave to shreds. "I am a princess born and raised," she said, lengthening her spine and facing Ermelinde as the crowd of women shifted and staked their allegiances, noting that Magna, Dagny, and Trine took their stances by her. "A queen born of queens."

"Was not one of them, your grandmother I believe, a slave before she became a queen?" Ermelinde said with a snide smile.

Alyssa chuffed. "Yes," she replied. "She was. My grandmother, Queen Oona, was a chieftain's granddaughter before she was captured and made a slave and a dowry gift for the Prince Black Mane's betrothal to a woman he did not love. The same prince who fell in love with her and made her a queen. A good and beloved queen, and faithful and loving wife."

"Well said," Magna muttered behind her, and Alyssa stood a little taller.

"Well," Ermelinde sniped, "whether you become such a good and beloved queen as well remains to be seen." She flicked her veiny hand at the bolt of blue. "What do you intend to do with all of this worm weave?"

Their contentious words apparently dismissed, she waited imperiously as Alyssa fought to find her tongue and her civility, certain that the older woman never forgot any slight, large or small.

"I will have several gowns made for myself and one each for the women of my husband's family."

"I claim the forest green," Magna said. "It goes well with my coloring."

"Which would you have, Aunt Ermelinde?" Alyssa asked by way of a peace offering.

"I will have to study them more carefully before I choose," Ermelinde answered. "Nothing in haste."

She turned her back on Alyssa, her queen, and started to walk in the direction of her family's longhouse. Several others, whom Alyssa had taken to thinking of as the yellow beard women, trailed obediently behind her, while some stayed to ogle the bolts of worm weave a moment longer before following after their queen bee. Of Ermelinde's swarm, only Marianne remained.

"You must understand," she offered as if she were asked, "Ermelinde and Fenrir and the other elders all wanted, expected, Jerrik to marry me."

"So I've been told."

Marianne's light blonde brows arched high. "Jerrik told you about me? About us?"

"He did."

"Did he tell you that we were lovers?"

Behind her, Magna and Dagny and Trine had gone so still, Alyssa wondered if they were even breathing. Before her, Marianne waited to see if her barbs had sunk in, and how deep.

"Jerrik told me that you've had sex," Alyssa said with the hint of a smile. "He never used the word 'lovers.'"

Marianne turned without a word and walked away to follow Ermelinde and her gaggle of clucking hens. Alyssa turned and burst into laughter at the expressions on Magna's, Dagny's, and Trine's faces. One by one, they closed their gaping mouths and started laughing along with her, until they spied something or someone over Alyssa's shoulder.

"Ladies," Jerrik said as their laughter died down. He held his hand out to Alyssa. "A word, wife."

Alyssa put her hand in his and let him lead her away from the wagons toward the paddock, Digger at their heels.

"What was that all about?" he asked when they were far enough away to not be overheard. "What did Ermelinde and Marianne say to you?"

"Nothing really," she replied with an unconvincing shrug. "Woman stuff."

"Alyssa?"

"Nothing I can't handle."

"Are you sure?" he asked. "Ermelinde and Marianne can be hard to deal with."

Alyssa chuffed. "I've dealt with worse," she assured him. He snorted and shook his head and glanced around the yard where it seemed every person there from royal to thrall were watching them. "Are you sure?" she asked him.

"About what?"

"All of this." She held both hands out to encompass the royal compound. "About giving up your life on the *Sea Eagle*. About being king. Marrying me and making me queen." She stepped closer and saw the storm clouds scudding across his gaze. "If you're not," she said, "I will gladly help you load all of this back onto the *Sea Eagle* and set sail anywhere you wish to go. As long as I'm with you."

The clouds cleared from his gaze and he took a deep breath in and blew it out. "Kiss me, Alyssa." He reached out and pulled her into him. "Kiss me, my wife, my queen. And you will know."

Alyssa smiled into eyes as blue and cloudless as a summer sky, wrapped her hands around Jerrik's neck, and kissed him. Kissed him so that he and everyone watching would know how much she loved him. He kissed her back, clasping her to him and kissing her as if he would never let her go. Eventually, the sound of loud cheering broke through the haze of their kiss and they pulled apart to see the men and women who had been unloading the wagons clapping and hooting.

"At least we know who's on our side," Alyssa said. She glanced over toward the feasting hall, where Ermelinde and Marianne and several others stood watching them as well. "And who's not."

"They'll come around in time," he assured her. "Once we have proven ourselves worthy."

She gave him a look that said, *If you say so,* and then took his arm and started back toward the wagons, where Pavel stood watching them approach, cap in hand, rocking from foot to foot.

"Pavel looks nervous," Alyssa said.

"Aye, he asked me if he could stay here with us instead of returning to the *Sea Eagle*. He fears he wouldn't survive another bout of seasickness."

"Not that I have much experience sailing," she said, "but I've never seen anyone as sick as he was."

"Nor I." He chuckled. "He was sure he was dying."

"Or at least wished he was," Alyssa said with a sympathetic shake of her head. "What did you tell him?"

"That I was certain I could find him a position that would never require him to set sail again."

Alyssa laughed, light and happy and content to be walking hand in hand with Jerrik. "Hamar was saying how he could use another stable hand," she told him. "Pavel is good with Storm and River. I'm sure they'd be more comfortable with somebody they're already familiar with."

"When did you speak with Hamar?" Jerrik said sharply enough that Alyssa held his gaze a moment before answering him.

"This morning at the stables when I was grooming River."

He muttered something about jealous fools and then he lifted her hand from his arm and kissed the backs of her fingers. "Do you wish to tell Pavel," he asked, "or should I?"

Alyssa took her seat beside Jerrik at the high table and heard him chuckle as her belly growled.

"Hungry, my little lynx?"

"Ravenous." Alyssa met the smile in his eyes with a smile of her own that let him know she wasn't necessarily speaking of food. They'd spent the entire day unloading the wagons and storing the goods in their longhouse, as well as helping situate Sven, Han, and

Bors in their new rooms down the hall from the king's and queen's suite. They'd had enough time to make love or bathe before supper. Although, as Jerrik had pointed out, as king and queen they could have made the entire household wait for them to sup, Alyssa didn't want to antagonize his aunt any more today, and chose to bathe first. They would have all night after supper to play. "You?"

"Ravening," he said with a hungry leer that made Alyssa's body react in delicious ways.

Their expressions promising a night full of lusty pleasures, they raised their horns of honey mead, a sweet, yeasty drink Alyssa found she preferred over beer, and took long draughts as the servants set trays of cut apples, pears, and herbed cheeses, along with freshly baked rye bread, early autumn greens, and roast goat on the table.

Alyssa filled her trencher and tucked into the tender, roasted meat, which tasted as succulent and savory as it smelled. She'd gotten no more than three bites down when Ermelinde, sitting to Jerrik's right with Fenrir, leaned over the table and caught Alyssa's gaze. "Tell us of Jerrik's marriage proposal, Alyssa," she said. "It must have been a dream come true for you, after waiting so many years for him to answer you."

Luckily, Alyssa had swallowed her last bite of meat, else she would've choked on it along with Ermelinde's snide innuendo. She took a swallow of her mead and met Jerrik's raised brows while thinking on what she would tell and what she would not, deciding in the end to tell the simple truth.

She took another sip of mead to wet her throat, when Jerrik spoke up. "When I first arrived," he said, "Alyssa was standing before a priest about to pledge vows of marriage to another man."

Those with food or drink in their mouths did choke and sputter, while Alyssa and Jerrik laughed softly and waited for throats to clear.

"Who?" Fenrir asked at last.

"His name is Kostya," Alyssa answered. "A childhood friend." She took another sip of mead and waited for the inevitable question.

"What happened?" This time it was Marianne who asked.

"When it came time to recite my vows, I couldn't," Alyssa said. "I stood before Kostya, the priest, and my family and told them I couldn't marry him."

"After you saw Jerrik," Marianne said.

Alyssa smiled at her husband. "No. I didn't know he was there yet."

"Then why?" Marianne said, sounding confused as to why a woman, any woman, would refuse marriage.

"Because he was not Jerrik," Alyssa explained. "I did not love him."

A soughing and murmuring filled the hall as Jerrik lifted Alyssa's hand in his and kissed the backs of her fingers.

"So, you chose love and personal happiness over honor and duty to your family and people," Ermelinde chided.

Jerrik's grip tightened on Alyssa's hand and the muscle in the side of his jaw ticked. Alyssa turned her hand in his and gave a slight shake of her head.

"Yes, Aunt," she answered. "I did."

"As queen," Ermelinde warmed to her lecture, "you must learn to put your people before your personal wishes."

"As queen, I will always consider the needs of the people in any decision I make," she told Ermelinde and anyone in the hall who could hear. "As a princess and my parents' seventh child, my marrying who I wished did not affect my city's people at all."

"Perhaps not." Ermelinde's voice was as stern and stiff as her bearing. "But it has affected ours."

The muscle on the side of Jerrik's jaw jumped. "Alyssa is my choice, Aunt," he said, his voice as cold and cutting as a winter wind. He eyed each person seated at the royal high table one by one. "If you recall, every single one of you, with the exception of Ermelinde, begged me to take this family's cursed throne, and I did, not because I wanted it, but for you, my family, and the people of this kingdom. Being king was not my choice; Alyssa is. She is my wife and queen, and I have every faith that she will be a good queen, a kind and fair queen, because she is all those things and more."

CHAPTER 11

Knots

Jerrik gave his wife a long, leisurely good-bye kiss at the door to their longhouse as Sven and Bors waited for him outside with big grins plastered on their faces.

"You and Alyssa look to have worked out the knots in your marriage, lad," Sven said as they headed for the stables.

"That we have." In the half fortnight since he'd defended Alyssa as his choice to his aunt, and before the entire royal household, they hadn't had one disagreement, and she'd been thanking Jerrik morning, noon, and night.

He grinned, thinking about their play that morning in bed, and glanced at the stables entrance where his uncle, Fenrir, whose wife had not been so pleased with Jerrik the past half fortnight, waited for them along with his eldest son, Rigil.

"You and your aunt and uncle?" Sven asked, following the direction of Jerrik's gaze.

Jerrik rolled his shoulders. He and Fenrir were getting along fine, as always. He and Ermelinde however… "Are still working out the knots."

Fenrir and Rigil would be riding out with Jerrik, Sven, and Bors today to meet the jarls and karls who owned and worked the farm holdings east of the city.

Over the past several days, Jerrik had met with the merchants and innkeepers, the fishermen and warehouse men of the city's port, as well as the skeppares and crews of the ships at anchor in the bay. He'd asked questions of them all and listened to their answers, and had learned that while most of the people had the same general needs and concerns of people the world over, here, in Sea Ridge, they also wanted to be reassured that Jerrik intended to see them prosper under his rule, and that his rule would last more than a year or three. A reassurance Fenrir had quickly and adamantly given them.

As far as Jerrik could tell, the kingdom had fared well enough under Fenrir's temporary rule, yet he'd also recognized a certain reticence in the people in general, which could be unease over yet another change in rule, which made him even more determined to see this whole king thing through. He no longer thought of escaping the throne, but of beating the curse and becoming a king who would make his family proud.

He was no fool. He knew it would be grueling work of a kind he had never undertaken before. Still, he was sure that with Alyssa, whom the townspeople had been instantly charmed by, as his queen, they would all of them learn and thrive.

"What about you and Fenrir?" Jerrik asked Sven, who, as Jerrik's counsel along with his uncle, had been watching and learning as well.

Sven gave Fenrir and Rigil a sideways glance as they approached the waiting men. "Still working out some knots of our own," he said.

Jerrik clapped Sven on the shoulder. As stubborn and opinionated as Sven and his uncle could both be, neither of them were unreasonable. "I'm sure you'll work them out soon," he said. He looked to Bors. "You?"

Bors shrugged. "Your uncle tends to keep clear of me." He flashed a grin as cold and sharp as the two short swords strapped across his back. "Though a few of his yellow beards have taken a stab at approaching me."

"What about?"

"Oh, this and that."

Jerrik chuckled. Few men were as naturally close-mouthed as Bors. The yellow beards, as Alyssa and his men from the *Sea Eagle* had taken to calling them, would get nothing out of him he didn't wish to give them. "You'll tell me if they speak of anything I should know about?"

"Aye, Skeppare."

If Bors realized he'd called Jerrik skeppare, he didn't correct himself, nor did Jerrik or Sven. In truth, it was good to have friends around who still thought of him as Jerrik or Skeppare. King would come in time, for all of them.

"Uncle, Rigil," Jerrik greeted the men as they entered the stables. "It looks to be a fine day for riding out."

"As good as any," Fenrir said sourly.

The people of Sea Ridge were sailors, farmers, and tradesmen who could ride a horse if they had to, but generally preferred to ride on a cart or wagon. With Aaron's influence, and now Alyssa's, who rode even better than Aaron had, Jerrik had learned to prefer a mount's easy gait and warm seat over the bone-jostling rattle of a wooden wagon bench.

Feeling the wind in his hair and the sun on his face on the back of a horse put him in mind of being on a ship's deck, another thing his uncle and cousin couldn't appreciate, not like Jerrik and his men did.

"King Jerrik." Hamar led Storm, saddled and ready, out of his stall and handed the reins to Jerrik as Pavel led a sturdy dun cob over to Fenrir and cupped his hands for Fenrir's boot.

"What's your name, boy?" Fenrir asked the lad as he settled onto the dun's saddle.

"Pavel, sir."

"Ah yes," Fenrir said. "The young thief my nephew took in."

Though Fenrir's tone hadn't been unkind, Pavel cast an accusatory glance Jerrik's way and then dropped his gaze to his new boots. "Yes, sir."

Jerrik wanted to tell Pavel it hadn't been him who'd told Fenrir the lad's story and named him thief, but now was neither the time nor the place. He swung himself up onto Storm's back and stroked the stallion's neck as Hamar and Pavel brought the others their mounts, impressed by how well Hamar had paired ride and rider according to size and temperament and abilities. When the men were all mounted, Hamar went to River's stall, and Jerrik saw that the mare was saddled as well.

"Queen Alyssa is not riding with you today?" Hamar asked.

"No," Jerrik told him. "She and the other women are choosing their cloth, and are being fit and measured for their gowns for our wedding a fortnight hence."

Hamar took hold of River's bridle as the mare craned her neck out over the stall gate and whinnied. "Sorry, girl." He rubbed the eager mare's cheek. "You must stay here for now. Maybe your mistress will take you out for a run later."

"I'm sure she will." Fenrir turned his cob for the open door and flashed a quick grin Jerrik's way. "I'm told she never misses a chance to visit the stables."

"The queen does dote on her horses," Hamar said, nonplussed, though Fenrir's words stayed with Jerrik for the rest of the day.

"Have you decided which color you want for your wedding gown?" Solveig, the head seamstress, asked Alyssa as various women of Jerrik's family inspected the colorful bolts of wool, linen, and worm weave displayed in the common room of the royal longhouse.

"I'm going to wear the same gown I married Jerrik in at our first wedding," Alyssa told the seamstress, who put her in mind of a wren with her darting eyes and flitting hands. "Though I would have you make me a shawl of the same amethyst worm weave." She lowered her voice to a whisper. "My husband has requested a nightgown of the same color, sheer, with no lining, and a tight, low-cut bodice."

"Oooh, yes." Solveig's brown eyes lit up as she took in Alyssa's figure. "Yes, I can do that. I can make you a gown that your husband will want to tear off you as soon as you don it, my queen."

"That wouldn't take much," Dagny, overhearing Solveig, said with a teasing grin. "Her husband practically undresses her with his eyes whenever he so much as gazes upon her."

Alyssa thought of how Jerrik had undressed her that morning before leaving with Sven and Bors, and her cheeks flushed with the memory, causing Dagny and Solveig to smile knowingly.

"I'd better leave enough seam to let out in the waists and bodices of your new gowns then," Solveig said, and Alyssa's cheeks warmed as her hand went to her still-flat belly.

"Already?" Dagny asked.

Alyssa dropped her hand. Her moon flow was a few days late, but after the hemorrhaging last time, she had no idea what to expect or when. Without her mother here to ask such questions, she would have to make a point of talking about it privately with Dagny sometime soon.

At thirty years of age, Dagny had gone from wife of a prince and mother of two young sons to queen and young widow. Her life's experiences and steady nature had made her indispensable to Alyssa and the royal household in a matter of days, and Alyssa trusted her wisdom and her discretion.

The crew of the *Sea Eagle* all thought Alyssa had miscarried while on the ship, and as far as she knew, they'd told no one here. At least she hoped they hadn't. It would raise too many worries and questions. She hated the lie she and Jerrik had started the night of their wedding, but it would do no good to correct it now. Besides, in the end, it was nobody's business but their own. She smiled shyly at Dagny and Solveig. "I'm not certain yet," she said. "Maybe."

"Well," Dagny said matter-of-factly, "if you aren't yet, you soon will be."

Alyssa's cheeks heated as Dagny and Solveig burst into laughter, the hard and knowing yet not unkind laughter Alyssa had heard her mother and sisters-in-law break into many times over the years.

Laughter that Alyssa was beginning to understand herself. She glanced across the room to where Ermelinde and her two daughters-in-law stood with Marianne, the four of them eyeing Alyssa with barely concealed disdain as they ran their fingers up and down bolts of worm weave Alyssa was gifting them with for gowns to wear to her wedding.

She bit back the giggle that threatened at the sudden thought of Ermelinde and Fenrir in bed together. How could two people make love, much less have sex, without ever bending their spines?

She met Marianne's cold, spiteful glare. The woman had stayed here in Sea Ridge as a guest of Ermelinde first in hopes that Jerrik would marry her, and now, Alyssa could only surmise, in the hopes that he would leave Alyssa for her or take her as his mistress.

Either way, Marianne and Ermelinde were not pleased that Jerrik and Alyssa were besotted with each other.

With a regal nod of her head, Alyssa turned away from Marianne. She could understand the woman's displeasure at losing Jerrik as a lover; however, he was Alyssa's husband now and Marianne needed to come to grips with it.

If Alyssa had been in Marianne's position, she would have left Sea Ridge and returned to her home where she was the daughter and widow of landed jarls. Yet Marianne had decided to stay at Sea Ridge indefinitely as Ermelinde's guest and friend, and although Alyssa would have been in her rights as queen to deny the woman abiding here, she didn't want to act out of pettiness.

Plus, she could afford to be magnanimous. Jerrik had sworn to Alyssa that he adored only her and had no further interest in Marianne or any other of his former lovers. As Dagny had so indelicately put it, by the way Jerrik and Alyssa had been going at it, she had no reason to doubt him.

"Oh, Magna," Alyssa exclaimed as the buxom redhead paraded around with the forest green worm weave draped over her shoulders and down and around her waist. "You were right. That green looks wonderful on you."

Magna beamed, and her grin grew wider at the approving smile on Hulda's face. To her credit, Magna, freeborn and part of the royal family, had agreed to share an upstairs bedchamber with Hulda, a thrall, saving Hulda the trouble of running up and down the stairs every time Alyssa needed her in her chambers. And though they were as different as night and day, for where Magna was bold and outgoing, Hulda was quiet and shy, they had become fast friends.

Hulda, too, had been admiring the bolts of cloth, her gaze returning again and again to a marigold yellow worm weave. She stood by it now, running tentative fingers over the cloth, and then snatched her hand away when she realized that Alyssa was watching her.

"With your blonde hair and coloring that yellow would look good on you, Hulda," Alyssa said. "What do you think, Magna?"

Magna nodded. "I agree."

"Are we dressing thralls in worm weave now?"

Ermelinde's snide voice clawed its way up Alyssa's spine and raised her hackles. Taking a slow, deep breath, she turned from Magna's reddening face and Hulda's horrified expression and met the woman's arrogant gaze.

"Hulda is my maidservant," she told Ermelinde and the other women with their noses in the air. "Would you have me dress her in rags?"

"I would have you dress her according to her station in life," Ermelinde said, her spine as stiff and unbending as her attitude.

"Her station is maidservant to the queen. Your queen. And as your queen, I will dress my maidservant as I see fit."

"Dressing a thrall better than the wives of the karls who will come to your wedding will not reflect well on you, my queen," Ermelinde scolded.

"There you would be wrong," Alyssa said. She looked to Hulda, who stood silent and deathly pale. "From this moment forward, Hulda is no longer a thrall. For her service to me, her queen, I declare her a free woman."

Alyssa was sitting at the table in her sitting room, arranging scraps of wool and felt in the wooden box that had been Digger's bed on the *Sea Eagle* but was too small for the growing pup now, when Jerrik came in and plopped down on the sofa.

"Good afternoon, husband," she said, smiling up at him.

"I thought we agreed to taking small, careful steps," he said, kicking off one of his boots.

Alyssa's smile flattened. "You heard already?"

Jerrik nodded and kicked off his other boot as Digger stuffed his nose into the first one. "Ermelinde found me at the stables."

"Ermelinde was in the stables?" Alyssa let out a low whistle that had Digger pulling his head out of Jerrik's boot and standing at full alert.

"She was yammering in my ear about you freeing thralls before I even set foot on the ground."

Alyssa stood and stepped over to Jerrik and knelt at his knees. "It was a rash decision on my part, I admit," she said. She placed her hands on his thighs. "But the woman rubs my fur the wrong way. She is arrogant and condescending and talks to me as if I were a child." She gnashed her teeth and actually growled. "I swear I bite my tongue ten times a day to keep from sticking it out at her like some petulant little girl still in side braids after she has pointed out yet another of my failings as queen."

Jerrik cupped Alyssa's chin and lifted her gaze to his. "I know she can be arrogant and condescending. However, she is the matriarch of this family, this city, and has been since my stepmother died five years ago."

Alyssa nodded. "I know. I do. I respect her for all her years and experience. The problem is, she does not respect me. At all."

"She will," Jerrik assured her. "In time, she will see what I and so many others see in you."

Alyssa smiled, his words soothing much of the sting. "What do you see in me, my lord and husband?"

Jerrik chucked her chin. "A feisty little lynx who will fight to the death for those she loves and has sworn to protect." Alyssa nipped at his fingers and Jerrik chuckled and pulled her up until she was straddling his lap. "No more freeing of thralls until we have established our rule as king and queen. Promise?"

"Promise."

"Good. Now give your weary husband a kiss. I have been listening to farmers speaking of crops and livestock all day while dreaming of your sweet lips."

"These lips?" Alyssa teased. She wiggled suggestively on his lap and then plied him with feather-light kisses until he pulled her hard against his chest and took her mouth with his.

A good while later, as they both lay sated and spent on the sofa, Jerrik glanced over at the box on the table. "What are you doing with Digger's old bed?"

Alyssa sat up and pushed her tangled hair behind her ears. "Hamar said there's a litter of kittens fully weaned in the thralls' longhouse. I was going to go pick one for our house tomorrow."

"Hamar said?"

"Yes, when I told him I wanted a cat for our house."

"When did you tell him this?"

"A few days ago." She sat back and eyed Jerrik, who was looking more and more displeased. "Do you not want a cat for the longhouse?"

"I hadn't thought about it one way or the other."

"A house is like a ship, Jerrik. A good mouser will keep the vermin out."

"Is Hamar going with you?"

"To pick a kitten?"

Jerrik nodded.

"He volunteered to."

"Tell him his services are not needed," Jerrik said, his voice short and clipped. "It'll be our kitten for our house. I'll go with you."

Alyssa watched the storm clouds scud across his eyes, and she reached over and laid her palm on his cheek. "You're right. It'll be our kitten for our house. I should have discussed it with you first, husband. As I should have discussed freeing Hulda with you. I'm sorry."

He took her hand in his and kissed her palm. "Thank you, wife."

"Here she is."

Alyssa handed the black and white bundle of fur over to Davin, Dagny's eight-year-old son, who had been waiting eagerly by the hearth fire for Alyssa and Jerrik to return with the new kitten.

Dagny and her oldest, Anders, were waiting as well, and they sat cross-legged on the floor as Alyssa and Jerrik, and Han and Bors did the same, forming a circle as Davin set the squirming kitten down in the center of it and tossed a ball of felt that Solveig had made for the newcomer's arrival.

"She's so cute," Davin exclaimed with a smile as the kitten chased after the ball and batted it. The first smile that Alyssa had seen on the boy's face since she'd come here.

"What shall we name her?" Alyssa asked Davin, who tossed the ball again and laughed out loud as the kitten leapt at the ball, landing on all four feet and sidling around it with stiff legs and an arched back.

"Hmm." Davin thought on it as Anders tossed the ball. The kitten ran after it, sliding face first into Alyssa's legs. Both boys and all the adults burst into laughter as the kitten sat back and flicked a white paw out and licked it with haughty unconcern. "Her paws look like she has on white boots," Davin observed.

"They do," Alyssa said. "Though she is naught but fluff and spit right now, I've noticed that the cats here grow quite large and furry."

"Everything here grows larger," Bors said, puffing out his chest as Magna and Hulda joined their little group.

"Bragging again?" Magna teased, kneeing Bors in the back.

"It's not bragging if it's true," Bors answered her with a sharp tug at his tunic's hem.

Magna chuckled and Alyssa saw her touch Hulda's hand pinkie to pinkie, long enough to be on purpose, while Bors and Han shifted to make room for the women. "Who is this little ball of fur?" Magna asked, wiggling her fingers for the kitten to pounce on.

"We were trying to decide on a name." Alyssa looked to Davin.

"Can we name her Boots?" he asked, and the kitten sat and stared up at Davin, ears erect and twitching.

Alyssa laughed lightly. "Boots it is."

"Can Boots live with me?" Davin asked, his eight-year-old eyes pleading with Alyssa, who looked from the boy to his mother. Dagny smiled and nodded her head.

Alyssa looked to Jerrik, who did the same. "Of course, she can," she said, and was immediately rewarded with her new nephew's beaming grin. "That means you will be responsible for feeding her and taking her outside to relieve herself and cleaning out her dirt box until she is old enough to go outside on her own."

"I will," Davin said solemnly. "I promise."

"Good," Alyssa said, and glanced at Jerrik, whom the boys usually gave a wide berth. "Maybe you and your brother can help your Uncle Jerrik build two dirt boxes, one for your and Boots's room, and one for down here."

"You know carpentry, Uncle Jerrik?" Anders asked, the first words the boy had spoken to Jerrik as far as Alyssa knew.

"I do," Jerrik told him. "I was a sailor, and a sailor must learn many skills."

"You were a sailor?" Anders sat up straight.

"Since I was a lad of ten and two, when I first sailed on my Uncle Knut's ship, the *Sea Eagle*. Han and Bors here were part of my crew." Anders's eyes grew big and round as he looked at the three men with awe. "How about after we finish building the dirt boxes, we go down to the harbor and I show you lads the *Sea Eagle*?"

"Can we, Mother?" Anders pleaded, and Alyssa wondered how Dagny was ever able to say no to her two sons with their big blue eyes that were so like their uncle Jerrik's, and, according to Jerrik, their dead father's.

"Of course, you can," Dagny said, her eyes glistening.

To Jerrik and Alyssa, she mouthed a silent thank-you.

"Did the boys enjoy the ship?" Alyssa asked as she stepped into the tub and lay back against Jerrik's chest.

"They did," he said, wrapping his arms around her belly and nipping the skin at the nape of her neck. "My mind is still swimming with Anders' endless questions. Reminded me of the first night I met Aaron. It wouldn't surprise me in the least if Anders decided he wanted to become a sailor when he's of age."

"Like his new favorite uncle."

Jerrik chuckled. "Davin, on the other hand, was more interested in Bones. Like his new favorite aunt." Alyssa grinned and Jerrik rested his chin on her head. "I don't understand you," he said. "I know how much you like cats, and still you let Lev keep Bones on the *Sea Eagle*, and then you let Davin claim Boots."

"What you don't understand," Alyssa told him, "is cats." She turned and straddled him, purring as he nestled his half-hard cock in her folds. "Unlike dogs, whose loyalty is given easily and wholeheartedly, cats are picky. It may not seem like it, but they choose where and who they want to live with for as long as they want, and not a moment longer. Bones chose the *Sea Eagle*, where he could rule over his own little kingdom, and Boots chose Davin, because she knows he needs her and will adore her." She wiggled her brows. "The little lynx chose you."

"Yes." Jerrik cupped her breasts and rubbed his thumbs over her peaked nipples. "She did." Alyssa mewled when he stopped his play. "Why?"

She settled back onto his lap with a smile and a shrug. "Because I fell in love with you at first sight," she told him. "Not for any one reason, but for thousands of reasons, all of which hold as true for me today as they did then." She leaned forward and kissed him, pressing her breasts against the hard breadth of his chest. "I knew you were mine as I was yours." She grinned against his lips. "I was right."

Jerrik sat back, his sky-blue eyes shining into hers. "Yes, my love, you were. You are right."

Alyssa's heart stopped, and then beat triple time. "You called me 'your love.'"

"I did." Jerrik smiled and touched his forehead to hers. "You are." He kissed her on the nose. "Aaron knew it would be so between us. I'm glad I listened to him."

"Me too," Alyssa said. Her brother's open smile came to her. His teasing voice calling her little lynx. "I miss him."

"I know," he said. "So do I. I still turn around ten times a day to tell him something."

"Only he is not there."

"No. He's not."

"Can we go visit him tomorrow?"

"You want to ride up to the ridge?"

"I do." She wiggled her hips, stirring up more than the tub's water. "We could take a basket of food and a skin of wine." She traced her fingernail down his chest to the light furring on his belly. "Have ourselves a little feast and a little fun."

He chuckled and bumped her pelvis with his. "I'll tell Hamar to have Storm and River ready for tomorrow."

"I'll tell Borgny to pack us some food."

"Good." He gave her a smacking kiss. "Now that is settled, hand me that tub of soap before this water grows cold."

Alyssa sat on her stool while Hulda combed the snarls out of her damp hair before supper. She smiled to herself, thinking of how Aaron used to pull on her braids when they were young, never too hard like the twins or Kostya, only a quick tug of the little lynx's tail, as he used to say.

"Do you have any brothers, Hulda?"

"Yes, mistress."

"Older or younger?"

"One older, two younger."

"Were you close to them?"

Hulda's hands stilled. "My mother died in childbirth with the youngest when I was ten and three. Helga was already married and my older brother apprenticed to a fisherman, so I raised my two younger brothers until they were six and four, until my father remarried and sold me to a farmer."

Alyssa whipped around on her stool. "Your father sold you?"

Hulda shrugged. "My stepmother did not like having another female in the house, and the farmer Orn and his wife were a kindly, older couple who fed me well and did not overwork me."

"How long were you with them?"

"Until I was ten and eight, when Farmer Orn died and his oldest son took over the farm." She hesitated a moment, and then continued. "The son was not so kindly without his father to keep him in line. A line his wife caught him crossing over one day when he caught me unawares in the milking barn."

Alyssa's chest seized as if the full weight of a man pressed down on her. She gagged on the smell of stale spirits and fetid breath and her skin crawled at the memory of rough, grabbing hands. "He raped you?"

Hulda's gaze dropped to her feet. "He did."

"I'm so sorry." Alyssa still had nightmares about her attacker. She could only imagine what fears and pain still plagued Hulda. "What happened, after?"

Hulda lifted her gaze, and her soft brown eyes glinted with a hard determination. "I ran away that night. It took me two nights and a day to make it here, to my sister, Helga, and her husband. I told her what happened and she told her mistress, Dagny, who told her husband, King Bard. He bought me from the farmer's son and his wife for a single copper coin." She gave a quick, feral grin. "A price the farmer dared not refuse."

"But you remained a thrall?"

Hulda shrugged. "King Bard at least was a kind master."

Alyssa didn't know what to say. She knew of slavery of course, more of the world practiced it than not. They had a longhouse full of thralls here. She knew too that slaves were treated as differently as their masters, and that most had little to no recourse if they were treated cruelly or even worked to death. Still, it was hard to fathom being that voiceless, that helpless, at the complete mercy of a person who considered you chattel.

"Your grandmother," Hulda said as she turned Alyssa's shoulder forward and started to separate sections of Alyssa's hair to plait. "It is true what Ermelinde said? She was a slave?"

"She was for about six moons before my grandfather, who became her husband, freed her."

"Like you freed me." Hulda laid a tentative hand on Alyssa's shoulder. "For which I can never thank you enough, mistress."

Alyssa laid her hand over Hulda's and gave it a gentle squeeze. "You are more than welcome." She dropped her hand and Hulda began to weave the separate plaits into one thick braid. "No one should be sold into slavery, or born into it."

"That is not what most people here think."

"Of the jarls and karls, I'm sure," Alyssa said. "What of the thralls?" She turned around so quickly that Hulda dropped the shank of her braid. "What do the thralls here think?"

She could see Hulda choosing her words before she spoke. "They think… No, they know they are treated well enough and better than most," she said. "There is a certain importance to being a thrall to the royal household, certainly more than being a field worker or a farm maid."

"But…"

"But it is hard to have no say in your own life, especially after having known the life of a freeborn. No matter how hard that life might be, it's yours. Yours to improve or to squander."

Alyssa nodded. "My grandparents and my parents thought exactly that. They didn't allow slavery in their kingdoms. Many people struggled, yet most thrived given the chance to work and provide for themselves and their families." She started to say that soon it would be the same here, but didn't. Jerrik was right. They would have to prove themselves as king and queen to the people first before implementing such changes. Changes that the slave-owning jarls would no doubt fight. Instead, she simply said, "Thank you for telling me all of this."

"Thank you for listening, mistress."

"Alyssa, please," she told Hulda. "At least here in the privacy of the royal longhouse. After all," she said with a slight laugh, "you've seen me naked. We cannot be any more informal than that."

CHAPTER 12

Poison

Jerrik kissed the back of Alyssa's hand before taking his seat beside her at the high table for supper. On the walk from their longhouse to the feasting hall, she'd told him Hulda's story of being sold by her father and raped by the farmer's son, and of her flight to Sea Ridge, her eyes and voice full of rage at the injustices suffered by women and slaves. A rage that still roiled their sea-green depths.

He'd promised her, again, that as king and queen they would end slavery in Sea Ridge, and he meant to keep his pledge. Before that though, they needed to have their wedding here, which would go a long way in getting the jarls to accept them as king and queen according to Fenrir, who knew the people of the kingdom better than he did.

Jerrik understood that the people wouldn't welcome a new king and queen without reservation. He and Alyssa would need to prove themselves as good, fair-minded rulers who could keep the peace and increase the prosperity of the kingdom, which he intended to do by building more ships and opening more trade routes between Sea Ridge and the rest of the world.

But no slave trading, which was something neither he nor his Uncle Knut had ever engaged in. Plus, he'd promised Alyssa.

His belly rumbled as the servers brought out trenchers of pickled herring, rye breads, and soft cheeses, along with roasted mutton and bowls of crisp autumn greens. He took a deep draught of his beer and eyed the last of the season's greens, which would soon be replaced by roots and tubers.

He'd forgotten how limited fruits and greens were here in the winter after years of sailing in southern climes and feasting on sweet, juicy, exotic fruits and bitter greens cooked with pungent herbs all year long.

He glanced at Alyssa and gave her a wicked grin that brought a pretty flush to her cheeks. He would simply have to feast on her sweet body all winter instead.

"We should meet with the jarls in the western valley tomorrow," Fenrir told him.

"Not tomorrow." Jerrik pulled his hungry gaze from Alyssa's tantalizing mouth to his uncle's thinned lips. "Alyssa and I will be riding up to the ridge to pay our respects to Aaron tomorrow."

"Cannot that wait?" Fenrir said impatiently. "We met with the eastern jarls today, we don't want to insult the western jarls by waiting too long after to meet with them."

Alyssa touched Jerrik's hand under the table. "I can wait."

"No." He shook his head. "You asked, others are presuming." He met Fenrir's narrowed gaze. "The western jarls can wait one day without being inconvenienced. If they feel slighted, they can take it up with me."

"I for one would like to ride up to the ridge with you tomorrow," Sven said, his deep voice booming out in the tense, silent hall, "to pay my respects to Aaron."

Jerrik looked to Alyssa. It was her day, her brother, her decision. She smiled softly and nodded her head.

"Your company would be welcome," Jerrik told Sven. He looked to Bors and Han. "Yours also."

They both nodded. "We'll come."

"Anyone else?" Jerrik asked.

Magna stood. "I go where my queen goes."

Jerrik bit down on a grin. Alyssa had done well choosing Magna to be her personal guard, an honor that Magna took seriously. "Meet here tomorrow morn at dawn to break our fasts," he said. "Bors, ride down to the docks tonight and ask Lev and Zoltan to join us if they want, then let Hamar know how many mounts we'll need for the morrow." He caught Pavel's eye, and though Pavel had never met Aaron, he had been part of the *Sea Eagle*'s crew. "Do you want to come with us, Pavel?"

"No, skeppare. I would only intrude." He looked to Alyssa, his big brown eyes wide and eager. "I could watch Digger for you?"

The late morning sun finally broke through the clouds as the riders made their way up the winding mountainside covered with towering, green spruce and pine trees, interspersed with brilliant patches of yellow gold larch. Riding Storm alongside Alyssa on River, Jerrik lifted his chin into a brisk autumn breeze that blew stray strands of hair around Alyssa's face.

She let her breath out in a long, happy sigh. "It feels good to be astride River again," she said. "To be out here riding with friends, breathing in the crisp, autumn air. Away from the politics of the palace."

"That it does," Jerrik agreed. He was learning to be king, to navigate the politics of ruling a kingdom rather than a ship, but it felt good to be Jerrik for a day.

"I hope Pavel feels better," Alyssa said, frowning. "He looked drawn and out of sorts this morning when we left Digger with him."

"The lad said he was fine, my little mother hen," he teased. "He and Digger will likely sneak a nap in the hay loft later."

"I suppose you're right," she said. "If he's ill, Hamar will take care of him."

"Hamar?"

She nodded. "Hamar's apparently quite knowledgeable in the healing arts. His father taught him."

"You are curiously knowledgeable about Hamar."

Alyssa tilted her head and studied Jerrik's stiff neck and clamped jaw. "We talk when I'm in the stables with the horses," she said. "That's all."

"I told you, you have nothing to worry about, lad," Sven, who rode ahead of them, said over his shoulder. "Your woman's Path Finder points true north and you are her Pole Star."

Alyssa smiled her thanks to Sven, while Jerrik bored holes into his back with his glare.

"How much longer until we get there?" Zoltan called out from behind them. "My ass is numb, and I'm not talking of the dumb beast I am bobbing around on like an unmoored ship."

"Quit your caterwauling," Bors chided. "It's only around the bend and up the rise."

"Easy for you to say," Zoltan grumbled back. "You've traded yer sea legs for a rider's ass. Me an' Lev here's still sailors though an' through."

"A fortnight on land don't make me less of a sailor, you curly-haired—"

"Cease your prattling," Jerrik commanded. He pulled Storm to a halt and nodded at the rubble of rocks still lining the edge of the narrowing path. "This is where the rock slide happened," he told Alyssa.

He dismounted and offered her his arm as she dismounted, and then he led her to the large rock lying in the middle of the path, the rock that had killed Aaron. He knelt down and laid his open palm reverently on the rock. "This is where Aaron died."

Tears welled instantly in Alyssa's eyes as she laid her palm over Jerrik's. "He died a hero's death," she whispered, her voice as ragged as her expression. "He died saving you, his friend and brother."

Jerrik turned his hand in Alyssa's and raised it to his lips, his gaze holding hers, absolutely serious. "He died telling me I could trust you."

"He was right, my love," she said through her tears. "You can. Always."

Jerrik stood at the rim of the ridge and looked down at the woods and the wild lands and the fields left fallow for the coming winter. He took in the farmsteads dotting the countryside, the longhouses of the royal compound, the ale houses, inns and warehouses, piers and docks that lined the bay's shore, the ships moored in the bay. He shaded his eyes and gazed out over the inlet that led to the wide-open sea and felt the wind stir, smelled the tang of salt air, heard the siren's song. *Sail away. Sail away.* A song that was losing its pull.

"Jerrik?"

He turned to the sound of Alyssa's voice and was anchored by the touch of her hand on his. She led him back from the brink to stand beside her and Magna and the crew of the *Sea Eagle* by the stone berm that was Aaron's final resting place beneath the gnarled, ancient pine that had stood sentry over Sea Ridge for a hundred years.

He took the wineskin Sven handed him and filled the horned cups held out for him. "To Aaron," he said. "The best friend and brother a man, or woman, could ever have. A man I was blessed to sail the world with and share many an adventure. A man of rare courage and honor who gave his life to save mine, and set me on the path to my wife and queen." He met and held Alyssa's sad, bittersweet smile for a moment, and then raised his cup high. "May the gods guide your steps to their gates, and may they always look upon you with good grace."

"To Aaron." Cups were raised and long, deep draughts of drink were taken.

"We shall not mourn our dear friend and comrade," Sven toasted, raising his cup again. "But rejoice for he who died the glorious death."

"For our brave, fallen friend," Bors added. "We will meet again where the drink never ends."

"To Aaron," Lev said. "Our comrade."

"To Aaron," they all rejoined and drained their cups.

"To Aaron, my adored and adoring brother," Alyssa said softly. "Thank you for saving my love." She swiped the wetness from her cheeks and sniffed and smiled up at Jerrik. "Thank you for sending him to me."

One by one they folded their legs and sat on the ground circling Aaron's grave, falling into their own thoughts as Magna refilled their cups, sipping their wine and picking at the cheese and flatbreads Borgny had packed for them.

"I told Aaron I'd dreamed of you as we were riding up that day," Jerrik told Alyssa. "Of the first night you and I met. Winter's Eve almost ten and three years ago now. He asked me why I thought I'd dreamt of you that night…reminded me of how you'd stowed away on the *Sea Eagle*, of how your father was so angry he made you jump ship and swim in the frigid water to his boat." He shook his head and chuckled at the memory. "Why did you do that?"

"Stow away on your ship?" Alyssa shrugged her shoulders and glanced around at the others, who were all listening intently. "I was eight years old," she said. "All my life my family had been telling me how akin I was to my Great-Aunt Lyrra in looks and temperament, and I knew from the stories my mother told me about her that Lyrra had sailed across the Mid Earth Sea to find her one true love, Nasim, the Cheetah, who became her husband. I thought I could sail away with mine, with you and my brother. And eventually," she said, smiling at Jerrik as she had that Winter's Eve, as if he were the gods of sky and sea combined, "I did."

The first thing Alyssa noticed as they rode back into the palace yard in the late afternoon was the group of six yellow beards congregated outside of Fenrir's longhouse watching them ride in, their faces cold and impassive except for the smirk on Rigil's face. The second thing she noticed was the lack of Hamar or Pavel coming out of the stables to meet them. She urged River to a trot and jumped off the mare's back as soon as they were inside the stable's door.

"Pavel?" she called out as Jerrik and the others filed in. "Hamar?"

"My queen?" Hamar poked his head up and over the wall of a stall at the far end of the stables. "We're in here."

He glanced down as Alyssa approached with Jerrik right behind her, both of them stopping at the sight of Pavel sitting cross-legged in the straw with Digger wrapped up in a blanket on his lap. Pavel was dipping a wet rag into a bowl of water and dripping the water into the moaning, glassy-eyed pup's spittle-crusted mouth. Alyssa covered her nose and mouth with her hands as the putrid smell of shit and vomit assailed her nostrils from a soiled pile of straw pushed to the corner of the stall.

She dropped down to her knees and tried to meet Pavel's gaze. The lad wouldn't lift his eyes from the pup in his lap. "What happened?" she asked.

"I… I don't know, mistress," he said, his voice as shaky as his hands as he dropped the dipping rag back into the bowl and tucked the saddle blanket tighter around Digger's prone body. He glanced up at Alyssa for the briefest of moments before lowering his gaze again. "I… I fell asleep around noon, and when I woke up, Digger was gone. I found him behind the kitchens, throwing up what looked to be a piece of bad meat. I carried him here, to Hamar, and we been seeing to him since." He looked up and met Alyssa's gaze with big, hangdog eyes. "I be so sorry, mistress. I shouldn't-a fell asleep."

Alyssa laid her hand on Pavel's slumped shoulder. "It's not your fault, Pavel," she tried to reassure him. "Puppies will eat any manner of things. At least you found him before he was too far gone." She moved her hand from Pavel's shoulder to Digger's head. The pup wagged his tail and lifted his head and then dropped it back down onto Pavel's lap with a whimper. Alyssa looked up at Hamar. "He's not, is he?" she pleaded. "Too far gone?"

"I cannot say for certain, mistress. I hope not."

Alyssa swallowed past the lump in her throat. "What can I do?"

"Keep him comfortable," Hamar said. He nodded toward a bowl of black, tarry-looking mush. "I was preparing a paste of coal and water to give the pup. It helps bind any poisons—"

"Poisons?" Jerrik exclaimed. "You think Digger was poisoned?"

"Not on purpose," Hamar explained. "I think whatever tainted the meat is acting like a poison in his little body. The coal paste should bind it and help it pass."

Alyssa sat cross-legged in the straw beside Pavel and scooped up Digger in his blanket and settled the pup in her lap. "I'll hold him for a while, Pavel. You look worn out."

"Thank you, mistress."

He looked like he was about to burst into tears. If Alyssa knew anything about boys his age, it was that they hated to be seen crying by anyone. "Perhaps you could go to the kitchens and get yourself something to eat."

Pavel glanced around the stables at Jerrik and the others with their still-saddled horses. "But—"

"Don't worry about the horses," Jerrik told him. "We'll take care of them. Go. The fresh air and some food will do you good."

"Bring back some clear meat broth for Digger," Hamar told him. "If…" he met Alyssa's worried gaze for a brief moment, "when he gets through the worst of this, he'll be needing some nourishment."

Alyssa held Digger and crooned wordless tunes to him while Jerrik and the others unsaddled their horses and Hamar finished making the coal paste. They all gathered round and watched Hamar and Alyssa try to dose Digger with the paste. The pup thrashed his head whenever Hamar started to pour the black concoction into his mouth and let at least as much if not more dribble out of his mouth than he swallowed.

"Is he getting enough of the paste in him?" Alyssa asked as she folded the blanket edge over the pool of paste and drool beneath Digger's head.

"He is," Hamar assured her. "I counted on him not swallowing a goodly amount of it."

Jerrik reached down and squeezed Alyssa's shoulder. "It's good Digger still has some fight in him, Lyssa." She nodded and sniffed. A tear dropped from her cheek to Digger's ear. Jerrik crouched down beside her and leaned his forehead against hers. "Don't despair, my little mother hen. If anyone can pull him through with pure love and determination, it's you."

"And Hamar," she whispered. "Digger will need all of Hamar's healing arts."

"And Hamar," Jerrik ground out. He dropped his hand from Alyssa's shoulder and she tilted her head and met his brooding gaze, wanting, needing him to tell her that Digger would be all right. "Do you want me to stay?" he asked.

"No." She shook her head. "You should go to supper." She glanced at Magna and the others who had gathered round. "All of you, go and eat. There's no reason for you to stay. Hamar and I can take care of Digger."

"I'll bring you both back some supper," Magna offered as she took hold of Jerrik's arm and hauled him to his feet. "Come, brother," Alyssa heard her say as they headed for the stable door.

"The sooner we eat, the sooner we can return with their food, and the sooner you can stop glaring daggers at Hamar."

Alyssa glanced up at Hamar, who dropped his gaze and mumbled something unintelligible as he suddenly found something in another stall that needed immediate tending to. She shook her head and repositioned Digger in her lap.

It all made sense now: Jerrik's sudden changes in mood whenever she mentioned Hamar. His cryptic remarks about Aaron telling him that he could trust Alyssa. His questioning that trust. Jerrik was jealous. Of Hamar. Apparently, Hamar was aware of it.

She'd seen it often enough with her father and brothers to recognize it, even though like her, neither her mother nor her sisters-in-law had ever done anything to encourage it.

She held Digger closer and swore softly. "Fucking men."

Alyssa wept and prayed and held vigil through the night, pacing back and forth with Digger bundled in her arms, sitting and dribbling water and broth into the pup's slack mouth, calling for Pavel or Hamar where they slept in their antechamber to change the pup's bedding when he soiled it, and only handing the pup over to one of them when she needed to relieve herself, despite their many offers to spell her for a bit. It wasn't for lack of trust in their care, but for fear that the pup would die without her, that he would take his last breath without her there to hold him and comfort him. That she could not bear.

"Lyssa."

She jerked up her head. "Jerrik?" It was sometime between midnight and the still, empty dark before dawn. "What are you doing here?"

"I find I can no longer sleep without you in my bed." He sat down beside her and laid his hand over hers. "Your hand is freezing." He touched the backs of his fingers to her cheek. "So is the rest of you." He took both his hands and rubbed them briskly up and down her arms, and then he pulled up the two blankets he had sent Hulda with earlier that night around Alyssa's shoulders and tucked them under her chin. "You'll do Digger no good if you become sick too."

"Or the—" she almost said baby, but stopped herself. She wasn't certain, not yet. Her moon flow was only a fortnight late and she hadn't noticed any other changes in her body. Plus, she'd decided if she were pregnant, she would tell Jerrik on their wedding day as a gift. "Or anybody else."

"Everybody else," he told her, tucking the blankets tighter around her and Digger, "myself included, can take care of ourselves, my little mother hen. You only worry about yourself and Digger."

Alyssa nodded and sniffed and burst into tears. She could keep from crying in front of Pavel and Hamar, but not Jerrik. He was her safe place. The one person in all the world besides her parents who she could be completely herself around. "What if Digger dies?" she mewled.

Still crouched before her, Jerrik met her gaze and held it. "I don't know for what purpose the fates brought you and Digger together," he said, his voice low and steady. "But I do know that even if the worst happens and he passes from this world to the next, you have given him two moons with a full belly, a soft, warm bed, and the love of a mistress he adores."

Alyssa sniffed, smiled, nodded, and hiccupped, and then hugged Digger close. Jerrik wrapped his arms around them and hugged them to him. He kissed Alyssa on the forehead and then Digger, and then he sat back on his heels and picked up the bowl of cold broth.

"I'll take this to the kitchens and warm it up," he said, standing.

"It's the middle of the night."

Jerrik slanted his eyes down at her and grinned. "Being king has its privileges."

"King Jerrik?" Borgny pulled the drapes to her bedchamber open and peered through the dim candlelight at Jerrik, who was feeding tinder to the glowing embers of coal in the kitchen hearth. "What are you doing?"

He indicated the pot of broth on the iron grate over the fire. "Warming up some broth."

"You should've woken me to do it," she said. "You're king."

"I was a sailor for much longer than I've been king," he said, though he gave way to the cook who had known him since he was a boy. "I'm used to doing for myself, and didn't want to wake anybody, although I seem to have woken you anyway."

"I was already awake," she said, though they both knew she'd been asleep. "Is the broth for the pup?"

"It is." He sat down on a stool by the worktable.

She let out a heavy sigh of relief. "He still lives then."

"For now."

The cook pressed her lips together, nodded, and stirred the broth. Then she looked over at Jerrik. "I'm so sorry, King Jerrik. I know Pavel says he found the pup eating tainted meat behind the kitchens here, and I don't doubt the lad, yet I can assure you, sire, that we keep a clean kitchen and meat house. I have no explanation for how the pup came across it here."

"Don't worry yourself, Borgny," he said, and then repeated Alyssa's reassurance to Pavel in the stables. "He's a puppy. Puppies will eat any manner of things. No one is blaming you or anyone else."

"That is not what your uncle said."

"What?"

"Fenrir told me and the kitchen maids and the butcher and the stable boy that if the pup dies, the queen will relieve us of our positions, if not our heads."

Jerrik sat back on the stool. "I can assure you, that did not come from me or the queen." Neither of whom had spoken a word to Fenrir about any of this yet, though Jerrik would definitely be speaking to Fenrir about it on the morrow. "Nor will anyone be punished if the pup dies. You have my word."

Borgny nodded. "Thank you, my king. The others will be relieved to hear it."

"Did they truly believe Queen Alyssa would react so harshly?" These people had known Alyssa for over a fortnight, and as far as Jerrik knew, she had never been anything except her usual kind self around them.

Borgny gave a sheepish shrug of her shoulders. "They didn't know what to believe, especially as Pavel, who's known her the best and longest of us all, looked the most frightened." She stirred the broth, and added, "What we did all know was how the queen dotes on the pup."

"She hasn't left him for a moment since we returned and found him ailing."

Borgny covered the bowl of warmed broth and set it on the table in front of Jerrik. "What that tells me, my king, is that your queen is a good and caring woman. If this is how she treats a sick pup, think of how good and loving a mother she will be."

Jerrik stood and picked up the bowl. "Thank you, Borgny, for this," he lifted the bowl, "and for speaking so honestly with me. I hope you always feel free to do so."

"I will, King Jerrik," she said with a dip of head and her knee. "You have my word."

The black night was giving way to the gray dawn when Jerrik stepped out of the kitchens and made his way back to the stables, the cook's words flying round and round his head.

He knew she'd inform the others of his assurances that none of them would be blamed or punished; what he didn't know, and was determined to find out, was why Fenrir had told them that in the first place, and why he had insinuated that the threat had come from Alyssa. Sweet, kind, caring Alyssa, who would sit up all night with a sick puppy and give away kittens to men and boys whom she thought needed them more.

Alyssa, whose smile warmed him like sunlight on water, and whose touch inflamed his passions.

Alyssa, who was standing in Hamar's embrace when Jerrik entered the stables.

"What do you think you're doing?" Alyssa startled at Jerrik's angry shout, and Hamar dropped his arms from around her as Jerrik strode toward them, the covered bowl of broth in one hand, his other clenched in a fist.

"Jerrik." Alyssa stepped forward and he thrust the bowl into her hands, barely slowing his stride as he raised his fist and slammed it into Hamar's face with a satisfying smack that sent Hamar falling back and left him sprawled out on the floor.

"Keep your hands off my wife," Jerrik growled as Hamar slowly sat up and swiped at the blood dripping from his nose.

"Jerrik," Alyssa said sharply, setting the bowl of broth on a stool. "Hamar did nothing inappropriate. It was I who hugged him."

The storm that had been brewing inside him since Kostya had accosted him in the stables broke. "You what?" he thundered.

"I was happy because Digger finally drank on his own, so I gave Hamar a quick, friendly, celebratory hug," she said. "Nothing more."

"There was nothing friendly about the way he was hugging you back," he said. He glared down at Hamar. "Was there?"

Hamar said nothing, but he stayed sitting and would not meet Jerrik's eyes.

"I swear to you, husband," Alyssa said. "It was nothing more than a quick hug or sisterly peck on the cheek that I would give to any one of my brothers."

"You kissed him?" he roared. The storm was now a gale-force tempest.

"No," she said with an exasperated huff. "I didn't kiss Hamar. I was speaking of the kiss on the cheek I gave Sven when we were camped by the river, and how you reacted to that, you jealous fool." She clapped a hand over her mouth, as surprised as he was by her outburst.

Alyssa looked at Hamar and pointed to the stable's door. "Leave us," she said. Hamar beat a hasty retreat. She stepped up to Jerrik and met and held his heated gaze. "I love you," she said. "I have given you my wedded oath and sworn my faithfulness—"

"Wives break their oaths all the time," he growled.

"Not me," Alyssa swore anew. "Why won't you trust me?"

"Why do you keep hugging and kissing men who aren't your husband?" he threw back at her. "If I act like a jealous fool, it is because you insist on acting like an innocent temptress instead of the wife and queen you are."

Alyssa sucked her breath in and narrowed her ice-green eyes on his.

"Fenrir warned me about this," he continued, heedless. "He told me not to let myself be led by my passion for you."

"Did he?" Alyssa's tone was as cold and angry as her gaze. "How temperate of him." She bared her teeth in a feral smile. "What else did Fenrir say about me? Please, tell me, dear husband, so I may strive to be more like his cold-hearted, stiff-backed bitch of a wife. Is that what you want?"

"You know it's not."

"No, I don't know," she cried. "One moment you praise my sweet nature and open heart, and the next you grow silent and moody or accuse me of...of—"

"Being a charming little flirt used to getting her way with men?"

Thwack.

He stood staring gape-jawed at the broth dripping down his chest to the empty bowl at his feet.

"Go ask your uncle's advice on how to deal with that," Alyssa hissed as she walked over to Digger and scooped him up in his blanket. Turning on her heels, she gave him her back and stalked out of the stables, and the gods help him, he grinned at the twitch of her skirts.

"Skeppare?"

Still dripping, he turned to find Pavel peering around the door of his and Hamar's room.

"Saddle Storm for me, Pavel," he told the lad, who must have heard the words hurled between him and Alyssa along with the bowl of broth.

"Aye, skeppare. I mean, my king."

"Skeppare's fine," he assured Pavel. In truth, at the moment, all Jerrik wanted to be was skeppare again, free to sail the world without any ties to anchor him down, his only cares and responsibilities to the ship and crew. Unbound from the duties of king, or husband to a twitching she-cat disguised as a sweet little puss, all the things he had become a sailor to avoid.

Pavel brought Storm around and Jerrik swung up into the stallion's saddle. "I'll be down at the *Sea Eagle* if anyone needs me," he said. "It damn well better be for something important if they come looking for me."

Jealous fool. Led by your passions. Jealous fool. Led by your passions. Jealous fool. Led by your passions.

Storm's hoofbeats pounded the words into Jerrik's head as they galloped down the road to the bay. *Just like your father.*

Was he? Was he fated to repeat his father's mistakes? To love a woman and put his trust in her, only to have her break that trust? Was Alyssa truly like his mother? Swearing her love and faithfulness to her husband, only to break that trust with another man, if Hamar's hug was exactly what it looked like to Jerrik? Or men, if Kostya had spoken the truth?

Jerrik pulled Storm up at the dock closest to where the *Sea Eagle* was anchored and paid a lad a copper to watch over the stallion, and then paid a fisherman another copper to use his rowboat. He braced his feet and rowed the oars through the water, his muscles relishing the familiar pull, his skin the feel of a brisk sea breeze, his mind churning along with the water beneath the oars.

When he made the *Sea Eagle*'s side, the only thing he was sure of was that he was going to have a long, private talk with Hamar when he returned to the palace. What to say or do with Alyssa, he still had no idea.

"Skeppare's aboard," Lev called out as Jerrik climbed up the ladder and stood on the deck of the *Sea Eagle*, even though Lev was skeppare now.

Jerrik took a deep breath of salt air in and blew it out. He looked around, taking in the clean deck, Zoltan stirring a pot of what smelled like porridge, one of the new men, whose name Jerrik couldn't recall, mending a sail, and another braiding rope. He eyed the mast, newly oiled and gleaming, and the lines of rigging swaying in the wind. "She's looking good," he told Lev.

Lev beamed. "Aye, she'll be ready to sail after your wedding in a fortnight's time, skeppare, er, King Jerrik."

Jerrik waved the title off. "Skeppare's fine, Lev. Do I still have any clothes stowed away on her?"

Lev eyed Jerrik's stained tunic and trousers. "Aye, skep. Your chest is still below deck."

"Good. I'll need to change before I return to the palace." He stripped off his tunic, relishing the bracing feel of the autumn breeze on his skin as Zoltan and the other new crew members gathered round, curious. "Right now, I feel the urge to do something physical. What does our girl need today?"

"Uh, well, her rigging could use a going-over."

By noon, Jerrik felt like himself again, which meant he knew he'd been an ass. He needed to tell Alyssa the truth about his mother. If he didn't, he'd lose the woman he'd adored since they were young.

After he cleaned up and was making ready to leave the ship, Sven came aboard and accosted him. "What the fuck is wrong with you?" Sven puffed out his barrel chest to twice its usual size, and he wore an expression full of thunder. "I gave you time to settle into being king. I gave you time to wrap yer head around being married. I gave you time to realize yer blind in love with Alyssa, who, in case you didn't get it into yer thick head, thinks you hung the moon, and I've warned you time and again about acting the jealous fool."

As Sven drew in breath to have another go, Jerrik held up his hand. "I know. I'm going to make it right."

"With yer wife and queen?"

Jerrik sighed. "Of course."

Sven grunted. When Jerrik didn't move, Sven growled, "Then what are you waiting for, lad?"

CHAPTER 13

Secrets

"Are you sure you won't come to supper at the hall?" Dagny asked Alyssa.

"No, I think not, Dagny. I'll stay here with Digger." Alyssa hugged the pup close and kissed his nose, smiling as he thumped his tail in response.

He'd been drinking water and broth since this morning, when the whole, horrible fight with Jerrik had happened, and she'd decamped from the stables with the pup to take up residence by the hearth fire in the royal longhouse, close to warmth and food and water for both her and Digger, and to the outdoors for when the puppy needed to relieve himself. Thankfully, the coal paste seemed to have worked: Digger had passed one small, tarry black stool around noon, and hadn't thrown up even once all day. "I want to try him on solids with a bit of bread soaked in broth in a little while."

Dagny squatted down and scratched Digger under the chin. "May I offer you some advice, my queen?"

Alyssa tilted her head at Dagny's use of her formal title. Dagny usually called her Alyssa when it was only the two of them or close family around. "Of course."

"Don't let them see you like this. Don't let them win." She gave Alyssa a quick, reassuring grin and then stood as her sons came running down the stairs, ready to join the rest of the household for the evening meal.

Alyssa nodded her understanding. If she continued to sit here and hide and sulk, she would only be proving certain people right that she didn't have what it took to be a wife and a queen. She was not about to give anybody that. "I'll leave Digger with Ranveig and join you in the hall shortly."

When Alyssa walked into the feasting hall, clean and coifed and changed into a long-sleeved undergown of dusky blue linen with an overtunic of midnight blue, all conversation stopped until she took her seat beside Jerrik, who was wearing a clean work tunic and trousers he'd often worn on the *Sea Eagle*.

"Husband," she said stiffly, though her smile could have dripped honey.

"Wife." He watched her warily as she picked up her horned cup and took a sip of honey mead but said nothing more.

"How is the pup?" Tryggr asked, leaning forward from his seat to the right of Ermelinde so that he could see Alyssa. "Better, I hope."

Alyssa looked from Tryggr to Jerrik. "May I answer your brother, my king?" she asked sweetly.

"You know you need not ask my permission," he answered.

"May I smile when I answer him, my husband?" she continued in the same vein.

"Alyssa," he growled low.

She blinked wide-eyed at him. "My lord?"

"What game are you playing at?"

"Game?" she said, batting her lashes. "I'm only making certain I behave according to yours and other's wishes. I wouldn't want to shame or embarrass you or your family by flirting with another man." She was aware, as was he, that everyone at the high table was listening to them, as well as more than a few straining ears at the lower tables. At the moment, she truly didn't care. "May I answer your brother?"

He inclined his head politely, though the muscle in the side of his jaw twitched. "You may."

Alyssa leaned forward and looked past him, Fenrir, and Ermelinde without giving them so much as a glance. "Digger is doing much better today, Tryggr. Thank you for asking."

She sat back and folded her hands primly in her lap, plastering a vacant half-smile on her face as she stared at the empty space over the heads of those seated at the lower tables until the food was brought out.

She served herself a spoonful of greens and roots, as well as meat, and cut the food into tiny little pieces and ate them one by one without tasting a single bite or speaking a single word. When she was done eating, she silently sipped her mead until her cup was empty, and then she sat back and folded her hands in her lap once again to stare out into the hall of buzzing bees without meeting a single curious gaze or being asked another question.

When he was finished eating, Jerrik stood and held his arm out for her, and she laid her hand on the sleeve of his forearm, her fingers stiff and her posture stilted as he led her from the table and out of the hall.

As soon as they walked out of the hall, Alyssa half expected him to brush her hand from his arm, instead he laid his hand over hers and led her to a bench by the gardens. "I need to tell you something," he said as they sat. "Something I should have told you before."

Alyssa was still angry at him, more than angry. She was hurt. Deeply hurt by what he had called her, of what he had accused her of being. Yet something about the tone of his voice and his expression, and that he was holding on to her hand so tightly, told her she needed to hear what he had to say. "I'm listening."

"You know my mother died when I was six years old," he said. "That she killed herself."

She nodded. "I know."

He took in a deep breath and blew it out. "What you don't know is why," he said, and she turned her gaze to him, though he stared straight ahead and wouldn't look at her. "I was the one who found her."

Alyssa didn't know what to say, so she simply laid her hand on Jerrik's.

"She ah…my ah…my father discovered she had been unfaithful to him," he told her. "That she had been having an affair with another man." Alyssa sucked a quick breath in and held it. "She denied it, of course," he said, still staring into the night. "But he wouldn't be swayed by her tearful pleas and protests."

Alyssa let her breath out in a whoosh. "He didn't believe her?"

He shook his head. "He had proof of her infidelity."

"What did he do?"

"By rights, he could have killed her, and swore he should have for what she'd done to him and our family. Instead, he denied her and claimed he would divorce her and banish her from her home, her family, and him." He looked out over the palace grounds and settled his gaze on what Alyssa knew had been his family's royal longhouse. "I found her later that afternoon, her wrists slit, lying in a pool of her own blood."

"Oh, Jerrik." Alyssa turned her hand and twined her fingers through his. "I'm so sorry. I had no idea."

He finally turned his head to look at her, and though it was dark, the pain on his face was starkly visible. "I know. I needed you to know, so that you'd understand..."

"Why you act like a jealous fool when I act like a charming little flirt?"

Alyssa woke stretching and purring, her body sated, her heart content. She reached a hand over to Jerrik's side of the bed, disappointed at first not to feel the warm, solid mass of him, then she remembered his tender kiss on her forehead after their morning romp and his whispering to her that she should stay abed as late as she wished. His grin was positively wicked as he encouraged her to rest up after their long and vigorous night of lovemaking. She smiled. Her brother's wives had been right: make-up sex was worth the fight.

Of course, you had to make up after the fight first, and she and Jerrik had. Sitting on the bench last night, listening to his story, her heart had broken for the boy who'd adored his mother and idolized his father, only to witness the jealous rage of his father and the shame of his mother, all of which had led to not only her death, but his family's in a way.

Knowing this helped Alyssa understand so many things, and understanding helped her to forgive him. Forgetting would take a bit longer.

Her breasts still sensitive and her body thrumming with the pleasurable memories of last night and this morning, she rolled over with a soft moan and burrowed her nose into Jerrik's pillow, breathing in the scent of soap, sweat, and sex.

She glanced at the sun's light peeking in through the edges of the oil skin stretched over the unshuttered window, tossed the bedding back, swung her legs over the side of the bed, and braced herself with her hands as the room swam.

She sat there until the walls stopped spinning and then she pushed herself up onto shaky legs and stumbled for the wash basin, where she threw up what little supper was still in her belly. Dipping the washing cloth into the water pitcher, she wiped her clammy face and mouth and plopped back down on the edge of the bed.

"Mistress?" A knock on the door heralded Hulda's entrance to the sitting room. "King Jerrik told me to let you sleep in," she said, her voice nearing the bedchamber. "I heard you moving around so, oh—" She stopped at the sight of Alyssa sitting and swaying on the bed, and quickly glanced over at the water basin full of vomit. "Are you ill?"

"No." Alyssa gave a slight shake of her head and smiled weakly when the room didn't spin in response. "I don't think so."

Hulda placed her palm on Alyssa's forehead. "You don't feel feverish," she said, standing back and eyeing Alyssa closely.

Alyssa took a deep breath in and blew it out and then another. She was no longer dizzy, and her belly, though no longer nauseous, was still queasy. She stood and her legs held, and her head cleared with several more slow, deep breaths.

"What can I get you, mistress?" Hulda asked, her expression a little less worried now that Alyssa was standing.

Alyssa placed both hands over her breasts, which had grown tender and heavier over the past several days. "A cup of water, a piece of plain bread, and Dagny," she said. "And Hulda, don't tell anyone else about this. Not yet."

"How long since your last moon flow?" Dagny asked.

Alyssa tore off a piece of warm rye from the platter laden with bread and fruit and cheese that Dagny had brought with her to Alyssa's chambers, and chewed as she counted backward in her mind. "It's been a moon and a fortnight since I bled," she said.

Dagny, who knew of the bleeding on the ship, nodded. "Your breasts?"

"Are heavy and tender to the touch."

Dagny took this in. "When you woke this morning, what happened?"

"I became dizzy when I sat up and then threw up what little there was in my belly."

"Now that you have some good, plain food in your belly?"

Alyssa tore another chunk of bread off with her teeth and broke off a piece for Digger, whose appetite had grown apace with hers this morning. "I'm ravenous."

"Good," Dagny said with a smile. "Have you noticed any change in the way things smell to you?"

Alyssa tilted her head. "Now that you ask, yes. Many things smell sharper, stronger. I'd thought it was the stench of Digger's sickness affecting me. Now that I think on it, I have noticed myself gagging at odors that never bothered me before."

"Such as?"

"The smell of brined fish, soured milk, and cooked eggs," Alyssa said with a shudder. "All of which I've eaten my entire life, and which even thinking about now makes me want to retch again."

Dagny laughed, not unkindly. "That's nature's way of telling you not to eat those things this early in your pregnancy, when they can harm your babe. Listen to your body, Alyssa, it knows what it does and does not need."

Alyssa speared a slice of pear on her knife. "I will," she said, popping the sweet, juicy fruit into her mouth.

There was a knock at the door, and Alyssa speared another slice of pear as Dagny went to answer it.

She cracked the door open and peeked out. "It's Hulda and Magna," she said.

"Let them in."

"Don't be angry with Hulda," Magna said as soon as she entered. "I badgered her into bringing me here to your secret meeting."

"It's fine," Alyssa assured them both, and then narrowed her eyes. "However, what happens here this morning stays between the four of us for now. I want it to be a wedding present for Jerrik."

"You're pregnant?" Magna shouted and then clapped her hand over her mouth. "Hulda was right, you're pregnant. I'm going to be an auntie." She danced a little jig, grinning from ear to ear as Alyssa eyed a blushing Hulda.

"I am sorry, mistress," Hulda said. "I..." She looked to Magna, who, grinning even wider if that was possible, took her by the hand and faced Alyssa and Dagny.

Alyssa glanced at Dagny, who seemed neither surprised or upset, and then she wagged a finger at Magna and Hulda, laughing. "I knew it," she said.

"You don't mind?" Magna asked, her grin gone, her expression serious.

"Not at all." Alyssa smiled with genuine happiness. "Love is love. I'm happy for the both of you."

"What about Jerrik?" Magna asked. "Do you think he'll mind?"

"Your brother has seen more of this world than most," she told Magna. "I think you'll find that he's open-minded about such things. Bors, on the other hand," she teased, "will be sorely disappointed. He's had his eye on you since the day we got here."

Magna shrugged. "He'll get over it soon enough. All I need do is point out the gaggle of maidservants ogling him whenever he so much as twitches one of his big, manly muscles."

They all laughed, because it was true. The maidservants had all been sizing up and ogling Sven, Han, and Bors from the day they had landed, including more than a few whom Alyssa had caught eyeing Jerrik. Not that she blamed the women, the men from the *Sea Eagle* were a virile, handsome lot, and none more so than her husband.

"Well, this has been quite the morning," Alyssa said. "Me pregnant. Magna and Hulda in love." She glanced at Dagny, whose soft gray eyes welled with tears of deep and abiding sorrow. "I'm so sorry, Dagny," she said, suddenly close to tears herself.

Dagny nodded, sniffed and smiled, sad and bittersweet. "Life goes on," she said. She blew a breath out and tucked both hands in her lap as she sat straight and erect. "I may have lost my husband, but at least I knew his love, and he mine." She met Alyssa's sympathetic gaze and gave a rueful laugh. "Resulting in my two rascal sons who are the spitting image of their father."

Alyssa laid a hand over her womb. "I only pray the gods see fit to bless me and Jerrik with sons as fine and strong as yours and Bard's."

"And a daughter or three to drive Jerrik stark raving mad," Magna added gleefully.

Jerrik sat with Fenrir, Tryggr, and Sven at the table in the council chambers, a room that his father's father had built in what used to be the king's longhouse and was now where Fenrir and his family lived. This was the room where Jerrik's parents had argued the day his mother had killed herself.

"How is the queen?" Fenrir asked.

"She's well," Jerrik answered. "Why do you ask?"

"She seemed to be feeling out of sorts at supper last night and didn't break her fast in the hall this morning," Fenrir said. "Though I suppose spending a night in the stables would do that to a person."

Jerrik glanced over at the closed door, where Bors and Han sat, erect and instantly on guard. "She was tired and worn out from tending to Digger so assiduously," he told his uncle. "Now that the pup is recovering, I suggested she sleep in this morning."

"So the queen and her stable master managed to save the cur," Fenrir said.

Jerrik glanced at Sven, who had confirmed his suspicions on the walk over that the entire royal household, from jarl to thrall, knew about Hamar's broken nose and how he'd come by it. Whatever game his uncle was playing at, Jerrik wasn't having it.

"You know they did," Jerrik told Fenrir, who sat back at the tone of Jerrik's voice. "As you know that I broke Hamar's nose because I caught him embracing my wife. As you know that's why Alyssa was out of sorts at supper last night and that we talked it out and made up after. Why are you pretending ignorance?"

Fenrir held both hands up, palms out. "Don't take offense, nephew—"

"Your nephew doesn't; however, your king does," Jerrik said, earning Sven's gruff humph of approval.

"I was attempting to get your side of the story," Fenrir explained. "To suss out truth from rumor."

"Then ask me straight out," Jerrik told him. "I may have been a sailor these past ten and two years, but I'm not ignorant of the games and politics of palace life. In truth, I've been privy to the politics of kings and their households from all four corners of the world through my years of travel and trade." He pinned Fenrir with a level gaze. "I don't like games, Uncle, and as king, I will not tolerate them."

"As you command." Fenrir dipped his head. "I am here to serve you, my king." He gave Jerrik a half-smile. "And might I say, well done, King Jerrik."

"You may," Jerrik said, relieved and proud that his uncle had approved of his handling of the situation.

Jerrik may have been privy to the goings-on and politics of many kingdoms, but he was still new to being a king.

He respected his uncle, who had been counsel to his father, his two brothers, and now him. It would make what he had to say next go down easier. "The reason I called this meeting," he said, emphasizing the word *I*, "was to get a few things settled between all of us. Chain of command and what that entails. As well, I wanted to talk to you, Uncle, about your conversation with the kitchen staff about Alyssa and Digger. Specifically, what you told them Alyssa would do to them if the pup died."

"Which was what?" Fenrir asked.

Jerrik blew an exasperated breath out. Was this some sort of test? Hadn't he expressly told his uncle that he didn't like these games a few moments ago? "That she blamed them for the pup getting sick and would have their heads on a pike if he died."

Fenrir pressed his thin lips together and shook his head. "What I told them when they asked me if the queen would blame them was that I did not know," he said. "I told them there were several possibilities, ranging from the queen not blaming them at all to the last and most extreme, which I emphasized was the most unlikely."

He splayed his hands. "I cannot help it if their poor peasant minds latched onto the worst outcome."

Jerrik considered this. He knew firsthand how the fears and superstitions of the unknown could cause people to dread the worst. He, and especially Alyssa, were still unknowns to most of the people here.

"From now on," he told Fenrir and every other man sitting in the room, "if you're approached by someone with a question about what I or the queen may say or do about a situation, you're to tell them you don't know, and then come to myself or the queen with the question and we will decide how to answer." Heads nodded and assents were mumbled. Jerrik held his uncle's neutral, well-studied gaze. "Your duty is to counsel me, not to speak for me or the queen. Is that understood?"

Jerrik sat in the empty council chambers with only the ghosts of his past for company. He'd dismissed the others, wanting some time alone to think and plan for the future. The first thing he had to get through was the wedding in ten days. To that end, he had set Fenrir, who knew the visiting jarls, their likes and dislikes, allies and enemies, to the task of organizing rooms and housing and servants. Tryggr was to work with Borgny on the stores of foods and cooking fuel and all the other essentials needed to feed five hundred people for three days of feasting, and to hire extra cooking staff. Sven was to coordinate with the innkeepers, townfolk, and skeppares of the ships in port. Jerrik would go with Han and Bors to hunt for game.

After the wedding, he wanted built a separate small house next to the feasting hall to serve as his council chambers. It would keep him from having to be in this room full of memories, and it would move the seat of power from Fenrir's longhouse to a neutral location while providing the privacy he'd felt lacking today while a whole company of yellow beards hovered outside the room.

He intended to hold regular assemblies in the new council chambers where arguments and grievances could be discussed and dealt with, and where the king's laws were set and enforced. Meeting not only with his counselors and heads of households, but with his jarls and karls as well.

He smiled. Knowing Alyssa, he would need to hold assemblies where thralls were able to bring their complaints forward without fear of retribution, a good start to introducing the idea of a slave's rights to the kingdom, with the ultimate goal of declaring all men and women free. A worthy goal he agreed with. One he'd discussed with Fenrir and Tryggr, along with his other plans, earlier this morning.

While his uncle had agreed with Jerrik's plans and had offered several suggestions about how to implement them, the elder had also cautioned him against moving too fast, especially when it came to freeing the thralls. He'd warned Jerrik the jarls could rise up in arms against him, and Jerrik agreed to take his time and move slowly toward such a monumental change.

He also intended to ride out into the countryside and meet with the farmers on a regular basis. To speak with them personally about their needs and wants, and to see for himself the fields, crops, stores, and stock animals. He'd learned long ago from his Uncle Knut for a ship to run well, a skeppare must have a well-trained crew he could trust, as well as knowing every rope, sail, plank, and nail himself. He must know how she handles in a storm as well as in calm weather, to be prepared for sand bars and rocky shoals, and rain squalls and day upon day of windless skies. In short, a skeppare must be ready for anything. Jerrik figured a king was no different.

Except as king, Jerrik was responsible for thousands of people, a wife, and eventually children, not a crew of eight adventure-seeking sailors.

A soft knock on the door broke his musings. "Enter."

The door pushed open and Marianne walked in. "Jerrik."

"Marianne." He sat back in his chair as she sauntered toward him with a predatory smile. "Is there something you wished to talk to me about?"

She hiked her hip onto the edge of the table in front of him and perched, one long leg tucked up under her and the other swinging as she leaned forward, exposing the gap between her breasts. "Your wife," she said.

"What about her?"

"I hear she's found herself a lover already." She leaned in closer and whispered in his ear. "I am offering myself as yours."

Jerrik sat back to put some distance between them, and saw Alyssa standing in the open doorway, her face white and her mouth open.

"Alyssa." He stood so abruptly that Marianne jerked back and almost fell off the table. "Alyssa," he said as she whirled in a swirl of yellow skirts and ran out the door. "Alyssa, wait." He started after her, shaking off Marianne's grasping fingers. "Alyssa."

He didn't miss Ermelinde's smug smile as he strode out the door that she was still holding open, or the household full of yellow beards and servants watching him chase after his wife.

He clamped his jaw shut to keep from yelling at them all to mind their own fucking business, knowing that this little scene would be all over the palace before he even caught up to Alyssa, who was already out of the longhouse and running at full speed for the woods beyond the grounds.

He ran after her, not really caring who saw him. If she got too far ahead of him, he'd never find her, and storm clouds were moving in from the north. He followed her into the woods, where he'd already lost sight of the she-cat who was as at home in a forest as he was on the sea. He stopped and listened and heard the snap of twigs and crunching of underbrush from deep in a copse of oak, and caught a glimpse of yellow flitting through the trees.

"Alyssa," he called out. "Alyssa, wait."

Silence, and then the rapid sound of boot-fall, the shaking of leaves, and silence again. He followed the faint signs of boot prints until they stopped, and then, recalling stories Aaron had told him of how his little sister would climb trees to hide out in when she was upset, he looked up into the thick branches of a gnarled old oak.

The little lynx was treed.

"Alyssa, let me explain."

Her answer was to climb higher, and he climbed up after her, half afraid she'd try to jump down before he reached her. She was so high up in the tree it would have meant a broken foot or leg if she jumped.

His worry eased some when he pulled himself up onto the branch below her and sat with his back against the oak's trunk, taking the time to slow his breath and form his words. "I know how it looked," he began.

"It looked like you and your old lover were taking up where you left off."

He blew out his breath. At least she was talking to him. "I'm sure it did. Believe me, I did nothing to encourage her. She came into the chambers asking to speak with me and then she propositioned me. Which was when you walked in."

"Hmph."

"I swear on my life, Alyssa. Nothing more happened."

"What was her proposition?"

"She offered herself as my lover."

A slow hiss emanated from his she-cat. "Why would she think you wanted a lover, so newly married?"

He rubbed the back of his neck. He'd hoped to avoid this part, but he wasn't going to lie. "She told me she'd heard you already had a lover of your own."

"She what?" Eyes as bright and hard as cut emeralds glared down at him. "That bitch." She shook her head and growled an unintelligible curse. "What did you say to that?"

"Nothing. That was when you walked in." To a place she had never set foot in before. "Why did you come to the council chambers?"

"Magna wished for me to tell you something, in private, before it became common knowledge. Han told me I could find you alone in the council chambers."

So, bad timing it was, or good, he supposed. Better Alyssa had seen it with her own eyes than hear about it later from some gossipmonger.

"What was it that Magna wanted you to tell me?"

"It's about her and Hulda."

"Will you come down a branch and tell me?" he cajoled. "Maybe give your husband, who has been nothing but true to you in thought as well as deed, a kiss or ten in the telling?"

"Only if I get to bloody Marianne's nose."

He laughed and patted the branch in front of him. "Come on down, my bloodthirsty little lynx."

Jerrik stood from the supper table and offered Alyssa his arm as the servants started clearing the trays and trenchers, catching more than one curious glance as she stood and placed her hand in the crook of his elbow and walked with him to where Marianne sat at one of the low tables with the other women of Fenrir's household. He and Alyssa had been watching Marianne whisper and speak behind her palm to the women throughout the meal, and to Alyssa's credit, she'd suffered their snide smiles and knowing glances without comment the entire time. She remained silent as Marianne's smug expression wilted under Jerrik's scowl.

"My queen and I would have a word with you," he told Marianne, "in the council chambers. Now."

"King Jerrik." Ermelinde stood from her seat at the high table. "Marianne is a guest in my house. Your uncle and I would like to be present for this meeting."

"Of course," Jerrik agreed. He'd expected such a request. "Tryggr, Sven, Bors, you will be present as well."

"Aye, skep…ah, King Jerrik," Sven answered.

Jerrik and Alyssa led the way out of the hall to Fenrir's longhouse, past curious servants and a few yellow beards, and then into the council chambers.

He took the seat at the head of one end of the long table with Alyssa, Tryggr, Sven and Bors. Fenrir sat at the other end with Ermelinde and Marianne.

"I will speak first," Jerrik said, "without comment or interruption, and then your queen will have her say. After we have spoken, you may, each of you, speak in turn. Am I understood?" Heads nodded all around. "Good." He fixed his gaze on the three at the other end of the table. "I realize that you expected me to marry Marianne and make her queen, and that you, Aunt Ermelinde, especially wanted it. However, I did not. I chose Alyssa. I married Alyssa. She is my wife and your queen. It is done." He pinned Marianne with his glare. "I've said this before, and this is the last time I expect to have to ever say it again. I am well pleased with my wife in all ways. I have no need nor want of another woman."

Marianne nodded and dropped her gaze, and Alyssa smiled and laid her hand over his under the table. Jerrik turned his attention to Fenrir and Ermelinde.

"I know you act out of concern for our family and city, Uncle," he said. "Alyssa and I might be new in our roles as king and queen, yet I am no ignorant, stripling lad. I was raised a prince. I understand my duties as king. I skeppared a ship and have dealt with royalty all over the world. When I need help navigating the waters of kingship, I will ask for it. I will welcome your honest opinion, but any decision will be mine, as will the results of my decisions, good or bad."

"Of course, my king. I only meant—"

He held up his hand, and Fenrir pressed his lips into a thin line and remained silent. Jerrik looked to Ermelinde, whose usual haughty expression was even more so. He clamped down on an unbidden smile. His aunt was obviously unused to being dressed down and was not pleased.

"Alyssa is a princess born and raised," he said. "By a father and mother whom I admire greatly as parents and monarchs. She has been taught what it means to be queen, to treat people with fairness and the respect they deserve, which you, neither of you," he swept Ermelinde and Marianne with a fierce glare, "have done for her."

Sven humphed for emphasis while Tryggr smiled and dipped his head. Ermelinde's countenance grew haughtier. Fenrir's face was an unreadable mask, and Marianne's was one of desperation.

"From this moment on," he told them, "I expect that to change. I expect you to quit undermining her and quit scolding her," he said to Ermelinde. "You," he told Marianne, "are to quit competing with her. You will lose. Both of you. Every time." He turned to Alyssa. "Do you have anything to add, my queen?"

"My husband expressed himself quite well," she said. "Therefore, I have only two things to add. Until I say otherwise, you," she told Ermelinde, "stay away from me. And you," she told Marianne, "stay away from my husband."

CHAPTER 14

The Water Scrying

Alyssa grinned at Jerrik, who sat by the hearth fire in the main room of their longhouse, his back leaning against the warm bricks, his legs sprawled out, sipping a cup of beer and humming along in his deep baritone to the tune she and Han were playing on the harp and flute. Sven was trying to sweet-talk Ranveig into giving him another piece of bread with honey and butter from the larder, and Bors was laughing with Magna, Hulda, and Dagny as they watched Anders and Davin chasing Digger and Boots in circles around the table. Even Pavel had joined them for the evening, having come to tell them that the cots were set up for the extra stable hands they'd hired for the wedding. The boy wound up staying for some music and company at Alyssa's invitation, though he seemed especially on edge tonight. Not that she blamed him. Tomorrow, the guests would start arriving for the wedding, followed by three days of celebrating. This evening, they could all relax and enjoy the quiet of family.

"Auntie Lyssie, Auntie Lyssie, look," Davin squealed as Boots climbed up his leggings and tunic to perch on his shoulder. "Look what I taught Boots to do."

Alyssa laughed, her mood as light and lilting as the tune she and Han had been playing. "Well done, Davin," she said, clapping her hands as Davin paraded around with the kitten balancing on his shoulder. "That's quite a trick."

"Auntie Lyssie," Anders called for her attention. "Look what I taught Digger to do." He held a piece of jerky up over Digger's head and moved it in a circle, grinning proudly as the pup danced around on his hind legs begging for the choice treat with which Anders rewarded him.

"How did you teach him that?" Alyssa asked. "All I can teach him to do is bark at the door when he wants to go out." She caught the twitch of Jerrik's lips. He'd been watching her train the pup to dance on his hind legs in their chambers for the past several nights.

"I hold it up for him like so," Anders said, holding up another piece of jerky and beaming as the pup danced for it again. "And he tries to get it."

"Boots can dance too," Davin said, setting the kitten down and dangling a string above her until she jumped up and swatted at it. "See, Auntie Lyssie," he said, vying with his brother for her attention.

"Oh, you boys are so clever," Alyssa said, grinning from brother to brother. "How lucky we are, Uncle Jerrik, to have two such clever nephews."

"Very lucky," Jerrik agreed with a wink at Alyssa.

"Do you hope your baby will be clever boys like us, Auntie Lyssie?" Davin said, twirling the string for Boots.

"Baby?" Jerrik's expression was one of pure astonishment as he met Alyssa's gaze. "You're pregnant?"

Her cheeks flushed as she smiled at Jerrik. "I'd wanted the news to be my gift to you on our wedding day," she told him.

"I'm sorry, Alyssa," Dagny said. She glanced fondly at Davin, who still played with the kitten, oblivious to the drama playing out. "Little pitchers have big ears and open mouths that tend to spill secrets as easily as water."

"It's fine, Dagny," Alyssa assured her, and then she looked to Jerrik, suddenly unsure. "Isn't it?"

Jerrik set down the cup he'd been holding in mid-air on the hearth's edge and crouched in front of Alyssa, placing his hands on her knees. "It's more than fine, my love," he said, taking her face in his hands and kissing her. "It's the best gift you could ever give me, besides yourself."

Alyssa grinned from ear to ear, and then burst into tears.

"Alyssa?" Jerrik's brows furrowed. "What happened? Why are you crying?" He pushed a stray lock of her hair behind her ear and wiped a tear from her cheek. "Is it the baby? Are you all right?"

"Nothing happened," she said, laughing through her tears. "The baby is fine and I'm well." She threw her arms around Jerrik's neck and pressed her forehead to his. "I'm crying with happiness and relief because I love you and our babe so much already, I couldn't have borne it if you hadn't been pleased."

"I am beyond pleased, my love," Jerrik said. He stroked her hair, his worry dissipated. "I fear I have no words to describe how I feel."

Alyssa giggled and kissed his nose. "You will have eight moons to think of them," she told him.

The guests had arrived and been situated and the entire royal household was getting ready for the feast on the eve before Alyssa's and Jerrik's second wedding. A ceremony that would unite them before and with the people of Sea Ridge.

Jerrik donned his tunic of harvest gold linen Solveig had embroidered with leaves of green and gold, as well as red worm weave. Alyssa wore her new, long-sleeved gown of forest green linen, the sleeves and hems embroidered with green and gold vines, and an apron of golden worm weave.

Hulda wore an undergown of cream linen with a woolen apron of moss green and new kid boots Alyssa had gifted her with that morning. Tomorrow, she would wear the gown of yellow gold worm weave, the gifting of which had so upset Ermelinde and ended with Alyssa freeing Hulda then and there.

Alyssa allowed herself a small smile of satisfaction. Ermelinde had taken her at her word and had stayed away as had Marianne. Ten days of relative peace, despite all the preparations for the wedding celebration.

"Mistress?" Hulda said from behind her, sorting through Alyssa's jewelry chest. "I cannot find your mother-of-pearl hair comb."

Alyssa looked through the ornately carved jewelry chest that she'd been given on her tenth birthday by her parents. Hulda was right, the hair comb, Jerrik's gift the night he had proposed marriage, wasn't there.

"When was the last time you wore it, mistress?" Hulda asked.

Alyssa shook her head. "I don't remember, other than it was before Digger got sick. I do know I haven't worn it since." She swept a glance around the room at the chests, tables, and sofas. "It has to be somewhere in here," she said. "I never take it off anywhere else."

She twirled the sea green pearl on the chain at her throat between her fingers. "Use another comb for tonight. We'll look again before tomorrow." She hated the thought of being married without it. The hair comb had been Jerrik's gift on returning to her, and besides the pearl necklace he had gifted her on their first wedding day, it was her favorite piece of jewelry. She especially liked it when Jerrik removed it from her hair.

When Hulda was done pinning up her braids, Alyssa stood and smoothed her gown and turned to Jerrik, who stood with his hands behind his back. "Well?"

"By the gods, Alyssa," he said, his voice low and resonant. "You are stunning." He gave her a wicked grin. "I look forward to getting you back here to our little den where I can destroy all of Hulda's handiwork. But before we go," he motioned with his hand for Alyssa to turn around, and then he placed a fur throw around her shoulders and turned her back to face him.

"Oh Jerrik." Alyssa ran her fingers through the soft, luxurious fur of tawny gold with black spots as Jerrik pinned the neck with a silver clasp in the shape of a warship with an eagle's head prow. She ran a fingertip over the brooch. "This is your family totem?"

"No," he said. "It is *our* family totem."

Alyssa beamed and ran a hand over the short fur cloak.

"It's so thick and soft, and beautiful," she purred. "Is it lynx?"

"It is."

"I love it." She twirled around, twice, and then stopped. "I have no gift for you."

"You've given me the best gift of all, my little lynx," he said, spreading his big, strong hand over the soft swell of her belly. "I'm so proud to be able to announce my heir is on the way at the feast tonight."

"Are you ready for this?" Jerrik asked Alyssa as Sven stood at the door to their longhouse, waiting for the signal to push it open. Outside, the Harvest Feast had already begun. It was the first event of the three-day festival celebrating the harvest and their wedding.

Alyssa took a deep breath in and blew it out. "I'm ready," she said as she laid her hand on Jerrik's forearm. "Are you?"

Jerrik laughed and patted her hand. "I am."

Accompanied by Sven, Han, Bors, and Magna, all armed with blades and wearing chest plates and arm guards of lacquered leather, Alyssa stepped out into the courtyard hanging onto Jerrik. Hundreds of people were congregated around fires, roasting pits, and casks of beer, mead, and wine.

Twenty long tables with benches were set out, each one of them laden with baskets of apples, pears, and the last of the late summer greens. There were loaves of ryes and flatbreads, and wheels of cheese, trays of pickled herring, and trenchers of roasted goat, mutton, and beef. They hadn't taken more than five steps when cheers rang out.

"Hurrah for King Jerrik and Queen Alyssa."

"May their reign be long and prosperous."

"May the queen be as fertile as our harvest."

"May the fates bless them with sons of ash and daughters of elm."

"Hurrah for King Jerrik and Queen Alyssa."

They smiled, nodded, and waved their way through the throng to the Feasting Hall, where the jarls of the kingdom and neighboring lands were gathered. Their tables were laden with the same bounty as those outside, with the addition of the elk, venison, and pheasant Jerrik and his hunting parties had supplied.

As ranking royals of neighboring kingdoms, King Olaf and King Torald and their wives were seated at the high table to Jerrik's right, while Tryggr, Trine, and Dagny were to Alyssa's left. A stiffly formal Fenrir and Ermelinde sat at the far end of them.

Jerrik led Alyssa to their places and they took their seats. He raised his horned cup, winked at Alyssa, and took a drink of beer. "Family, friends, neighbors," he said, officially starting the celebration. "I thank you for coming here to celebrate this harvest and my marriage to my beautiful bride, Queen Alyssa." He dipped his cup to hers and Alyssa raised hers to him. "Although we were married in her family's palace three moons ago, we look forward to our ceremony here on the morrow with all of you in attendance." He waited until the claps and whistles died down, and then he offered Alyssa his hand, clasping it tight as she stood. "There is more," he said. He lifted Alyssa's hand in his and pressed a kiss to the backs of her fingers. "I am pleased to announce that Queen Alyssa is with child. We will welcome our firstborn come early summer."

Well wishes and congratulations echoed off the rafters and turned to shouts of encouragement as he pulled Alyssa into his arms and gave her a rousing kiss. They sat down, grinning like fools at each other, and then tucked into the feast.

Many courses and cups of mead later, her belly stuffed and her cheeks sore from smiling and laughing so much, Alyssa pushed back in her chair, wondering why she'd dreaded this night.

After the servants cleared the tables and brought out the spiced wine, Fenrir stood, puffing out his chest and adjusting his bear skin cloak around him. The hall quieted. "I call Olaug, the Water Scryer," he announced.

She watched the white-haired crone walk up the aisle between the two sides of tables with the help of a walking staff with a mixture of curiosity and awe.

Jerrik had explained earlier how Olaug, a woman who had been old and wizened when he was a lad, would pour water into a ceremonial bowl and then gaze into it, where she would be shown any manner of visions or omens.

The venerated elder shuffled up to the high table, bowed her snowy head to Jerrik and Alyssa, and then turned to the small table that had been brought out along with a silver pitcher and shiny black obsidian bowl. The table's top was ornately carved with the Tree of Life in the center and framed by images of air, water, earth, and fire in each of the four corners.

Leaning her raven head staff against the table, Olaug slowly poured the water into the bowl, her voice low as she recited an incantation to the gods of water and foresight.

The hall went silent as she set the empty pitcher down and stirred the water with a shaft of intertwined ash and elm, and then stared into the water as it swirled and settled.

Nobody in the hall spoke or moved, all of them watching Olaug as intently as she studied the water for a hundred breaths exactly, and then she straightened and faced the high table. Alyssa felt a chill wind blow, though they were in a draft-free hall.

"What did you see, Olaug of the Ancestors?" Jerrik asked.

Olaug's wizened gaze moved from Jerrik to Alyssa and back again. "I saw a lynx in her birthing den. Suckling at her teat was a mongrel cur with curly brown hair and eyes. Standing proudly at her side, a roan stallion. In the gray storm clouds above, an eagle screamed." She lifted her face to the rafters and emitted two piercing, high-pitched screeches and then lowered her gaze to Jerrik's and let out three harsh "cuckoo, cuckoo, cuckoos."

The hall went as still and silent as a tomb. Alyssa tried to swallow past the stone in her throat as she felt the warmth leave Jerrik's hand, felt him stiffen in his seat beside her. She turned to him and saw the muscle tic in the side of his clamped jaw as the clear blue of his eyes clouded up and stormed over.

Licking lips gone suddenly dry, she met the scryer's watching gaze and saw a flash of pity before the old woman blinked and dropped a veil of neutral nothingness over her face. A nothingness that threatened to overtake and overwhelm Alyssa from the inside out.

Without thinking or knowing why, Alyssa stood and walked on shaking legs to the scrying bowl, and with fingers gone clumsy with the numbing fear surging through her, she picked up the sacred shaft and stirred the mysterious waters until they were swirling in the black bowl with the force of a river eddy. She set the shaft down and gazed into the bowl's reflective depths as the eddy slowed and stilled.

For a long time, she saw nothing. Nothing beyond the blackness that she felt seeping into her soul. Then the black nothingness began to take the shape of a mountainside of barren, jagged stone jutting up to the sky.

On top of the mountainside an eagle perched on the uppermost branch of a dead tree, its skeletal limbs pale against a storm gray sky. The eagle surveyed the leafless trees, fallow fields, and abandoned, decaying buildings in the valley below with its piercing blue eyes, and then it blinked and let out a keening cry as the ebb tide flowed from the bay out to the sea, slowly, inexorably, until with a rushing swoosh the sea itself was sucked away.

Alyssa was the sea, unable to do anything as she was pulled farther and farther from the shore until there was nothing but black, stinking, oozing, mud all around her. She gazed up at the eagle in one last silent plea. The eagle sat alone and unmoving on a throne of stone as she was dragged over the abyss.

"Alyssa?" Someone far away was calling her name. "Alyssa?"

She tried to see where the voice was coming from, but her mind was floating somewhere outside her body, and her body was nothing but an empty husk. A dry, empty, hollowed-out husk that cracked and crumpled to dust as it fell.

She woke in Jerrik's arms, cradled against the breadth of his chest, his warm breath caressing her cheek, his eagle eyes searching hers. "Thank the gods, you've come back to me."

She lifted her hand and touched his cheek. Where her heart should've been there was nothing but a gaping maw. "I don't want to leave you, Jerrik. Please don't let it take me."

"Don't let what take you, Lyssa?" he rasped. "What was it you saw?"

Over his shoulder, Alyssa met Olaug's keen gaze. "What did you see, my queen?" the crone asked. "You must tell me."

Alyssa shook her head and buried her face into Jerrik's shoulder.

She shuddered, soul sick from the hold the vision had on her, afraid that she truly would be sucked into the abyss of black, empty nothingness, and not be able to find her way out. Not be able to find her way back to Jerrik.

Her body began to shake uncontrollably, and Jerrik scooped her up in his arms and carried her past the grassfire of whispers that had spread through the hall and out into the night, not stopping until she was safe in their bed, wrapped in blankets and sipping a cup of warmed mead.

Jerrik watched Alyssa sleep, her cheeks pink again, not deathly pale, her lips soft and rosy and slightly open, not grim and tight. Her breathing slow, deep, and steady, not rapid and shallow. Her eyes closed, not staring at him with a raw, primal fear that had chilled him to his marrow.

He lay on the bed next to her and stroked her thick, tawny mane, releasing his breath as she burrowed her nose deeper into her pillow. His pillow, actually, which the little minx stole whenever he wasn't in bed, because, she said, it smelled like him.

His breath caught and held, and his gut twisted. He wanted to hold her and fix whatever was wrong, but she hadn't told him what she'd seen in the scrying bowl. Not yet.

Olaug's vision, on the other hand, had been plainly spoken and understood. A lynx, suckling a mongrel child with brown curls, the stallion its sire, the eagle a cuckold. It didn't get much plainer than that.

Then Alyssa, with no training, no experience scrying, had gone into a trance and looked into the scrying bowl and had seen a vision of her own. A vision that had turned her ashen and sent her into oblivion. A vision that still had a hold on her.

He rolled his shoulders and blew out his breath, frustrated and hamstrung.

A man couldn't fix something if he didn't know what the problem was. He'd have to wait until Alyssa was ready to tell him what she'd seen, and why it chilled her so, before he could do anything about it.

At least he didn't need to be haunted by the chance that the babe she carried in her womb had been planted there by Kostya. Hard as it had been to keep from consummating their marriage until after she'd bled, he was glad now they had waited.

Hamar, the stable master, had brown eyes and brown curly hair. The thought came to him unbidden. The same thought he'd been trying to deny since the moment Olaug had described her vision. Or perhaps her vision had simply shown Jerrik's greatest fear. Visions and omens could be tricky things.

"Jerrik?"

"I didn't mean to wake you." He peered into eyes the color of a wind-tossed sea. "How do you feel?"

"Better." She sat up and laid her head on his shoulder. "I'm here with you." She nuzzled his neck and placed her open palm over his heart, her breath matching his. She straddled his naked hips, covering him with her wet heat.

"Are you sure?" he whispered, his cock already growing with need and urgency while his brain was telling him to slow down.

She'd fainted from shock not that long ago; she needed rest and quiet.

"I've never been surer," she said, doffing her night shift, her nipples hard, her breasts soft and heavy as she rubbed them against his chest. "I want to make love with you tonight, Jerrik. I need to."

She kissed him. Long, slow, and achingly sweet. When she pulled back and gazed into his eyes, the sadness in hers cracked his heart into a million shards of pain. "Alyssa?"

"I love you. I always have and I always will."

"I know you do, my little lynx," he said, pushing a lock of her hair behind her ear. "I love you too."

Her smile was like sunlight on water and her eyes glistened with tears. "Kiss me, wife," he said.

She kissed him with an urgency and a hunger that Jerrik felt to his bones. A hunger that he'd felt his whole life and had never come close to sating until now. Until Alyssa.

She kissed, nipped, suckled, and bit his lips, his tongue, his neck, his nipples, kissing her way down his belly to his cock, iron hard with need.

She licked the head and suckled the first milky drop of his seed, and Jerrik groaned through his teeth. He felt her smile around the tip and then she wrapped her soft, hot lips around him and suckled until he was gripping her shoulders.

When he thought he could take no more, she kissed her way back up his belly, his nipples, his throat, his mouth, her lips soft, gentle, and featherlight.

She sat back, her warm flesh covering his throbbing cock, and held his gaze.

She smiled, sad and bittersweet, and her eyes welled, but before Jerrik could ask her what it was that troubled her, she lifted her hips and took him in hand and slid down his cock in one long, sinuous move, sheathing him in her wet heat. She began moving her hips in delicious, torturous circles, riding him faster and harder and higher until they were soaring over the precipice, panting and gasping. Clinging together as they came crashing down to earth.

As they lay in each other's arms, their passion spent, their skin cooling, Alyssa told Jerrik what she had seen in the scrying bowl.

CHAPTER 15

The Wedding

Alyssa sat at the open window of their bedchamber, plucking the melancholy tune of the cowherd and the cloud weaver on her harp while staring out at the bay where the full moon high tide was still coming in. The *Sea Eagle* and three other trading ships bobbed peacefully in the water. The late afternoon sun had started its descent behind the mountains to the west, and the road from the bay to the palace was thronged with people on horses and on foot, or crowded onto farm wagons and trade carts.

In the courtyard, tables were set out much as the night before, with even more casks of beer, wine, and mead. The savory aroma of roasting meat filled the night air.

Almost all was in readiness for the ceremony that would wed Jerrik and Alyssa in the traditions of his land. A ceremony that would officially welcome the reign of King Jerrik and Queen Alyssa. A ceremony Alyssa had hoped would welcome her to her new home as well.

A hope that had been pulled out from under her by Olaug's scrying vision, and her own.

She, Jerrik, and every person in the hall who'd heard Olaug understood the implications of what the old seer said she saw. A lynx suckling a mongrel cur, the stallion sire standing at her side, the eagle's cry turning to a cuckoo's. Her child's parentage had been questioned in front of the entire household and visiting royalty and jarls.

She'd been publicly accused of carrying another man's child. She knew how hard Jerrik was trying to act like it hadn't affected him. Like he wasn't brooding over it or Alyssa's vision every time she caught him staring off into the distance. Like he meant it when he'd told her that visions could be tricky things and often only showed a person's fear of what could happen, not necessarily what would.

She shivered and lost her place in the song and didn't bother trying to resume where she'd dropped off, but started strumming the tune to "Somebody," the song her grandmother had sung to her grandfather the first night they'd met. The song she had sung as a farewell to him the night before she and her sister had left his city, sure that she would never see the love of her life again.

A feeling that Alyssa had become eerily familiar with since last night. She was supposed to wed Jerrik again tonight, yet felt as if she'd been saying good-bye ever since her vision in the scrying bowl.

"Why such a sad tune, mistress?" Hulda asked, dressed in her new gown of yellow gold worm weave. "Today is your wedding day."

"Of sorts," Alyssa said.

Hulda tsked. "Most women would be happy with one grand celebration, mistress. You get to have two. One at your old home and now one here in your new home."

"You're right," Alyssa said, setting Meadowlark down. She stepped out of her robe and held her arms up for Hulda to slip the amethyst gown with newly added long sleeves over her head, smoothing the worm weave skirts over her hips.

"Ohh, mistress, it is the most beautiful gown I have ever seen, next to mine, of course."

Alyssa gave a wan smile. "Thank you, Hulda." She ran her hands down her belly. "Another moon or two and it might not've fit."

"It does fit though, perfectly," Hulda said, guiding Alyssa to the stool at her dressing table. "King Jerrik will be growling off any man at the feast who looks at you twice, which will be every man there from eight to eighty."

Jerrik, who was getting dressed in Sven's chambers, had said almost the same thing earlier today as he'd watched Alyssa rising out of the tub, her hair dripping, her skin flushed from the hot bath water and their love play.

They'd awoken late, as had most of last night's guests, and spent the better part of the morning lazing away in bed, breaking their fast in their chambers at noon, and then bathing in preparation for tonight.

"I still haven't found your hair comb, mistress," Hulda said, pulling Alyssa from her reverie. "I've looked everywhere." She rummaged through Alyssa's jewelry chest again. "It is nowhere to be found."

"Pick another, then," Alyssa said, suddenly close to tears. She sat straighter and blew out her breath and swiped at her unshed tears. It was only a hair comb. Her favorite, to be sure. A treasured gift from Jerrik on the night he proposed marriage. In the scheme of all things, though, of little importance. "We're out of time."

She tried to think of anything other than her scrying vision as Hulda brushed and braided her hair into an elaborate coif.

Alyssa thought of her mother and father, of their fierce, passionate love for each other, for their children, their family, their people.

Of her grandmother and grandfather, her great-aunt Lyrra and great-uncle Nasim, of all the trials they had to overcome, and did.

She thought of the Winter's Eve she'd first met Jerrik, of his smiling, sky-blue eyes and low resonate voice, which had filled her heart as they sang together.

She thought of how he'd come for her almost four moons ago, of their joyous wedding, their strange wedding night, and all of the wonderful nights since.

She thought of her love for him, of how he'd told her that he loved her again last night.

She thought of their child, growing in her womb. She imagined a healthy, happy, blond-haired, blue-eyed son bouncing on his father's knee, and she actually smiled as Hulda placed the wreath of wildflowers on her head.

Dressed in her amethyst gown and lynx cape with the silver brooch clasping it around her shoulders, Alyssa descended the stairs to where Jerrik waited for her, the somber look on his handsome face breaking into a smile of pure male approval.

"Wife," he said, offering her his arm.

"Husband," she said, placing her hand on his arm as the others moved into place: Sven and Dagny ahead of them, Han, Bors, and Magna behind them, with Hulda trailing.

He drew in a deep breath and blew it out. "Shall we?"

The throng of people gathered outside cheered as they walked out the door, and then almost as one, the crowd stepped back and opened a path leading to the priest who stood at the arbor of ash and elm that had been adorned with the same wildflowers crowning Alyssa's head.

Their little parade made its way up the path amidst more cheers and blessings and stopped before the priest, where Alyssa dropped her hand from Jerrik's sleeve and met his piercing gaze with a tremulous smile. He grasped her hand and held it, twining his fingers through hers.

The priest cleared his throat and the gathering went quiet. He opened his mouth to speak, but the voice and the words that came were not his.

"King Jerrik," Fenrir called out as he stepped forward from the crowd. "I fear I must present you with some unwelcome information before the ceremony takes place." His gaze locked on Alyssa, and a cold dread took hold of her. "If it takes place."

"If?" Jerrik said. He looked to Alyssa, still holding her hand. "If you know what this is about, wife, speak now."

Alyssa shook her head. "I don't," she said, her voice scarcely a whisper.

Jerrik turned to Fenrir as Pavel stepped up beside his uncle and would not meet Alyssa's anxious gaze. "Tell me," Jerrik said.

Fenrir held his hand out and opened it, palm up.

"My hair comb," Alyssa said. "Where did you find it?"

"Pavel found it," Fenrir said. He met and held Jerrik's gaze. "In Hamar's bed. Where your wife has been lying with the man almost since the day you arrived here."

"You lie," Alyssa spat as the air around them buzzed and hummed like the droning of a thousand bees. She pulled on Jerrik's hand and grasped his arm to make him look at her, his sky-blue eyes turned storm gray. "He lies. I swear to you on our child's life. I have never lain with any man other than you."

"Considering the child that you carry may not be Jerrik's," Fenrir sneered, "your oath, the oath of an unfaithful harlot, means nothing."

Alyssa sucked her breath in and let it out in a hiss. "You are not a man, Fenrir. You are snake in the grass."

"Enough," Jerrik thundered. The earth swayed and moved beneath Alyssa's feet as if it were a ship in a storm-tossed sea. The only thing keeping her standing was Jerrik's iron grip on her arm. He turned to Pavel, who quaked and visibly paled. "Tell me, Pavel," he commanded.

"I...I seen the mistress, I mean, Queen Alyssa, comin' an' goin' from Hamar's room many a time, skep, King Jerrik."

"Pavel," Alyssa cried. "Why would you say such a thing?"

"Because it is true," Fenrir answered for Pavel, his snake eyes sneering at Alyssa. He looked to Jerrik. "I warned you, did I not? She is just like your mother. A lying, unfaithful whore."

"Nnnooo." Jerrik's roar was one of rage, pure, primal, animal rage.

"Jerrik," Alyssa cried, grasping his arm, trying to get him to look at her. "Husband. I did not do this. I swear to you." His jaw clamped tight and the white-hot anger in his ice-blue eyes froze her blood. "You must believe me, my love—"

"Your love?" He threw her hand from his arm. "You spread your love as easily you do your—"

Alyssa slapped him across the cheek. Hard. "How dare you."

"How dare I?" He grabbed her by the hank of her braid and pushed her down to her knees. "How dare you, you lying, cheating—"

The man who stood glaring down at her wasn't Jerrik. Not her Jerrik. He was a man she'd never seen before.

He was his father, denying his mother. Wrapping her braid around his fist, he pulled the ceremonial knife of horn and bone from his waist belt and held the blade to her throat.

By rights, he could kill her for her supposed infidelity, and by the look of pure rage on his face, Alyssa was afraid he would.

She clawed at his wrist, drawing blood as she fought for her life and the life of her unborn child.

"Stop fighting," he snarled, and Alyssa dropped her hands, all the breath, all the heart, gone from her.

Her vision blurred and a great buzzing sound filled her ears as her head was pulled side to side in a sawing motion, and then her braid was on the ground at her knees and the world went black.

Alyssa lay on the sofa in Magna's and Hulda's chambers, bundled up in a pile of blankets with Digger cuddled up beside her, yet unable to stop shaking. She had no memory of how she got here, or of how Digger came to be with her, or of anything except the look of betrayal on Jerrik's face the moment he'd decided to believe the accusations against her. His rage when he'd pushed her to her knees and cut her hair. Those memories were seared into her soul.

She closed her eyes against the anger and the hatred she had seen in his and sat up, trying to take slow, steady breaths to keep the panic from rising, but she couldn't stop the keening moan that rose up and out of her throat as she started to rock back and forth, back and forth.

"Alyssa." Faces blurred before her. "Alyssa." Worried voices. "Sister." Hands on her shoulders, pressing her back against something soft, stopping her rocking. "Mistress." Worried eyes. "Mistress, you must stop."

Something warm and wet licking her chin, whining softly. "Digger, no." Hushed whispers. "Cannot be good for the baby." Baby. Her baby. Jerrik's baby. A baby Jerrik didn't believe was his. Jerrik didn't believe her. Didn't love her.

She stilled, and her heart shattered into a thousand cutting shards, the pain taking the breath from her. "Alyssa? Alyssa."

Hands shook her by the shoulders and she gasped and sucked in a great gulp of air and burst into a torrent of tears and gut-wrenching sobs.

When she woke, she was in a bed with Digger curled up against her side, a candle on a small table between the bed she lay in and the bed where she could discern two heads poking out from the covers. Magna and Hulda.

Yawning, she ran her hand through her hair and stopped at her nape, where there was only skin and air. She ran both hands through her shorn hair, curious at how light her head felt without the weight of a waist-length mane.

She glanced at the table and saw her braid lying there, with the hair comb that had been Fenrir's proof against her tucked into it, and her throat constricted.

It wasn't the sight of her hair or the comb that made her want to vomit; it was the memory of Jerrik's face when he had cut it. He had hated her at that moment, and she had truly feared for her life.

Rubbing some blood back into her ice-cold hands, she roused Digger and pushed back the bed covers and swung her feet onto the floor. She wore a long-sleeved linen night shift that must have belonged to Hulda. Alyssa had no recollection of changing into it or the woolen socks she wore. Grabbing her lynx cloak from where it lay strewn on the sofa along with her amethyst gown, Alyssa threw it over her shoulders, stuffed her feet into her boots, and quietly slid the bolt to the door open, calling Digger to heel.

The longhouse was quiet except for the soft snores of its inhabitants as she made her way past the door to her and Jerrik's chambers, resisting the urge to push her way in and confront him. She needed to get her bearings before she faced him. Now that the worst of the shock had dissipated, she was beginning to get angry, which was the only thing keeping her from drowning in a sea of despair.

Picking up Digger, she continued down the stairs, past the smoldering embers of the hearth fire and out into the pitch of night. The first thing she noticed as her eyes adjusted to the dark was that everything, every table and bench and cask, had been removed from the yard, every fire doused, as if the debacle of her and Jerrik's almost wedding had never happened.

Which was what that snake, Fenrir, and his bitch of a wife had wanted.

Alyssa wondered what had happened to Hamar, and considered walking over to the stables to find out, to ask Pavel why he had lied about her and Hamar, but she knew if it were discovered that she'd gone there in the middle of the night, it would go bad for all of them. As bad as it was, it could still get worse.

She shuddered, remembering the cold feel of the blade as Jerrik held it to her throat, his face contorted with rage. He'd come close to killing her. He could still, by this land's customs.

Though he had to know that her father and brothers would come after him if he killed her. They still might, if they found out what he'd done to her today.

She shuddered again and wrapped the cloak tighter around her, holding on to the fact that he hadn't slit her throat or banished her or even divorced her. Much as she held on to the thin thread of hope that somewhere deep inside of him, where Fenrir's poison had not yet taken hold and festered, Jerrik still loved her.

It was that hope that had her on her feet now instead of lying in a mewling puddle of tears as she had been earlier, or at the bottom of the bay. Hope that Jerrik would believe her when the storm of his rage had calmed.

Shivering, she called for Digger, who came running from whatever smell had caught his attention. She patted her knees and he jumped up into her arms and covered her tear-stained face with puppy kisses.

"At least I have you," she told the pup. "They cannot take your love from me."

Or could they? Had they already tried?

Jerrik woke and reached for Alyssa, but she wasn't there. Her side of the bed was as cold and empty as the gaping maw in his chest. It was true, what they said, a person could actually feel their heart break. A rupturing that Jerrik had lived through once before as a child when his mother had chosen to leave him, his father, and brothers to their guilt and grief while escaping her own. A betrayal of love that Jerrik had spent his entire adult life avoiding, only to fall into the little lynx's trap.

Like his father had fallen into his mother's.

Curse the fates.

He stood and threw the bed covers off and dressed quickly, eager to get this thing that was gnawing at him done and over with.

He hadn't fallen asleep until well past midnight, and what little sleep he'd gotten had been fitful at best.

He strode down the stairs and stopped halfway down. Alyssa and the entire household were up and waiting for him by the hearth fire, and by the looks on their faces, they had all sided with Alyssa.

He glared at Sven, Han, and Bors. The women he could understand sticking by Alyssa's side, women always stuck together, but his own men, men who had sailed with him for years, who had sailed and fought and whored side by side with him, had known him better than his own family, had chosen Alyssa.

She stood as he approached. "I've sent for Fenrir, Ermelinde, Hamar, and Pavel to be brought here," she told him, her spine as stiff as her speech. "Tryggr and Trine as well. If I am to be tried, I want it to be a public trial. I want my family and friends to know the truth of what was said and done."

"As is your right," Jerrik agreed, cursing himself for noticing how her short hair made her eyes look even bigger in her gamine face. How the dark circles under her eyes and the grim lines around her mouth made him want to go to her and hold her, and kiss her sadness away. Yet beneath his sympathy for her, his rage still burned hot and angry.

How could a man still love a woman he hated?

"Is that for me?" he asked Ranveig as she set a tray down on the table.

"Aye, King Jerrik."

He sat at the table across from his men and tucked into the beer and bread and cheese, ignoring their heated glares and pointed silence.

When he'd finished, Ranveig cleared his tray and then brought out cups and pitchers of mead and beer and set them out on the table as first Tryggr and Trine arrived, soon followed by Pavel and Hamar, whose broken nose and bruised cheek were no longer black and blue, but a fading purple and yellow.

Han and Bors offered Tryggr and Trine their seats, while Pavel and Hamar stood together along the wall, looking as if they were trying to disappear into the woodwork.

Alyssa had given them both a quick glance when they entered, yet other than that, she hadn't looked at her friend or lover once, the callous little bitch.

At last, Fenrir and Ermelinde arrived, accompanied by Marianne, whom Alyssa had not mentioned asking for, and who had no reason to be here as far as Jerrik knew. They, of course, walked straight over to where Magna and Dagny and Hulda sat, standing imperiously until the women gave up their seats to them.

"Now, what is this all about?" Fenrir demanded.

"Your queen," Jerrik said, defending her despite himself, "has called for her trial to be held here, with those in attendance as witnesses."

"I thought her guilt had been established," Fenrir said.

"That will be for me to decide," Jerrik told him. "That, and any punishment to be meted out."

He saw Alyssa's hand go to the nape of her neck and then drop to her lap. Her eyes met his for a moment, as green and fathomless as the sea.

He stood and cleared his throat. "The charges against you are of infidelity and unfaithfulness to your marriage vows. Of lying with the stable master, Hamar, who is *not*," Jerrik emphasized the word, "your wedded husband." He swallowed his bile. "It is claimed that the child you carry in your womb may not be of your husband's seed. That you may be carrying a common bastard, not a royal heir." He held her gaze, his own demanding the truth. "What say you, wife?"

Alyssa stood and smoothed her skirts. She looked at no one else, spoke to no one else, but Jerrik. "I say that the charges laid against me are lies," she said, her voice, her manner, calm and collected. "Lies concocted and spread with malice by your uncle and counselor, Fenrir, and his wife, Ermelinde, to make you cast me aside." Her voice broke. "As you have done."

"I lie?" Fenrir shot up out of his seat and jabbed a finger in the air at Alyssa. "The bitch lies." He turned on Jerrik. "I brought you proof. Hard proof of your faithless harlot's lies. I did it to save you and our kingdom from the same fate that your cuckold father suffered from." He sneered at Hamar, who jerked his head back and up. "Better to find out now than after raising another man's child."

Jerrik took a moment to unclench his fists and calm the storm building in him. "Hamar," he said when he could speak without raging. "When I punched you in the face, did you deserve it?"

Hamar nodded. "Yes, my king. The queen's hug was nothing more than a friendly gesture on her part. Mine, on the other hand." He shook his head. "You had the right of it." He blew a breath out and continued, unasked. "I admit I, and most of the men in this city, are half in love with Queen Alyssa." Alyssa's eyes widened and her jaw dropped. "I also swear that she has never given me, or any other man that I know of, any reason to believe she returned our regard." He pulled himself up to his full height and met and held Jerrik's gaze. "If I may say, King Jerrik, even a blind man can see she only has eyes for you."

Sven coughed loudly, twice, and glared meaningfully at Jerrik from beneath bushy brows.

Ignoring Sven, Jerrik turned back to Hamar. "Have you ever lain with my wife?"

"No, my king," he answered without hesitation. "Never."

"Of course, he would say that." Fenrir flicked his veined hand at Hamar. "Remember, I have proof and a witness."

The witness. Jerrik eyed Pavel, who dropped his gaze to his feet. Pavel, whom Jerrik and Alyssa had rescued from an abusive father who had taught him to lie, cheat, and steal. Pavel, whom his crew had taken in and treated like a little brother, and whom Alyssa had never been anything but kind to.

"Pavel?" Jerrik said.

Pavel toed the floor with his boot before finally looking up and meeting Jerrik's questioning gaze. "Aye, skeppare?"

Jerrik didn't correct him. Maybe it was better the lad thought of him as skeppare and not king right now. "Were you telling the truth last night, about finding Alyssa's comb in Hamar's bed?"

Pavel licked his lips and nodded his head.

"And you saw them together, the queen and Hamar in…" Jerrik couldn't bring himself to say it.

"Aye, skeppare," Pavel said, glancing down at his boots. "I did." He looked up at Jerrik. "I seen them together with me own eyes." Eyes that darted back and forth between Jerrik and Fenrir.

Jerrik nodded and said nothing, not trusting himself to speak. Alyssa stood and approached Pavel, standing no more than a few paces from Jerrik, who, the gods help him, breathed in and was instantly calmed by the sweet scent of winter lilies and summer rain.

"I'm not angry with you, Pavel," she said, catching the boy's full attention. "Truly." She smiled, and he took a shaky breath. "I know you were coerced into this. I have no proof. Yet I know." He opened his mouth as if to speak, glanced briefly in Fenrir's direction, and snapped it shut. "Do you wish to tell me about it?" He dropped his gaze and shook his head. "Very well then," she said, using the same soft, steady voice Jerrik had heard her use to calm a nervous horse or a spitting-mad cat. "You say you saw me and Hamar having sex." Pavel's head shot up and his face went beet red. "When, exactly, and where, and how many times?"

"Wha…what?" Pavel stuttered.

"When did you see us?" Alyssa asked him. "What day? What night? What time? How many times? How many places?"

"The boy cannot possibly be expected to remember all the details," Fenrir said dismissively from behind her.

"Why not?" she asked, her green eyes narrowing on Fenrir. "He witnesses his queen, the wife of a man he idolizes, cheating with another man, and he cannot remember where or when? Why did Pavel come to you with what he saw? Why not Jerrik? Did he report to you each time he supposedly saw us together? Or only—"

Fenrir shot up out of his seat. "He came to me the day he found your comb in Hamar's bed," he snapped. "Which was when he confessed having seen you two together all the other times." Fenrir turned to Jerrik. "He said the queen and Hamar had been meeting secretly almost from the first day you arrived here, that he didn't want to say anything, but that once you announced her pregnancy, he felt it his duty to expose her, in case the child was not yours, especially since she had already miscarried a child on the journey here, that may or may not have been yours."

Jerrik felt all the air go out of him.

Alyssa gasped. "How did you? Who told you?" She glared with green fire at Sven, Han, and Bors, all of whom looked as surprised as she did that Fenrir knew about it. She shook her head. "I did not, I was not…" She caught Jerrik's gaze and set her hands on her hips with a huff. "Whose child would it have been if not yours?" she demanded.

"Kostya's." Jerrik hurled the name at her with the cutting precision of a blade. A blade that hit its mark by the sudden look of surprise on her face.

"You think I slept with Kostya?"

"He told me you had. In the stables, the day you took me to see Storm, when you went to fetch Bones' belongings."

Her eyes widened with understanding, and then narrowed with betrayal. "You believed him?"

"I had no reason not to."

Lengthening her spine and squaring her shoulders, she stepped up to Jerrik and whispered so that only he could hear. "That was why you didn't consummate our marriage until we arrived here. Until after I had bled. You thought I might carry Kostya's babe."

"I thought it a possibility."

Alyssa chuffed. "And now you think I might be carrying Hamar's child," she said, speaking loud enough for all to hear.

"I think it a possibility."

She took a slow, deep breath in and let it out. She lifted her gaze and met his accusatory glare with her own. "Why do you believe everybody except me?"

"Why would Kostya lie?"

"Anger, spite, revenge."

"And Pavel?"

"Fear."

"Why would Fenrir lie?" he asked. "He is my uncle and counselor to the king. He has served me well, as he did my father, my brothers, your brother—"

"And where are they all now?" Alyssa cried. "They're dead. All of them. Dead and buried in an early grave."

"How dare you," Fenrir yelled.

"Are you accusing my husband?" Ermelinde screeched.

"You lying whore," Marianne screamed.

More angry shouts and denials and slurs erupted from Fenrir's side of the room, while whispers grew to a low insistent buzzing from Alyssa's as she and Jerrik stood staring at each other.

"Out," he commanded. He swept the room with a glare. Nobody had moved a muscle. "Out," he yelled. "Everybody out." He scowled at Alyssa. "Except for you."

The others shuffled out the door, mumbling and cursing among themselves and leaving him alone with Alyssa.

"Why didn't you ask me?" she said.

"Ask you what?"

"If I had slept with Kostya?"

He snorted. "In my experience, most women tend to lie about their lovers."

"I am not most women. I'm not your mother. I have never lied to you, nor would I ever." She leveled her gaze. "I have only ever lied for you."

"When?"

"Our wedding night. Our first night together here. On the *Sea Eagle*, letting the crew, and now your uncle and whoever else he chooses to tell, think that I miscarried on the ship."

He listened until she mentioned miscarriage and then he clamped his jaw and chewed on the inside of his cheek.

"You still don't believe me," she said, her voice, her expression full of bewilderment. "Why did you marry me if you thought I'd lain with Kostya?"

Jerrik rolled his shoulders. "I told myself it didn't matter. That as long as any child you bore was mine, it wouldn't matter."

"Except it did matter, didn't it?" she said. "It does matter."

"Yes," he admitted. "More than I ever thought it could or would."

Alyssa pressed her lips together and nodded. She closed her eyes, took a deep breath in, and opened her eyes as she released her breath, fixing her crystalline green gaze on him. "I love you," she said, "but I want a divorce."

"What?"

"I'm divorcing you."

"You can't."

"I can," she said. "I asked Dagny about it this morning. Your land, your customs, give me the right to divorce you."

He stood at his full height and glared down at her. "What about my child?"

"Oh," Alyssa snorted. "So now it's your child?" She stepped up and stood forehead to chin with him, glaring up at him. "This child is my child, and mine alone. I and my child will sail on the *Sea Eagle* as soon as she is ready, back to *my* home, where I will raise *my* child amongst my loving family and *my* child will never need to worry about being believed by its own father, or slandered, or murdered by your aunt and uncle."

CHAPTER 16

Deceit

"Thank you for sharing your chambers with me and Digger," Alyssa told Magna and Hulda as she shut the chest at the foot of the bed where she'd put her clothes and personal belongings.

"I would say it was our pleasure," Magna said, sitting on the other bed beside Hulda. "But..."

"But," Alyssa echoed. She plopped down on the floor and leaned her back against the bed as Digger climbed into her lap and licked her chin. The pup seemed to sense her unhappiness and had barely left her side since her "trial."

"Are you certain you want to divorce him?" Magna asked for the third time that morning. "I know he can be a hot-headed, judgmental idiot, but he loves you. I've never seen him so besotted with a woman before. Give him time," she pleaded. "He'll come to his senses."

"No." Alyssa shook her head and kissed Digger's nose. "If he truly loved me, he would believe me."

"You have to understand," Magna said. "His mother's lies, his father's jealousy, the circumstances of her death, her abandonment... He learned to mistrust love at an early age."

"I understand," Alyssa assured her. "I do." As humiliated and angry as she was, she loved him. She loved him so much it hurt. But she refused to live with him if he couldn't trust her and believe in her. In her love. Her mother's words, *Do not lose yourself,* came to her. "I can't. I won't be his wife if he thinks I'm a lying whore."

"Did he say that?" Hulda gasped.

"He may as well have. He believed Fenrir when that lying sack of yellow shit spewed his lies about me." Alyssa shook her head and swiped at the hot tears stinging her eyes. "How can he be so blind? How can the people here be so blind? Fenrir is a snake in the grass, slithering here and there spreading his venomous poison where it will do the most harm and serve him best. He, Ermelinde, and Marianne, all of those slinking and skulking yellow beards following him around like dullards, are nothing but a pit of vipers."

"Tell us how you truly feel," Magna said with an exaggerated arch of her brows, and Alyssa burst into laughter. It was either that or give in to more tears. She was entirely sick of tears.

Magna and Hulda joined in on the laughter, and even Digger picked up on the lightened mood, jumping up and down and barking, enjoying this new game. A loud knock on the door brought it to a halt.

"Yes?" Magna said. "Who is it?"

"It's Sven," his voice boomed. "Along with Bors and Han, come to offer our services to the queen."

Magna slid the bolt free and opened the door. "Come in." She stood aside as the men crowded into the room. Alyssa got up and sat in a chair by the table, offering Sven the other chair while Magna resumed her seat beside Hulda. "Sit." Magna waved Bors and Han toward the sofa.

Sven cleared his throat and faced Alyssa. "We, the three of us," he said, indicating Han and Bors, "have come to tell you we'll sail back to your home with you, lass. Make sure you get back to your people safely. You and the babe."

Alyssa sniffed back yet more tears. "Thank you," she said. "I can't tell you how much this means to me." At least they believed her. "Does Jerrik know?"

Sven nodded. "Aye, lass. He knows. He was all for it. If you truly are intent on going back?"

"I am."

"Then the skep, ah, king, wants you making it home safe and sound. He said as much."

"What did he say about the babe?"

Sven rumbled something low and unintelligible into his beard.

"I see," Alyssa said.

Jerrik cared enough about her to want to see her home safe, but he wouldn't claim the babe in her belly, despite naming it his when they'd argued earlier. She glanced at Han and Bors, good sailors, good fighters, good men whom she trusted with her life, and her babe's, and then she met Sven's waiting gaze.

While not old, and still as strong and formidable as an ox, the graybeard was not a young, spry man. He'd admitted to looking forward to an easier, more comfortable life when he'd agreed to stay and be Jerrik's right hand and counsel.

Jerrik needed him here.

"I accept Han's and Bors' offer to sail with me gladly." She gave the two men a quick smile of thanks and then turned back to Sven. "You must stay here and watch after Jerrik. Help him become the king he is meant to be."

Sven opened his mouth as if to argue, and then clamped it shut.

"He's going to need you, Sven, and you, Magna, to watch his back and protect him."

Nobody asked who he needed protection from.

"What did she say?" Jerrik had been pacing his chambers, waiting for Sven to return from speaking with Alyssa, and trying and failing not to notice how empty the rooms were without her presence. How empty he was.

"She thanked me for the offer," Sven said, "and said that she would gladly accept Han's and Bors' protection, but I was to stay here to watch after you. To help you become the king you are meant to be."

Jerrik didn't know what to say. He'd half expected her to fling the men's offer back at him, though he shouldn't have. Her emotions may run deep, but she wasn't a vindictive person. That she'd thought of him and his needs proved it.

"She also asked that we start moving her belongings down to the *Sea Eagle* today or tomorrow," Sven said.

Jerrik glanced at the shelf in the sitting room that held the trinkets he and Aaron had given Alyssa over the years of their travels, all of which she'd kept and treasured. His gaze settled on the little ivory statuette of a wild cat. The last gift Aaron had bought for his beloved sister. The gift that Jerrik had presented Alyssa with, along with the news of her adored brother's death, on the night he'd proposed marriage to her, ten and two years after she'd proposed to him.

He thought of her smile that first Winter's Eve, of her many smiles since, how those smiles could make him feel like a god.

He thought of their first kiss, so pure and passionate he'd stayed away from her for four years for fear of ending up exactly where he was now.

He thought of all their kisses since, of how making love with her was like diving into deep, warm waters one moment and soaring through the skies the next. Of how not only their bodies met and melded, but their hearts and souls as well.

He thought of how openly and freely she gave herself, all of herself, to him, holding back nothing of what she felt. He'd earned the bite of her anger. His, which had consumed him for the past twenty years and two days, had flamed out, leaving him a hollow, burnt-out husk.

He was the eagle in her vision, sitting alone in the dead tree, watching the tides take his love away.

"I've lost her," he told Sven.

"No," Sven growled. "You threw her away. You denied her, denounced her, and discarded her. Her love, her faith, her light. You broke her heart, lad. But you have not lost her, not yet."

"You believe her." It was more statement than question.

"I do. As you should."

He wanted to. He truly did. "What about all of the men who have spoken against her? Kostya? Pavel? Fenrir?"

"A jealous man jilted at the altar. A young lad easily controlled. An old man used to wielding his power through others who cannot control her. What about them? Their motives are clear." Sven tugged on his beard and eyed him. "What you really want to know is what about your father and mother," he said. "If you are fated to make their same mistakes."

He already had. He'd married for love, even if he hadn't admitted it at the time. He'd abandoned his wife, his love, in a jealous rage. Yet what Alyssa had told him was also true. He was not his father, and she was not his mother. Mistakes could be corrected.

If you knew the truth of a matter. He'd been a fool, not asking her about Kostya that day in the stables, letting his jealousy fester and grow. He only hoped and prayed that he still had time to right his wrongs.

"Let's go find Pavel," he told Sven.

After speaking with Pavel privately, Jerrik went searching for Bors, and found him outside of the thrall's longhouse, surrounded by a group of young boys listening raptly to one of his tales of seafaring adventure. This one of sailing into a port on the Great Sands River and being chased by a giant, slithering, scaled serpent that could run as fast on land as a man and swim even faster, snapping at his heels with teeth as big as a bear's claws.

One of the younger boys tugged on Jerrik's tunic. "Is it true, King Jerrik?" he asked. "Did you see this serpent too?"

"See it?" Jerrik said, crouching down to the boy's level. "The only reason it almost ate Bors and not me was because I can run faster, and the creature could see that Bors had more meat on him."

The boy's eyes grew even bigger in his imp's face as he looked from Jerrik to Bors and back again, bringing a well-needed smile to Jerrik's face.

"What's your name, lad?"

"Aaron."

The name stood Jerrik straight up. By the curly, blond-haired lad's height and the gap where his top two small teeth were missing, Jerrik guessed him to be about seven or eight years old. Which would have been around the time that the *Sea Eagle* had spent the summer in port here.

"Who are your mother and father, Aaron?"

"My mother is Rika and my father is Lang."

"Who do you look like? Do people say?"

Aaron puffed his bony little chest out. "I look like my older brothers, and we all look like my father did as a lad, so says my grandmother."

Jerrik let his breath out, not knowing if he was disappointed or relieved. "I knew an Aaron," he said. "We sailed together for many years. He was like a brother to me. He was the queen's brother."

"Queen Alyssa's?"

"Yes."

"I like Queen Alyssa," Aaron said. "She always says hello and smiles at me."

Jerrik swallowed past the fist-size stone in his throat. "I'm sure she likes you too." He ruffled the boy's mop of blond curls, jerking his hand away as the image of himself ruffling the gold blond curls of a boy with big blue eyes came unbidden to him.

He stepped back, clearing his throat. "I need to speak with Bors now," he said, waving over the hulking Northman who made full-grown men quail at the sight of him, yet always ended up with children and animals hanging onto him like remoras on a shark.

"Skeppare?" Bors ambled over to him.

"I want you to go down to the *Sea Eagle*, tell Lev I'll be coming down later to go over what needs to be done for Alyssa and River to sail with them."

"You really going to let her go?"

"I'm going to make preparations for her to go. Whether she does will be up to her."

"Aren't you even going to fight for her, skep?"

"I'm king now," he reminded Bors, and himself. "As king, I must do what is best for my people."

"How is letting Alyssa leave best for the people? The people love her."

Jerrik met Bors' contentious glare with his own. The big, burly, normally terse Northman had been charmed by Alyssa from the first. Of course, he would believe Alyssa over Fenrir, even with all the evidence that Fenrir had brought forth, even without having been present when Jerrik questioned Pavel earlier. Only Sven had. Only Sven knew what Jerrik had found out, though they'd be letting Bors in on it soon enough.

He, Han, and Magna would be essential to their plan.

Jerrik glanced around to make sure there was no one around to hear what he was about to tell Bors, and heard his name being called.

"King Jerrik, King Jerrik." It was Pavel, yelling at the top of his lungs as he came running toward them from the direction of the stables. "Sven needs you. It's Queen Alyssa."

"Where?" Jerrik yelled back, running to meet up with Pavel, who pointed to the royal longhouse.

"He carried her to your house."

"Carried her?" Jerrik turned for the house and Pavel cut across the grounds to meet up with him. "What happened?"

"Me and Sven, we came out of the stables, and Queen Alyssa was out in the paddock, brushing River one moment and keeling over the next."

That was the last thing Jerrik heard. He ran as fast as he ever had, even faster than when he and Bors had been chased by the scaled serpent. He pushed open the door to the longhouse and took the stairs two at a time, panting as he flung the door to his and Alyssa's chambers open, only to find it empty.

Fuck.

He ran out and over to Magna's and Hulda's chambers and tried to push the door open, only to find it bolted from the inside. He banged on the door. "It's Jerrik," he yelled. "Let me in."

"Hold your horses, lad," Sven's voice said from the other side of the closed door as Jerrik heard the bolt slide.

He pushed the door open, growling at Sven, who jumped aside to keep from being knocked over, and strode in past the others, straight for where Alyssa lay in a bed, propped up with pillows. "What happened?" he asked. "Are you all right? Pavel said you keeled over."

"I'm fine," she told him, though her eyes were red and puffy as if she'd been crying. "I became a little dizzy is all."

"Dizzy enough that Sven had to carry you all the way here and put you to bed?" He was angry and scared and not handling this well, yet at the moment, he didn't care.

"You know how protective he can be," she said with a shrug.

"I do. Especially when it comes to you."

"Careful, lad," Sven warned him. "You know Alyssa considers me like a favorite uncle, and I of her as a favorite niece. Nothing more, and certainly nothing less."

"So you keep telling me, old man."

"Old man." The still hale and hearty graybeard crossed arms that were as thick and corded as an anchor rope across his chest. "You care to find out if this old man can still whip your ass, lad?"

Jerrik stood to his full height and glared at Sven. "Are you threatening your king?"

Sven laughed, short and harsh. "No. I'm threatening you, you stubborn, blind, jealous fool." He threw his hands up and stomped out of the room, slamming the door behind him.

Jerrik turned his attention back to Alyssa and stepped closer to the bed. As tempted as he was to sit down beside her and fold her into his embrace, he took hold of the bed linens instead and pulled them down to her knees. "There is no bleeding this time?" he asked.

"No. I told you, I became a little dizzy. Probably because I haven't been sleeping or eating too well of late."

"The babe is still…is all right then?"

Alyssa laid her hand over her belly. "Yes."

He blew out a gust of breath. "Good," he said, more relieved than he could say. "I was afraid you had miscarried ag—"

"Again?" Alyssa snarled. "Were you about to say again?"

He stayed silent.

"Get out." Alyssa glared at him. She pointed at the door. "I said, get out."

"No. I'm your king—"

"You're my husband," she hissed at him. "My husband, damn you. Whom I have never lied to. Ever. Who still refuses to believe me."

"So," he said, jutting his jaw out. "I'm still your husband?"

"Yes," she snapped. She held his gaze, her own as green and deep and as fathomless as the sea. "You're still my husband, and will be until the day I step onto the *Sea Eagle* and sail away from here."

He whirled around, strode out, and slammed the door behind him, leaning his back against it and kicking it with his heel for good measure.

Sven, waiting for him in the hall, laid his hand on Jerrik's shoulder. "You did what you had to do, lad."

In his head, he knew that was true, but his heart was sore at having to hurt Alyssa again. "I may have done an unforgiveable thing," he said.

Sven squeezed his shoulder. "That woman will forgive you anything," he told him. "Once all is explained."

Jerrik wasn't so sure. He'd never seen Alyssa that angry before. Not even when she'd thrown her blade into the thief's chest with deadly precision. Which was probably what she'd like to do to him right now. He stood and squared his shoulders and blew out a determined breath. "I'm off to the *Sea Eagle* to make our plans."

Sven gave him a hearty slap on the back of his shoulder as they headed down the stairs. "I'll be wandering around here, complaining loudly about the queen's plan to sail and the king's stubborn refusal to believe anything she says. Along with a good oath or ten for the fates playing their tricks on your poor, cursed family."

A stabbing pain pierced Jerrik's chest at the memory of his mother lying in her bed, her eyes that used to smile at him as if he were her reason for living, fixed and staring into the abyss. "You don't think Alyssa would hurt herself or the babe, do you?"

"No," Sven said without hesitation. "Never. I think it's good that she's angry."

"Angry." Jerrik laughed, short and harsh. "The little lynx is spitting mad." Still, he understood what Sven was saying. His mother had been distraught the day she took her own life. Anger was better. Anger would warm Alyssa's blood and keep her alive. He clapped Sven on the shoulder. "It shouldn't be too hard to keep her angry with me. I only hope I can survive it."

"You'd better explain to Magna what you're up to soon then, lad," Sven said as they started down the stairs. "Before your sister takes matters into her own hands."

"You're right about that," Jerrik murmured.

Magna had taken being Alyssa's protector to heart, and her glare when Alyssa had kicked him out had been no less angry and a lot more aggressive. He had no desire to fight his sister over his wife's honor, or to pull her blade out of his back. "I'll tell her when I get back from the *Sea Eagle*. If I can pry her from Alyssa's side."

"What about Hulda and Dagny?" Sven asked.

Jerrik shook his head. "The fewer people who know the better. I'll have to make Magna swear not to tell Hulda as it is."

"That'll leave many angry tongues wagging on about you, King Jerrik."

They stopped at the door as the weeping strains of harp music wafted down from upstairs. "Good," Jerrik said as they both stepped outside. "I'm counting on it."

Alyssa woke to low voices and dimming daylight in an unfamiliar room without the solid, familiar warmth of Jerrik's body next to hers. She sat up, confused for a moment, and then she remembered. She remembered that he thought her unfaithful. He thought she had lain with Kostya and lied about being a virgin bride. That she'd miscarried Kostya's babe. He thought she'd slept with Hamar, that the babe she carried in her womb might be Hamar's and not his.

A low, keening moan rose from the empty, aching maw in her chest and up past the burning fist lodged in her throat. Tears stung and she started to rock back and forth, her hands holding her belly as if she could give some small comfort to the unborn babe whose father had denied them. Them.

Alyssa stopped rocking. She sniffed and swiped at her tears and took slow, deep breaths in and out, in and out. She smiled. Then she laughed. She was pregnant with twins. She knew this as surely as she knew that her son would have white-blond hair and sky-blue eyes, and her daughter would have hair of golden brown and eyes as green as spring grass.

She took comfort knowing if her children were destined to grow up without a father, they would at least have loving grandparents and five adoring uncles to help raise them to adulthood.

"Alyssa?" She lifted her gaze and met Magna's worried frown. "Are you all right?"

Alyssa nodded. "Yes." She shook her head. "No." She shrugged. "I don't know."

She smiled down at her hands cradling her belly and then back up at Magna and Hulda, both of them watching her intently. *Do not lose yourself.* "But I will be," she told them. "I will be."

Magna released her breath and dropped her shoulders from her ears. "Good," she said, plopping down on the bed. "I'm glad to hear you say it." She looked to Hulda, who nodded back at her. "I, we, think you need to show it as well."

"Show it?"

"Aye. Show Fenrir, Ermelinde, and Marianne that they haven't beaten you."

Alyssa let out a shaky breath. "But they have," she said. "I will leave here, I will leave Jerrik, and they will have won."

Magna grabbed her by the shoulders and turned Alyssa to face her. "You haven't left yet," she said. "You are still my stubborn jackass of a brother's wife and their queen. You've told me you're the daughter of warrior queens. Act like it."

Alyssa felt more like a wrung-out washrag than a warrior queen. Still, she understood what Magna meant. "What do you suggest?"

"Fight back."

"How?" Alyssa knew she sounded pathetic, she couldn't help it, her brain was as wrung out as her body.

"To begin with," Magna said, "take a bath, put on one of your best gowns, let Hulda fix your hair, and then go sup in the hall, sitting beside your husband, spine straight and head high."

Alyssa nodded, started to stand, and sat right back down. This was the time of day she and Jerrik usually bathed together. She closed her eyes against the image of him standing naked as he took her hand and helped her out of the tub. His broad shoulders, slim waist, long, well-muscled thighs gleaming wet and slick, and his cock, half hard from simply looking at her as she stepped out of the tub, wet and naked.

She pressed her lips tight, suppressing a groan as her body remembered the feel of his, pelvis to pelvis, skin to skin, his big, strong hands roaming the length of her backside, holding her close. She opened her eyes to Magna's peering gaze. "You'll need to check the bathing room for me," she said. "He usually bathes this time of day."

Magna stood. "I'll go check now." She tossed something to Hulda, who caught it and glanced down into her palms and smiled. "If I were you," she told Alyssa, "I'd be sure to wear that comb in my hair tonight."

Alyssa entered the feasting hall dressed in a gown of yellow gold worm weave, soft leather boots, and the lynx cloak Jerrik had gifted her on the eve of the Harvest Feast. Accompanied by Magna, she walked past the whispers and wagging tongues, head high and spine erect, up to the high table, where she took her seat, the queen's seat, beside Jerrik. He acknowledged her presence with a stiff nod, but didn't speak to her, nor she to him.

"Mead, please," she told the serving maid, who filled her cup as Jerrik watched her out of the corner of his eyes, his gaze fixing on her hair, which Hulda had trimmed into chin-length curls, and the hair comb that Fenrir and Pavel had presented as evidence of her infidelity keeping the curls under some semblance of control.

She glanced over at Fenrir and Ermelinde, who looked rather displeased at her appearance, lifted her cup to them and took a long drink of her mead, earning tight-lipped frowns from them and the quick twitch of Jerrik's lips.

Servants brought out trays of fish and meats, and greens and roots, most of which was likely left over from the wedding feast that hadn't happened only two days ago, though it felt like a lifetime.

Not really hungry, Alyssa made herself eat, as much for the twins' sake as to show her enemies that she was still alive and kicking. When she had eaten enough to prove her point, she pushed her plate aside and sipped her second cup of mead.

"I talked with Lev today," Jerrik said, the first he'd spoken to her since she'd sat down beside him. She gave a slight tilt of her head, the only indication that she was listening. "He said the pen for River would be complete three days from now, and that you could send Han and Bors down with your chests anytime you were packed and ready. They plan on sailing in six days' time, on Freya's day next."

She said nothing.

"I assume you'll be taking Digger with you."

"Of course."

"You have my leave to take anything you brought here back with you."

She dipped her head.

"Including the worm weave gowns off Ermelinde's and Marianne's backs."

Alyssa's lips twitched.

"Let me know when you want to pack up your things and I'll be sure to be absent from our...my chambers."

She closed her eyes and pressed her lips tight.

"Since my presence is so distasteful to you."

She glared at him. "You are the one who exiled me from your presence," she hissed. "Don't try to turn this on me."

"It is on you," he said. "You were the one who broke our marriage vows. Not I."

"I. Did. Not."

Jerrik grinned.

"You think this is funny?" she snarled. "You enjoy humiliating me in public like this?" she growled low and gnashed her teeth. "I never thought you a cruel man until now."

Jerrik sat back, his expression unreadable. "I never thought Aaron a liar before," he said.

Alyssa bristled. It was one thing to call her a liar, but now he was calling Aaron one too? Aaron, his best friend, who'd been more a brother to Jerrik than his blood brothers. Aaron, who had sacrificed his life for Jerrik's. "Because he was not," she said.

"He told me that I could trust you."

Alyssa didn't know whether to scream, cry, or slap her husband in the face.

"Thank the gods my brother is already dead. It would've killed him to hear you say that, to see what you've become." She stood and looked down at him. "You are right in one thing, King Jerrik," she said coldly. "I do find your presence distasteful."

"He's not who I thought he was," Alyssa told Magna as Hulda removed the lynx throw from her shoulders. "How could I have been so wrong about him?" she asked, looking from one woman to the other as if they knew the answer. "You spoke to him this afternoon," she said to Magna, who had saved her from running into Jerrik in the bath chamber. "How was he?"

"He was much the same as he has been," Magna said. "Hurt, angry, and trying to figure things out."

"*He's* hurt and angry?" Alyssa harumphed.

"Here, slide this sleeve down," Hulda told her, helping pull the gown down to Alyssa's waist and over her hips.

"I've known him for ten and two years," Alyssa said as she stepped out of the gown. "While it's true the total number of days that we've spent together is only a matter of four or five moons, the time we did spend together was wonderful." She smiled sadly, remembering. "We walked, we talked, we played, we sang. He told me of his adventures in faraway lands and I told him of my home and family, which he always claimed he admired. He taught me how to sail, and I taught him how to ride, and we taught each other how to…"

"Arms up," Hulda said, sliding a night shift down over Alyssa's raised arms.

"I've known him from boy to man, and he's known me from girl to woman. He made me a woman," Alyssa said, her cheeks and other body parts flushing with tactile memory. "He told me that no other woman has ever compared to me. That while I wasn't his first, I'd be his last, and he was content with that."

"Boots," Hulda said, and Alyssa lifted first one foot and then the other as Hulda pulled her soft kidskin boots off.

"He told me he loved me," Alyssa said, the words wringing her dry. She plopped down on the side of the bed and asked the one question she had no answer to. "So why?" She sought Magna's steady gaze. "Why did he turn on me? I have loved him, and only him, since I was eight years old. He's the only man I have ever lain with. Why won't he believe me?"

"I wish I could tell you," Magna said with a slow shake of her head.

"No one can," Alyssa said, "except Jerrik."

"So, ask him," Hulda said as she was hanging Alyssa's gown to air out.

"No," Magna said quickly. "Not yet. I think it would be better for both of you to keep your distance for another day or two, wait until your tempers have cooled."

"My temper is the only thing keeping me warm right now," Alyssa said with a heavy sigh. She plucked at the hem of her linen night shift, thinking of the sheer shift of worm weave that Solveig had sewn for her and Jerrik's wedding night. "Without it, my blood would grow cold and sluggish and my heart would turn to stone and sink into the abyss that is my soul."

She felt more than saw Magna and Hulda exchange a look between them as she lay on the bed, wanting nothing more than to curl up in Jerrik's strong arms and rest her head on his broad chest, listening to the steady beat of his heart as he whispered words of love into her hair. But Jerrik wasn't there. He wasn't with her. Nor would he ever be again.

She'd lost him.

She closed her eyes against the pain and tucked her knees to her chest, her mind even more weary than her body. A weight settled by her feet, and she opened her eyes to Magna's worried gaze.

"You wouldn't..." Magna couldn't bring herself to say what worried her.

Alyssa knew what it was. Jerrik wasn't the only person haunted by the ghost of his mother. The whole cursed family was. "Don't fear for my life, sister," Alyssa said with a melancholy smile. She cradled her still flat belly. "I would never do anything to harm my childre—child."

They would be the only thing she'd have left of Jerrik, other than her memories.

CHAPTER 17

The Ridge

It had taken all of Jerrik's will to stop from jumping up and chasing after Alyssa to apologize for being cruel. It may have been necessary, and best for all in the long run, but the hurt in her eyes had pierced the armor of pain and distrust Jerrik had worn with stubborn determination for too long. The little lynx had gotten so deep under his skin he couldn't hurt her without hurting himself. He'd hurt her badly enough for her to publicly denounce him, something he never thought she'd do. He'd been so sure and confident of her love for so long, he'd never considered her leaving him by choice.

Of course, she hadn't been given a choice. She'd been driven to her decision by deceit and jealousy. The jealousy had been all Jerrik's, the deceit… Jerrik emptied his second cup of beer and eyed Fenrir, who sat at the end of the table, sipping wine and speaking with his son Rigil and another yellow beard named Brandr, kaptein of Fenrir's personal guard.

"More beer." Jerrik slammed his empty cup down on the table, and a serving maid came scurrying over with a full pitcher and filled his cup. "Leave the pitcher," he said when she started to carry it away. "In fact, bring two more."

He waved Sven, Bors, and Han over as most of the people, having finished their supper, were leaving the hall. "Bring your cups with you," he told them. "You too, Pavel," he told the lad, who sat at the far end of the men's table, where he'd eaten alone.

Jerrik pushed back from the table and stretched his legs as they chose seats around him. "Make yourselves comfortable." He lifted his cup. "I plan on drinking until I can neither see nor piss straight tonight."

"Well then." Bors grabbed the pitcher and filled his cup and the others' as well. "To who, or what, are we drinking?" he said loudly as the serving maid set down two more pitchers. "Shall we drink to women?" He lifted his cup to the blushing maid. "The fairer sex by far."

"'Tis true, they are fairer in looks by far," Jerrik agreed as a pair of sea-green cat eyes framed with thick, sooty lashes smiled as warm and bright as sunlight on water at him one moment, only to narrow into slits of green ice the next. "Ruffle their fur the wrong way, and they'll use that fairness against you. They'll smile and simper and swear their everlasting love and loyalty one day and then stab you in the back clear through to your heart the next."

"Careful, lad," Sven cautioned. "You sound like a man who has tasted the sweetest of honey wine and declared it soured grapes."

Jerrik slammed his sloshing cup down. "Why shouldn't I? I was promised the sweetest and purest of maids and given a brazen hussy who would cuckold me, a king, with a stable hand's child." He drained his cup with one long, angry swallow, wiped his mouth with his sleeve, and pushed his cup over to Bors to be refilled. "At least I found out about her treachery before I claimed the bastard as mine, thanks to Pavel here." He grabbed the cup that Bors shoved over to him and took another swig. "Drink up, lad," he told Pavel. "You've earned it."

"Jes' repaying the kindness you did me, skeppare," Pavel said, lifting his cup to Jerrik before taking a drink. "Doing my duty to my king."

"What of your duty to your queen?" Bors demanded. "What of the kindnesses she's shown you?"

Pavel paled under the big Northman's glower.

"Leave him alone," Han said. "Boy only do what he had to. Not all our eyes blinded by her beauty like you."

"She is a beauty, no doubt about that," Bors said, earning a glare from Jerrik. "Maybe I'll stay in her homeland after we sail her back there, offer to marry her." He laughed at Jerrik's murderous glare and shrugged. "I'd be willing to raise another man's child if it meant getting to lie with—"

"Enough." Jerrik slammed his fist down on the table, glaring daggers at Bors, who shrugged and hid his smile in his cup as he gave Fenrir and his rapt cohorts a sidelong glance.

"Speaking of the queen," Sven said to Jerrik, deftly steering the conversation to a different tack. "She's told me she wishes to visit her brother's grave one last time before she sails on the *Sea Eagle*."

"Fine," Jerrik said.

"With you, and only you."

Jerrik took a long, slow drink of his beer, aware of seven pairs of eyes and ears watching him and listening for his answer, some openly, others covertly. He made a show of setting his cup down with deliberation and then rolling his shoulders back and growling through gritted teeth. "Tell my wife I will ride to the ridge with her the day after tomorrow. The two of us. Alone."

Jerrik entered the feasting hall as the servants were setting out trays of fresh baked ryes and cheeses, and took his seat beside Alyssa, who refused to acknowledge his presence. They hadn't spoken since supper the night before, or even seen each other, as Jerrik had spent the day on the *Sea Eagle*, stowing Alyssa's chests in the hold and helping ready the pen on the deck for River. The servants set platters of roasted goat on the table, and Jerrik smiled as Alyssa's belly rumbled loud enough for him to hear.

"I'm glad to see your appetite for blood hasn't lessened," he teased.

"Are you?" she answered archly.

"Contrary to what you might think, I don't wish for any harm to come to you or the child."

"*The* child?" she said, her brows arching into her hairline. "How considerate of you."

"I'm a considerate man."

Alyssa chuffed and said nothing.

"Thank you for agreeing to ride with me tomorrow," he said softly, and then added much more loudly, "We'll leave for the ridge tomorrow morn after we break our fast. Borgny will pack us a midday meal."

"Fine."

"Why is it when you women say fine, you mean anything but?"

Alyssa held her knife up, glaring daggers at Jerrik. "Why are you trying to goad me into a fight?"

"Am I?" He eyed the knife now pointing at him.

She narrowed her eyes and shook her head. "Who are you?" she asked him.

Jerrik clamped his jaw and shook his head, unable to tell her. Yet.

"King Jerrik," Fenrir said loudly from the other end of the table. "Did you find the ceremonial blade that went missing?"

Jerrik pressed his lips into a grim smile. "No," he told his uncle. "I did not."

"Perhaps you misplaced it?"

"No. I'm sure it was in my chambers." He turned to Alyssa. "You didn't pack it up with your belongings, did you?"

"What? No. I may be a cuckolding, lying harlot, my lord and husband, but I am no thief." She smiled so sweetly at him that honey could have dripped off her lips. Honey that turned to venom as she glared down the table at Fenrir. "You may check my chests on board the *Sea Eagle*, if you don't believe me."

Jerrik swallowed the laugh that came unbidden, gritting his teeth and chuffing instead. This was a side to Alyssa that he'd only seen glimpses of before. The sweet, adoring, bright-eyed girl he'd married hadn't been named the little lynx by her family for nothing.

Normally kind and easygoing, his sassy she-cat was not afraid to show her claws when threatened, or to bite if necessary, as it had been when she'd killed the brigand with her blade to defend Jerrik. He liked this side of her. Though not the avalanche of events that had caused her to show it.

"As I'll still be down on the *Sea Eagle* tomorrow," Sven said, "I'll be happy to inspect the queen's belongings." He gave Fenrir's end of the table an affable grin. "Bors, Han, and I'll be driving a wagon with some barrels of wine and beer down to the ship this evening soon as we can get Borgny to pack us some leftovers for the night's festivities."

"Are all three of you planning to stay the night on board then?" Jerrik asked.

"Aye, skep, ah, King Jerrik," Sven answered. "We figured that seeing as how you'll not be needing us tomorrow."

"And since we plan on toasting the gods and goddesses of the skies and the seas until we can't hold our cups up tonight," Bors added, "it made more sense to sleep over on her." To which Han lifted his cup and clanked it against Bors'.

"It's a good thing you're taking two barrels each of beer and wine then," Jerrik said, "else there'd be none left for the crew's journey back to Alyssa's home." He lifted his cup to her. "May the winds fill your sails and the tides ever flow in your favor," he said, and saw her go pale, remembering, too late, her vision in the scrying bowl.

"If you will excuse me, King Jerrik," she said, pushing her chair back and standing, her hands visibly shaking. "I think I'll retire for the night."

"Magna," he called, watching Alyssa's head lift and her spine lengthen as she left the table. "Have Borgny fill a tray and take it to Alyssa. She didn't eat much and may get hungry later."

"Of course, brother." She started for the kitchens and then stopped. "You won't mind if I spend the day tomorrow visiting a friend to the west, since you and the queen will have no need of me?"

"Go." Jerrik waved her on. "Enjoy your visit. I don't expect us to be back from the ridge until sundown."

"Wait, mistress," Hulda told Alyssa as she was about to pull her long outer tunic on over her undertunic. "Put this on first," she instructed, holding up a vest of lacquered leather.

"Why?"

"It never hurts to be too careful." Hulda held the vest out to Alyssa. "You won't have any guards riding with you. I'd feel safer knowing you wore this."

"In case Jerrik decides cutting my hair wasn't punishment enough for something I didn't do?" Alyssa quipped as much to herself as to Hulda.

"Oh no." Hulda shook her head as Alyssa pushed her hands through the vest's arm holes. "I don't think King Jerrik would do anything to harm you."

"Any more than he already has, you mean," Alyssa grumbled as Hulda stepped behind her.

"Which I am sure he regrets," Hulda, ever the optimist despite all she'd been through, said, pulling the laces on the vest tight.

Alyssa ran a hand through her shorn hair, the sight of which seemed to shock Jerrik whenever he looked at her these past few days. She was no vainer than the average woman, but she knew her hair had been one of her best features. People had told her so throughout her life, including Jerrik, who had called it her mane of burnt honey.

He'd often insisted on unbinding it for her, admiring the thick wave of curls cascading down her back as he would gently run his fingers through it, or revel in the feel of it as Alyssa trailed it over his bare chest and belly, and other body parts, in bed.

"Magna left early," she said, changing the subject from what'd brought heat to her cheeks and elsewhere. "Is the journey to her friend's place a long one?"

"Long enough," Hulda said, tying off the laces. She stepped back and eyed Alyssa. "It's a good fit," she said with a pleased nod, and then picked up a pair of leather wrist guards from the tables. "Hold your arms out, mistress."

Alyssa quirked her brows and obeyed her maidservant, who quickly laced up the guards, and then helped Alyssa don her linen outer tunic and woolen apron.

"There," Hulda said. "How does that feel?"

"A little confining," Alyssa said, swinging her arms and twisting from side to side. "Yet not uncomfortable."

Hulda handed her the lynx throw. "The weather can change quickly up there."

"Don't I know it," Alyssa said as she draped the throw over her shoulders, though she was thinking of how a pair of clear, sky-blue eyes could fill with storm clouds rather than the mountains outside.

Having already partaken of some bread and mead upon rising from her bed, she decided there was no reason for her to go to the feasting hall where Jerrik would be breaking his fast.

She sent Hulda to tell him that she'd meet him at the stables, and went downstairs, where she handed Digger over to Anders and Davin for the day and had Ranveig wrap up a chunk of cheese and a thick slice of bread for the ride up to the ridge, along with an apple each for River and Storm.

She hadn't been to the stables since the day after what should have been her wedding night, and would have been, if not for that lying snake, Fenrir, and Pavel. She still didn't know why Pavel had lied about her and Hamar, and had only asked him the one time at her "trial." His lie wasn't the crux of her problem. Jerrik not believing her was. She stepped into the dim light of the stables and called out, "Anyone here?"

Pavel came out of Storm's stall, leading the stallion to a tie-off post. "Mistress?"

"Are you the only one here?"

"Aye, mistress, the other hands is breaking their fasts. It's jes' me to saddle Storm and River."

"Where is Hamar?"

"Gone," a deep, familiar voice said from behind her.

She whirled around and found herself standing face-to-face with Jerrik. "What do you mean, gone?"

"He chose to leave," Jerrik said, his piercing blue eyes watching hers. "To go live and work on his cousin's farm to the east of here."

Alyssa nodded and ran a hand though her shorn hair. "Good for Hamar," she said. "It's hard to live in a place where people choose to believe the worst of you."

After they saddled up, Jerrik took the lead on Storm and Alyssa followed on River, keeping the mare far enough behind Storm she wouldn't have to speak to Jerrik. She ignored him when he looked over his shoulder, which became more and more frequent as they climbed the winding road up the mountain's side. What she couldn't ignore was the short sword sheathed at Jerrik's waist along with his usual dagger, and the long sword strapped across his back.

When they came to a straighter, wider section of the path about halfway up, Jerrik pulled Storm to a stop and waved impatiently at Alyssa. "I want to talk with you."

Alyssa nudged River forward, glaring at Jerrik. "What about?"

"I want to ask you to wait until summer to sail back to your family."

"Why?"

"It'll be much less dangerous to sail come the summer, and safer to sail with a babe than pregnant."

"You don't have to pretend to be worried about me sailing pregnant anymore," she said. "Or have you forgotten I know the real reason you didn't consummate our marriage until we reached your home?"

"I haven't forgotten, nor should you forget I was and am a king. I had to be sure that any child you carried was mine and not Kostya's. My worries about you sailing pregnant weren't completely false. As it turned out, pregnant or not, you did almost bleed to death. Which is why I wish you would wait until after the babe is born to sail back."

"Pregnant or not?" The bastard. He still believed Kostya. He still believed she might've been pregnant with Kostya's child.

"What matters is that you are pregnant now," he said. "I'd feel better knowing you weren't sailing pregnant, especially with winter coming."

"You'd feel better if I stayed here until the babe is born so you can see if he has your blond hair and blue eyes or Hamar's brown."

"There is that."

Alyssa went cold all over, his words hitting her with the sleeting, stinging force of a winter storm. "Did you hear that, my love?" she said, her voice cracking.

"Hear what?" He cocked his head, listening to the chill wind soughing through the trees.

Alyssa placed her hand over the gaping hole in her chest. "This," she said. "The sound of my heart breaking."

"Alyssa, wait." Jerrik sent Storm charging after Alyssa, who had sent River into a reckless gallop up the mountain road that was quickly becoming a narrow, winding path. "Alyssa," he yelled as he caught the flick of River's tail disappear around a sharp corner. "Alyssa, slow down. It's not safe."

As big and strong as Storm was, the stallion was barely keeping pace with the slighter, fleeter mare, and Alyssa was a much better rider than Jerrik was. He urged Storm on, afraid of losing sight of them, even more afraid of what they were riding into blind. He'd pushed Alyssa too far, and now she was running away from him into almost certain danger.

He had broken her heart.

"What did you think was going to happen, you callous idiot," he cursed himself as he chased after her. "Even a heart as open and giving as hers can only take so much before it breaks." As his father had broken his mother's. And she, his. "Fuck."

Jerrik leaned forward in the saddle, straining his ears for any sounds of men or other horses over the pounding of his heart and Storm's chugging breath as he struggled to keep the stallion within sight of River's flying hooves, not missing the tracks of numerous hoof prints leading up, and not a single one down, the mountain.

Fuck, fuck, fuck, fuck, fuck.

When Jerrik made the ridge, there was nobody there except Alyssa, who had already dismounted and was tying River to a bush. She looked up as he trotted Storm over and then she turned her back on him and walked to the edge of the cliff as he quickly tied off Storm next to River.

"That was a cursed foolish thing to do," he rumbled as he strode to her, and then stopped dead in his tracks at her expression as she turned to face him. "Alyssa?"

"Is this not what you wanted?" she said, standing at the precipice. "To be rid of me once and for all?"

"No," he exhaled, his legs as shaky as his breath. "No, by the gods, never."

She tilted her head and smiled, sad and bittersweet. "Don't worry, husband," she said, stepping away from the cliff's edge. "You may have broken my heart, but you haven't broken me. I haven't lost me."

"Good," Jerrik said. "I'm relieved to hear it." More than he could say. "I will need my bloodthirsty little lynx by my side this day."

She tilted her head. "Why will you need her?"

"I will tell you why, little lynx," he said. "First, you must come closer." She took one hesitant step toward him. "Closer still," he coaxed. "Close enough that I may whisper into your ear."

She eyed him from head to toe, her gaze taking in the long sword at his back, the short sword at his waist, the leather guards on his wrists, and the vest of lacquered leather beneath his short cloak.

"Trust me, Lyssa," he said, using her favorite pet name.

She snorted and took a step back. "As you trusted me?"

"No." He shook his head, met and then held her gaze. "As I should've trusted you." He held his hand out to her, willing her to step to him and not away. "Please."

She stepped forward and put her hand in his and Jerrik clasped his fingers around hers and pulled her to him. "Thank you, Lyssa." He felt the edge of the leather guard on her wrist and splayed his other hand across her back. "Good," he said. "You're wearing the wrist guards and vest."

"What are we doing here, Jerrik?" she asked. "Why are you armed and both of us wearing armor?"

He stared into eyes as wide and wary as a cat's being coaxed into a snare, but this snare wasn't for her. "We've set a trap," he said softly. "Sven, Han, Bors, Magna, and I. They wait in hiding to spring it."

"For who?" she whispered, her eyes flicking around and behind him. "Or what?"

"For the yellow-bearded snakes in the grass doing my uncle's dirty work."

Her eyes lit and her mouth opened in a delectable *oh* before she clamped it shut.

Jerrik leaned in close, whispering in her ear, "Now embrace me, Alyssa. Embrace me like you still love me."

"I do still love you." Alyssa sighed, her whispered words his absolution. "I always have and I always will."

He wrapped his arms around her and pulled her to him. "Ahh, Lyssa." He ran a hand back through her short curls, his eyes searching hers. "I've missed you, wife."

She shook her head, her confusion evident. "Jerrik, I—"

He stilled and cocked his head. "Shhh," he whispered. He touched his forehead to hers. "Do you hear it? The sound of boot-fall in the leaves behind us?"

She listened intently and nodded her forehead against his. "I hear it."

Jerrik lowered his mouth to her neck. "Do you see anything?" he asked.

Alyssa peered over his shoulder. "No. Wait. Shadows moving in the tree line."

"How many?"

He nuzzled her neck while Alyssa counted. "One, two, three. I cannot see." He lifted his head and nuzzled the other side of her neck. "Four, five, maybe six. I can't be sure."

"Even odds then," he said, lifting his head and giving her a smacking kiss on the lips. He turned them around so that he was facing the tree line, and unclasped her lynx throw, letting it drop to the ground. "Do you want my waist blade or short sword?"

"Short sword," she said. "I have my own waist blade."

Jerrik flashed her a fierce grin. "There's my little lynx," he said, slowly pulling the sword from its sheath and handing it to her between their bellies. Then he pushed her behind him and pulled his longsword free as six yellow beards came running at them with swords raised high, their shouts of victory cut short as Han and Bors dropped down from the ancient oak, and Sven and Magna came out from the tree lines on each side, blocking an easy escape.

"I give you a choice," Jerrik yelled as the yellow beards stopped their rush and repositioned into a defensive circle. He eyed Brandr, kaptein of Fenrir's ersatz guard. "Surrender to your king now, or die."

"You are not my king," Brandr spat back. "Nor any of ours here."

Jerrik gave his broadsword a one-handed swing. "Does Brandr speak for all of you?"

"I do," Brandr answered with a general grumbling and nodding of yellow heads. He glanced around at the men circling them, at Alyssa and Magna, and grinned. "We like our odds."

"You've never seen my sister or my wife fight then," Jerrik told him. "They are equal to your yellow maggots, if not better."

Brandr charged like an enraged bull, blowing and bellowing and counting on his size and bulk to overtake Jerrik. "Move," Jerrik yelled to Alyssa, who leapt out of the bull's path as Jerrik sidestepped his charge. He could've easily sliced Brandr's hamstring as he blundered past, but Jerrik wanted him alive for questioning. He slashed the back of the man's vest open from shoulder to shoulder and planted his feet, waiting for the bellowing bull to round on him.

"Alyssa?" he yelled, unable to see her without taking his eyes off Brandr. "You all right?"

"I'm fine," she yelled back as Brandr turned.

Jerrik tightened his grip on his long sword as Brandr raised his sword high and charged again. He slashed his sword down sideways, aiming for Jerrik's neck, and Jerrik blocked the worst of the blow with the flat of his sword, taking the brunt of it on the shoulder pad of his vest.

He pushed up with his sword, hard and fast, sending Brandr stumbling backward, barely managing to hold his sword up against the blows Jerrik rained down on him. The searing image of betrayal on Alyssa's face, her pleas of innocence against Fenrir's false charges, the image of her under Brandr's blade urged Jerrik on with vengeance and fury until at last Brandr dropped to his knees. Panting, Jerrik held the tip of his sword to Brandr's throat. "Do you yield?"

Sucking in great gasps of air, Brandr nodded and laid his sword down at Jerrik's feet. "I yield," he said as sweat poured down his face.

Keeping his sword at Brandr's throat, Jerrik pinned the man's sword under his boot and turned to look for Alyssa. She was under the oak, engaged with a yellow beard who stood a head taller and four stone heavier than her, feinting with her waist blade and jabbing with her short sword as the man swung his long sword at her, only to slice through air. "Alyssa?"

"He's the one bleeding, not me," she shouted back. "A slug is no match for a lynx."

Jerrik didn't dare leave Brandr alone, and the others were all still fighting their opponents one on one, so he knocked Brandr up the side of his head with the hilt of his sword, grinning at the satisfying thunk as metal hit skull and Brandr sank to the ground unconscious.

Jerrik turned to help Alyssa and hadn't taken two steps toward her when the yellow beard she was fighting took his sword in both hands and thrust it at her. Jerrik flew for them, her name a voiceless scream in his throat as she leapt to the side of the slug's grunting thrust and twisted midair, coming down with the short sword in both hands and cutting into the soft, exposed inside of the man's elbow. The man screamed, dropped his sword, and tried to slow the blood spurting from his severed artery with his other hand.

Alyssa staggered back, her eyes wide and wild, and her face almost as ashen as the yellow beard's who was bleeding out at her feet. Jerrik stabbed the man clean through his heart, finishing him.

"He would've killed you, Alyssa," Jerrik said, tucking her into his shoulder as he kicked the dead man's sword away. "You had no choice."

She looked up at Jerrik and nodded. "I know."

She started to shake, and he held her close as he took in the scene around them. Han was wiping his blades clean on a dead yellow beard with a knife in one eye and a slit throat, while Sven was pulling his sword out of another's belly. Bors spat down on a headless yellow beard's body at his feet, and Magna stood over another yellow beard who lay legless and lifeless in a pool of blood.

"Everybody all right?" Jerrik called out, grinning at their varied and profane answers, assuring him that any scratches they had received from the yellow-bearded bastards were of no concern. He started to walk Alyssa over to a fallen log, but she barely made it two steps before stumbling. He scooped her up in his arms.

"I can walk," she protested weakly, but she wrapped her arms around his neck.

"You're shaking like a leaf in the wind," he shushed her as he tucked her into his chest. "And weigh as little. I fear if didn't carry you, you would be blown away." She burrowed her nose into his shoulder and Jerrik slowed his steps, loath to let go once they reached the log, fearful she truly might blow, or run away.

"Magna," he called over his shoulder as he set Alyssa down on the log. "Fetch Alyssa's fur and come sit with her while I have a word with Brandr."

Jerrik laid the lynx throw over Alyssa's shoulders and looked from her pale face to Magna's and back again. "Han," he called over his shoulder, "bring one of the waterskins and a wineskin as well."

When Han returned with the skins, Jerrik handed the one with wine to Alyssa. "Take a good drink or three, both of you," he told her and Magna. "It'll help to settle the shakes."

He watched them, making sure they each took several long pulls from the skin before he took a drink himself, and then he stood and walked over to Brandr, uncorked the waterskin, and trickled the water over Brandr's face until the man woke up coughing and sputtering, his gaze wandering and unfocused.

Jerrik kicked his boot. "Brandr," he said, and again, more loudly, "Brandr."

The yellow beard leaned his head back and stared up at Jerrik for a long moment. "Ah, fuck."

"Ah fuck is right," Jerrik said, angry and deadly serious. "Your men are all slain and you're my prisoner. Unless you wish to make your wife a widow and your children orphans, you will answer me truthfully. Do you understand what I'm telling you?"

Brandr nodded and lifted a hand to the side of his head where a red knot was already forming.

"Where are your horses?" Jerrik said. "How many men are with them?" He kicked Brandr's boot when the man didn't answer. "Where are your horses," he repeated, "and how many men are with them?"

"In a copsh of firs 'bout five hunred paces shtraight up from here," Brandr answered, his words slurring. "Only Rigil's with them."

"Same as his father, afraid to do his own killing," Jerrik spat. "Does he have the ceremonial dagger?"

Out of the corner of his eye, Jerrik saw Alyssa sit up straighter. "Aye," Brandr said, grabbing his head in his hands. "Rigil's hash it."

Jerrik and his men exchanged glances. "Bors, Han, you know what to do," he said, and then added over his shoulder as they headed off. "Alive if you can."

"Aye, skep."

Jerrik glanced over at Alyssa and Magna, both of whom had been listening intently to everything being said, before turning his attention back to Brandr. "What were your orders?"

"Wha?"

"How were you supposed to kill us, Alyssa and me?"

"With blades," Brandr said. "Make it look like you killed her an' then yerself."

"After you killed us, what then?"

Brandr rubbed the back of his neck, circled his head, and made a motion toward the waterskin. Jerrik handed him the skin and waited while Brandr took a drink, swished the water around his mouth, and then spit out the blood-tinged water.

"What were you supposed to do with us after you killed us?" Jerrik repeated.

Brandr pressed his fingers against the side of his jaw and opened and closed his mouth, twice. Jerrik kicked Brandr's boot hard enough to jerk the man's leg to the side. "Do not try my patience, yellow beard. I can get the same information from Rigil."

Brandr lifted his head and peered up through swelling lids at Jerrik. "We were to ride down after setting up your bodies with the bloodied dagger," he said. "Then ride back up with Fenrir and Rigil this afternoon after Fenrir worried loudly and publicly about the two of you coming up here alone, what with you and your parents' history."

"I see," Jerrik said.

Alyssa rose from the log and walked over to stand beside Jerrik. She linked her arm with his. "Unfortunately for you and your master," she told Brandr, "you have both sorely misjudged my husband and me."

CHAPTER 18

The Trial

They rode down the mountain single file and silent. Sven took point with Jerrik and Alyssa behind him. Behind them, Magna led a bound and gagged Rigil on his horse, and Han led Brandr on his. Bors took up the rear, the line of five horses carrying the bodies of the five slain yellow beards tied to his mount.

It was high noon when they reached where the path widened into a road, the place where Alyssa and Jerrik had argued this morning over when, not if, she would sail away from him, pregnant with a child he still wouldn't claim as his.

She glanced back at Rigil and Brandr, recalling Brandr's words about Jerrik's parents, about how Fenrir had planned to use their history to explain their son going mad and killing his cheating wife and then himself. She urged River forward until they were even with Storm and Jerrik. "How did you know?" she asked. "How did you know what Fenrir was planning?"

"Do you remember what you said to me the day you called Fenrir and Ermelinde to our longhouse, demanding a public trial?"

"I said many things."

"Yes," he said with a wry grin, "you did. But do you remember what you said after I defended Fenrir's motives for accusing you of being unfaithful to me? After I claimed he had only ever served my father and brothers for the good of the kingdom?"

Alyssa remembered. The words, the accusation, had flown out of her mouth without conscious thought, though she had thought of them often since. "I asked you where they all were now, your father and brothers and Aaron."

"Then you answered your own question. Dead, you said. They were all dead. Dead and buried in early graves."

"I had no idea you gave what I said any credence."

He gave her the full slant of his piercing gaze. "I've always given what you say credence, Alyssa."

She eyed him beneath arched brows. He may have always given her words credence, but he hadn't always believed them. The fact that they were in this mess proved it.

"After I had time to cool off and think about what you'd said," he continued when she said nothing, "I talked to Pavel again, privately."

"And?"

"He confessed all. He told me that Fenrir had threatened to claim he'd stolen jewelry from Ermelinde, and that I would have no choice except to punish him by taking away his free status and declaring him a thrall, unless he poisoned Digger."

Alyssa's belly flipped. "Pavel poisoned Digger?"

Jerrik nodded. "I think he felt worse about that than the rest of it."

"The rest?"

"He admitted to stealing your hair comb and saying he found it in the stables, as well as lying about witnessing you and Hamar together."

"You believed him?"

"Why wouldn't I?"

"Why wouldn't you believe me?"

"I did believe you. That's why I questioned Pavel."

Alyssa shook her head and turned away from Jerrik, who had completely misunderstood her. She glanced ahead at Sven, and swore his ears were pinned back like a horse's, trying to hear what she and Jerrik were saying.

She looked over her shoulder at Magna, who had edged her horse closer to them, and at Rigil, who glared back at her. This was not the time or place to correct Jerrik's understanding of what she'd meant. That conversation would have to wait. In the meantime, she could get a few other things cleared up.

"Last night at supper," she asked, "when you basically accused me of stealing the ceremonial dagger?"

"Was a setup," Jerrik said. "I already knew that Pavel had stolen the dagger on Fenrir's orders. It was all a trap, as was the invite to ride up to the ridge, only the two of us, without any guards."

"The horrible things you said to me?"

"Were all a part of it."

"You could have confided in me."

"No, my little lynx," he said with a smile and a slow shake of his head. "You're a terrible actress. You wear your heart on your sleeve, and all a person has to do is listen to the music you play on your harp to know how you're feeling. I needed you to be seen as still angry at me in order for the trap to work."

Alyssa chuffed. "I would've still been plenty angry with you."

Jerrik cocked his head. "Even after I'd admitted I'd been wrong about and to you?"

Alyssa laughed, short and harsh. Apparently, he'd thought that once he admitted to finding out the truth of the matter that she would fall adoringly at his feet, grateful that he would want her back. That all would be forgiven.

The conceited ass.

She clicked her tongue and urged River forward, riding the rest of the way down the mountain alongside Sven, who wisely said not one word about what he'd overheard.

When they made the palace grounds, Alyssa reined River back so that she rode alongside Jerrik as they entered the courtyard. She was still queen and he king. For now.

It would be best to show their solidarity to the people. Sven dropped back and rode to Alyssa's other side, their gruesome parade collecting a crowd as they headed for Fenrir's longhouse, a crowd that rapidly grew in size and excitement as the dead men were recognized and names called out. When they pulled up outside Fenrir's door, Tryggr and six men whom Alyssa recognized as loyal to Jerrik met them there, armed and at the ready. Jerrik nodded to Tryggr, who pounded on the door.

"Uncle," Tryggr called out over the loud grumblings of men and the keening wails of women. "Uncle Fenrir, come out. Rigil and Brandr have returned with grievous news."

Fenrir came out quickly, followed by Ermelinde and Marianne and three yellow beards, the masks of feigned shock plastered on their faces cracking as they took in the scene before them. Ermelinde started toward Rigil, but Fenrir held out his arm, barring her way.

"What is the meaning of this?" he demanded. "Why is my son bound and gagged like some common criminal?"

"Because he is," Jerrik answered. "He is a thieving, lying, murderous criminal." He glared down at Fenrir. "Don't look so surprised, Uncle. It was you who made him so."

"That is preposterous, I—"

"Seize him," Jerrik commanded. "Seize them all."

Tryggr and his men, who already had their long swords pulled, surrounded Fenrir and his yellow beards before they could unsheathe a single blade.

Alyssa took in the angry faces and shouts of the growing crowd and was heartily glad of Jerrik and Sven flanking her. She saw Bors, Han, and Magna had pulled their long swords, and when she glanced at the bodies of the dead men they were guarding, her heart wept for a woman with two young daughters clinging to her skirts as she lifted her tear-streaked face from the shoulder of her husband's body.

Jerrik stood in his stirrups and addressed the agitating crowd. "People," he yelled over the angry shouts and keening wails. "People, listen to me." He looked to the woman with the children and three others crying over their dead men. "I'm sorry for your grievous loss this day," he told them, bowing his head to them." He lifted his gaze and his voice to the gathering crowd. "I'm sorry for any and all of you who lost their husband, father, son, this day. However, these men lay in wait and attacked the queen and myself at the ridge this morning. They did this on my Uncle Fenrir's orders, and they paid the price with their lives."

"Fuck the whore queen," a man shouted, and the grumblings of the crowd grew angrier.

Alyssa sat silent as Sven and Magna edged their mounts closer to her, though she tightened her grip on River's reins and eyed a gap in the crowd that opened to the woods beyond.

Jerrik held a hand up and the crowd quieted a little. "The queen is innocent of all charges made against her," he proclaimed loudly. "False charges laid by my uncle."

"Prove it," the same man, his hair and beard yarrow yellow, called out.

"We will," Jerrik said, "and more." Still standing in his stirrups, he swept the mob with his gaze. "We will be holding a public trial for my uncle and my wife in the feasting hall shortly. Any and all of you may attend who wish to."

He turned to the women and children, the fathers and mothers and brothers and sisters gathered around the dead yellow beards. "You will be able to see to your men afterwards," he told them. "To see them off to the netherworld with honor for serving their liege, if not their king. For now, they will be guarded closely, no further harm will come to them. You have my word."

Alyssa sat beside Jerrik at the high table, with Dagny sitting to her left, and Trine to Dagny's left, with the seat next to Trine's kept open for Magna, who'd left the hall after having a few words with Jerrik. Tryggr sat to Jerrik's right and Sven to Tryggr's. Facing the high table were three low tables. Tryggr's men stood guard at one table where Fenrir, Ermelinde, Marianne, and the three yellow beards sat. Han and Bors sat to either side of Rigil and Brandr, who remained bound and gagged, at the second table. The third table, which was closest to the open aisle leading from the hall's entrance, remained empty.

"Thank you, Borgny," Alyssa told the head cook as she and another maidservant set a light repast of mead, bread, fruit, and cheese in front of her. She poured herself a cup of mead, put a piece of bread, a few slices of apple and cheese on her plate, and passed the tray to Dagny.

"Would you like anything else brought out?" Jerrik asked, eyeing her sparse plate. "Some cold meat perhaps?"

"No." Alyssa shook her head. "I'm too nervous to eat much."

He laid his hand over hers on the table and gave it a gentle squeeze. "There's nothing to be nervous about. All will be revealed and your good name restored."

Alyssa gave him a weak smile and ran her other hand back through her cropped hair.

Jerrik lifted the hand he had hold of and placed his warm lips on the back of her cold fingers. "I'm sorry I cut your hair."

Alyssa pulled her hand from his and tucked both into her lap. "It's only hair," she said. "It'll grow back."

Would love, trust, and faith? These were what she wanted her marriage based on, along with the lust and passion that she and Jerrik had a surfeit of. She was determined not to settle for less. Yet like so many other things unsettled between them, this discussion would have to wait.

The door to the hall swung open and Magna entered with Pavel, Hamar, and Olaug. The gathering burst into a combustion of whispers as they made their way to the high table. Alyssa turned to Jerrik. "I thought you said Hamar left to go live with a cousin."

Jerrik flashed her a quick smile. "It was all part of the plan, little lynx."

Alyssa chuffed. "The plan that I couldn't be trusted to be a part of, though apparently everyone else here was."

"Not everyone," Jerrik said as Magna stopped at the empty low table and Hamar, Pavel, and Olaug took seats there.

"Don't be too angry with Jerrik," Dagny told Alyssa. "We all thought it best you didn't know. It was imperative Fenrir and his conspirators thought you and Jerrik were at odds. We couldn't have you walking around smiling and playing happy tunes on your harp day and night."

Alyssa eyed the woman whom she'd considered a close friend and ally. "When did you all decide this?"

"The afternoon you slept in Magna's and Hulda's chambers after you kicked Jerrik out and played songs sad enough to make half the household weep," she said with a sly grin.

Alyssa narrowed her eyes at Dagny, yet couldn't muster any real anger toward her. She'd conspired with Jerrik to help trap Fenrir and disprove his accusations against Alyssa. Accusations that she knew Dagny never believed.

Magna took her seat and Jerrik turned to Alyssa. "Are you ready for this?" he asked.

Alyssa nodded. "Let's get on with it."

Jerrik stood and the hall quieted. "Today, I have brought witnesses forward who will speak against Fenrir and the charges that he has laid against my wife, Queen Alyssa. The same witnesses he extorted to steal and lie in order to prove his vile, untrue accusations."

Fenrir said nothing and looked at no one, not even his son, Rigil, bound and gagged at the table next to him.

Beside Fenrir, Ermelinde sat with her usual haughty manner, nose high and lips pressed tightly together, though she at least glanced at her son, and pressed her thin lips even tighter. Next to Ermelinde, Marianne fidgeted in her seat, reached for a cup that wasn't there, and then licked her lips and swallowed.

Alyssa hoped Marianne's mouth was as dry as a desert in drought.

"This morning," Jerrik continued, "those loyal to me and the queen sprang a trap for those who chose to follow my uncle, who had conspired to have us murdered up at the ridge." The crowd buzzed and whispered loudly as Jerrik glared down at the accused, the muscle in the side of his jaw ticking. "I have heard their confessions, and soon, so will all of you."

He sat and took a drink of Alyssa's mead. "Do you have anything you wish to say?" he asked her.

"No." She shook her head. "I'm eager to hear what Olaug and Pavel have to share though."

"As you should be." He cleared his throat and took another drink of mead. "I call the scryer, Olaug of the Ancestors."

Olaug rose and stood, leaning on her walking stick of ash and elm with the raven's head. She dipped her chin to Jerrik and then bent a knee to Alyssa.

"Tell us of the water scrying you performed for us on the eve of the Harvest Festival," Jerrik said.

Olaug's wizened gaze met and held Alyssa's. "I lied," she said. "I lied about what I saw in the scrying bowl."

"Why?" Alyssa asked as a hush rushed through the gathering.

"I lied because Fenrir came to me the day before the festival and demanded that I do so," Olaug said, her voice loud and clear enough for all to hear. "Fenrir told me that I was to say I saw Queen Alyssa with a child not of King Jerrik's seed."

"What did he threaten you with if you did not?" Jerrik demanded.

"Fenrir would accuse me of witchcraft and would see me burnt at the stake."

"She lies," Fenrir hissed as a collective gasp sucked the air from the hall and then released with the sound of a hundred angry bees buzzing.

No," Olaug said, her voice as calm and steady as her demeanor. She turned her crones gaze on Fenrir. "I did lie, on the night of the Harvest Feast, as you extorted me to; however, I do not lie now." She smiled serenely, her cheeks rising and the corners of her wizened eyes crinkling. "Would you like me to tell you what the scrying bowl showed me of you, Fenrir, brother to a dead king and his dead sons?"

"I would know, Olaug of the Ancestors," Alyssa said, and Fenrir blanched and went still. Olaug said nothing, waiting, a small half smile playing at the edges of her mouth. "I would know what you truly saw in the scrying bowl the night of the Harvest Feast."

Olaug nodded and filled her chest with air for the telling. "I saw an eagle sitting on a throne carved into the stone face of a mountainside," she said, "alone, except for the yellow-furred squirrel chattering in his ear as the eagle peered out over the lands and across the seas, searching, ever searching, until at last he spied a lynx, snug in her den on a bed of thick furs and fine worm weave, nursing a boy child with hair the color of winter wheat and eyes the blue of a summer sky at one breast, and a girl child with curls of golden brown and eyes of green at her other breast."

"Twins?" Jerrik looked from Olaug to Alyssa. "We're having twins?"

Alyssa smiled and placed a hand over her belly. "Yes," she told him. "I've seen them too, much as Olaug describes them." What she did not say was how in both her and Olaug's visions, Alyssa and the babes had been far away from Jerrik.

Jerrik sat dumbfounded for a long moment, and then he laughed. "A twin boy and a girl," he said, and laid his hand over Alyssa's on her belly. "I shouldn't be surprised. They run in your family."

"They do," Alyssa said. Though whether they would be their twins or hers was still to be decided. At least Jerrik was accepting them as his now. She looked to Olaug, whose placid half-smile reminded Alyssa of a cat who had eaten a fat, juicy vole. "Thank you, Olaug," she told the scryer, "for coming forward with the truth."

Olaug dipped her head and bent a knee. "You are most welcome, my queen and king."

That Olaug, a seer and venerated elder, had addressed them as king and queen was not lost on Alyssa. She'd given them her loyalty in the most public of manners. Alyssa smiled and dipped her head to Olaug in return.

"Do you wish to question Olaug the Seer, Uncle?" Jerrik asked Fenrir, who took one look at Olaug's enigmatic smile and shook his head. The corners of Jerrik's lips twitched up and he cleared his throat. "Thank you, Olaug," he said. "You may take your seat."

Olaug dipped her head to Jerrik but did not sit. She stood leaning on her staff, eyeing Alyssa. A little unsettled at first by the seer's unblinking gaze, Alyssa became easier the longer she held it. "Remember, my queen," Olaug said at last. "What the water shows us is only a possibility, not a certainty."

Jerrik knew what the water had shown Alyssa. She'd told him of her vision of the eagle sitting alone in the tree, of the lands below him dying, of the tides pulling the sea away, pulling her away with it, pulling her away from him. To his shame, he'd almost let them. He'd let his jealousy get the better of him and had believed his uncle's schemes and lies over Alyssa's protestations of innocence. He'd been wrong. Now, he was about to put wrong to right.

"Pavel," he called out. "Stand and tell us the truth of your dealings with Fenrir."

Pavel stood and took his cap off, worrying it between his hands and shifting from foot to foot as he cleared his throat. "Yer uncle, Fenrir, that is, came to me in the stables the night I told Queen Alyssa I'd watch over Digger for her whilst you and she rode up to visit her brother's grave," he said, his words spilling out. "He told me I was to give the pup some tainted meat, else he'd claim I stole jewelry from his wife and have me banished from here and back to the life of a street thief." He looked up at Alyssa from beneath his brows. "I was ever so glad Hamar was able to save Digger."

"What happened after Digger lived?" Jerrik asked. "Did Fenrir come to you again?"

"Aye, skep, ah, King Jerrik. Fenrir came back at me, crazy mad the pup'd lived. He told me I was to steal the queen's favorite hair comb and give it to him. I was to say I found it in the stables when asked. To say I'd been seeing Hamar and the queen meeting up and being...together, else Fenrir'd tell it was me who poisoned Digger, and he'd poison River and Storm too and blame that on me as well."

Beside Jerrik, Alyssa sucked in her breath and let it out in a slow hiss, glaring daggers at Fenrir, who sat sneering smugly at Pavel.

"Did you do his bidding?" Jerrik asked Pavel. "Did you steal the queen's hair comb?"

"Aye, King Jerrik, I did," he said, rocking from foot to foot.

"To be clear, Pavel," Jerrik said. "Did you ever see the queen and Hamar lying together?"

"No, sir. I never seen them do anything more than talk." He bit down on his lower lip and looked about to cry as he met Alyssa's gaze. "I be so sorry, mistress. I was so afraid of going back to what I was. Can you ever forgive me?"

"Of course, I forgive you, Pavel," Alyssa said with a tender smile for the lad. "Digger and I both do."

Jerrik lifted Alyssa's hand in his and kissed the backs of her fingers. He'd never doubted that she would forgive Pavel; it wasn't in her nature to hold grudges. He, on the other hand, could and did. "What have you to say about these charges, Uncle?" he demanded.

"The boy is a thief and a liar," Fenrir said with a dismissive flick of his hand. "I deny and resent his accusations."

"It's true enough," Pavel burst out before Jerrik could say anything. "I was a thief and a liar, that's what my father taught me to be." He turned to face the people in the hall. "Yet, despite it, or maybe because of it, the king and queen took me in and made me part of the *Sea Eagle*'s crew, where I learned the value of an honest day's work and a man's word." He turned back to face Jerrik and Alyssa, twisting the cap in his hands. "I swear on my life, King

Jerrik, Queen Alyssa, the only lies I've told since were the ones forced on me by Fenrir."

"Thank you, Pavel," Jerrik said. "You may sit." He looked to Hamar, who stood without being asked, back straight and chest out. "What have you to say, Hamar?"

"Queen Alyssa and I have never shared anything more than conversation and a friendly hug, which you walked in on and near broke my nose over, King Jerrik."

"I admit to being a jealous man when it comes to my wife," Jerrik said with a shrug and a grin that brought a spurt of laughter from the gathering, and a frown from Alyssa. "Look at her," he said, unapologetic. "Can any man here blame me?" More laughter followed and Jerrik grew serious once more. "Has anyone here ever witnessed the queen being anything other than friendly to a man other than myself?"

Heads shook to loud murmurings of *no* and *never*, and Jerrik indicated that Hamar should sit back down.

Jerrik stood and waited for the crowd to quiet. "On the charges of infidelity laid against my wife, Queen Alyssa, I declare her innocent." He gazed down into eyes swirling with all the colors of the sea and lowered his voice so that only she could hear. "I'm sorry for letting my uncle use my history and jealousy against you. I should've known better."

Alyssa blinked and nodded. Jerrik owed her so much more than simple apologies. All of which would have to wait.

"Remove Rigil's and Brandr's binds and gags," he told Han and Bors. "Give them some mead," he said, sitting back down as both Rigil and Brandr rubbed their freed wrists and licked their dried and bloodied lips. "They will need it to answer my questions."

Questions that Jerrik already knew the answers to. He glanced at Fenrir, the lying snake, who couldn't know that Rigil and Brandr had both confessed all up at the ridge to save their own skins. Jerrik had kept Rigil and Brandr bound and gagged to keep it that way, until now.

"Brandr," Jerrik said. "Stand and tell us what Fenrir ordered you and your five dead companions to do in regard to the queen and myself up at the ridge this day."

Unlike Rigil, who cast a quick look his father's way, Brandr didn't even acknowledge Fenrir's presence as he stood and faced the high table. "Our orders were to ride up there at break of dawn and lie in wait for you and the queen," he said. "To kill you with blades and make it look like you had killed the queen in a murderous rage and then yourself."

Loud gasps filled the hall and then quieted as Jerrik held up the ceremonial dagger that was to have been part of his and Alyssa's wedding ceremony. "With this dagger?" he asked. "The dagger that has been in my family for ten generations and which Fenrir had stolen from my chambers and publicly accused the queen of taking?"

Brandr nodded. "The same."

"What was your reward to be?"

"I was to be made Kaptein of the King's Guard."

"King Tryggr?" Jerrik said.

"No." Brandr shook his head. "King Fenrir."

The crowd burst into a chorus of what's and who's and how's until Jerrik raised his hand, still clasping the ceremonial dagger. "How did Fenrir plan to bypass Tryggr, the next in line and rightful heir of the throne?" he asked, not trusting himself to even glance his murderous uncle's way, else he jump over the table and do to Fenrir what he'd intended to do to Jerrik, Alyssa, and Tryggr.

Brandr took another drink of his mead, set the cup down, and cleared his throat. "He said he would find a way to kill Tryggr after he had you killed, as he'd had Bard and Alviss killed, and then the people would have no choice except to name him king."

"Lies," Fenrir cried as angry shouts and the thumping of fists on tables echoed through the hall. "Everything Brandr has said is a lie." Fenrir stood and pointed a bony finger at Brandr, who had been his man until now. "What did Jerrik promise you to lie about me?"

Brandr turned and looked at Fenrir for the first time since the trial had begun. "King Jerrik offered me life and banishment for speaking the truth," he said. "Death if I lied."

"You gave me your oath," Fenrir accused Brandr, as if he were the victim of a murderous plot and not the plotter. "You chose your own selfish life over honor."

Brandr turned around and faced his wife, who sat directly behind him with their young son and daughter. "I chose to speak the truth for myself and my family," he said as his wife wiped her tears and smiled bravely at him. He turned around and glared at Fenrir. "My only dishonor was in attempting to carry out your murderous orders, twice."

"Twice?" Jerrik said. "Explain."

Brandr glanced at Alyssa, who'd already heard him confess this morning, and then quickly looked away. "Me and Gunnolf, one of the men killed this morning, dislodged the boulder that was meant to bury you, King Jerrik, and Aaron."

"It would've buried us both if Aaron hadn't sacrificed his life to save mine," Jerrik said, his voice breaking as he gazed down at Alyssa. Her beloved brother and his best friend hadn't died in some accident of nature. He'd been murdered. On Fenrir's orders.

"You cannot prove any of this," Fenrir said with a smug sneer that Jerrik couldn't wait to wipe off his face. "It's this man's word against mine."

Jerrik sat back and smiled. "You may be seated, Brandr. Rigil, stand. Stand and tell us what you told me this morning after the attempt on my and Queen Alyssa's lives."

Rigil turned in his seat and nodded to his wife, Linnea, who sat as still and silent as stone along with their son, who couldn't have been more than three or four. Turning back, he took a drink of his mead and then slowly stood and faced Jerrik and the high table.

"Brandr has spoken the truth," Rigil said. "My father, Fenrir, ordered Brandr, me, and the five dead men outside to lie in wait for King Jerrik and Queen Alyssa and to kill them both."

"And?" Jerrik prompted.

"He had Brandr and Gunnolf attempt to kill you with the boulder that killed Queen Alyssa's brother, Aaron."

Jerrik laid his hand over Alyssa's, clasped tightly in her lap. "What about my brothers, Alviss and Bard?"

"Fenrir ordered Gunnolf and two of the others who died on the ridge to kill Alviss and to make it look like a hunting accident." He looked up at Dagny beneath his brows. "Bard was poisoned."

"Poisoned?" Dagny gasped. "How?" she cried. "By who?"

"By Grima," Rigil said. "A maid who served in your royal longhouse, and my father's bed." He glanced at his mother. If this was news to Ermelinde, she didn't show it. She sat as still and erect as ever, her usual mask of haughty indifference plastered on her face. "My father paid her in gold to add water hemlock to Bard's mead each morning for two moons. Gold she then used to start a new life in a new land."

"Why?" Dagny said. She was looking at Fenrir, not Rigil.

"To become king," Rigil answered when his father did not.

Dagny stood and faced Fenrir, her eyes narrowing. "You thought it right to kill my husband, the rightful king and heir, to make my sons fatherless, so that you could become king?" she spat.

Fenrir gave Dagny the briefest of glances and shrugged, as if all the grief, pain, and loss he'd caused meant nothing. Alyssa stood and folded the shaking Dagny into her embrace.

"I want to kill the bastard," Dagny whimpered into Alyssa's shoulder. "I want... I want my husband back. I want Bard."

"I know," Alyssa murmured into her hair. She glanced up at Jerrik, her eyes welling with tears. "I know you do. Think of your sons. Think of how you see their father in them. Of how they will grow into men as good and strong as Bard." Dagny sniffed and lifted her head, the raw grief in her eyes almost taking the legs out from under Jerrik.

The same grief that he'd felt when he'd thought Alyssa lost to him. He and Alyssa had only been married for three moons, Dagny had lost her husband of ten and three years. "Sit, sister," Alyssa said, gently pushing Dagny down into her seat. She met Jerrik's gaze, hers blazing green fire. "Jerrik will deal with Fenrir. He will pay for what he has taken from you. From all of us."

Taking a deep breath to steady the storm building in him, Jerrik faced Fenrir. "Do you have anything to say about your son's charges against you?"

Fenrir stood and met his son's steady gaze with the patronizing air of a man sitting in judgment, not a man about to be judged. "What did your cousin promise you to lie against me, my son?"

"The same as he promised Brandr," Rigil said. "Life and banishment to speak the truth of what I know. Certain death if I lied."

Fenrir spread his hands out, palms up, and turned to face the gathering, smiling as if he were the benevolent, all-knowing father who must explain things to his ignorant children. "Of course, my son and Brandr would say anything that my nephew, Jerrik, new and inexperienced as he is in the role of king, would have them say about me to save their own lives," he said. "Who can blame them?"

"Are you saying that they're lying?" Jerrik questioned. "That I should kill them, I should kill your son, and spare you?"

The entire hall went deathly silent. Fenrir glanced at Rigil for a brief moment, and Rigil froze. As did Jerrik's blood.

"If death is the penalty for lying, then yes," Fenrir said, "Rigil and Brandr must both suffer the consequences."

"Nnnooo," three distinct female voices cried out as Rigil's and Brandr's wives and Ermelinde all shot to their feet.

"He is lying," Ermelinde screeched. She glared at her husband. "Fenrir is lying. I know it all. What Rigil and Brandr say is true."

"Shut up, bitch." Fenrir slapped Ermelinde across the face, and only Alyssa's hand on his arm kept Jerrik from leaping across the table and strangling his uncle. "She would say anything to save her son," Fenrir appealed to the crowd. He turned to Jerrik, his smile as slick and oily as his words. "Who are you going to believe, a woman who hated your wife on sight, or me, your uncle, who has only ever served your father and brothers and yourself to the best of my abilities?"

Jerrik snorted. "I would believe anybody except you," he said. "You, who had it all, family, wealth, rank, and respect, yet would kill for more, who would sacrifice his own son for his twisted ambitions." He stood and pinned Fenrir with his gaze. "To be king?"

"To rule as king," Fenrir answered. "As I always should have. I, who had to counsel your father, your brothers, you. To hold your hands and lead you by your noses to act as kings, when your women led you by your cocks." He turned and addressed the assemblage. "Do you know that he and his Rus wife want to free all of the thralls of this kingdom? To make the blooded jarls and freeborn kralls pay them for their work?" The hall filled with rumbles and whispers, and he turned back to Jerrik, a smug smile on his face. "The only thing I have sacrificed is my life for the good of this kingdom. What would you know of it? You, who have never had to sacrifice anything."

The storm building in Jerrik broke. "I have lost a mother, a father, two brothers, and a friend who was my brother in deed if not blood," he raged. "I accepted the throne and became king when I would have gladly remained skeppare of the *Sea Eagle*." He glanced at Alyssa, who had suffered Ermelinde's and Fenrir's lies and accusations almost from the day she had arrived at Sea Ridge. "My wife left her family, a good, loving, happy family, to be my queen here." He fisted his hands. "I may have sacrificed my marriage because I believed you and your lies over my own wife." He shook his head. "You knew exactly how to play on my mother's memory—"

"It was Fenrir," Ermelinde shrieked. "It was all Fenrir. He killed your mother and your father."

CHAPTER 19

The Reckoning

"What?" Jerrik stood so abruptly that the rush of blood to his head left him swaying on his feet like an unmoored ship. He blew out his breath as he anchored his fisted hands on the table and focused on Ermelinde's pinched face. "Are you saying that my mother didn't die by her own hand? That Fenrir murdered her?"

"Yes, my king. That is what I am saying."

"She is a lying bitch," Fenrir swore. "She will say anything to save her son's life."

"As you will say anything to save yours," Jerrik countered, "and nothing to save your son's." He spat his distaste for the man he and his father and brothers had all trusted to help them rule this land. Had trusted with their lives. Lives that they had all lost, all except Jerrik, who likely would have lost his as well if not for Aaron and Alyssa. "How?" he asked Ermelinde. "How did he kill my parents?"

Ermelinde shook off Fenrir's hand as he grabbed at her and stepped forward. "He…he held a blanket over your father's face as he slept," she said, "until Anders had no breath left in him."

Jerrik's father, King Anders, had seen forty and two winters before his death. Though his death had been unnatural and untimely, he'd at least lived a full life by most measures. Not so his mother. The memory of red blood pooling in white linens, of his mother's white-gold hair fanned out on her pillow, her beautiful sky-blue eyes staring lifeless and unseeing at him, almost took his breath away. "My mother?" he rasped.

"I gave Queen Alina a dose of belladonna to calm her after her fight with Anders," Ermelinde said. "When she was too drugged to fight him, Fenrir slashed her wrists with her blade and left it beside her to look as if she took her own life."

A rage as red as his mother's blood engulfed Jerrik. "My mother's last thoughts were of fear, betrayal, and shame," he stormed at Fenrir, "because of you."

"She died because your father thought her a cheating whore," Fenrir said.

"Aye," Jerrik snarled, "because of your lies and accusations."

"They weren't lies," Fenrir said. "I know. I was one of her many lovers."

He stood there with a little half-smile on his face, looking as smooth and unruffled as a calm sea. Yet Jerrik knew how deceptive such a sea could be. How its glassy surface could hide a deathly undertow beneath its waters.

"You lie," he ground out. "My mother never cared for you. Even as I child I knew that much."

Fenrir shrugged and smiled and held his hands palms up. "A lovers' spat—"

"You lie," Jerrik roared. He jumped over the table in one leap, closed the distance between him and Fenrir in two strides, grabbed his uncle by the neck of his tunic and held his blade to Fenrir's throat. "It will be the last lie you ever tell."

"Trial by combat," Fenrir wheezed out. "I demand trial by combat."

Jerrik shoved him back and spat at his feet. He knew that as king, he had the right to kill Fenrir there and then. Witnesses had been brought forward and exposed his lies and murderous deeds. His guilt had been proven. Still, guilt and loyalty were two different things, and as king, it would be best if Jerrik had the loyalty of his people, all of them.

Killing Fenrir in a trial by combat would do much to sway those still grumbling and undecided. "Say your farewells to any here who may still care for you, you treacherous snake," he told Fenrir. He turned and gave him his back as he walked to the high table. "Sven," he said, "loan Fenrir your long sword."

"Nah, skep," Sven said with a shake of his head. "I'll not be giving my sword to the likes of him." He jutted his chin toward the table where Rigil and Brandr sat between Han and Bors, their weapons confiscated and lying on the table. "Let him ask one of them."

Fenrir walked over to the table his son and kaptein sat at, and without saying so much as one word to either of them, he took a long drink from Rigil's mead and then lifted a long sword and a short sword from the table. Swinging the swords in both hands, he walked to the middle of the open space between the high and low tables, where he stopped and saluted Jerrik with the short sword. Jerrik laughed, quick and sharp. He had to give his uncle credit. The man knew how to put on a show. "I will be with you momentarily, Uncle," he said.

He strode over to the high table and took a swig of Alyssa's mead.

Alyssa leaned across the table and said, "I don't trust him, Jerrik. He knows you're stronger and quicker than him. He will not fight fairly."

"No," Jerrik put the cup down, "I don't suppose he will." He smiled into her worried eyes. "I don't plan on giving him a chance to pull any of his dirty tricks."

"Be careful of the snake, my eagle."

"Kiss me, my little lynx."

Alyssa leaned closer, took his face in her hands, and kissed him as sweet and lovingly as any wife had ever kissed her husband. "I love you, Jerrik," she whispered urgently as he broke their kiss.

He smiled and nodded. "I know. I've always known, my Lyssa."

He stepped back with a purposely cocky grin, dipped his head, and then turned to face Fenrir, noticing that Sven, Bors, and Han all rested their hands on their swords' hilts. He tapped the tip of his long sword to Fenrir's. "To the death," he said.

Fenrir nodded solemnly, and then spit a mouthful of mead into Jerrik's eyes. Jerrik jumped back and aside, and the thrust of Fenrir's blade only grazed his ribs instead of stabbing Jerrik square in the chest. Shaking the mead from his face, he dodged the wide arcing swing of Fenrir's long sword, which hit the floor with a dull clang. With a ferocious cry, Jerrik leapt up and then swooped down on Fenrir, slicing through the shoulder of the arm that held the short sword. He landed with his booted foot on the flat side of Fenrir's long sword, ripping it out of his hand and pinning it next to the short sword Fenrir had dropped from his dangling, useless hand.

Fenrir stood swordless, his shoulder sliced open and bleeding, his mouth hanging slack as he stared dumbly at Jerrik.

"You killed my mother, my father, my brothers, my friend," Jerrik ground out. "You tried to kill me, my wife, and my unborn children. You would have let your eldest son die for your crimes." Jerrik spat in his face. "Now is the time to pray to any gods who may have mercy upon your worm-eaten soul. Your body is about to become the same. My only mercy will be a quick death."

Fenrir lifted dead eyes to Jerrik's. "I only did what I thought best."

"You did what you thought best for you." Jerrik shook his head. "Only for you." He'd had enough. "Kneel," he commanded. "Kneel to your king. You don't deserve to die standing."

He could hear a pin drop as Fenrir slowly started to lower himself to one knee, almost toppling over and righting himself with his good arm along with much grunting and groaning. Jerrik would've felt badly for the man when nobody, not even his wife or son, made a move to help him, were it not for the fact he'd brought all of this on himself through sheer greed for position and power.

Fenrir was on both knees now, facing his wife and family. "Do you have any last words?" Jerrik asked as he took his position to Fenrir's side.

"No," Fenrir said. "None."

He hung his head low and Jerrik gripped his long sword in both hands and raised it high. "May the gods of the underworld welcome you."

"Jerrik," Alyssa screamed. "He has a blade in his left hand."

Fenrir jabbed up at Jerrik's belly as Jerrik jumped straight up, sucking in his belly so that Fenrir's blade found only air. He hung weightless for a moment as the crowd drew in a collective gasp, and then dropped back to his feet, slashing his long sword down with such force that Fenrir's head dropped and rolled onto the floor, his twitching body following.

Jerrik stood over Fenrir's severed head and body and wiped the sweat and blood from his face with his sleeve. He nodded his thanks to Alyssa, and then he faced the low tables, still holding his short and long swords at the ready.

"I am Jerrik Anderson," he said, his voice ringing loud and clear. "Rightful king to Sea Ridge by birth and by combat. If anybody else cares to challenge me for the throne, now is your chance." He waited, his sword dripping with Fenrir's blood.

Not a soul moved or spoke. "If anyone here does not wish to accept me as king, then they are free to take what is theirs and leave. However," he glanced purposely at the four yellow beards sitting amongst the gathering, "if you attempt to usurp my rule or harm me or any member of my family, your penalty will be death." He looked down at the grisly visage of his uncle's face, staring unseeing into the void, framed by a pool of congealing blood. "Such will be any traitor's fate."

"Hail, King Jerrik," Sven called out.

"Hail, King Jerrik," the gathering chanted back. "Hail, King Jerrik. Hail, King Jerrik."

Jerrik sheathed both of his swords and looked at Rigil and Brandr and each of the three yellow beards still bound and gagged. "Brandr," he said. "You and your fellow yellow beards have two days to pack up your families and your belongings and leave here. Any thralls you claim will be given the choice of leaving with you or staying here as free workers. If you're ever seen in Sea Ridge again, the penalty will be death. Do you all understand and agree?"

"Yes, King Jerrik," Brandr said, as the three yellow beards all nodded their heads vigorously.

"Rigil," Jerrik said, "you and your family, along with your brother and his family and your mother, will all leave under the same terms, with the added condition that you will pay the widows of your father's dead yellow beards a silver weight of ten ounces each for the loss of their husbands and another silver weight of eight ounces for each child their husbands left them with."

"That is outrageous," Ermelinde complained.

"Outrageous?" Jerrik pinned her with his glare. "Outrageous is losing the care and protection of a husband and a father."

"It will make beggars of us," she whined.

Which Jerrik doubted. Knowing Fenrir, his uncle had amassed and hidden a fortune. Whether his wife and son knew where or how much was another thing altogether. Not his problem. "You, your husband, and son should've considered that before you murdered my family and theirs," he said, lifting his head toward the weeping widows.

"They died by your swords," Ermelinde argued. An argument that Jerrik was in no temper to take up.

"They died following Fenrir's orders," he thundered. "Now, accept my terms or leave this night with nothing more than the clothes on your back."

"What about me?" Marianne said, with a simpering smile. She'd been silent throughout the proceedings.

Jerrik chuffed. How had he ever considered her for his queen? She was nothing more than a selfish, self-serving bitch. "You have a home with your dead husband's family," he told her. "I suggest you return to it. Tomorrow. If they'll take you."

"If they do not?" she asked, imploring him with her big blue eyes.

"Then you'd better hope that your father will take you back into his house," he said. "Either way, you aren't my problem any longer."

Alyssa lowered her body into the welcoming heat of the bath water with a long, weary sigh, and leaned her head back on the tub's edge. So much had happened since this morning her mind was still spinning trying to make sense of it all. In the end, all she knew for certain was that Fenrir was dead, his family and those of the traitorous yellow beards banished, Marianne was leaving tomorrow morn, and nothing had been settled between her and Jerrik.

She scooped a handful of soap from the tub, lathered her hair and face, and then dunked her head under the water to rinse the soap, sweat, blood, and grime away. When she came up, Jerrik was sitting on a stool next to the tub, eyeing her full breasts with a hungry grin.

"Twins, huh?" he asked, lifting his eyes to meet hers.

"If Olaug's and my visions are true," she replied, slinking down in the tub so her breasts were covered by the soapy water, which hid next to nothing.

"If it's all right with you, I'd like to name them Anders and Alina, after my parents."

"So," she said, "now you believe that the babes I carry are yours? Now that Olaug has admitted to seeing them in her vision, and Pavel has admitted that he never witnessed Hamar and me lying together?"

"I do."

"Because you believe them before me. As you believed Kostya about me, and would not lie with me until I'd bled."

"As I've explained before, as king I had to be sure you weren't carrying Kostya's babe. Any babe you birthed had to be mine."

"You could have asked me."

"Perhaps," he said with a shrug. "Perhaps I didn't want to know the answer."

Because he'd believed Kostya. "You should have asked me," she said miserably.

He shook his head. "I couldn't chance your lying to me." He met her gaze and held it, his own bare and raw. "I couldn't have borne it."

Because of his mother. "I've never lied to you, Jerrik," she whispered. "Ever. As it turns out, neither did your mother to your father."

"No," he agreed. "It turns out she did not. She'd been innocent of the charges laid against her by my treacherous uncle." He swallowed, hard. "It seems the hurt, anger, and betrayal I've carried with me all these years were of my uncle's doing, not my mother's. The things I've blamed her for…all this time—"

Alyssa sat up, exposing her breasts, her heart. She clasped the pearl and said, "Tell me."

Jerrik took a big breath in and let it out slowly. "I was there," he said. "I was six years old and had snuck into the council chambers, a room my brothers and I had been forbidden from being in many times before, which made it perfect to hide in from my eldest brother, Alviss."

He gave Alyssa a wry grin and she smiled and nodded in understanding. She'd grown up with six brothers, she knew how it was with boys and forbidden places.

"I heard voices approaching, loud, angry voices, and I hid under the table." He closed his eyes as if listening to those voices. "I heard it all. My uncle accusing my mother of being unfaithful to my father, telling my father of all the evidence against her, my mother wailing and sobbing as she pled her innocence and begged my father to listen to her, to believe her." He let out a ragged sigh. "But he wouldn't. He cursed her as a wanton whore who cared not for the good name he'd given her, for the love of her husband and sons, and he cast her aside."

"Oh, Jerrik." Alyssa's eyes welled with tears as her heart bled for the boy he'd once been. "No child should ever have to hear such things."

"On that," he said, "we agree wholeheartedly."

"What did you do?"

"I stayed hidden until they all left, and then I crawled out from under the table and ran to my mother's chambers, where she lay crying on her bed." His voice caught and his gaze went somewhere else for a long moment. "When she saw me, saw my face, she knew. She knew I'd heard my father's condemnation, her pleas, her shame."

"What did she do?"

Jerrik started to smile, and then his eyes welled with tears and his smile crumpled. He coughed and swiped at the threatening tears. Alyssa knew how hard it was for him, how it pricked his pride to cry in front of her. "She, ah, she held me in her arms and told me not to cry. She told me she loved me, that she would always love me, no matter what, and I... I asked her if what my uncle said was true, because if it wasn't, my father would never have believed it." He sniffed and coughed and tears ran down his cheeks. "She told me over and over that she loved me, loved my brothers, loved my father, that she would never do anything to hurt or harm us. She kissed me on the cheek and told me to go play, not to tell anyone else what had happened and that all would be well." He squeezed his eyes tight against his falling tears and his voice cracked. "I did as she told me, but somehow, somewhere inside me, I knew that something was wrong, so I returned to her room." He met Alyssa's watching gaze, and the pain in his nearly undid her. "I found her...her wrists cut... bled out...her eyes unseeing..." Alyssa reached out and took his hand in hers. "She, she left me," he cried. "She left me, after promising me that she...she loved me. Promised she would never leave me."

"She didn't leave you," Alyssa said. "She was taken from you."

Jerrik nodded, dropped his head to their hands, and wept.

He wept as she knew he hadn't wept since the day he'd found his mother dead in her bed, openly and unashamedly, burying his face into her neck, his body shaking as badly as hers had after the fight on the ridge.

When his tremors finally lessened, Alyssa stood and stepped out of the tub and wrapped a linen towel around her chest and tucked the hems tight between her heavy breasts.

"Turn and hold up your arms," she told him, pulling his leather vest and then his tunic up and over his head and tossing them to the floor. "Now stand," she said, smiling as her fingers touched his bare belly and he sucked in his breath.

She untied the stays to his breeches and let them drop to his knees. "Now sit." He sat and she knelt to pull off his boots one by one, followed by his breeches.

"In the water." She lifted her chin at the tub. "Go on."

Jerrik stepped into the tub and lowered his body into the bath water. "Sit forward," she told him, and Jerrik half groaned, half sighed as she poured a pitcher full of warm water over his head and down his back and chest. She poured several more pitchers over him and then she scooped a handful of soap from the tub and rubbed it in slow circles round his head.

He moaned as she kneaded and rubbed her way down the back of his neck and into his shoulders, and then groaned when she pressed her thumbs into his spine where his neck and shoulders met.

"Marry me," he said, letting his head loll.

Alyssa laughed softly and ran her soapy hands over his shoulders and down his chest and back. "Dunk," she said, and giggled lightly when he came up spitting water at her. She walked to the foot of the tub. "Lift your leg."

She scooped a handful of soap and lathered up his foot, his calf, his thigh. Jerrik pretended to pout when she stopped at the water line. "Now your other leg," she said, eyeing his hard cock under the water. They'd made love in this tub so many times, it could've been their second bed. Tempting as it was to dip her hand under the water and rub his cock, to step into the tub and lose herself with him, there were still too many unresolved issues between them.

She pushed his leg back into the water and held a clean drying linen out for him.

With a disappointed groan, Jerrik stood and stepped out of the tub. "Thank you for the bath," he said as she wrapped the towel around his shoulders. He took the hems in his hands and drew them tight. "And for listening. I've never told anyone what I told you about that day. About my mother."

"Thank you for telling me," she said. "I know how hard it was for you."

They dried themselves and Alyssa put a clean linen night shift on. Jerrik hadn't brought any clean clothes with him, and wrapped the towel around his waist.

"Will you stay the night with me?" he asked her. "In our bed?"

"I don't think—"

"To sleep only, I swear," he promised. "I miss you, Lyssa. I miss having you next to me."

Alyssa woke in the snug cocoon of Jerrik's body wrapped around hers, warm, rested, and content. She smiled as Jerrik's big hand cupped her breast and his teeth nibbled at the nape of her neck. True to his word, he'd done nothing more last night than whisper sweet endearments into her ear and nestle her body close to his until they'd fallen asleep. He'd woken hard and randy, as he did more often than not, and her body was responding to his touch, a touch that Alyssa had neither the will nor the desire to deny. She turned in his arms and smiled.

"I can stop now if you wish," he said.

"What I wish for, husband, is you." She ran her hand down his belly and his cock, which thickened with each stroke of her fingers. "All of you."

"Your wish is my command, wife," he said, moving with her hand until he was fully aroused, and then rolling her over onto her back and kissing her, his mouth slanting and slaking. "Gods, I've missed you in my bed, Lyssa," he whispered roughly. "These past days and nights have felt like an eternity." He kissed away any reply she might have made, and as he kissed his way down her throat and took one aching nipple in his warm, wet mouth, any coherent thought she had flew from her mind. All she knew, all she wanted, was Jerrik.

Taking him in hand, she rubbed his soft, fleshy tip along her woman's cleft in delicious, tortuous circles, spreading her wet heat over him, over her, spreading her legs beneath him, welcoming him as he entered her with one slick thrust. "Ahh, Jerrik," Alyssa moaned as her inner muscles embraced him. "I've missed you too."

He smiled down into her eyes and began to move inside her, slow and easy, his grin growing apace with his rhythm. They moved together in a dance as raw and primitive and old as time itself, skin to skin, soul to soul, soaring, falling, rising up out of the abyss together.

When Alyssa woke again, her head was nestled on Jerrik's shoulder and his fingers were trailing lightly up and down her arm.

"Welcome back, sleepyhead," he said, kissing her forehead. "I hate to leave our snug little nest," he said, starting to slide his arm out from beneath her. "Unfortunately, this day's business will not wait."

"Nooo." Alyssa held on to Jerrik's arm and nestled her nose into his neck. "Don't leave, not yet."

He chuckled, and Alyssa smiled as the sound reverberated in his chest. "Much as I wish otherwise," he said solemnly, "it would not be wise to make six widows wait to send their husbands off to the netherworld." His chest rose and lowered with a heavy sigh. "They've been building the funeral pyres since dawn."

"You're right, of course," Alyssa said, leaning on one arm and admiring her husband, who was alive and well, unlike the dead yellow beards whose wives would be saying farewell forever today. Jerrik was right. It would be cruel to make them wait. "I'll go to my room and get dressed. Digger must be beside himself, wondering where I've been all night."

He swung his legs over the side of the bed and stood. "After the funerals, I'll have Han and Bors bring your belongings back to our chambers from Magna's rooms. They can get the rest from the *Sea Eagle* tomorrow."

Alyssa sat up, spine straight and chin lifted. "Why would you do that?"

Jerrik cocked his head. "What do mean, why would I do that, after what we just—"

"Just what? Had sex? You assume that because we had sex that I'd come running back to you? That all would be forgiven and we could go back to where we were before," she waved a hand around the room and beyond, "before everything that's happened?"

"You are my wife, Alyssa."

"Not if I divorce you."

"You are carrying my children."

"Whom you denied were yours up until last night."

"Publicly," he said. "I've known they were mine since Pavel confessed his lies."

"Because you believed him. You believed everybody except me, your wife," Alyssa snapped.

She stood, grabbing the bed linens and wrapping them around her shoulders, picked her night shift up from the floor, and stormed out of the bedchamber and into the hall, slamming the door behind her. Pulling the linens tighter around her nakedness, she stomped down the hall to Magna's and Hulda's rooms, where she stopped in front of the door and fisted her hands in the linens as she doubled over and screamed out, "Fucking men."

Jerrik sat at the main hearth fire with Sven, Han, and Bors, drinking beer, discussing the day's events, and listening to Alyssa strumming the melancholy tune of the cowherd and the cloud weaver up in Magna's and Hulda's rooms, which she'd disappeared into after supper, where she'd sat next to Jerrik, stiff, seething, and silent.

Draining his third cup of beer, Jerrik wiped his mouth with his sleeve and stared into the empty cup. "I fucked up," he said.

"No, lad," Sven assured him. "You handled things in a kingly manner. Your decisions were fair and merciful, the funerals went off without a hitch, and Fenrir's wife and sons were able to pay off the widows quite handily, despite Ermelinde's cry of poverty. I heard no grumblings of dissent amongst the people; in fact, quite the opposite."

"I meant with Alyssa," he said. "I fucked up royally with my wife."

"Oh, that," Sven said, chuckling into his cup. "Yes, we heard."

"The entire household heard," Bors said.

"You two think this funny?" Jerrik snapped. "My wife intends to divorce me and sail away with my unborn children and you two are laughing?"

"Did she say that?" Sven asked, his countenance suddenly serious.

Jerrik nodded. "This morning, after we… Before she stormed out of our chambers."

"Do you think she meant it?" Bors asked. "She hasn't mentioned sailing back to her homeland with Han or me in days. She stood by you as stately and loyal as any good queen and wife through the funerals and the settling of debts."

"She stood by me without saying a word to me all day," Jerrik said. "Alyssa always says what she means and means what she says. I swear the woman couldn't lie to save her life." A fact he had callously forgotten in his jealous haze.

"Tell us exactly what you said to her and what she said to you this morning," Sven ordered.

"I told her that I'd have her things brought back up to our rooms from the *Sea Eagle*."

"Without asking her first?" Sven said. Jerrik nodded and Sven shook his head. "Big mistake, lad."

"Apparently. She accused me of assuming she'd return to our chambers. That I was wrong to think everything bad that's happened was forgotten because we'd lain together."

"Why wouldn't you assume that if she slept with you?" Bors asked.

"Right?" Jerrik shook his head. "She's my wife, carrying our children."

"You didn't say that, did you?" Sven asked.

"It's true," Jerrik answered.

"Uh-huh." Sven pulled on his beard. "What was her response?"

"She threw my doubts about our children's parentage back at me," Jerrik said. "How I hadn't believed her until Pavel's confession. How I'd believed everyone over her. Then she stomped out of our bedchamber and, well, you heard."

"Oh aye, lad," Sven said with a chuckle. "We did. I do believe you're right. You fucked up. You fucked up royally."

"I know I did," Jerrik groused, pouring himself another cup of beer. "What I don't know is what to do about it."

"You need to make amends," Sven said.

Jerrik chuffed into his cup. "No shit."

"You love her," Sven said. "Don't you?"

Jerrik closed his eyes and saw Alyssa's smile, heard her lilting voice, felt her touch. "More than I ever thought I would or could," he admitted. "I can't imagine my life without her. She's the air I breathe, the wind in my sails."

"Tell her," Han said, who tended to listen more than speak. He raised his brows to the weeping strains of the harp wafting down. "Appeal to goddess of love. Prostrate youself. Offer gifts, offer you heart. Ask her stay, or you be like cowherd, alone, without wife or children."

Alyssa pulled her lynx throw tighter around her shoulders as she strode across the empty courtyard where yesterday the entire compound had watched Fenrir's extended family along with Brandr and the other three yellow beards and their families drive their wagons laden with their household goods out of the city and head west for the nearest port. She wondered where they would go. If they would choose to settle somewhere new together, or go their separate ways. She sighed. They weren't her concern anymore. What concerned her was whether she would be staying here at Sea Ridge or sailing for her homeland tomorrow.

She imagined the answer to that question had been the crux of Jerrik's request last night, when he'd pounded on the door to Magna's and Hulda's chambers, smelling of beer and as unsteady on his feet as she had never seen him, a crooked grin on his face as he'd asked her to meet him in the stables this morning for one last ride together.

One last ride together. Words that swam around her head all night. Words that didn't give her much hope of staying here with him.

"Yes, Digger," she told the eager pup as they made their way to the stables. "You can come with me, wherever I end up."

She was still angry enough with Jerrik to leave. He'd treated her badly. Worse than badly. Abominably. He'd believed the lies about her and denounced her publicly. What hurt the worst though was that he'd believed that she'd been unfaithful to him when all she had ever done since she was eight years old was love and idolize him. He was all she'd ever wanted, and while she'd had him it'd been like living a dream come true. Until it wasn't.

Even now, she couldn't think of his smiling eyes, strong profile, and lean, muscular body without aching deep in her core. She could remember every word spoken between them, good and bad, and would for the rest of her days and nights, which were looking to be long, cold, and sad. At least she would have his children to raise and love, and to remind her of their father every moment of every day. She'd have her memories of him. Most importantly, she would still have herself. Heartbroken and in pieces, but there. She hadn't lost herself. Not completely. Not yet.

Would she even be herself if she wasn't loving Jerrik?

She had a sinking feeling she was about to find out as she stood outside the stable's door, not quite ready to step in and face the man who had given up trying to get her to speak to him yesterday. Would he give up on their marriage too, or would he fight to save it? With a long, shaky sigh, she pushed the door open and walked in.

"Digger," she called the pup as he gave a yelp of excitement and ran straight into a stall near the back of the stables that was used for storage. The stall that had been his sick room.

She stopped at Storm's and River's stalls, which were next to each other, and where both horses were comfortably munching on fresh hay, neither of them saddled.

"Pavel? Hamar?" she called out, but there was no answer. Where were they? Had she misunderstood Jerrik?

She could have sworn he said to meet him here after breaking her fast. "Digger?" she called again when the pup started yipping, and she heard a cat meow. "Digger, leave Mouser alone." The stable cat didn't especially care for the pup, and was equal his size, with more sharp points. "She'll scratch your eyes out," she said as she turned into the stall and stopped in her tracks.

Jerrik sat on a stool in the middle of the stall, his hair shorn and his beard shaved, holding the stable cat in his lap. "Jerrik?" Alyssa tilted her head, as if changing her view of him would change what she saw. "What's going on?"

He set down the cat, which Digger set off chasing, and stepped up to her. "I'm here to beg your forgiveness," he said. "To make amends for what I have said and done to you."

She opened her mouth and said nothing.

"I love you, Alyssa," he said. "I know you love me, and have, since you were a little girl in side braids and I was a young, brash, stupid boy who basked in your adoration and came to take it for granted as I grew into a brash, stupid man, while you grew into a kind and beautiful woman."

"Jerrik." Her breath came out in a sigh.

"Please," he said. "Let me get out what I have to say." He gave her a sheepish grin, reminding her of the boy he'd been when they first met. "I've been practicing it in my mind all night."

Her heart beat triple time and she nodded.

"First, I want to say how sorry I am for listening to Kostya and not asking you straight out for the truth about you and him. For roping you into lying about when and where our marriage was consummated, and for not believing you hadn't miscarried his babe." He let out a short, harsh laugh. "I'd never been so jealous of anyone or anything in my life, and I handled it poorly."

Alyssa tilted her head at his last bit of confession and gave him a small smile. "Thank you," she said.

"Also, I want to say I'm even sorrier I let my uncle play on my jealousy and my foolish belief that I was fated to repeat my father's and my mother's sordid history. I believed his lies, and others', over your word." He took a shaky breath and met and held her gaze. "Though I've never admitted it, even to myself, all I've ever wanted from a woman was love and trust, and it seemed too good to be true that I'd found it with you. When I started to believe it, to believe I'd found it, and maybe I could keep it, I let my old fears and doubts convince me you'd broken that trust. So I broke yours. I broke your trust and your sweet, loving heart, and it turns out, in doing so, I broke mine as well." Tears stung the back of her eyes as he reached out and ran a hand through her shorn hair. "I'm so sorry I cut your beautiful hair," he said with a rueful smile.

Alyssa reached up and ran her hand over the short, prickly hair on his head, down the sharp angles of his cheek and the smooth, beardless line of his jaw, all meant, she knew, to be his public display of self-punishment. "It's only hair," she said. "It'll grow back."

"Will your love for me?"

Alyssa stared into eyes as blue as a summer sky with clouds of doubt dimming their brightness. "It never went away," she whispered.

He smiled, more hesitant than she had ever seen him. "Will you stay with me, my Lyssa? Will you stay here with me and be the mother of our children. Be my queen. Be my wife. Be my love."

Alyssa smiled through welling tears. "Kiss me, husband," she said. "Kiss me, and you will know."

EPILOGUE

The full moon shone down on the courtyard, its light reflecting on the first dusting of snow covering the ground as Jerrik and Alyssa stood before the priest under a bower adorned with boughs of fir and holly. Winter's Eve, ten and three years from the night Jerrik had first lain eyes on his little lynx, the night she'd proposed marriage and he'd found his true love, though it had taken him all these years to realize it.

He swept his gaze over the hundreds gathered to witness their king and queen pledge their troths to each other, to their family, and their people, and didn't spy a single yellow beard among them.

In the two moons since Jerrik had killed Fenrir and banished his family and their followers, he and Alyssa had come into their own as king and queen. If household gossip was correct, and according to Alyssa, household gossip was always correct, they'd become quite popular among their subjects, especially after their edict declaring all thralls free people who had the choice of their trade and to work for fair pay.

The edict brought some grumbling from the jarls, but none of the anarchy or chaos Fenrir had predicted came to fruition.

In truth, the kingdom of Sea Ridge had lost few workers, and had gained a thousand men and women working twice as hard now that they were working for themselves and their families. As word of their new world order spread, more and more free men and women were choosing to live, work, and trade in Sea Ridge's bustling port and farmlands.

The priest cleared his throat, and Jerrik squeezed Alyssa's hand as they stood straight and proud.

"Do you, Jerrik, son of Anders and Alina, take Alyssa, daughter of Aleksandr and Sahar, to be your wife? Do you swear to honor and protect her, to remain faithful to your marriage vows, spoken before these witnesses here tonight?"

Jerrik gazed into Alyssa's eyes, as green, deep, and fathomless as the sea. "I so swear."

"Do you, Alyssa, daughter of Aleksandr and Sahar, take Jerrik, son of Anders and Alina, to be your husband? Do you swear to honor him, to be the caretaker of your family life, to remain faithful to your marriage vows, spoken before these witnesses here tonight?"

Alyssa met Jerrik's waiting gaze with a tremulous smile. "I so swear."

"You may place the rings that symbolize the bonds of marriage on each other's fingers," the priest said.

Jerrik turned to Sven, who held the rings out in his palm, and took the ring he'd designed before he'd set sail to collect his bride, the ring engraved with the symbols for love, fidelity, and trust, and placed it on Alyssa's finger. Alyssa placed the matching ring made for Jerrik on his, and laid her hand atop his.

They held their hands bearing the symbols of their union out to the priest, who laid his hand over theirs and intoned the blessing of sacred union between man and woman, elm and ash. "Jerrik, son of Anders, King of Sea Ridge, will you trust your family dagger to your wife as keeper of the hearth and family?" the priest asked.

"I will." Jerrik pulled the ceremonial dagger that had been in his family for ten, soon to be ten and one, generations from his waist belt and held it out in both hands as he went down on one knee.

"Alyssa, daughter of Sahar, Queen of Sea Ridge, will you accept this dagger and vow to always keep a warm hearth for your husband and children?"

"I will," Alyssa said as she took the dagger from Jerrik's hands and knelt beside him.

"Then I declare you husband and wife," the priest intoned, and they stood. "You may now kiss—"

His words were drowned out by cheering as Jerrik pulled Alyssa to him and kissed her, long and deep, with all his heart, and then he bent down and kissed the soft swell of her belly.

"Thank you, Lyssa," he whispered as he stood beside her. "Thank you for loving me all these years and waiting for me, for not leaving me."

"I love you, Jerrik," she said with a smile that made him feel like a man, a man full, complete, and content. "All I ever wanted was to walk through life with you hand in hand."

"I love you, my little lynx," he swore solemnly. "I'm proud to sail the calms and the storms with you for the rest of our lives."

TURN THE PAGE FOR A SNEAK PEAK AT
THE LION & THE SWAN

THE LION & THE SWAN

"What ails you, Black Mane?" his brother, the Cheetah, asked as Asad pulled harder at his robe.

"My betrothal nears," Asad said with a low growl, "and I can see no way free of it." He glanced back over his shoulder at the women's table and eyed the Fox, his intended, who wore a gown of russet weave that pushed her fleshy breasts up to almost spilling out of the tight, low-cut bodice. The last time he had seen her, she had been a girl of ten and five who had liked her sweets as much as she disliked the word no, and by the way she had indulged in the honeyed dates that were the last of the seven-course feast, she had not changed much in the three years since.

"Duty and honor to family and kingdom," Asad said as much to himself as to his brother, "all require that I sit here like a sacrificial goat and let myself be bound and caged."

"At least the Fox will be your first wife of seven," the Cheetah offered with his cursed calm.

Asad huffed and then cocked his head. There was a rustling beyond the path that led from the stage of polished sandstone into the dark shadows of the garden. The still air moved, and he caught the sweet scent of night-blooming jasmine. He sat forward on his haunches as the Jackal, a thin, balding man with a nervous twitch of a smile, stood from his stool at the king's table and held his cup high. The Jackal had threatened his household with beatings if the secret of his dowry gift was revealed before this evening, but Asad's manservant, the Crab, knew every servant in every palace of the Seven Tribes, and had the entire story before sunset, though they had only arrived that noon.

The gift, the first and most valuable of seven to be given, were two sisters from the far north called the Swan and the Dove, whose pale, otherworldly beauty left the menservants speechless, the maids jealous, and the women of the household sour with envy, especially the Fox of the Swan.

The sisters had tried to escape twice already, and had made it as far as the city's third wall the first time, and the stables the second, after which they had both been thrown into hot holes. They had been sentenced to three days in the deep pits dug into the ground and covered with tightly slatted palm fronds that could sweat the water out of a full-grown man in five days, but the Swan had become ill in two and the Jackal had been forced to pull her out or lose her. Tonight, she would sing and dance for the gathering, and her sister, the Dove, would play the harp and sing. Then they would be given by the Jackal to the Panther as dowry for the Fox's betrothal to the Black Mane: eldest son to eldest daughter, as was tradition.

"Welcome, friends," the Jackal said, his tongue darting out and sweeping across his thin lips. "Welcome to my home on this Summer's Eve." Claps and loud murmurs broke out all around the courtyard and the Jackal raised his cup higher. "I am honored to host this, the hundredth gathering of the tribes. For the next twenty and one days my home is yours." His lips twitched up and he licked them again before nodding to the Panther. "And now, my honored guests, I bring to you the Swan and the Dove."

A bare foot, as white as milk, arched out of the garden's shadows and stepped onto the torch-lit path, the trim ankle turned just so, the calf long and leanly muscled, the knee as well turned as the ankle. Asad sucked in his breath as shimmering panels of white weave parted from a thigh as long and lean as an alabaster column. He let his breath out slow and measured, watching the graceful sway of shapely hips that nipped up to a slim waist draped with a finely wrought gold chain. A sheer bodice gathered beneath breasts as round and firm as pomegranates, and collarbones of chiseled ivory winged out from the one-shouldered gown to arms as long and lean as the legs they swung in time with.

A veil of hair as pale as moonlight framed high, angular cheeks, and finely drawn brows, a darker shade of pale, arched over eyes as big and round as mossy river rocks. Eyes that met his and held, and studied him as keenly as he studied her.

ABOUT THE AUTHOR

Michele James lives in a southern California beach town with her understanding husband, two lazy house cats, and two crazy cattle dogs. She is the proud mother of an adult son and daughter, and is Oma to the world's most adorable grandson.

A mostly retired veterinarian technician, she enjoys reading everything from cereal boxes to serious tomes, watching movies without commercials, cooking, gardening, walks on the beach (especially in winter), and practicing yoga.

CONNECT WITH MICHELE:
website: michelejamesauthor.com
instagram: @michelejamesauthor
facebook: facebook.com/michelejamesauthor

www.BOROUGHSPUBLISHINGGROUP.com

If you enjoyed this book, please write a review. Our authors appreciate the feedback, and it helps future readers find books they love. We welcome your comments and invite you to send them to info@boroughspublishinggroup.com. Follow us on Facebook, Twitter and Instagram, and be sure to sign up for our newsletter for surprises and new releases from your favorite authors.

Are you an aspiring writer? Check out www.boroughspublishinggroup.com/submit and see if we can help you make your dreams come true.

www.ingramcontent.com/pod-product-compliance
Lightning Source LLC
Chambersburg PA
CBHW070859180626
46817CB00003B/829